Age of Valor: Heritage

D. E. Morris

CreateSpace

All characters appearing in this work are fictitious. Any resemblance to real
persons, living or dead, is purely coincidental.

Printed in the United States of America

First Printing: December 2014

Second Edition Printing: October 2015

ISBN: 1503340139
ISBN-13: 978-1503340138

For Dad,

It's your fault I got into this crazy writing mess in the first place.

And I love you for it.

ACKNOWLEDGMENTS

Without the support of family and friends, this book would never have seen the light of day. But it took three special people to give me the courage and the confidence to share this world of mine with all of you.

Mackenzie – my most steadfast and sincerest cheerleader. Jessica – who made it through the first and last drafts without killing me and told me to keep writing. Laura – who made it through the rest and helped me fine tune what was surely a mess to start with. Hopefully I made it better. And everyone else who has had a hand in this long journey – I love you. Thank you. You mean the world to me.

PROLOGUE

Her legs were beginning to wobble and her chest burn. Each breath in felt like it could be her last. The doleful church bell was calling to her, leading her through the thick forest and the cold, driving rain. Just a little farther. There was already clearing in the trees ahead. Just a little farther.

Behind her, the thunder of the horses' hooves moved with a threatening speed in her direction.

She'd been at the gate of the village just moments ago, sitting in the rain in her worn trousers and tunic, long blonde braid hidden under her cap. It was uncanny, the timing of the church bell and the cries of panic from the back of the village. She could hear what they were saying and it was enough to get her on her feet. The wail of the horn on the wind made her move even faster, the sound echoing around her before getting lost in the thick trees of the forest. She beat out a steady cadence with her pace, running for the safety of the church, avoiding the main pathway in hopes of losing any pursuers in the overgrowth. Sanctuary could be found within those stone walls and it was the only hope left.

A low branch seemed to come out of nowhere, leaving a long bloody scratch on creamy skin. She tripped on an upturned root in her haste and fell to the forest floor, landing on her hands and knees, her cap dangling from an oak branch above her weary form. She wanted to sink into the muddy ground, to be swallowed up by the woody scent and the prickling pine needles, but she had to run.

There was an unmistakable trembling of the ground and the young woman knew the horses were close. She had to get up or they would be upon her and all would be lost. With every last ounce of strength, she got to her feet and ran.

A tall pine tree, all but hollowed out from years of rot, provided quick shelter. She ducked inside the thick trunk and huddled against the woody wall as one of the horses rushed past her. There were more coming, and still the church

1

bell rang. She had to get there before the riders did or all would be lost. Sharp green eyes took in the texture of her shelter. She lifted her wrist to touch her soaking sleeve to the cut on her face and came away with a slight blood stain. There was only one option left now. A diversion was needed. The wood was dry enough so it should burn for a few minutes at least. If she was quick about it, the riders would notice and give pause.

A silent prayer was sent up before her body was engulfed in blue and gold flames. She only had time to hear a cry of alarm before it all went dark and warm. In the next instant she was once more chilled by autumn rain and biting winds. The thickest part of the forest was now behind her and she ran for the church again.

The cobblestone under her feet was promising, even if it was sparse. It meant she was there. Her leather boots sloshed through a puddle and she was suddenly in the small open courtyard of the church, the bell ringing in her pulse. The horses were closer now, not held up long by the strange spark she'd started in the woods. She could hear the urgent cries of the riders pushing their mounts to their limits, but she could make it. She had to make it. The tall wooden doors of the old building opened heavily and she didn't stop moving until she was safely inside. As soon as the doors were closed, she leaned against them and looked at the two who had been waiting for her, wide-eyed.

Breathless, she reported, "The king is dead."

CHAPTER ONE

The village healer ran as fast as he could through the castle hallways and up the stone stairways. It had been reported that King Tadhg was ill. Racing into the king's chambers the healer found the king on the floor, surrounded by the queen, the prince and princess, and Tadhg's most trusted advisers. When the queen saw the healer enter, her sobs became desperate. In her arms lay her husband, frozen forever with a slackened mouth and brows drawn together in what could only be an expression of pain. Where his eyes should have been were empty sockets, blood wet on his face from his eyes, nose, and mouth. Upon further inspection blood had also leaked from his ears to slick the hair at the back of his neck. This was an evil the healer had only read about in stories and ancient medical books. He crouched to investigate.

"He was given Rabia powder," the healer reported grimly after several long moments. "Ingested in small doses it kills with slow torture. It shuts down and decomposes organs, muscles, and bones one by one, setting blood to boil. To achieve results such as these, I can only imagine how much he was given at once."

"The king has been murdered," said one of the advisers slowly, visibly shaken. He looked at one of the guards by the doors. "Sound the alarm and find the one who did this!"

The rush of armored footfalls down the castle hallways seemed to compete with the thunder outside. Men with swords strapped to their belts were hurriedly tying cloaks around their necks and pushing helmets down over their heads in the armory below the castle. Squires dashed from one man to the other to assist where needed. A man being dressed in older and darker armor seemed the only one calm among them. Ashen hair and fair skin served a perfect contrast against the black of his horse. He tied a black and red cape around his neck before mounting. Once adjusted in the saddle, he looked at the other men with heavy-lidded dark brown eyes.

No words needed to be exchanged. As soon as the others were ready on their horses, the man on the black horse gave a commanding, "Ha!" and kicked his heels into the ribs of his steed. The horse raced out into the terrible afternoon weather with three men close behind, several other guards peeling away from the group to search down muddy streets and darkened alleyways. Once away from the shelter of the stables, the rain stung their faces like icy needles, clouds covering any chance of sun to warm them.

The woods were quiet and deceivingly peaceful. Even the birds had stopped singing, huddling into nests to keep warm and dry. As the men rode between the trees, fanning out in a wide line to search the bushes and shadows, the leader of the knights searched the thick branches overhead. They provided a small amount of cover from the elements but also could have been used as a place for their prey to hide. With a hawk-like gaze, he looked a little ways ahead and spotted something hanging from an old tree branch. "What do we have here?" he murmured, nudging his horse forward.

The other three men, observant of their captain's moving, drew up near him. As the sopping cap was pulled free, the lead rider narrowed his eyes in speculation. There was only one place the one they chased would go from there. "The church."

"He could have run farther," suggested one of the other men. "There was a caravan leaving Montania for the port of Amme not long ago. Perhaps he was with them."

"No," said the first rider, certainty in his dark glance toward the direction of the church and the sound of the bell. "We have no leave to seize the church. If he was smart enough to be able to poison the king, he will be smart enough to hide in the church." Taking the cap and tucking it into his belt, the rider whipped his horse with the reins and was off again.

Finding the cap was only helpful in confirming suspicions. When the alarm sounded, several people reported seeing a boy run from the gate. His description had been taken from these witnesses by castle guards and given to the riders before they left. A cap just like this had been included in that description.

A flash of flames, blue, gold, and hot made the horses rear up and cry out in fright. The lead rider tugged hard on the reins and pulled his own mount around to investigate. The tree on fire sizzled in the cold rain and died in the space of a breath. The rider in battle proven armor dismounted to take a closer look. The ground around the tree was blackened as was the hollow inside. His brow furrowed. He touched his gloves to the soot and rubbed the black ash together between his fingers. After a moment he said, "Keep riding. He cannot have gotten far." With one more analyzing glance at the tree he made for his horse and followed his men.

4

They reached the old stone building only minutes after the great wooden doors had closed. The rider with the cap in his belt dismounted and ordered the others to stay where they were in the open courtyard. If there were outlaws waiting for an easy opportunity to attack they would be woefully disappointed; his men were the best knights in Caedia and they knew how to fight any attacker.

Raising a fist he pounded on the doors and stood back, glancing around as he waited for an answer.

A tall, round monk in long brown robes answered the door looking confused. "Blessings, good sir. How may we be of service this dreary day?"

"You are giving sanctuary to a boy who has committed a crime," claimed the leader of the riders, his voice so low and gravely that it sounded unnatural. "I demand the church give him to us freely."

The monk shook his head. "I'm afraid I know not of what you speak. The only male in this church is standing before you now."

"I thought the holy men were not supposed to lie."

"I tell you nothing but the truth. But what of this boy? What crime has he taken part in that would be serious enough to have four of the king's men out in the rain to chase him?"

"He has slain the king." The reply came as a low growl and the monk gasped. The rider scowled. "Do not pretend with me, old man. If you hold no boy within your sacred walls allow me and my men in to see for ourselves."

"And muddy the floors with your boots? I should think not. I will pray for the soul of the king, but now I must bid you good day." It would not be so easy as that. The knight extended a hand that stopped the door from closing shut. Behind him the other three dismounted and walked forward, hands resting threateningly on the hilts of their swords. "I see you will not be content until you search," said the monk, "so I will allow you to do so. Please, all I ask is that you respect the house of the Giver."

Needing little else to give him permission to enter, the knight pushed the door aside. He walked past the monk and peered into the great stone cathedral. Tall windows of colored glass lined the walls and torches lit the hall with warm flickering light. At the front of the sanctuary stood two girls, one taller than the other but both blonde and wearing kirtles that were simple and worn. They stood together and watched as the church was invaded. "Who are you?" the knight asked lowly.

The taller of the two girls stuck out her chin, green eyes lit with anger. "We have no business with you, sir."

The knight raised his eyebrow at the girl, taking in her dirty patched dress. "Do you have any idea who I am? I am Merrik, Captain of High King Tadhg's knights." He took a step closer to the girls. "What is that in your accent...you're

5

of the Celtique Clans." Jaw set, he pressed, "I will ask no more. Tell me your names."

"I am Ashlynn Stuart," she told the knight begrudgingly. "This is my younger sister, Kenayde. We were born in Siness but have lived here in Caedia for most of our lives."

Merrik narrowed his eyes, his gaze trailing over her with scrutiny before returning to her face. "Stuart?" He stared hard at her for a long moment as though trying to see her thoughts through her eyes. At length, he finally blinked. "The Gaels never leave their kind. Why are you here?"

"Being Celtique does not make me a Gael by default."

"They were my sister's children," the monk offered quickly, coming down the aisle with the rest of the riders accompanying him. "Both she and her husband were slaughtered by raiders. I collected their girls to live here with me."

Merrik's eyes did not leave Ashlynn for but a second and that was to glance over the quivering frame of Kenayde. "Why does she shiver, and why is your hair wet?"

"She shivers because it was men like you who raided our home. She shivers in fear."

He looked at the younger girl in assessment. What reason would there be to fear him if there was nothing to hide? Lifting a brow he returned his attention to the elder sister once more. "I asked you two questions yet only received one answer."

"We needed wood to dry for the fire and it is raining...*my lord*," Ashlynn growled, no small amount of annoyance in her tone.

Having no tolerance for wasting time, the riders split up at a meaningful nod from their captain and disappeared down the different annexes of the church. Merrik remained with the other three in the sanctuary. "Tell me," he said, turning to the monk now, "how it is you escape scandal, being here alone with two young girls?"

"Sir, they are my sister's daughters! How could you think of such things?"

Merrik smirked and turned around to face the girls again for a moment. He seemed more amused by the wilting figure of Kenayde than anything else but said nothing more. Instead he walked past them to the altar glancing up the rough stone walls and putting a hand to its coolness. It had been a very long time since he'd been to any sort of church and he'd forgotten how intricate the work of the masons could be. On the altar behind him were elaborate carvings of knots and loops that seemed to have no beginning or end. Touching the top of the altar with his thigh, he pushed forward and the top of the stone table slid slightly. A light of interest went on in his dark gaze and he turned around. "What is under here?"

The monk appeared confused at this question. "It is where we keep the sacramental wine and bread. It keeps the mice away."

"Show me."

Ashlynn left her sister long enough to step in front of the monk. "You do not have to do this, Uncle Briac."

"Yes he does," rumbled Merrik, looking down on them now from the altar platform. "Come, Brother. Move this tablet and show me you have nothing to hide."

Briac gave Ashlynn an apologetic look and moved beyond her, but before he could even join Merrik one of the guardsmen came back. "My lord." He held out his sword and hanging from the tip was a soaked wad of clothing. "This was found in one of the back rooms."

"Well, well, well," Merrik said softly, obviously delighted. He left his recent target of interest and reached for the clothing. "What do we have here?"

"The cloak I wore to gather the wood," Ashlynn's words were biting as she reached out for the clothing. Merrik, however, was quicker and grabbed them first.

"Is it then?" The one they sought was described to be wearing a tunic and trousers of the same cream and faded brown as this. Now he had proof. Unclumping the clothing in his hands he stiffened when it was revealed that what he held was indeed a sodden cloak. Ashlynn didn't bother to hide the smugness of her expression. "What is this?" he asked.

"My cloak," Ashlynn repeated, loud and slow as if she were talking to someone hard of hearing. She reached out and snatched it from his hands. "My uncle has been kind enough to let you look around and soil the floors of this holy place for too long. Quite obviously we do not have what you are looking for and I think it is time you left."

Merrik was displeased about the cloak and looked at it as though he couldn't believe it was actually what the girl had claimed. After a moment's silence the others came back. Merrik gave a small wave of his hand and all four of them stomped back through the church and out the doors without so much as another word.

"We ride for the castle," were his orders to only one knight as he mounted. "I will tell the prince of our findings and you will see to supplies." His horse turned impatiently and Merrik looked at the church. "You two will stay here and keep watch. We will be returning here before nightfall and will not leave until we have the king's murderer."

The three men cast uneasy glances at one another before one of them decided to be bold enough to talk. "But...it's an old monk and two girls. Do you really think..." His question was left unfinished; Merrik turned to face the knight with a cold glare. "Of course," the knight finished with a quick nod. "Forgive me, my lord."

7

"Do not question my orders again," Merrik threatened quietly. He urged his horse on, leading the way back through the forest to Montania.

The village itself was quiet, as if afraid to make any noise or sudden movement. News of Tadhg's death had not yet spread but the town's citizens knew something was afoot. The king's captain did not ride out as quickly as he had for simply any reason. There were faces at windows and bodies blocking door frames as the two men rode through town. All wanted reassurance from imagination born threats, but none wanted to ask for comfort from Merrik. He was not known for his kindness or generosity; Tadhg would not have a man like that serving directly under him. Both men shared the cold, uncaring and unfeeling qualities that made them great leaders of war. In fact, Tadhg liked to call himself a "King of War," a title with which no one would argue.

He was a braggart of casualties and was known to bathe himself in blood and still wish for an adversary to run his sword through. He was skilled in tactics and was forever coming up with the best ways to surprise the enemy.

His castle, Montania, the high kingdom of Caedia, had been decorated in the finest silks and fabrics, all stolen from lesser kingdoms he'd bested in battle. These fabrics were hung and used like trophies and the lands of the kingdoms left in the hands of stewards appointed by Tadhg. Every kingdom he conquered, he ruled from afar.

These silks and dressings did nothing to win over the people of Caedia. Neither did they gain the affections of his children, Prince Laidley and Princess Luella. The king was always so busy that there was never any time for his offspring. Even his wife, Finola, had to beg for his time. Now the prince would take the throne and everything would change. It was Laidley whose company Merrik now sought as he hurried through the castle.

The future king had not been pleased to discover the captain of guards had no prisoner to present. He was even less amused upon hearing Merrik's only suspects to be two girls and an old monk.

"The girls are from Altaine of Siness, my lord. I suspect from his accent that the monk is from somewhere in Cieria." Merrik was on bended knee before the prince.

Laidley was dressed in dark court clothing, his coal black hair left loose and hanging just past his shoulders. He sat in the smaller throne that was to the left of the much grander one in which his father had always taken residence. His blue eyes were heavy-lidded with the knowledge that he would eventually have to sit in his father's place, on the king's throne, but he was not yet ready. Looking at Merrik, a man who had been in Tadhg's services for twenty-one years, as many years Laidley had been alive, the prince scowled. "A Brother from the Isles I can accept - they come from everywhere. How did he explain the girls away? Why do you think it was them? What proof have you?"

"The monk said they were his nieces." Merrik noted the look of concentration about Laidley's face. "When the villagers were questioned they described a young man, what he was wearing and where he was running. Except for a caravan long since gone, there is nothing out there besides the church. There were footprints in the woods that did not continue farther than the old building." He thought of the tree and the strange colors of the flames but decided to say nothing about them for the time being. "All we found was a cap, but I cannot shake the feeling that these three had something to do with the murder of the king. The elder of the two girls - she told me their surname is Stuart."

Laidley's brow furrowed immediately. "As in Nir Stuart, deceased High King of Siness?"

"It is a fairly common name, My Prince, and could be a coincidence." It needn't be said how he felt on the matter. His gut was almost never wrong. He paused for Laidley to speak, but when the prince offered nothing Merrik spoke once more. "If I may, Highness, I will take supplies back to the men I have left there." Laidley's gaze finally flickered to Merrik, questioning. "There was little we could do," the older man explained, "while they were under the protection of the church, but if my suspicions are correct then I believe they will try to leave under the cover of night, or even in the early hours just before dawn."

Laidley said nothing for a moment but kept his eyes on Merrik. The silent thought process that could be seen behind the seemingly placid expression was much like the one Tadhg so often wore. Yet there was also something behind Laidley's eyes that gave away a certain instability. For a moment this thought distracted Merrik, but he was trained enough to keep his features unreadable. When Laidley did finally speak his voice was low and thick with concentrated emotion.

"My father never trusted anyone as he trusted you Merrik. Sometimes I think he loved you more than his own family for all the time he spent in your counsel."

Merrik bent his head respectfully. "Your father could not have been more a brother to me did the same blood run through our veins."

"I suppose that happens when you grow up with someone." Merrik didn't answer and the prince didn't seem to mind. With pursed lips he pushed his hair from his face, stark against the contrast of his pale skin, and leaned forward in his throne. "The rain will not stop before tomorrow and your men will need supplies. We should make haste."

Now Merrik looked up. "Your Grace?"

"You pledged your life for King and Country when my father still lived. When I am King, even now before I am made so in the eye of the people, does your word still bind you?"

Merrik did not blink or hesitate before he answered. "Until I no longer draw breath."

"Then I ride out with you. I will have the head of my fathers' murderer on a pike when I am crowned." Merrik lowered his gaze once more, but the prince continued. "They called my father the 'Red King' for all the blood that was shed under his rule. He knew this and reveled in it. Some of it was your own doing Merrik and in that you should take pride. What will they call me? How will the history books remember me?" Laidley sat back in his throne, his lips curving into a small smile, attention far away. It was only the sound of footsteps and the familiar swish of skirts that brought him out of his reverie.

Luella could have been Laidley's twin for the bond the siblings shared as well as the physical similarities. He'd been only a year old when Luella was born so the two had grown up with a deep understanding of one another. He didn't even have to look at her now to know she was not happy. Like her brother, Luella had eyes the color of a summer sky and raven hair. The only physical difference was her honey complexion to his creamy skin. As she came into the room, even in her state of grief, she was lovely in her dress of midnight with little rivers of dried tears stained into her cheeks. But there was no grief on her face at the moment, only anger.

"You want to know how the history books will remember you?" Her question was quiet and quivering with animosity.

Laidley looked first to Luella, then to Merrik with a small wave of his hand. "Leave us. Ready my horse." Merrik rose bowing his head to the prince and then to Luella as he passed her on his way out of the throne room. She completely ignored him and the handful of courtiers as they began to slink out of the room. With an expression of both annoyance and a certain level of patience, Laidley looked at Luella. "Do not make this into something it is not."

Luella blinked before letting go of a chuckle of disbelief. "Something it is not?" she repeated. She took a few steps closer to her brother so that she could easily reach out and touch him if she wanted to but did not move to do so. "Laidley, have you been listening to yourself? I have heard every word you have spoken since Merrik came back and you sound *just* like Father."

"And that is a bad thing?"

"He was murdered." The reminder was barely audible but it was enough to make Laidley flinch. "The funeral pyre is not yet lit and you are already planning your legacy. Trying to figure out how to best him; or to be worse, I cannot quite figure out which." Luella shook her head, loose strands of hair framing her face. She reached forward and placed a hand over Laidley's. "You can end this. You don't have to make it worse."

"I would not expect you to understand." Laidley jerked his hand away and stood to pace the length of the throne room, leaving Luella to stare after him

10

with wide eyes. In all his twenty years Laidley had been gentle with her, never raising his voice or saying anything hateful to her. As he looked through an open window to the rainy world outside, a part of him wanted to turn around and apologize. But then she spoke.

"How dare you say that to me! You think because I am a woman, because I am the second born perhaps, that I cannot possibly understand the pressure that has been thrust upon you?"

"That is exactly what I think!" Laidley closed the shutters and turned to face Luella, a foreign anger in his expression as he stalked back across the room to close the distance between them. "You will not have to run kingdoms Luella! You will not have to make decisions over who is worthy enough to live and who deserves death!" He pointed at Tadhg's empty throne, face red with emotion. "You will not be the one who chooses the fate of your own kingdom with a simple word." He gripped her shoulders hard, his cheeks flushed with heat. "You will not have to make war so that war is not made against you!"

Luella reeled as though she'd been slapped and shoved him away. For a moment her words simply wouldn't come and all she could do was stare at her brother. If he had gone too far it had not yet registered with him and there would be no time for it. Luella was recovering from her shock quickly. "I have lived inside these walls, hearing my mother weep every single time Father decided a victory was sure enough to let him ride out with his men and wage his own battles. I have been here every time our food has been delivered with rats and their excrement or spiders or snakes! Where have you been, Laidley? Where were you when three of the kitchen staff died of bites from insects we've never seen before? Where were you and Father the day the entire west wing of the castle was blown to nothingness and we lost a baby brother we will never know? Playing war? Do not tell me that I cannot understand the pressures you face! Do not even dare to try because you cannot begin to know what it is to be in my shoes. To be the one to stay behind and try to pick up the pieces and make all of us whole again!"

Laidley shifted his weight uncomfortably, bested but not willing to openly admit it or back down. He couldn't afford it if he was to be crowned soon. "It is not the same," he insisted quietly. "See a man you have trained with slain in battle and then come to me with your tears."

"Do you see me crying, brother?" Luella shook her head, equally as stubborn. "Go then. Ride off with your champion knights and slay the enemy. May it be an easy victory for you because I do not think Mother could live through losing you as well." She seemed done with the conversation and turned, her steps and the sounds of her skirts moving over the floor announcing her leaving as they had her arrival. But just before she was gone from sight completely Luella glanced over her shoulder.

"What will you do?"

Laidley looked at his sister. When it was easy to read in his face that he didn't understand the question, she expanded. "With this trio, if they are the ones who killed Father. Two little girls and an old monk. What will you do?"

At this Laidley gave a sloppy shrug that belied his royal status. "Do not concern yourself with it." He lifted his eyes and settled on Luella's face, holding her gaze with silent authority. They had been equals for so long, age never being an issue. Now he was her king and no longer her brother. If he did not stand up to her and make her acknowledge his superiority now she would never willingly be under his leadership. "Do you love me sister?"

There was still obvious anger in her expression and Laidley could almost feel her growing resentment toward him. He was, however, her king now. Respect was to be given when it was rightfully due, even if the crown fell to the son of a slain man and not one who earned it. "Of course I do." But for the first time in her life the love was not evident in her tone or her eyes.

"Then do not question me."

Luella said nothing, only bowed her head in a moment of silent submission before taking her leave. She would do as requested, Laidley knew this. But that did not mean she would be the dutiful little princess waiting for the next order from her brother and her king while he continued down a path she disagreed with so greatly. She was trained in the same battle skills as Laidley and only lacked the actual field training. Despite this small handicap she was not without confidence. For a moment he wondered if she would be bold enough to act on her own, to go against him. No. Not Luella. She had never been a timid little princess, but there was not strength in her to actively go against her king. She could not possibly be a threat.

Still in the same spot by the empty thrones Laidley waited until he could no longer hear Luella's receding footfalls before letting go of a hiss. He raised a hand to scrub it over his face. "Merrik!"

Heavy boots came quickly, just as the prince knew they would. Though he'd been sent away the captain of guards was never too far out of earshot. "Your Highness?"

"Have you everything needed for your men?"

"The packs have been sufficiently loaded."

"And my horse?"

"Has been saddled and is waiting for you."

"Good." Laidley fell silent in thoughts of his sister. Luella was always the one to look after everyone. Since an attack six years previous on Castle Montania, the one to take the life of the youngest of Tadhg's children along with several others, the queen had not been quite right. Even simple tasks seemed to take too much effort to think through. Part of Finola had died with her child and losing her husband - what would that do to her? Perhaps Luella did know something of the pressures after all. Laidley had become king of an entire nation in a mere moment whereas his sister in essence had been performing the political and mothering duties of a queen for much longer. There was no questioning that the siblings would have to work together and come to some sort of accordance. But smoothing things over would have to wait until later.

"My mother will not be well enough to carry out her duties as Dowager Queen." Laidley was being diplomatic in his statement and they both knew it. "I must take a wife, and the sooner the better." Merrik nodded sagely but said nothing as Laidley continued to muse aloud. "Until I find a woman worthy of my attention and strong enough to be my queen much more will be placed upon Luella's shoulders. This will make her more of a target as well. See to it that when we return there are double the guards to protect her. Pull them from other battles, take them from my personal retinue, I care not. But make no mistake these men must be loyal to me. I will not have another stranger come in under the guise of friendship to take anymore lives."

"Yes, My Prince. I will arrange it as soon as we return."

Laidley nodded with a sense of accomplishment. His first real order as king would be fulfilled and that was something to give him a much needed boost of confidence. "Now...let us go to that church and be done with this mess."

It had been a long time since the young prince took a ride through the forest. The last time had been in a carriage to the port town of Amme where a ship sat waiting for departure. Even then he'd been able to take a few glances out the window and look at the scenery. Today he noticed his surroundings, but they were more of a bother than a beauty. He hated how cold and wet the rain was, scowled at the color changing leaves on the trees and cursed the slick and sodden ones on the ground that could easily trip up one of the horses.

As was custom, Merrik took the lead keeping Laidley safely in the middle of two skilled swordsmen. Not that Laidley couldn't have taken care of himself if they were attacked. He knew his way around a sword fight better than the average prince. When much sought after time with his father became elusive once he was too old to be cuddled and coddled, Laidley turned to raising his skill level in combat. It was what his father loved most and had the potential to bring them together. Luella joined in the learning as well, and both of Tadhg's children grew up quick and agile in combat.

"Merrik." Laidley looked at the back of the older man. "You knew my father when he was younger. Were we ever alike?"

"Your father was never like you, Prince Laidley. He was always thinking of battles and who or what he could conquer." He glanced over his shoulder. "Permission to speak freely?"

"Of course."

"The only time I ever saw the human side of your father was during his courtship of your mother, their marriage, and the birth of his children."

Laidley nodded slowly. "Then it would seem I am more my mother's child than my father's."

Merrik stared ahead, pausing before adding in a light tone, "If I am still speaking freely, Your Grace, I pray every day that you are more like your mother than your father."

They rode on in silence, Laidley thinking over Merrik's words. High Queen Finola was rather feeble-minded but she had a good heart. He thought of Luella and their argument. She had a good heart as well and she was one of the most intelligent women he'd ever known. It was wrong of him to raise his voice to her as he had. The loss of his father, however absent his father had been, cut him deeply. He had to remember it was not only his loss and that all spirits would be tender for awhile. Hopefully catching the culprit would bring some closure and they could all move on as a family.

The two men left behind had found sheltered places under thick, heavy branches to lash their horses and bunker down for the night. They were thankful for the food and wineskins provided and updated the others as they filled their stomachs. So far there had been no movement, but night was falling fast and it would not be surprising to witness an attempted escape.

Fresh vengeance pulsed through Laidley's veins as he stared at the tall wooden doors to the church. Trusting Merrik's instincts, he was certain his father's killer was inside. As soon as any one of the three suspects stepped foot into the forest it would be all over. All he had to do was wait, and waiting was never enjoyable.

A storm rolled in subtly, bringing darker clouds and a quicker night. All of the men watched the candles being methodically blown out through the colored glass windows. For every appearance the three inside were going to bed. Laidley shifted his position under the thick bushes that concealed him. Any moment now...he was sure of it.

The escape did not come as quickly as Laidley would have liked. In fact, he ended up resting back into a more comfortable position as they waited. Nothing happened. The men slept in shifts and without any real rest, waking in the early morning to a slightly warmer breeze and a misting drizzle of rain.

All of them were caught off guard when the doors of the monastery opened. A small group of mourning doves took flight vocalizing their surprise at the sudden intrusion of their gathering. The monk was alone and did not appear to be aware he was being watched. He folded his arms over his rounded stomach and tucked his hands into the long sleeves of his robes.

There were bushes to the lee of the old building full of small red berries. The monk moved toward those bushes now. He pulled a few berries free and stuck them in his mouth to chew. A whinny of a horse made him right himself and slide his hands back around his stomach to disappear into the large sleeves.

Their cover blown by a rather unhappy mare, the three guards who had been camped outside all night long showed themselves, drawing their swords as they moved closer to where the monk stood. "I can't remember the name for these berries but mash them with a bit of honey and it is splendid on toast."

"You do not seem surprised to see us, Brother Briac," said Merrik as he too stepped out into the open.

"You?" asked Briac innocently "No, not you. Him perhaps." Laidley stepped from his cover and stood beside Merrik matching the older man in height and stern expression. Briac gave a respectful nod to the prince. "Your Majesty." Hands still tucked away and looking completely undaunted Briac ignored the three guardsmen and focused on the other two. "Something tells me it's not the berries that have brought you out here this early morning."

"Where are the girls, old man?" Laidley had no patience for pleasantries.

"Asleep in their quarters where I left them."

Merrik gave a nod to his men and one disappeared into the church. Briac said nothing and made no move to stop the man. Merrik surveyed the monk. "You seem calm for a man about to be strung by his neck."

With a casual shrug Briac answered, "I have yet to be accused of anything. What is there to fear when the knowledge of impending death had not yet even been given to me?"

"You are accused of conspiracy," Merrik explained patiently. "It could not have been you to run from us yesterday since you're too big to run anywhere, but I would wager that it was one of those Celts who did."

Briac nodded impressed. "That is a bold wager, sir." Thoughtful, he tilted his head. "The way you say Celts...is it meant to be an insult?" Merrik didn't answer. "The girls are very proud of their heritage as I am proud of mine. I do not take it as an insult and neither would they."

One of the two soldiers still outside spat on the ground. "Full of Gaels...dirty witches using magic and talking to those cursed winged lizards..."

"Interestingly enough," Briac said, now addressing the soldier, "not all females on the Celtique Isles are Gaels. And not all Gaels are female. Isn't that something?"

"Enough of this," Laidley huffed. "Confess to your part in this and you may yet be spared. Continue with this babbling..." His hand moved menacingly to the hilt of his sword.

But Briac was still unaffected. "You will kill me either way my good prince. Let's not fool ourselves into thinking otherwise. Besides I know where it is I am going and would gladly see the Giver in Heaven than stay in this world of sorrow and misery."

15

The guard emerged from inside and looked at Merrik. "They're not here."

"As I suspected they would not be," sneered Merrik. "Take him back to the castle. Lock him in the dungeon and pull his fingernails out one by one until he tells us where the girls are. Until then, we will search for them on our own." He and Laidley turned to find their horses as the guardsmen closed in on Briac.

Even as three swords approached, Briac's expression was placid. He waited for the men to be just within his reach before withdrawing his hands from inside his long sleeves. But his hands were no longer empty. From sheaths strapped to his arms and hidden by the long robes he withdrew two daggers. Despite his age and girth he was quick enough to slit one throat before anyone knew what was happening. Blood spilled down the front of the soldier as he fell and the other two froze in a moment of shock. Hearing the sputter of the first man, Merrik and Laidley turned around in time to see Briac sink both daggers into the heart of one of the other two soldiers. The last one threw himself at Briac and barely missed cutting off the old man's ear as he ducked out of the way. Merrik grabbed his own dagger from his belt and threw it. The dagger found its mark in Briac's right shoulder.

"Stupid move old man." Briac fell to the ground, his weapons cast from his hands as he grabbed at the dagger in his shoulder. The guard still alive shoved his sword forward resting the tip of it under Briac's neck. It was enough to make Briac stop, and Merrik stooped over him. "Very stupid."

Laidley glanced around, unconcerned with the fallen men but not wanting to be surprised by anything else. "We have no need of him Merrik. We can find them on our own."

"Yes," agreed Merrik, crouching down so that his face hovered over Briac's. "Say hello to the Giver for us."

16

CHAPTER TWO

There was an immediate sense of urgency when Merrik and his men had departed from the old monastery the previous day. Briac rushed to lower the heavy wood and iron latch, then sank to the floor with relief.

"Lynnie, how did you know?" Kenayde questioned in awe, taking the wet dress Merrik's men had found.

"I didn't," Ashlynn admitted, walking over to help Briac back to his feet. "I was just cautious. Your nieces?"

Briac shrugged. "They believed I was a monk, why not that as well?"

Kenayde rushed toward the altar to move the stone back and reached in for the wet clothes they'd managed to shove in before the knights entered. "We should burn these. Just to be safe."

Ashlynn's lips set into a tight line. "Fine. They shall be our offering to the Giver since it's all we have. We must leave before morning or they will be back, and with more men."

"Leave?" Briac looked confused and wide eyed. "For where?"

"I don't know," Ashlynn confessed. "I am making this up as I go. We just can't stay here."

Kenayde nodded. "She's right." Without waiting for further argument she set the sopping clothes atop the altar, adding sticks of incense before stepping back and kneeling. Briac took up the same position beside her and Ashlynn stood on the other side of him. Without a torch or a word to mutter a magic spell, the clothes that should have been too wet to burn were set ablaze in a fyre of brilliant sapphire blue and gold. Ashlynn knelt and bowed her head.

"Great Giver, hear Your children. We beg Thee for divine protection against those that would mean us harm and halt us on our course. Be with us this night while we prepare for the journey tomorrow. Guide our hands and our

17

hearts so that we may know what is right and what is true to Your word but most of all what it is You would have us do. Be near us while we are in the restful moments so that fear may not creep into our hearts. Make our feet swift when the time calls. We ask for these things in Your blessed and most holy name. Amen." Ashlynn opened her eyes to stare at the fyre, breathing in the thick incense that was filling the room. Briac rose to his feet and shuffled away down one of the annexes, but Kenayde stayed with her head bowed and her eyes closed.

"Don't be afraid, Nadie."

"I'm not," the younger girl answered, still unmoving. "I am simply adding in what it was you forgot."

Ashlynn blinked and looked at her sister the same time Kenayde opened one eye to look at Ashlynn. "What did I forget?"

Kenayde closed her eye again, her head bowing just a bit more. "To ask for your own protection. You are the one who killed the king, Lynnie. If they find that out..."

"They won't." True to Ashlynn's character her tone was sure and confident. "But I thank you for your added prayers. When you're finished you should rest. We'll be leaving before sunup."

Now Kenayde's eyes opened and she looked at her sister. "No, I wanted to help you and Briac ready the packs and the horses."

"No horses," Briac announced as he came back into the main hall. "They'll attract too much attention."

"So what do we do?" Kenayde asked. Both Ashlynn and Briac looked at her and she shook her head, curls bouncing about her face. "Oh, no. No, Lynnie. We can't! You're not experienced enough!"

"Yes I am," Ashlynn replied harshly. "Kenayde, it is either that or we are caught and hanged. Or worse."

"But what about Briac? He can't come with us. He'll be burned to death!" Ashlynn turned to Briac and Kenayde looked at them both in triumph. "We have to figure out another way."

"You'll have to leave me here."

"No," Ashlynn argued. "If we leave you here they will know something is amiss. Our only hope is to head for Amme on foot and barter for passage aboard the next ship out."

"Out to where?" Kenayde asked.

"Home if we can manage it. If not..." Ashlynn frowned. "As long as it is out of Tadhg's kingdom, we'll be safe."

"For now." Briac's expression was grim. "Get some rest. We leave in a few hours."

Age of Valor: Heritage

~*~*~*~

When war came to the high kingdom of Altaine on the island of Siness of the Celtique Isles, they knew there was no way of winning. But to simply give in would mean being crushed and even with a sure defeat they would not lie down to simply die. With Tadhg it was fight or be obliterated. So they fought for as long as they could, until their own king, Nir, died while trying to save his two daughters. His wife had passed while giving birth the their youngest and he knew if he fell, his children would be taken to Tadhg as trophies and unspeakable things would happen to them. It was only to secure their safety should something happen to him that Nir made sure they would be sent away if he should perish.

Ashlynn and Kenayde, three and one, were dressed as simple peasant children the day black horses, thick with muscle and weighted down by armor and knights, stormed into the village surrounding their castle. Altaine had been warned of the oncoming war and the town was in a panic. As the capital was taken over by the black knight of Tadhg, the girls were smuggled out with the smaller, weaker children, aided by an elfin counselor in Nir's court. They were sent east to an even smaller kingdom before being separated from the other children and sent south and away from Siness.

The small shipping village of Nivar in Caedia earned most of its income through trade of boating supplies, ships, and seafare. The port's backdrop was the majestic Oceana Palace, sitting high above on a cliff that reached out to the ocean like an old friend. Nir's younger brother by seven years, King Wessely Stuart and his young bride, Emiline, could not have children. It had been a great controversy in the small kingdom for a time after Wessely had taken her for his wife, yet Wessely refused to send her away. There were mutterings of conspiracies and plots to get someone else on the throne, but Oceana's kingdom was so small that the talk died down after awhile and the most fantastic ideas were reserved for drunken babbling. Ashlynn and Kenayde's arrival at the palace helped calm the minds of those left worrying. With no one to look after them but the king and queen, they had become next in the line of kin to inherit Oceana as well as Altaine when it was safe.

The truth of who they were and how they'd come to the palace was never kept from the girls. Wessely and Emiline raised them as though they were their own. never letting them want for anything. Eventually Ashlynn lost the ability to be satisfied with her simple life as a pampered princess. She would overhear daily reports on where Tadhg's men were attacking, new reports to say that some had given up on trying to rebuild and simply fallen to his hands, content to let him leave men there so as not to risk any further war in years to come. Altaine was close to becoming one of them and Ashlynn rallied. She was young, but there was a strong sense of duty in her. If she could prevent her homeland from being taken over by the Red King she would do whatever was in her power to stop it, even if that meant killing him to be free of him.

She trained with the knights, much to the disgust of her sister, and took a keener interest in politics and social economics. A maid at the castle by the name of Cailin, a young girl from the island of Ibays and Ashlynn's closest friend, had said more than once that her people were the grunts of the Celtique peoples, looked down upon by everyone else. That was something Ashlynn committed to changing.

Her goals were lofty, but both Wessely and Emiline knew if anyone could do it, it would be Ashlynn.

Now passing through the rooms of the church, she remembered how her decision to leave Oceana had confused and hurt Kenayde, thinking she was abandoning their parents and abandoning her. It took many late night conversations to convince Kenayde that she was abandoning no one, but setting out to try and change the world. Kenayde said she was foolish, but ultimately agreed it was Ashlynn's decision and that she would support her no matter what. Little did she know that her support would be taken so far as assisting in murdering Tadhg.

With a lantern in one hand, Ashlynn pushed open the door to the church library and peered in at Briac with scrutiny. The old man had his back to her as he searched for something by lantern amid the books on the shelves. "You should be asleep."

Briac turned briefly at the sound of her voice before returning to reading the spines of the old tomes. "And you shouldn't be?"

Ashlynn shrugged. She walked farther into the study and closed the door behind her. Lifting the lantern higher, she squinted in the poor light. "What are you doing?"

"In every monastery there are hidden passages. I didn't want to say anything in front of your sister, but I doubt very much that this church has been left unguarded." Briac's fingers ran over the books, moving them back and forth. "If we can find an alternate passage out of here it would be preferential to the front door."

"Agreed." Ashlynn set her lantern down on the desk and joined Briac, tilting her head thoughtfully. "Wouldn't a false book be typical, though? If anyone came through here looking for a secret passageway, wouldn't this be the first place they looked?"

Briac paused and lifted his lantern to look at Ashlynn's face. "I hadn't thought of that." He frowned, sighing through his nose. "Where would you put a secret passage if you were a holy man?"

At this, Ashlynn grinned. "I have never even been close to being holy or a man, so you are asking the wrong person. I do have an idea though. Come with me."

Out in the sanctuary Ashlynn set her lantern on the altar so she could take two of the un-lit torches from the wall. A thought had them ablaze with blue and gold flames. "What we need to do is look for a draft."

Briac shook his head slightly. "This place is like a castle. There are drafts and breezes anywhere you go."

"Yes," Ashlynn agreed, "but if there is a passage somewhere that's contributing to any sort of air current, then the push or pull to the fyre will be greater than any old draft. Stick to the walls, avoid the windows if you can in case we truly are being watched, and mind the flames."

Briac held his torch aloft and moved to the wall. As he walked, he ran his knobby fingers over the stones, dark brown eyes glancing at the flames of his torch every so often for a hint of some kind of breeze. The rain had not let up outside, turning the cold church even colder now that it was night. Briac pulled his robes closer around his neck and a shiver passed over his spine just as Ashlynn spoke.

"I may have found something."

Turning, Briac saw Ashlynn setting her torch back into one of the sconces. She was peering curiously at the lantern she'd set on the altar. "What is it?"

"I can't believe I didn't think of this in the first place. Come help me." Briac crossed the sanctuary to return his torch to its rightful place before joining Ashlynn at the altar. "Help me get the top off," she instructed, setting the lantern aside. The old man hastened to the other side and together, they moved the heavy stone tablet to reveal the inner compartment.

Briac shook his head in obvious confusion and looked at Ashlynn. "There's nothing in here but communion bread and wine." She gave him no reply yet again but grabbed her lantern once more. As soon as she bent over the opened altar the fire danced as if caught in the wind. "Well I'll be," Briac exhaled.

"They hid it under the altar," Ashlynn grinned. "No one would think to look there. Come on. Help me get all of this out so we can see where it leads." Lantern still in hand, she grabbed some of the flatbread wrapped in cloth and set it on the floor out of the way. Once the inside of the altar was free from the communal elements, Ashlynn handed her lantern to Briac and climbed inside to get a closer look. The stone was smooth and in-ornate, almost seamless to the touch and Ashlynn frowned to herself. "I do not see how this was ever used or how air is even moving underneath. There's no way to lift the bottom of this up. We will have to break through."

"Break through a holy altar?" Briac gawked.

Ashlynn lifted her head running a hand through a curtain of messy hair. "Do you have another suggestion, then? Briac, need I remind you that there are men waiting out in the rain to capture us the second we set foot outside these sacred walls? We do not have time to look for the thing that will open this for us."

"But this is an altar of the Giver, Ashlynn."

"Surely the Giver will grant us His forgiveness for a thing as small as this. If He has not already forgiven us for the much larger sins we have committed up to this point, then our souls are already damned." She stood and looked down at Briac from her altar perch. "You were never as pious as this before. Do not start on me now when our very lives are at stake."

"Not pious," he defended stubbornly. "It's superstition that makes me fearful."

"Well whatever it is," said Ashlynn, climbing out, "swallow it down. How well can you see in the dark?"

Briac shrugged one shoulder stiffly, handing her back her lantern. "Well enough on any normal night."

"And a night with no moon? I'm nervous that anyone outside will be attracted by the light and try to see what we are doing. I need you to be the one to break through the rock, Briac. I may have the brains, but you have the brute." He did nothing to mask his displeasure, but Ashlynn hardly gave it any notice. A thought from her extinguished all light and the vast sanctuary was flooded in darkness. "Use the end of the torch. The metal should be pointed enough so that you may break through."

"And you?" Though his face couldn't be seen, a frown could easily be heard in Briac's tone. "What will you do?"

"I will keep watch by the window. If I see movement..."

"They can't come in without permission."

Ashlynn scoffed quietly. "Yes, so says the law of High King Tadhg. Work quickly, Briac. I fear we may yet have to fight before this night is over and I would not see blood shed in these halls."

Though the task didn't sit well with him, Briac wouldn't argue. Ashlynn moved on quiet feet to the window. Nothing could be seen past the glass, save the cold little rivers of water that ran down the outside of the colored pane that separated her from the elements outside. But she didn't need to see faces to understand they were there. Somehow knowing they were wet, cold, and miserable gave her some small amount of satisfaction. At least she, Kenayde and Briac were warm.

A sharp clang of metal rang out through the air and she turned her head.

"Sorry," Briac groaned. "I tripped." There was a scraping sound as he picked up the unlit torch and eventually the first thud of metal against stone was heard. It wasn't nearly as loud as metal against metal; the stone was much softer than expected and helped him work faster. This did nothing to put Ashlynn at ease, however, and her attention stayed trained on the outside.

Lightning gave a brief moment of illumination and Ashlynn narrowed her eyes to try and see any movement. "I don't think I'm getting anywhere," Briac said from the altar's chamber.

"Keep working." Ashlynn was no longer so soft in her tone but more stern in her order. Though she hadn't seen anything outside she wanted to be out of the church as soon as possible.

"Lynnie?" Briac stopped working and Ashlynn looked away from the window as though she could see her sister in the dark. "Lynnie, what's going on? Are you all right?"

With a sigh and using her hands to guide her, Ashlynn found Kenayde and ran her fingers over soft messy curls. "Everything is perfectly fine," Ashlynn soothed in a hushed motherly tone. "I keep forgetting how light a sleeper you are." The older man took that as his cue and started chipping away at the stone once again while the two girls went back to where Ashlynn had been keeping post. "Briac and I agreed that if we wait until morning to leave then we'll be inviting trouble to accompany us."

"But I don't understand. What's he doing? Where is he?"

"You need not concern yourself with that now, little Nadie. Just stand here with me for awhile."

The digging of metal against rock, the rain against the glass, and the occasional roll of thunder became the only sounds for a long time. Eventually Kenayde, sitting with her back against the wall, fell back asleep. Every time there was a flash of lightning Ashlynn would unwittingly hold her breath and search the outside as quickly as she could, relaxing only slightly when they were covered in darkness once more.

"I can't tell exactly how far I've gotten," Briac said after one long rumble of thunder, "but in one of the corners I think I'm through to the other side."

Ashlynn went across the sanctuary to the altar, a small ball of blue and gold flames forming in her hand as she walked. Briac's face was cast in eerie shadows as he looked at her, smeared with dirt from his work. "See?"

She looked in, holding her hand away from her friend so as not to harm him. As he'd assumed there was a lot of damage done to the inside of the altar, but a lot more than Briac expected. In one of the corners there was a blackness where the rock had completely fallen through to the hidden chamber below. "What about using the heel of your boot on that corner?" Ashlynn suggested, glancing at Briac. "If you stand up so that you're bracing yourself on the sides of the altar and kicked while holding yourself steady, you might get a bit more out of the way."

Briac gripped two sides of the altar and stood as Ashlynn instructed. With a mighty drive of his foot, he kicked downward and the two of them watched as the bottom gave way. Briac's elbows locked before he could fall through and he was hanging over a dark pit to an unknown exit. Ashlynn extinguished her fyre so she could help him out and called to her sister. "Nadie, wake up! We have a way out. All right Briac?"

"Did you hear the rock hit?" he asked when his feet were on the secure ground of the church floor. "I didn't hear it hit anything but water."

"Neither did I," Ashlynn admitted. "That means we may have a long and wet way down. Hand me one of the torches." Once the torch was in hand and lit with her fyre, Ashlynn peered inside the now broken altar. Ladders of wood and rope hung down two sides. Little else could be seen. There was no telling how safe either ladder would be and that made her more nervous for Briac than Kenayde or herself, for he was nearly twice their size and close to it as well in weight. Curious, she let go of the torch and all three watched the light fall into the unknown. Like the rock Briac had kicked in moments ago, it eventually found rest in murky water.

"Not too far a climb," Briac said with optimism.

"But a far fall," Ashlynn muttered. "Kenayde and I will go down first, each taking a ladder to test the strength and determine the best way for you down."

"We don't know what's down there," the old man argued.

"It is a risk we must take, Briac."

"There won't be any fresh air down there, will there, Lynnie?" Kenayde asked.

"We have no other choice."

"If we are trapped down there..."

"I know, Nadie. I know. But I won't let anything happen to you, I give you my word. We'll find a way out and you will see the sun again if I have to dig through stone with my bare hands." Hanging on with one hand she kissed her other and touched Kenayde's face. "Down you go."

The descent was slow, filled with intentional movements and the occasional crying out as a particularly rotted rung gave way. When a muffled crack and a scream came up through the darkness as one of the ladders split, followed by a splash, Briac practically threw himself over the side of the altar to try and see what was going on. "What happened?"

"Kenayde!" Ashlynn cried.

"I'm all right..." she replied weakly after a moment. "But I'm all wet."

"It's all right lass," the old man laughed softly. "So long as you're still in one piece, that's all that matters. Are you almost to the bottom, Ashlynn?"

"Almost. How far up is the water, Nadie?"

"To my calves. It's cold."

"Good to know. Briac? Take my ladder down. I had fewer breaks in mine than Nadie had in hers." She felt the bottom of her dress hit the water and the cold creep up her legs as she splashed down into it. Kenayde reached out a hand to steady her before looking for the torch that had been thrown down earlier. "I'm down. I want you to drop the torch down just the way you're holding it. I should be able to catch it. It will take less energy to keep the fyre going on one of them than it would be for me to carry it on my own."

Briac let go of the light he'd been holding onto. Ashlynn caught it with both hands and lit the one Kenayde had successfully fished from the water.

"What can you see?" Briac called down, not even yet begun his descent.

Both Kenayde and Ashlynn looked around in the torch light, though there wasn't much to see. The walls were too close on three sides and covered in slimy growth, leaving them only one way to go and the light didn't travel far enough to show them anything but a long narrow passage. "Nothing exciting," Ashlynn reported. She glanced at her sister. "How are you doing?"

Kenayde nodded distractedly, holding her torch aloft. "Just don't let the flames go out."

Looking up, Ashlynn waited for Briac. "Are you planning on joining us, or what?"

"That's what I'm trying to decide."

"What?" Both girls looked up in alarm. "Briac!" gasped Kenayde. "You cannot leave us to go on our own!"

"If you stay behind and they find we've gone but you're still here, they will kill you!"

Briac sighed. "Someone has to cover the altar back up or they'll know where you've disappeared. I can't do that standing on that ladder. I've already thought it through. Besides, they wouldn't kill a man of the Giver."

Ashlynn was livid. "Do you think that matters to them Briac? That captain – Merrik - he will kill you!"

"Ye of little faith."

"This is no time for jokes, Briac. I may not be the queen of your nation, but as someone to whom you pledge fealty, I command you to get your arse down here this instant!"

In the darkness above them, Briac's deep laughter could very well have been meant for some trick by a court jester. "Such language from a refined lady. With all due respect, Your Majesty, I do believe this is in your best interest. I'll be all right."

"No, Briac!" cried Kenayde, now on the verge of tears.

"Pray for me and we'll meet again on the misty mountains of the heavens."

Even as they protested, the heavy stone was hefted back atop the ruined altar.

Ashlynn and Kenayde stared up at the way they had come down for a very long and silence filled moment. Neither could believe what Briac had done, and though she understood his reasoning, Ashlynn was growing angrier by the moment.

"Come on," she said eventually, perhaps a bit too harshly to her weeping sister. "Staying won't make him change his mind and we need to get out of here." Turning, she sloshed through the cold water in the only direction that was open to them. As she moved, a silent prayer went up to the Giver that nothing was alive in the waters that could harm them, nothing dead to trip them up, and nothing hidden to swallow them into darkness and make them drown. She found herself praying for Briac's safety as well, not wanting any of them to find their final resting place to be in the very one they all thought would save them.

CHAPTER THREE

Ashlynn had long since lost all feeling below her waist. The cold crept up her legs and gripped her thighs and hips, setting them ablaze in an icy pain. She was weary as she and Kenayde moved through the underground passageway that was their escape route. Her arm was tired from holding up her torch and she switched hands, glancing at her sister as she did so. Soft golden curls were matted and wet and Kenayde hadn't spoken for awhile. Ashlynn fully expected a complaint or two at least, but there had been none and she was starting to worry.

"It can't be much further, Nadie. We'll be out soon." Kenayde nodded, but didn't speak. She, too, was tired of wading through cold water and holding up a torch.

For a while the passageway had gone straight and both girls were optimistic of a fast opening into the forest. After the first turn, they were even surer of their escape. Five turns later, six, seven...their optimism had severely diminished. Ashlynn had promised they would soon be out so many times that Kenayde's nodded reply was now mechanical. She knew Kenayde was only moving because she was following her. If Ashlynn stopped, as she desperately wanted to, Kenayde would sink into the water and be done for.

They came to a three-way split where the water was shallow and offered a small island of rocks to the right side of the tunnel. Ashlynn sloshed her way over and Kenayde did the same. Both of the girls were exhausted and managed to curl up against one another on top of the rocks and sleep, the torches shoved between the cracks to give them light and warmth. When they awoke it was impossible to tell the time, and whether it was night or day. Kenayde held her torch high and looked at her sister. "Which way, Lynnie?"

"I don't know," Ashlynn answered softly. If she was figuring the turns correctly they had been heading into, or even under, the mountains. "It would help if the water had a current or was moving."

"But...the water is moving."

Ashlynn looked at her sister, confused, then followed the blue eyed gaze to

27

the left tunnel. Lifting her torch higher didn't show her what Kenayde was seeing at first, but then the water did indeed move. Not in any certain direction, but rippling and swirling like something had surfaced and gone back under. Kenayde made a small sound like a whimper and moved closer to her sister as something swam past her legs. "Lynnie..."

In a quick protective movement, Ashlynn put her younger sister between herself and the wall, both of them facing the direction of the rippling water. Farther back in the tunnel from which they'd come, a half-seen shape jumped from the water and made a slap like a fish throwing itself against the wall. Ashlynn realized she'd been holding her breath and exhaled. "Stay here." She moved in the direction of the sound, Kenayde very close behind, ignoring the order given to her. Nothing could be seen in the limited torch light and the waters were so dark that it was impossible to tell what had made the sound. "I don't know what it was. A fish maybe?"

Kenayde shook her head vigorously. "That was no fish." She glanced behind herself, making sure the wall was still close by. Turning to get a better look, she narrowed her eyes and reached out with her free hand. "Whatever it was hit here. Look. The wall is all wet."

"Kenayde, don't!" The idea hadn't formed quickly enough in Ashlynn's mind to figure it out before, but now she grabbed Kenayde's hand and pulled it back just in time. The droplets of water, stationary until that moment, now sank into the wall as though being absorbed by a sponge. In the same instant appeared the head of a beast, scales black and blue, shining exactly like the water on the wall had, eyes white and sightless. It spat, hissed and snarled. Kenayde screamed, pulling her hand away from her sister and into herself. "Easy," Ashlynn soothed. "It's a water dragon." She pulled Kenayde back so that the creature would stop sputtering. His head wasn't large at all, the size of a small horse at best. "Can you understand me?"

The dragon blinked his empty eyes and calmed some. A rumbling came from his throat, the promise of an ill nature if she came any closer. *I understand your words, Gael. What are you doing down here?*

Ashlynn flinched at the intrusion into her mind. *My apologies, great lord of the waters. It was not our intention to intrude or disrupt. My sister and I are simply looking for a way out.*

You must have gotten down here somehow. Go back the way you came and you will get out.

His head started to sink back into the wall, but Ashlynn reached out with her thoughts. *Wait! Please, we cannot go back that way.*

The dragon stopped, halfway gone into the wall. *Why not?*

"What's going on?" Kenayde whispered. "Is it talking to you?" Unlike Ashlynn, Kenayde's abilities were not very strong. She could create fyre on her own on very rare occasions, but that was the extent of it.

"Shh," Ashlynn instructed. *Death awaits us if we return from whence we came. Please, great dragon, we are in need of your permission to pass...and if you would be so kind, perhaps your help.*

The dragon considered the request a moment before turning to gaze at the girls. *You smell like ashes and it bothers my senses.*

Ashlynn smiled despite herself. It was a very juvenile thing to say for a creature who had the ability to live for hundreds of years. His size would not have given his age away as it varied from dragon to dragon, but now Ashlynn was more amused than intimidated. *Forgive me. Even with the water, I cannot escape the way I seem to smell to the drags.* The dragon snorted and pulled his head completely into the wall before coming back out into view and bringing the rest of his body with him. The girls moved back, Kenayde hanging onto her sister's arm as they saw the dragon in his entirety. Like his head, the rest of his body was black and blue, and slick with slimy buildup. He had no wings and was shaped like an over-sized snake. Fully before them now, he had to hold onto the wall with his stumpy legs to keep himself above water.

Tell me more of this supposed death that awaits.

"He wants to know why we're down here," Ashlynn told Kenayde.

"Can he understand me?"

"Yes." Ashlynn kept her eyes on the dragon. "He can hear you but he can only speak telepathically." She pursed her lips for a moment. "He is still a young one from what I can tell and wants to know why we can't go back the way we came."

Kenayde let go of a soft sigh of wonder. "What are you going to tell him?"

"The truth."

Well?

The dragon didn't seem to have much patience and Ashlynn had to keep herself from letting her own impatience leak into her thoughts. *We pass here to escape men who seek to place the death of Tadhg on our heads.*

Rightfully?

Yes, she admitted boldly. *He was an evil man that needed to be put out of our misery.*

The reaction from the young dragon was not one she'd expected. He was laughing and it felt like something tickling somewhere in the back of her mind. *Death amuses you.* It was more of an observation than a question.

Mortal death is always amusing. Especially when one believes he has the right to kill the other.

Ashlynn scoffed. *That is rather impertinent.*

I am older than you by several years, Gael. I have every right to be.

And as a water dragon, you should be showing respect to those before you

29

with the ancient blood in their veins.

The dragon gave a warning rumble in his throat, shifting his position on the wall. Kenayde watched breathlessly, eyes going from her sister to the dragon as the silent conversation went on. *Respect? You are the ones invading my territory!*

And with your help we would gladly leave it.

This caused the dragon a brief moment of pause. His white eyes blinked to show he was considering what had been said.

We cannot find our way out without a guide.

Still the dragon was unresponsive, but after a moment he melted into the wall he had been clinging to. "What happened?" Kenayde asked eagerly.

"I don't know." Ashlynn stepped forward and touched the cold and slimy wall. "I told him we needed his help to get out." Both girls heard a movement up ahead of them and turned in time to see the dragon stick his head up out of the water. Ashlynn smiled slightly. "Come on. He's leading us out."

Following the dragon, they turned for the right passageway and the last one Ashlynn would have chosen on her own. Being down in the dark and taking turn after turn had disrupted her sense of direction. Going right felt like they would only be heading back toward the castle but she also knew the dragon wanted them out of his place of seclusion and wouldn't lead them astray. She let Kenayde go first, more comfortable knowing her younger sister was in the middle and not left to bring up the rear.

Upon request, the dragon surfaced at another rocky area and let the girls rest again. He left them while they slept, returning when he felt them moving around in the water. For the first time since they'd been down there it seemed Kenayde had lost her fear. She held her torch high, the light flickering on the walls and bouncing off the ripples they made in the water as they walked. Her eyes stayed on the dragon when he'd occasionally stick his head above water and kept walking and looking for him when he was swimming below the surface. She was completely enchanted with the little thing, whereas Ashlynn just wanted to be done with him.

"He's a good spirit, to show us out like this."

Ashlynn snorted softly. "You weren't privy to the conversation. A good spirit is not quite the way I would choose to describe him."

"I wonder how he got down here. And how does he get about to eat? There's nothing alive down here except us. And there aren't even any bones in the water of what he might have eaten."

"I don't know."

Why does she look at me like that?

Even under the water, he was talking with Ashlynn and she smirked to herself. *I do believe she may be a little smitten with you.* That got him to leave her alone for awhile and this time when laughter was felt through thoughts, it was the dragon feeling Ashlynn's laughter.

"Lynnie?" Kenayde spoke softly. They'd spent another night in the cold water, and were feeling weak from the lack of food and parched with nothing to drink. "What do you think will happen to Briac? Do you really think he'll make it back home?"

Another question to which she did not have a sure answer. "Briac has been around much longer than we have and has been through a few battles in his time. Merrik may try to bring him down, and may even temporarily succeed, but you and I both know that Briac is far too stubborn and determined to get back to the Isles to stay a prisoner for long."

This answer temporarily satisfied Kenayde and she fell silent for a few minutes. Soon however, she questioned her sister again. "If you knew what he was going to do by not coming down here with us would you have still left?"

Ashlynn had been asking herself the same question for almost as long as they had been abandoned by Briac and her answer was always the same in the end. "Yes." She couldn't see her sister's reaction to the answer and didn't give her time to say anything in reproach. "It would have been one or all of us, Kenayde. Were it a choice between him or me, that I cannot tell you the outcome. Briac wouldn't have let me stay behind to take you home himself, so it would have been him to stay behind and I would not sacrifice our lives for a 'what if' to see us all stay together."

Kenayde trudged on ahead thinking over the answer her sister offered. "That's why you'll be high queen in Siness and why I am content to stay at Oceana."

"Why is that?"

"Because Oceana is peaceful and there are no decisions as important as life and death. Siness is one island, a part of a greater nation and that requires diplomacy. I do not know that I could have made the decision you claim you would have."

"No one knows what they can or cannot do until the time is upon them." Ashlynn frowned slightly. "What I say I would have done may not be true at all if the situation were before me. Diplomacy, decrees...it's all just pretty words."

"Words are not so pretty when they speak of death."

For once it was the younger sister to silence the older. Ashlynn studied the back of Kenayde's head and wondered how she could have missed her sister growing up over night. For so long Kenayde had been the little girl that clung to Ashlynn's shadow. She much preferred to let Ashlynn speak whatever harsh words needed to be said, then come along afterward to heal a broken heart with soft words. She never seemed to mind being the follower, the child. Now she was getting older and becoming independent of her older sister. In a small way, the realization of this left Ashlynn feeling a little unbalanced.

With nothing in their stomachs to sustain them, the girls tired easily and needed to stop and rest again. Their slumber was restless, but they woke to find bread, still dry, and some sort of salted meat. They didn't ask how the dragon had gotten it to them, but ate quietly and gave him their thanks before moving on once more.

"Do you remember the day you went on your first hunt?" Kenayde asked sometime later. Ashlynn did indeed remember it and she grimaced ever so slightly at the memory. "Mama and I were so worried for you, but Papa was confident that you would come home in one piece."

"And I did, didn't I?"

"You did," Kenayde agreed, "but nothing was ever the same after that day. Everything changed."

That was the day Ashlynn had used her strange magic in front of those she'd been training with. When she killed a mountain lion with her fyre alone they knew to take her seriously from then on and no longer questioned her ability to hold her own. Ashlynn may have been a princess, but none could tell it from the way she trained and learned. She was serious in her studies, trying to learn all she could about the Celts and the Gaels and what sort of power she had. When the men went into town for a night of drinking and women, Ashlynn disguised herself as a young knight in training and went with them. She would ignore the debauchery of her comrades, taking the opportunity to gain information from anyone she could about the Celtique Isles and the tales of the old magic that the Gaels possessed. Eventually Wessely caught on and called for her one morning before she started her daily studies.

She always felt he'd never trusted her, never believed she was mature enough to know the truth about who and what she was. Looking back on her memories she realized he had simply been afraid and wanted to protect her for as long as he could. She could still hear him saying to her the day he tried to show her, "Do not fault me for wanting to keep you safe. It has been my motive since the day you and Kenayde arrived."

Her reply had instantly been, "I would never, Papa," but she had spoken too quickly.

It was the first time he'd told her to use her fyre. For as long as she could remember she had been commanded never to use her magic. That day was different. It was as if he needed to see it. "Light the candles," he'd prodded. A simple thought had the room they'd been standing in aglow. "Sit and I will try to explain all that I can."

As king, Wessely was commanding and ever sure of himself. That day he'd been so soft spoken, almost nervous. It had unsettled her, especially when he began asking questions that made no sense. "What do you remember from your life in Siness?"

"I don't remember very much at all. Most of it is fuzzy. I remember being scared when Nadie and I were given to some woman to hide. I remember all the soldiers coming into town and the vibration of the floorboards from so many heavy horses riding by at once."

"What else? Do you remember anything before that?"

"Well...I was very young, Papa."

"I know." Wessely had looked at her, more serious than she'd seen him for a long time. "But you must try and remember. Anything. Please, it is most important."

All she really remembered of her life before the invasion were faces, her fathers' face being the most prominent in her memory. "I remember my father...a little anyway."

"And what before that?"

"Papa, I was only..."

"Think, Ashlynn." His insistence had been gentle, but there was a certain urgency to his words even as he'd placed an old scroll before her.

"What is this?" Wessely hadn't answered but grabbed one of the candles to bring it closer over the printing. "Papa, what's going on? You're scaring me." This small plea almost seemed a shock to the king. He'd looked at Ashlynn, who shook her head. "I can't remember anything and I do not know what you want me to remember so badly. What does it even have to do with anything?"

"Everything." Wessely pursed his lips together a moment. "Look at this scroll and tell me what you see."

Ashlynn couldn't understand what had gotten into her father, or the way he was acting now, but leaning over the table, she obliged. What was on the scroll meant nothing to her. "It is one of the ancient languages. I can't read it."

This seemed to almost disappoint the king. "Nothing?"

"Not a word of it." Ashlynn looked again, more than certain that the writing on the scroll was not something she had studied. In fact, even the way it had been written seemed somehow old. But then something caught her eye. "Wait. It does look a little...that word there..." She pointed to a group of lines, eyes narrowing slightly. "That...I think it says *time*." Ashlynn blinked, a little surprised to recognize anything but now motivated to keep looking. She ran a finger over the parchment, intrigued. "Um...water. That right there is water. And earth. No, maybe...no, I think it is..." Finally looking up, Ashlynn shook her head. "What is this, Papa?"

Wessely seemed almost unable to speak. It was hard to tell whether he was pleased, surprised, or in complete shock. He, too, shook his head, and even for a moment looked on the verge of tears. "I do not know what language this is," he answered at length, "nor does any scholar to see this since it has come into my possession. Even the most educated are at a loss."

Silence filled the room and it only took a few seconds of it to make Ashlynn laugh. "No, really. What is it? It has to be one of the old boring languages I looked at with my tutor before." Wessely did not speak but continued to gaze at his daughter with the same complex expression. This made Ashlynn uncomfortable and her tone grew slightly in decibel. "What language is this, Papa?"

"I truly do not know."

"What do you mean?" She slammed open hands on the table and rose, no longer even slightly amused. "How can I know a language you do not? How is that even possible?"

"Lower your voice." She was feeling riled but not beyond the ability to listen. "Sit, please. I will try to explain." Wessely started to gather up the scroll, but Ashlynn stopped him by placing a hand on top of it. He left it alone and sat down. "I will ask you to remember your tone. I have no doubt that at one point or another you will feel the need to express that rather audible temper of yours, but please..."

Ashlynn nodded soundlessly and sat back in her chair, fully prepared to listen.

"Before your father had you," Wessely began carefully, "there was an island just off the northwestern coast of Ibays - Magroh Island; you've heard it mentioned in your studies." Ashlynn nodded once more. It was a place she'd heard of only a handful of times and not much had ever been said about it. "The island was small," Wessely continued. "If it was as large as Nivar, I would be surprised. But it needn't have been large to be intimidating or a threat to anyone. There was nothing on Magroh but trees and one small mountain. Again, nothing at all to concern oneself with. It was what the mountain contained that made the island so important."

She'd guessed a dragon.

"Yes, heartling," said Wessely, "a dragon. And she was a terrible beast to anyone that would enter her domain. For generations she was there, and she became a target for game long before she became a legend."

"I've never heard this legend."

"For good reasons, I assure you." Wessely looked at the flame atop the candle closest to the scroll. "Countless men, kings, nobles, simple county peasants...many lives were lost in the pursuit of this dragon."

Ashlynn's eyes narrowed. "Why? Was she a danger to people?"

"Not at all."

"I would be pretty grouchy if someone tried to enter my cave, too."

Wessely smiled. "As would I. Especially if I were protecting something precious to me."

"Like a baby dragon?"

"Some wondered, and you know how priceless hatchlings are to poachers."

Ashlynn made a face. "Don't remind me. I think hunting dragons is disgusting. Especially the Gaelic ones."

"I could not agree more, but many still hunt them. Money is a powerful motivator to even the gentlest of men, and there was a high reward for every part of a dragon. In most places there still is, though not as high as the payment for Unicorns. But they pursued this dragon for the sheer sport of it. The more men to die at her talons, the greater the challenge. The greater the challenge, the higher the reward. As years passed and her dracklings would have grown, it became very apparent that there were no offspring. Never were they seen to take to the skies for hunting and, for that matter, neither was she."

"Then how was she getting food?" Ashlynn looked thoughtful. "If there were always men coming to hunt her as you say, then it would be folly to leave, even to sustain herself. Her treasure would be vulnerable, just as she herself would be."

"But then, as you ask, how did she stay alive for so long? And what was she protecting, if not her own young?" There was an odd light to Wessely's eyes, a strange excitement.

"You tell me," Ashlynn said with a nervous giggle. "I don't know this story."

"No one ever knew how she lived, but she thrived even in the continuous hunts. It was your father who solved the mystery. Part of it, at least. Your father went to Magroh Island with a skeleton crew, and when they returned to Siness, none of them were quite the same as before. When they were asked about what they had found, all remained silent on the matter."

Ashlynn wet her lips and sat forward. "So...what happened? What happened to the dragon? Did he kill it? And why wouldn't any of the men speak? Why wouldn't *he*? Did he find what she'd been protecting?" There came a slight wrinkle of confusion to her forehead. "And why have I never heard this story before?"

The excitement Wessely had before had faded, replaced once again by the solemn look of apology. "Your father was never one to take a life for sport or bragging rights. What truly happened on that island, only your father knew. I would like to believe that he told me the truth of it, but I cannot be certain. What my brother told me was that he left Siness with three men to his crew and no more. Upon reaching Magroh Island he left strict orders, telling those men to stay on the ship no matter what they saw or heard. And if at any moment they feared he had been lost, they were to sail for home. But there was never a need

35

to worry. The dragon, as it would turn out, had been waiting all along for your father." Ashlynn blinked her surprise and Wessely nodded. "Countless years of being pursued only to wait for the moment she met him. When he approached the mouth of the cave nothing could be heard or seen of her but the reflection of her eyes, like a cat who's been caught in a shadow gazing at you. She didn't snap at him, didn't growl. At first she did not even move but looked at him in her disembodied darkness. It was a moment of judgment on both parts: your father trying to decide whether or not to get closer, the dragon deciding whether or not to let him."

"I can picture it," she said softly. The memories she had of her father were fuzzy, but his face was something she would never forget. He'd had a kind and gentle face, beautiful hazel eyes and blonde hair that was always soft and just brushed his shoulders when he wore it loose. In her mind, Ashlynn's father actually looked like a younger version of Wessely, though Wessely had been the younger of the two. "He went in, didn't he?"

"He went in. At least, he started to. As soon as his feet touched the darkness the dragon made the strangest sound..."

"She was thrumming," Ashlynn ventured, her voice somewhat distant and dreamy.

Wessely's smile was soft. "That beautiful vibration of peace coming from her very core, making the walls and the ground of the cave tremble ever so slightly, was her way of welcoming him. He entered and the cave was lit in a fyre more amazing than he'd seen in his life. The heat of it was grand, but not overpowering, and the colors were like nothing he'd seen before. Looking at the dragon, he finally saw her in all her glory. Her scales were golden and almost too dazzling to look at in the light of the fire. When she moved, her eyes stayed on him, blue-green probes to take in his every breath and the thrumming did not stop. There was no danger there, and both knew it. When she drew upon him and put her giant maw very close to his face, he didn't flinch. Instead he reached out a hand and placed it on the side of her head. The scales felt like living heat but did not burn, and they were hard as steel. She closed her eyes and leaned into him.

"All at once her figure changed, shrinking and turning into that of a human in the space of but a few breaths. The dragon was no longer there but instead, a maiden more beautiful than words could ever express."

Ashlynn's smile was wide and her green eyes full of understanding. "She was a Gael, a human who is also a dragon! Oh, how wonderful!" Except, she realized at once, how much of a risk she'd taken by revealing herself to Nir. "But that's dangerous. There aren't any ordinances off the Isles to protect them from poachers."

"I believe she chose to reveal herself despite the danger because she was tired. Not in the physical sense, but of the wait and the fight."

Ashlynn rested her chin in her hand. "But what was she waiting for?"

"Someone to take her home. Someone to love. That was what she told your father when he asked her years later. Beautiful and small; she always looked gentler and more frail than she really was. Her hair was long, reaching down to her waist and curling at the ends, golden as her scales had been." Wessely smiled, almost to himself. "The only thing that gave away her true temperament was her eyes. There was a fire in them, a light of hidden mischief."

Ashlynn's head tilted slightly. "You speak as if you knew her. Or know her. Is she still alive?"

Wessely sighed softly. "I did know her. Rather well, in fact. She was someone a person could never forget. Beautiful beyond description, charming, winsome, and fiercely loyal. Once she was by your father's side, she never left."

"By his..." Ashlynn sat straight and stiff with brows drawn together. "Wait, are you telling me this...this dragon was my..."

"Your mother," Wessely finished for her. "Yes. Her name was Siobhán and she came home with your father disguised as one of his crew."

Nothing came from Ashlynn's lips and she stared at Wessely, dumbfounded. Dozens of questions, demands for answers, a gamut of emotions ran through her head; it was nearly impossible to choose any one to begin with. "How..." It was as far as she could go before other words, other thoughts distracted her. Finally blinking, Ashlynn shook her head, running a hand over her braid and wetting her lips. "I don't even know what to say."

Wessely looked at his daughter with a small amount of pity. "Do you believe me? Because that's what is most important. You must know that I have never once lied to you and I would not change that now."

"I know," Ashlynn answered softly. "That is why I don't know what to say." She lifted her eyes from the table. "If Siobhán was my mother and she was a Gael, what about me? And Kenayde? We've never...I mean, I can make fyre, sure, but I've certainly been angry enough to lose control and turn into...and we don't even know if Nadie has the ability of fyre because she won't even try."

"There is much we don't know," Wessely replied calmly. "There were times we were afraid that any given tantrum would be the one to trigger something and you would change. It was one of the reasons I was so nervous to let you train in combat."

Ashlynn's eyes narrowed. "If my mother was Gaelic, then it should have passed on to me. Nadie and I should have known what we were inherently and we should know how to use it by now." She looked at Wessely again. "Right?"

"There is more to the story, Ashlynn." Wessely pulled yet another book from his vast collection. "It has been written that there was once, before humans ever inhabited the land, a world where many living beings existed. Giants, goblins, faeries, rocs, sphinxes, merfolk, creatures unmeasured in number except for the dragons. Only six dragons with abilities uncharted. One dragon for every element..."

As the page was turned, Ashlynn's fingers moved in silent calculation. "Earth, Water, Air, Fire, Light, and Darkness. But what do these six Elemental dragons have to do with me or my mother?"

Wessely turned his eyes back to the book in his hands for a moment and read aloud. "The dragon of Water was low to the ground and long in body. No wings did it have for no wings would it need.

"Fire was blood red, with teeth as sharp as iron. She could withstand the most brutal of attacks and her scales would burn to the touch.

"Air had breath that was cool and fresh, his glorious body the color of clouds. He was gentle and kind but brought storms and dark skies when enraged. His counterpart, Earth, had scales of gold. She had a temper that was contained on the fair days and deadly on the foul."

"Wait a minute..."

"Light and Shadow were hardest to control," continued Wessely, ignoring the interruption. "Both thought they were the best of the pride, both vain in their looks and their gifts. All six were able to change their forms later on in their lives, taking on the shape of humans, as well as..."

"Papa!" Wessely stopped and looked at Ashlynn. "Are you trying to tell me that my mother was one of them, one of the Elemental dragons? Are you telling me she was Earth?" Her tone no longer held that new excitement, but was low and quiet. "How much of this did you actually think I would believe?" Reaching over the table, she grabbed the book from Wessely's hands and closed it. She closed the other book as well and left them atop the scroll with the ancient language. "You actually had me convinced for a little while, but then you went just a little too far with this last part." Wessely's pursed lips parted as he started to speak, but Ashlynn stood up, disappointment in her expression. "If you wanted to make me think that my magic comes from a dead bloodline so I'd stop asking questions and searching on my own, it didn't work. You lied to me for the first time, and it didn't work. Now I'm just going to work harder, and I'm going to do it alone."

There was nothing Wessely could say to stop her or reason with her. Ashlynn brushed past him and ran. Within moments of her exit, the candles went out and Wessely was left alone in the darkness.

CHAPTER FOUR

Luella left almost as soon as the confrontation with her brother had ended, only lingering long enough to catch a few words of what was being exchanged between Merrik and Laidley. The older man's counsel was wise, but it would take more than that for Luella to ever trust Merrik. Something about him always made a cold chill run down her spine. No matter the atmosphere of the room, he somehow changed it with his very presence, as if a cloud of darkness shadowed him wherever he went. He had never once touched her or said anything inappropriate, but his eyes lingered too long on her sometimes. It was why she tried to avoid even being in the same room with him whenever possible.

No one had accompanied Luella as she set off from the castle. She'd gone down to the stables with enough money to keep the stable boy quiet, saddled her own black palfrey, and left with no guard in her company. She found she was more comfortable on her own, enjoying the freedom of choosing where to go; one of her retinue was bound to tell her any given direction might not be the wisest of choices otherwise. It was an easy guess to assume that her brother and Merrik would take the fastest and most direct route to the church, so to avoid any detection, Luella decided to take the long way around. If the three Laidley sought were clever enough to use Rabia powder to kill her father, surely they would realize that every monastery had more than one way in and out. If Laidley had been thinking a little more clearly he probably would have realized this as well. Though Luella had no idea where a secret exit might end up, she could only assume it would bring them closer to the port town of Amme.

It was strange for Luella to be out on her own, defying orders, such as they were. She'd expected a certain amount of anxiety, guilt even, for what she was doing. Her entire life had been spent in accord with her brother; never had there been any large thing they disagreed on. Now, however, Laidley was bent on

39

vengeance. It was the very same thing that turned Tadhg into the man he had been.

"We have to catch them before Laidley does," she told her horse. She dug her heels into his ribs and he snorted, picking up his speed. If Laidley found the trio first he would most certainly kill them without a second thought. If they were truly Celts as Merrik had said, a war would then be started, though perhaps that was what Laidley wanted. It would be a way to prove himself, a chance to show everyone that he could be just as heartless and callous as Tadhg had been. What better way than to wage war with the Celtique Nations? They were islands of mystery and deep loyalty to one another; a family where blood did not matter. During his lifetime, Tadhg hated the Celts more than any other and sought to destroy every last tribe on the Celtique Isles. Their camaraderie was a threat to his reign. Though they did not actively seek to overthrow him, the very knowledge that they could was enough to make him act in fear and begin making his wars.

Galloping at breakneck speed, it came as a sharp surprise when the horse whinnied a loud protest, digging his hooves into the damp soil and rearing. Luella pressed her knees tight to the stallion and leaned forward, narrowly avoiding being thrown. She jerked the reins when he tried to turn and run back the way they had just come. The horse pranced nervously, shuddering beneath her and spooked by something Luella couldn't see. "Hush!" she commanded in a sharp hiss as the horse snorted loudly. She swung a leg over the saddle and jumped to the ground, the reigns still held tightly in her grip.

"All right, calm down." The horse threw his head when Luella tried to soothe him with a gentle hand to his nose. Her curiosity piqued, Luella tied the reins to a tree so she could explore. Nothing seemed odd to her, but the palfrey was a sensitive horse. He had to have seen or smelled something troubling to be so startled. Either way, she could be in danger. Blue eyes scanned the trees and the dark green shadows around her. Perhaps there was a better way to go about this.

She looked at the horse and stroked the side of his face. "Run, and run quickly," she whispered. Once he was free, she slapped his flank and sent him galloping back through the forest. Luella knew what she had to do now and her horse would not be safe where he was, especially tied up. She paused a few moments to listen to the fading hoof-beats. As soon as she was sure the horse was far enough away, Luella stood tall and locked her knees.

A pain ripped through her body to her very core and she cried out. It seared when her fingers elongated and joints formed where humans should have none. Her clothing melted into her skin, iridescent black scales in its place. Toes turned into claws, wings spanning sixteen feet wide when fully extended erupted from her shoulder blades, followed quickly by a tail at the base of her spine. As her face lengthened and her lips went from mouth to maw it took everything in her not to cry out. Dropping to all fours, the transformation from human to dragon was now complete. Five times her normal size, Luella had to move from where she crouched in order to have room for her new girth.

In draconic form it was much easier to see the three sets of hoof-prints in the shadows, though the sunlight bothered her eyes more; one of the drawbacks to being a kindred to the dragons of Darkness. She would need to be cautious as she moved about the woods and watch for any predators or hunters.

Luella had shifted into her dragon form only a small handful of times and for no longer than a few minutes. No one in her family knew she could do it and she prayed they would never find out. Tadhg had not been a Gael, and that meant her mother, who was most certainly not a Gael, had to have been intimate with another man to produce a daughter who could become a dragon at will. It also meant that Luella was part Gael. It was one of the reasons she'd been so quick to try and stop Laidley from killing the three he now sought. In part, they were her kin. She would risk a night in the rain if it meant finding them.

One of the few benefits to Tadhg being a crazy warmonger was his constant thirst for knowledge. He needed to know everything about everyone, and therefore had a literary collection that filled two separate rooms. With the Gaels being his biggest opponent, at least in his mind, his library was extensive. Stealing books one at a time, Luella learned about her gift and what it meant for her. She also learned that dragons and Gaels could speak to each other with just a thought. There was never a reason to test this before, but now the idea was rather enticing.

She'd found the church easily enough, and stayed perfectly still in the shadows when Laidley and Merrik passed her. They were headed back to the castle with three soldiers and something being dragged behind the trailing horse. The sharp tang of blood filled Luella's senses like old metal on her tongue. That did not bode well for her mission of mercy.

When morning dawned on her third day alone in the woods, she decided it was time to try a new approach. It would be her first time using mind-speak, but if she reached even one other creature it could aid in her search. Lashing her tail in anticipation, Luella tried to remember what the books had said about it. Just...think.

~*~*~*~

Far beneath the ground Luella stood on, the water dragon leading Ashlynn and Kenayde poked his head above the surface and froze. The sisters exchanged glances as they, too, stopped. "What's wrong with him?" Kenayde whispered.

"I don't know," Ashlynn replied, watching the dragon with slight concern.

41

Are you all right?

Did you hear that?

Ashlynn's eyes narrowed and she glanced around. *Hear what?*

On the surface, Luella snorted in excitement. She could hear the young water dragon. *Give me your name and your exact location.* Her voice sounded much more commanding than she'd ever heard it, almost like it was coming from another being entirely.

How can you not hear that? the water dragon spat in Ashlynn's direction. Surprised, he turned his attention to the new voice in his head. *I am Elas McGee, my lady, and am fully at your service. Currently I am in the tunnels under ground that lead away from the house of the brethren, shepherding two irritating young girls to the surface.*

Ashlynn glared at the dragon she now knew was named Elas but said nothing.

Why do they not respond? Luella asked. *Tell me your names.*

I believe they cannot hear you, my lady. Elas turned in the water to look at Ashlynn and Kenayde. *They are but pests seeking to avoid the hand of justice.*

Where will you come above ground? These children may be the two I seek. She waited for the answer but instead of words, a picture was forced into her mind of a spring that came up close to Amme. *Thank you, my friend. We shall meet there.*

Ashlynn held her hand aloft and a ball of blue and gold flames lit up the murky tunnel. Elas hissed fiercely and disappeared under the water. *What is going on?* she demanded.

Kenayde shied away, wide eyes going from the fyre in her sister's hand to the spot where the dragon had disappeared. "Lynnie?" she ventured, but it appeared that Ashlynn was too focused to hear her. "Ashlynn!" Finally, green eyes blinked and Kenayde relaxed slightly. "Control, remember? There is not enough room in here. You'd kill us all."

Ashlynn stared at her sister a moment, taking the words in one at a time and processing them slowly. Eventually she nodded and closed a fist over the flames, extinguishing them instantaneously. "Very well." Her voice was soft in the darkness. "Let's turn around and go down the other tunnel." Ashlynn started back and Kenayde followed with confusion on her face.

"Why?" the younger sister asked. "What happened?"

"Because." Ashlynn's tone was suddenly cold and flat. "Following the dragon will now take us to our captors." Kenayde let go of a gasp of betrayal and then another gasp when Elas appeared from the wall like a sponge oozing excess liquid.

For all your fancy words and haughty attitude you certainly act more like a whelp than I would have expected. Ashlynn glared at him, his words in her head like the soft buzzing of a bee caught in a jar. She reached for Kenayde's hand, poison in her glare at Elas, and tugged her sister along. *The other tunnel leads farther underground and stays there,* Elas continued, clinging to the wall and unfazed by her venomous looks. *Your only other option is the way you came, and there is no telling if that way is yet clear for you.*

The words hit her and Ashlynn growled, low in her chest at first and then building audibly. In her frustration, she threw her torch down the tunnel where it went out as soon as it hit the water. Darkness became a heavier blanket over them, but Elas appeared amused at the little tantrum.

For a long moment no one breathed a word. Kenayde drew closer to her sister, one hand in Ashlynn's, the other clutching their only torch left alight. Ashlynn's angry and uneven breathing bounced off the walls, amplified and making her sound much bigger and more dangerous than she was at the moment. Ultimately she turned to Elas with hurt and defeat on her face. *Why did you tell them we were here?*

Elas shifted his weight on the wall, white eyes blinking before partially closing. *I had no choice.*

There was obvious shame in his tone, albeit slight, and Ashlynn watched him closely. *What do you mean you had no choice?*

The dragon swished his tail. *Do you understand nothing of what you are?*
"Lynnie?"

Ashlynn held up a finger, silencing Kenayde. *Please, Elas. I need to save my sister, if nothing else. I am sorry for my temper, but this situation is not as amusing for us as it seems to be for you.*

Something in her mental tone made Elas duck his head. He didn't respond for a moment and when Ashlynn started to turn away, sure of his silence, he gave a soft whine. Ashlynn stopped and looked at him once more, surprised by the feeling of submission that came with the sound.

I have lost track of the way my people live, he explained slowly, *how I am supposed to live. I know we have our rules, and alliances, and levels of command, but I have been down here for so long that I have forgotten them.*

Sensing Kenayde's growing sense of unease, Ashlynn repeated his words. "Why?" she asked aloud. "Why have you been down here so long? And what does that have to do with anything?"

Elas dipped his tail into the water as though seeking comfort from it. *Because,* he began, then paused thoughtfully. *Tell her to put her hand on me. This will take us days if you have to repeat everything.*

Ashlynn eyed the dragon for a moment, considering. With pursed lips she nodded in his direction, her gaze never leaving him. "Put a hand on him, Nadie. You'll be able to hear him." Kenayde moved forward slowly, letting go of Ashlynn. *If you hurt her, I **will** kill you.*

43

You have my word, Elas replied, humbly sincere but quick before Kenayde's small hand was on his back and all three were open to the conversation.

"It's going to hurt," Ashlynn told her, referring to the foreign voice that would soon be in her head, "but you'll get used to it after a little while."

"I know," Kenayde replied meekly. "I remember the last time you tried to speak to me like this."

Ashlynn nodded once before turning her attention back to Elas. "Now, start talking."

You are young, he began, but immediately recoiled at the look of disapproval on Ashlynn's face. *What I mean is that there is still much for you to learn about our kind. Like humans, there are those of us who are fickle and vain. We care only for things that make our personal world a little more comfortable. I was not such a source of comfort to my family and ended up down here to protect myself. If my disfigured body could not be looked upon then I could not be looked upon.*

"How awful," Kenayde said softly, head bent and eyes closed.

"So what you're saying is that we serve you no purpose and so you must rid yourself of us?" Ashlynn inferred.

No, Elas hissed. His serpentine head swiveled, turning white eyes to Kenayde. *Remove your hand so that I may show you.* Kenayde did as she was told, eyeing the dragon curiously. He let go of the wall and fell into the water with a graceful splash. The sisters shared a glance when it took him a moment to reappear.

I must ask you one thing. Ashlynn turned her gaze down the tunnel, knowing Elas was there but unable to see him. *Please do not scream.*

"Do not..." Ashlynn reached for her sister, pulling her from near the wall to keep her close. "Stay calm, Nadie," she whispered. "He asked us to stay calm." Standing close together, Ashlynn felt the shiver that ran down Kenayde's spine. She scared so easily, it was a wonder she'd lasted so long without having some sort of a breakdown.

The water up ahead of them moved and Kenayde lifted her torch to get a better view of what was coming. When Elas stepped into the light, she covered her mouth with her free hand to hold in a cry of pity. The figure before them was no longer a dragon, but not quite a man either. One side of his face was smooth and lovely, with pale skin and an eye so blue it could have been a direct reflection of the ocean. Long blue hair brushed his shoulders in damp clusters and tangles, and thin red lips seemed carved into a permanent frown. The left side of his face, from hairline to his neck and below the collar of his tattered shirt, was a mask of the same scales that covered his body when he'd been a dragon, his left eye just as white as it had been before.

"Please..." His voice was higher than it had been in Ashlynn's head, and she recognized the accent for the first time as it echoed around them. It surprised her to hear the vulnerability in his tone. He clenched his left fist, or what should have been a fist but was another extension of his dragon form. "I'm sorry. I know how hideous I am. I didn't mean to frighten you."

Kenayde seemed frozen, still staring with a hand over her mouth. Ashlynn, on the other hand, peered at him with curiosity. "You're a Gael from Ibays. I know that accent. What...happened to you?" Her question was barely audible, and Elas looked down at his taloned hand.

"I was attacked by wild dogs when I was a boy. It was my first time shifting alone and they caught me right in the middle of it. When my family saw that the damage done would be permanent..." He trailed off, letting the girls figure the rest out for themselves.

"And you've been down here ever since," Ashlynn surmised, looking at his torn and poorly patched clothing. He nodded and looked down at the water with obvious shame. "I'm sorry that happened to you, Elas. I am. But it neither explains nor excuses you telling whoever it was that we were down here."

"I'm surprised you couldn't hear her," Elas remarked thoughtfully. "We are limited in our abilities when we are in human form, though I thought for you it would be different."

"I suppose it may have been simply because she was unfamiliar to me."

For a long moment Elas simply stared at Ashlynn, half his face frozen under lustrous scales, the other free from any discernible expression. "Perhaps," was his only reply at length. He seemed to decide something then, and it appeared to put him a little more at ease. "She is young in her gifts, this one you cannot hear, but she gave me an order and I had to obey it."

"Why?"

It was the first thing Kenayde had said since Elas had shifted, and his eyes went to her. She is of the dragon of Darkness. A simple Gael like myself cannot willingly disobey a direct order from a direct descendant."

"An Elemental?" Kenayde looked up at her sister with worry. "Why would an Elemental be after us?"

The frown Ashlynn had been wearing deepened and she looked down at her sister. "I don't know; it doesn't make any sense. Why would an Elemental be on Tadhg's side?"

"If it helps," Elas offered, "I felt no malcontent in her words. Just determination."

This did nothing to change Ashlynn's thoughtful scowl. "Are you sure it was an Elemental?"

Elas nodded. "I know the difference between my kind and theirs."

"Perhaps," hedged Kenayde, "she's here to protect us. Maybe she knew

45

somehow that we needed her and she's here to protect...her...kin...." She trailed off, shrinking from the glare her sister was giving. "Sorry."

"I know the difference between my kind and theirs," Elas repeated. Both girls looked at him, one with hopefulness and the other with a mixture of pessimistic disbelief and irritation.

"Really?" The doubt was heavy in Ashlynn's single-worded question.

"Really," Elas confirmed, unaffected by her tone. "Why do you think I didn't attack you? You invaded my home, my solitude. If it had been anyone else they would be dead by now. You...you just sent my temper racing because it was so unexpected. I began with discourtesy and for that I apologize, but when you started giving it right back..." The corner of his mouth twitched into a small smile. "It's been so long since I've had anyone to talk to."

Kenayde looked up at her sister with a trace of amusement as well, but there was hardly a refection of the levity the others shared. In fact, Ashlynn appeared to be quite the opposite of humored. Slightly irritated with her sister, Kenayde returned her attention to Elas. "We need to get out of here, Elas. We need to find our friend and go home. Do you truly believe that this dragon means us no harm?"

He shook his head slowly. "I felt no ill will in her thoughts, though I cannot say for certain there was anything positive either."

"Well...that's good enough for me."

Ashlynn balked. "Good enough for you?"

"What else is there to do, Ashlynn?" Now Kenayde was getting frustrated. Ashlynn had to sit and look at every angle, weigh every option. Kenayde had never been like that. She reacted with her emotions more than her head and trusted her gut feeling. It was a thing Ashlynn would never be able to do because she was too analytical. "We have three options open to us right now, correct?" questioned Kenayde. "We let Elas take us to the surface where we meet the Elemental. Maybe it's blind optimism because I'm your sister, but I feel quite secure in the fact that you could defeat her if it came down to it. Option two: we go back the way we came and risk Merrik and his men still being there. And Briac..." She couldn't bring herself to finish that thought. Kenayde may have been young and a bit on the naive side, but she understood full well what they might find of Briac if they went back. "Option three," she concluded in a much less enthusiastic tone, "we become hermits and stay down here with Elas for the rest of our lives."

It was quiet for a long moment and Elas stood watching the girls, his mismatched eyes trained mostly on Ashlynn's face. She hardly noticed, lost in the process of weighing the options her sister presented. At length, her tongue swept over her lips to moisten them, tasting the stale air around her. With a small sigh, she looked at Kenayde. "I think we should go back."

The surprise was evident in the other two, but Kenayde recovered quickly. With determination on her child-like face she took an emboldened step away from her sister, then another until she stood on the left side of Elas. He flinched away from the torchlight, his white eye closing almost all the way. Kenayde quickly switched hands and held the torch further away so as not to bother him. "I'm going with Elas, then."

"What?" There was shock in Ashlynn's voice and she stared now, incredulous. A glare at Elas had his head down, not wanting to be caught in the middle of it. "Kenayde, do you know what you're saying? You would place your trust in a stranger over me? Your sister?"

"It's not about that." Elas ventured a look at Kenayde when he heard her small voice break. There were tears shining in her eyes and her bottom lip quivered. "It's not about that, Lynnie," she repeated, her voice just above a whisper. "I cannot go back there and see Briac killed. I can't do it. I'm not as strong as you are." Her tears spilled over and Ashlynn was there in the next second, wrapping her arms around her little sister.

"It's all right," she soothed, running a hand over Kenayde's soggy curls. "It's all right, I understand." She took the torch from her sister and handed it to Elas so she could embrace her better. Resting her chin on Kenayde's head, she gave Elas a stern look. "Do not betray us."

"I may have no choice," he said honestly, though there was obvious sympathy on half of his face. "I am just a lowly Gael. She is an Elemental and therefore out-ranks me in any of my personal decisions."

"And what about me?" Ashlynn asked harshly. "Since you claim to be so insightful."

"It will come down to who gives the order first, I suppose."

"Then I order you to..."

He stopped her with a shake of his head. "Right now? You're just a human."

If Ashlynn could have killed him with a glare, she would have had him dead before another breath passed his lips. "Stop it," Kenayde mumbled from inside Ashlynn's embrace. She straightened herself, swiping at her tears with frustration. "Stop, Lynnie." Looking up at her sister, her gaze was pleading. "The best we can do right now is keep going and take this meeting with the Elemental one step at a time. What good are we doing standing here?"

"Fine," Ashlynn hissed, snatching the torch away from Elas. "Then this is how it will go. You, dragon, will exit first when we get there, and meet with this Elemental before we even emerge." His lips parted in protest, but Ashlynn continued without room for him to speak. "Through your words I will be able to judge the situation, so choose them carefully. If and when I decide it is safe for us to come out, we will. If not, then you will take my sister, and you will leave

47

while I distract this Elemental."

Kenayde's eyes went wide. "What? No!"

"There is no room for argument, Kenayde. It may be the only way for you to escape."

"I won't go without you! What if she's stronger than you? What if she kills you?"

Ashlynn's brows pulled together. "What happened to that blind optimism you had just a few moments ago?" Kenayde said nothing, but wrapped her arms around herself. Reaching out with her free hand, Ashlynn took Kenayde's chin and made her look her in the eye. "It's going to be fine. Elas will protect you."

"I will," he promised, not even needing the prompting glance Ashlynn shot him. "You have my word. If there's a battle, I will get you safely away."

Kenayde sniffled and looked at Elas when her chin was free. "I know," was her weak reply. "I trust you."

Elas seemed surprised by this and Ashlynn smirked, almost caustic in her gaze. "She trusts everyone." Dipping her head she kissed the top of Kenayde's curls before trudging on to find another dry place to rest.

CHAPTER FIVE

Things were silent for a long time as the trio made their way in the dark, heading toward either a bitter end or an exciting beginning. Ashlynn led the way with the torch in hand while Elas and Kenayde followed behind her side by side. Every so often, she would glance over her shoulder at the pair, looking more at Elas than her sister. As sincere as he sounded and for all she wanted to believe him, Ashlynn was not so easily won over as Kenayde.

"How long has it been since you've been home?" Kenayde asked, dissolving the silence with her timid question.

Elas didn't answer at first, taking the time to think so his reply would be accurate. "It's been thirteen winters since I have seen the green hills of Ibays. Soon to be fourteen by the feel of the waters."

"That's a long time to be alone. Weren't you afraid?"

"At first," he admitted. "I found this place by pure accident. I had been running for nearly six days, trying to get away from the shame I brought my family, eating little and sleeping even less. Eventually I found a ship that hired me as a deckhand after I promised to stay down in the galley during the day and only come on deck at night when most everyone had gone to sleep. Once the boat was docked, I just wandered through the port town and eventually out into the woods. The water down here called to me and eventually I was able to find the tunnels."

Kenayde's brows rose slightly. "The water called to you? How?"

Again, Elas was quiet in his thinking. When he finally ventured an answer it was slow and deliberately spoken. "It's almost like being cold through and through and nothing can warm you. You search for heat and even the smallest shift in the temperature, the tiniest hint of warmth draws you and the closer you get the warmer you feel. When you finally have that source before you or

49

around you and you begin to thaw, you know you're safe. A human's heat is my water."

It was a good enough explanation and Kenayde looked thoughtful. "Do you feel cold? Is that what land is for you?"

"Sometimes," Elas answered with a small shrug. "I can be on land in this form and even as a dragon, but the farther I am from water the more foul my state and the greater my aggravation." He looked at the back of Ashlynn's head. "What is your water?"

"Water is my water," Ashlynn answered curtly. In a much softer and subdued tone she added, "Earth."

Elas only nodded as though he'd expected as much for an answer. Looking at Kenayde, he studied her face. "May I ask you a question?"

"Of course."

"How..." He faltered, frowning. "How can you walk on that side of me?"

The question seemed to surprise Kenayde and she blinked. "Do you want me to walk on the other side?"

"No," he answered quickly. "I just thought you would be less disturbed and more comfortable with the human side of my face."

Kenayde looked over at him, half of her expression masked by the darkness but the other, highlighted by the torchlight, revealed a smile. "I could not be further from disturbed, Elas. You are beautiful in my eyes."

The compliment embarrassed Elas and rendered him speechless. Ahead of them Ashlynn rolled her eyes. She knew Kenayde found beauty in everything, but to have her warming up to someone who could very well betray them in the end instead of sticking with her own sister was downright insulting. "How much farther?" she demanded.

"Not far." Elas offered Kenayde a small smile of thanks, only succeeding in brightening her own smile. "May I ask you something else?"

Kenayde nodded. "Ask me anything you like."

"Can you make the fyre too? I know you couldn't hear me without touching me, but are you able to do other things?"

She shrugged dispassionately. "Yes, but Lynnie can do much more than I can. She always could. I know I can make fyre because I have done it once before. Like her, I can travel through the flames without getting burned, but that is the extent of it as far as we know. I think Ashlynn got all the gifts and to be perfectly honest, it doesn't bother me in the least."

"Because she was first-born," Elas guessed.

"She didn't always have her abilities," Kenayde continued. "At least that is what we were told."

"No. She wouldn't until the parent passed would she? You can't have two of the same Elementals at the same time. It would throw the balance off of everything." He pushed his damp hair behind his ear. "Was it your mother or your father?"

"Mother." Kenayde didn't hesitate in answering despite the glare tossed over Ashlynn's shoulder. "But our father also died when we were very young."

"I'm sorry."

Kenayde smiled her thanks. "It is sad in its own way, but we were raised by our uncle and his wife and they were our parents. We never lacked family or anything, really."

"Are we finished with the questions?" Elas and Kenayde looked at each other before falling silent. A light could be seen farther down the tunnel. "Is that it?" Ashlynn asked, blinking to making sure she wasn't seeing things.

Elas moved a bit faster, walking past Ashlynn. "Yes." His voice was low. "I will go first as you said to survey the situation." Ashlynn's eyes narrowed, showing she was still wary of him and this sudden willingness to do as she'd ordered.

"Lynnie." Kenayde put a gentle hand on her sister's arm, eyes asking for trust that was not yet earned.

Ashlynn scowled, unhappy with this momentary loss of control but recognizing the necessity of it. "Go," she agreed in a tight voice. "But I swear, if you betray us..."

"You'll kill me," Elas interrupted. "I know." Without waiting for any type of reply, the scales on the dragon side of his face started to spread and he sank down into the water. Within seconds he was climbing out and up the incline to the outside, no longer half human but all dragon.

~*~*~*~

Luella had never been so close to Amme without guards in her entire life. Then again, she'd never spent several nights alone in the forest or been outside the palace courtyard in her dragon form either. Yet here she was, no more than a hundred yards from civilization, covered in luminescent black scales. The excitement from all the firsts on her adventure had hardly lost their effect. She lashed her tail as she waited, overjoyed and a little nervous in the knowledge that at any moment she was going to meet her first dragon. The thought was more than a little amusing given her current form, but none the less thrilling.

The head that popped up from the hole in the earth just a few feet away had her flatten herself to the ground, almost like a cat getting ready to pounce. This dragon was a lot smaller than she was expecting and Luella lifted her neck slightly to peer at him.

Elas looked left and right, finally seeing the great black dragon as he climbed out of the tunnel completely. *My lady.*

51

Luella would have grinned if she could. *You are a water dragon.*

Yes, Elas confirmed with a respectful dip of his head.

And you most certainly are not from Caedia.

Correct again, my lady.

Luella now looked over his small frame to peer suggestively at the hole from which he'd come. *And the others?*

Will not come out until I can assure them safety.

The surprise registered in Luella's dragon eyes. *Are you their guardian then? What has happened between now and before when they were only petulant children to you?*

They became human to me.

Despite never having been in the situation before, Luella actually did understand. It was one of the cardinal rules of war that the dragon had broken. He'd gotten too close to his enemy. *Tell me your name again, my friend.*

I am Elas McGee of Ibays, from the Celtique Isles.

Well Elas of Ibays, please tell your charges that no harm shall come to them in my presence. I am a neutral party.

Down below, Ashlynn frowned as Elas repeated the last thing the dragon had said to him. Kenayde looked at her sister as it was translated once again, searching. "What do you think, Lynnie? Should we trust her?"

"No one is simply given my trust," Ashlynn replied darkly. "She will have to earn it." With lips set into a thin line of stubborn determination she took Kenayde's hand and climbed up the steep incline to the outside. After being in the dark for so long both of them had to blink several times to adjust their eyes. It was Kenayde who saw clearly first and it was she who now froze in wonder more than fright.

"Oh, Lynnie!"

Ashlynn rubbed her eyes once more after throwing her extinguished torch down. When she could finally see clearly, the massive black dragon hulking before them also took her breath away. For a moment the fear was forgotten, as was the responsibility of keeping herself and her sister safe. She too, was taken in by the sheer beauty of the ancient beast. "My lady," she felt compelled to say, and bowed her head. Kenayde did the same.

Luella's head tilted curiously to the side. *They cannot hear me?*

No, my lady, Elas answered, going to stand beside Kenayde. *But I have told them all you have said, and the older one,* Ashlynn glanced at the great Elemental as she was mentioned, *can hear me.*

But not me, Luella mused. *Curious.*

Elas took a quick look at Ashlynn from the corner of his eye. *The younger one...she was able to hear me through touch. Perhaps...* Ashlynn glared at him though her head was bowed demurely.

Luella only hesitated a moment before stepping forward and lowering her head before Kenayde. The younger girl stared at her for a moment, dumbstruck, before Elas tucked his head under her hand.

Do not be afraid, he encouraged. *She only wishes to speak and have you hear her.* Kenayde swallowed and nodded. With a quick glance at her sister, Kenayde lifted her hands and placed them on either side of the the great black maw.

Do not fear me, child.

It was a soft suggestion, but Kenayde squeezed her eyes shut and she staggered. This new voice in her head was much more powerful than Elas had been.

"Kenayde?" There was worry on Ashlynn's face as she tried to brace her little sister.

"I'm all right," Kenayde breathed. "She's just a lot bigger than Elas." With that statement, Luella pulled away from Kenayde's grasp. She seemed to hesitate for a moment as if trying to decide how to proceed. "Come back," Kenayde urged, determined. "I'll be all right."

The dragon shook her head. *No, this will be easier in my human form.* She looked pointedly at Elas. *But as I have promised no harm, so, too, must they make the same vow. I want their word.*

Elas relayed the request, still touching Kenayde's hand. This brought a look of confusion to Ashlynn's face. "Why would we harm you? This is neutral ground. If you keep your promise, we will keep ours. You have our word."

"Wait!"

All eyes turned to the youngest in the party; she looked down at the dragon beside her. "Please?" The one word was enough to convey what she wanted, at least to the two flanking her. Elas looked uncertainly at the much bigger dragon, and she simply dipped her head in permission.

Forgive my appearance, my lady. He stepped away from Kenayde so they were no longer touching, already increasing in size. He stood on his hind legs, spine straightening, talons turning into fingers and toes. Again, the scales receded from half of his body leaving the other like some sort of costume. Kenayde's small smile for him was one of encouragement, one that he returned uncomfortably as he stood by her side once more.

There was no form of acknowledgment this time but a look of curiosity from the large dragon. Her tail lashed once before her body began to shrink. The change was much the same as the one they had all just witnessed, but this time black scales disappeared completely to reveal smooth olive skin, long raven hair, and an exquisite black riding dress, making the simple peasant clothes Elas had, as well as the sodden clothes the girls wore, seem paltry in comparison.

Within the space of a breath, Ashlynn pulled her sister behind her, standing in a defensive position between Kenayde and Luella. "Lynnie!" Kenayde complained.

Luella brought her hands together, deferential before her. "You know who I am."

Ashlynn's lips were nearly bloodless, they were pressed together so tightly. "You deceived us," she spat. "*Princess* Luella...say you mean us no harm..." Ashlynn's green eyes darted from side to side. "Where are your men? Let them come forth so that I may burn them to cinders."

"You do not understand," Luella started taking a step forward. Ashlynn raised a hand, her palm empty one moment, a threatening ball of blue and gold flames there the next. Luella's eyes widened and the step taken forward was now reversed. "You..."

The fyre grew covering Ashlynn's hand in a warning. *Take Kenayde,* she commanded Elas. *Get her out of here now!*

He looked at Kenayde, his face a mask of scales and confusion. "But I..."

"Go!" Ashlynn yelled.

"Stop!" Luella had everyone's attention with her demand and what they saw when they looked at her had Ashlynn shocked speechless. The princess also had a hand raised, holding the same exact type of fyre. Ashlynn recoiled, completely stunned. Her own hand began to lower, her flames dying slowly in the process. "Will you listen to me now?" Luella asked, her tone much softer.

"How..." For a moment it was all Ashlynn could say. "I thought I was the only one."

"I thought *I* was the only one," Luella agreed, her fyre going out and a small smile on her face.

"I can do it sometimes," Kenayde reminded in a small voice.

Ashlynn shook her head, blinking as though this were all some sort of elaborate dream. "I don't understand." Her brow furrowed. "Besides my sister and me, I have never known another with the ability to summon fyre."

"Have you ever known another Elemental? The books say we have many things in common." Luella shook her head. "I really mean you no harm. There is so much to explain, so many questions I have for you and I am certain answers you need from me."

"But if you are an Elemental..." Ashlynn's stature relaxed some allowing Kenayde to come out from behind her. "...that means Tadhg was...." Her eyes narrowed. "But that makes no sense. If he was a dragon he would have used that very much to his advantage and destroyed more than men on horses alone could." Luella said nothing, her expression patient and somehow reminding Ashlynn of Wessely. He always had that look when he knew she would figure it out on her own if she really thought about it. And as Ashlynn did think, her narrowed eyes showed her sudden understanding. "Tadhg was not your father."

54

Luella shook her head. "No one knows this. Tadhg himself did not even suspect."

"But why tell us?" Ashlynn questioned. "We...I am the one responsible for his death. You must know that already."

"I do. But I tell you as a token of my trust in you. That you would allow me to be part of this."

"Why?" Ashlynn asked again, convicted in her suspicions.

"My brother is out for your blood. He is truly Tadhg's son, even down to his very way of thinking. His way of solving this problem is taking your life as you took the life of his father. An eye for an eye, as they say. I tried to speak with him, tried to dissuade him from starting another war, but he is set in his ways. He is just as stubborn as I am and I know he is, at this very moment, hunting for you. He and the captain of his guard will not stop until they find you."

"Merrik," Kenayde said with a small shudder. "He has a black soul. I knew that just from the brief time he was inside the church. Even the torches quivered under his eye."

"He is very good at what he does," Luella agreed. "He was also the chief supporter of the wars my father waged. It was his lust for power, I believe, that sparked the want of it in my father."

"If you are trying to convince us that Tadhg was once a great man I feel it cruel to let you continue. There are no words that would ever convince us of that." Ashlynn was no longer antagonistic in her tone but far from friendly. "He killed our father when we were children. A great man would not slaughter innocent people like sheep, all for the love of power."

"It wasn't all for," Luella argued amicably. "There was a legend he sought to prove true."

"A legend?" Ashlynn asked.

"The legend of the Elementals." Lifting a hand, Luella swept her hair from her face. "It is said in times of brutal war, the Elementals would return to seek revenge upon those that would willfully harm those most innocent. They are the keepers of the peace but also the Giver's warriors, His wrath in tangible form."

"I have heard a different version of that legend." Elas seemed almost hesitant to share what he knew, simply because of the way Ashlynn's gaze demanded information.

"When I was a boy, I was blessed enough to have stories told to me by a visiting elfin matron. She, along with several other elves, were often in my village and this particular elf liked to tell us children different tales each time she came. I remember one about the Elementals particularly because of the enthusiasm with which she spoke." Kenayde, exhausted and clearly tired of being on her feet, sat on the ground. Luella smiled at the younger girl and did

55

the same, leaving Ashlynn and Elas the only two standing.

"She said it was written in the old scriptures that the Giver sent His son to walk upon the earth - the Deliverer they called Him - a piece of the Giver Himself in flesh. It was His son who created the Elementals, the curious fyre makers, to protect the followers of the one God. The Elementals were to care for these mortal men, to protect them from harm but to never interfere with their mission to spread the Giver's message of good news and love."

Now Ashlynn sat as well, reproachful. "I didn't take you to be a follower of the Giver, Elas."

His expression was one of confusion. "Does that matter? Anyway, Elementals were given the gifts of fyre, of mind-speak, and the ability to become like mortals themselves in appearance."

Ashlynn asked, "Why give them the shifting ability?"

"Because they were to spread the word of the Giver as well, and in their Elemental form alone they would be hunted," Elas explained. "Though there has not always been a Tadhg there has always been someone like him; someone who believes he should be feared and worshiped by everyone."

Again, it was Ashlynn to speak up. "Every man has his own truth. Who but the Giver Himself is to say that He is the one god to follow? Does not every man in his lifetime dream of power? What makes the Giver so different from someone like Tadhg, but that we cannot see Him?"

Kenayde looked at her sister, appalled. "Ashlynn! Why must you be so confrontational and antagonistic? You are a believer in the Giver yourself!"

Ashlynn's shoulders rose in a slight shrug. "Sometimes."

"Oh?" There was obvious disbelief in Kenayde's expression. "And who was it you prayed to before and after your little suicide mission? Who do you remind me to pray to when I am either afraid or worried? You cannot choose to believe in Him one day and disregard Him the next. That would be like believing that a sword can kill you once and not the next time."

"Excuse me," Luella broke in. "There will be plenty of time to discuss theology later. If it's all right with you, I would like for Elas to finish so that we may decide upon the next step. What of the Gaels, Elas? How did they come to be?"

When neither sister said anything, Elas continued gingerly. "I suppose they were the offspring of the Elementals, the second-born, third, and fourth born, and so on."

"And the legend?" Luella pressed.

"Oh yes!" Elas had almost forgotten why he'd started speaking in the first place. "The elf said that when all twelve Elementals are found and come together, the word of the Giver will have been spread according to command and the Deliverer will come again to make this world new and to take his

56

followers home to be with him and his Father."

"And those who choose not to believe?" Kenayde asked timidly.

Elas frowned. "Will face the wrath of the Giver Himself."

For a moment no one said anything more, each processing the tale in their own way. It was Luella who spoke first, a frown on her face. "It sounds more like a prophecy than a legend."

Ashlynn nodded, agreeing. "You believe your father was seeking the Elementals because he wanted to see if there was any truth to it?"

"Not at all," Luella said. "I believe he wanted to find the dragons to slay them, and any offspring they may have. If this legend was proven true or given too long to spread among the people, there would be less fear in him and more hope in someone else. If he could not destroy the Giver, he would destroy those that represented Him."

"That makes sense." Ashlynn's gaze was to the ground. "When I was younger, Papa told me that Tadhg invaded Siness because he was after Kenayde and me. I never understood, even when he tried to explain it to me. But I understand now. Our mother was the Elemental dragon of Earth."

"Making you her heir when she passed."

"Yes." She looked at Luella. "But if both you and I are direct descendants of the chosen, why is it we cannot hear each other?"

For some reason they all looked at Elas, as though he should have the answer. In turn, his eyes widened and his shoulder rose and fell. "What makes you think I know?"

"Maybe, like the second coming of the Deliverer, all the Elementals have to be together again before it can happen." Every so often, Kenayde would say something so completely right that anyone in her company would have been shocked to hear it come from the young girl. This was one of those instances. She looked around at all the eyes on her. "What?"

"That makes sense," Luella agreed in the next moment. "It has been generations since they have all been together. If a talent goes unused for too long, it eventually goes away."

Ashlynn shook her head. "I speak to the Gaels all the time through telepathy."

"Didn't you hear Elas? Beasts with special abilities. Perhaps the way the Elementals communicate with each other is completely different from normal telepathy."

"Telepathy is not normal," Kenayde grumbled. This finally drew a smile from Ashlynn and she tugged a lock of Kenayde's hair.

"Only because you can't do it. You would think otherwise if you could." She looked at Luella once more. "So you think if we found the others it would be restored?"

"It is only logical." Blue eyes turned to Elas, a thin line of concentration on Luella's brow. "You said twelve Elementals? I was always taught there were only eight."

"I was taught six," Ashlynn added.

Elas shook his head. "No, I distinctly remember her saying twelve because I always heard after that there were only eight."

"Briac would know." Kenayde chewed on her bottom lip as Ashlynn squeezed her shoulder.

"Was Briac your third?" Luella questioned gently, remembering what she'd seen in the woods.

Ashlynn nodded. "He stayed behind and let us escape. We all knew that Merrik was out there..."

"And that my brother would join him shortly," Luella finished. "It was brave of him to stay behind. He must have loved you very much." Kenayde offered no reply but Ashlynn gave a small smile of thanks. "The best thing we can do now," Luella continued, "is get as far away from here as possible."

"We are going back to Siness," Ashlynn told her, standing and brushing her clothes off. "If your brother means to engage us in battle it is where we should be." Her glance at Kenayde was regretful. "We will be strongest in our own lands."

"I agree," Luella nodded. "There are ships going in and out of Amme all the time, at least so I have been told. It shouldn't be too hard to find one sailing for your homeland."

There was an odd expression on the human side of the water dragon's face. As Luella and Ashlynn discussed how to best approach finding a ship, Kenayde stood and went to him. "You look sad."

Elas frowned. "I cannot say for certain what I am." He looked at Kenayde, a strange mixture of emotion in his gaze. "It feels like my world has been turned upside down. For so long I've been alone and then you and your sister come along. Not only do I converse with another living being, but I also share this human side of me. And then I end up in the presence of not one, but two Elemental dragons." He attempted a smile but failed halfway through. "I'm afraid my life will seem rather dull for awhile after this. I almost feel as if I've made a friend."

"Oh, but you did!" Kenayde took his right hand between both of hers. "Elas, you did. And Lynnie, she'll be a different person when she's home, she always is."

"She is protective of you," Elas said, looking at their hands together. "I cannot fault her that."

Kenayde smiled. "Come with us." Elas blinked, startled by the suggestion, and Kenayde nodded. "Come with us."

"I...that would be impossible." He pulled his hand back, frowning. "I have not been to the Isles for too long, and I haven't changed. They won't want me now any more than they did then."

Kenayde was not so easily dissuaded. "Then you will stay with us in Siness. The people there are embracing, Elas. They will look on you as a kindred and not what it is you've convinced yourself that you are. You will be among your own kind again. You will have friends and a family."

"A family?"

Kenayde nodded once more. "It is what we are there. We are all family. We look out for and take care of one another."

Elas took a long moment to consider and when he spoke, his tone was hesitant. "Will you stay with me? Or...let me stay with you?"

The smile that spread across Kenayde's lips was spectacular. "Yes."

"Then I will go with you." His tone was begrudging, as though he had lost a bet and now had to pay up. "You may need added protection anyway."

Surprising everyone, Kenayde squealed in delight and threw her arms around Elas. He was shocked to the point of not moving, especially when he saw the guarded way Ashlynn now looked at them. "It will be wonderful!" Kenayde was whispering, seemingly unbothered by the fact that she was embracing a stone statue. "I promise."

"Kenayde." She let go of Elas and turned to look at her sister just as Luella was leaving the group. "Luella has gone to find someone to get us dry clothing," Ashlynn explained, "and safe passage from here."

"To home?"

"Eventually." Ashlynn frowned. "There may be other stops along the way, depending on the vessel, but we will get there. I suggested using fyre but that is no longer an option..."

"Because Elas is coming with us," Kenayde interrupted. Ashlynn nodded and Elas drew his brows together.

"Do not put yourselves in more danger than is required, especially on my account." His gaze flickered between the two sisters. "I can cross the sea on my own and much faster than any ship you find. Or I will stay here. I will do what is required if only you will keep your safety in mind."

Kenayde began to say something, but it was Ashlynn that argued his chivalry. "I am keeping our safety in mind. And yours. If the prince somehow finds out you helped us and catches you, he will kill you without a second thought. If we use fyre to travel he will see the scorch marks left behind and know we are not normal Gaels. If I shift and fly us home, it would be the same as becoming a living target for an archery contest."

"And the princess?" Kenayde questioned.

This made Ashlynn frown. It would be going against her very nature to

59

simply accept this stranger into the fold. Yet what choice did she have? It was with a stern reminder to herself that trust was not the same as acceptance that she spoke. "By aiding us she knows her life is now forfeit as well. If and when her brother finds out what she is, he will kill her anyway. The burdens of the father are always placed on the child when the father is no longer there to bear them."

Kenayde shook her head. "But she is his sister!"

"It does not matter," Ashlynn said evenly. "Blood loses to power every time. So now we stick together. We protect each other no matter the cost."

"And when we are home again?"

"When we are home..." Ashlynn looked at her sister with determination. "When we are home we will seek council, regroup, and put an end to this war before it has a chance to even begin."

CHAPTER SIX

Luella stood at the bow of the ship, the wind blowing her hair in salt water tangles. This was her first time on a boat and leaving her homeland. Rational thinking told her she should be afraid of all the unknowns and the uncertainties, but there was a thrill of the unexpected in her veins. Her small protected world was growing by leaps and bounds and it was more exciting than anything the young princess had ever experienced before.

Luella had found a boat with the help of a local, an average sized shipping vessel that let them ride with the promise of payment in the way of labor. They would be making several stops before reaching Siness and there were letters and parcels that needed to be sorted before they could be delivered. It was quick work split up among them and they knew the price for their transport had been just so the old captain could argue he hadn't fallen victim to three pretty faces and given them a free ride.

At the first stop, not more than a day after they set out from Amme, they had two hours ashore in a village Luella had never heard of. It wasn't anywhere near as large or beautiful as Amme, but it had an inn where Kenayde and Ashlynn were able to wash up and purchase cleaner clothing. Luella even bought newer things for Elas which, to his surprise and humble thanks, were presented to him when they met at the beach. Now, sailing into the setting sun four days later, they had only one more stop to make before reaching Siness the next morning.

Ashlynn came up beside Luella, silent and calm. The two looked like night and day in comparison. Luella with her long dark hair, chestnut complexion, and crystalline eyes. Ashlynn with golden waves, fair skin, and a piercing green gaze.

"I love sailing," Ashlynn said after a long while. "It feels like a whole other world at sea, like things on land couldn't possibly effect you." Their faces were cast in the brilliant orange light of the setting sun and they had to look away after a moment. "How are you doing, Luella?"

Luella's answer at first was a smile, but it didn't last long. "When we started out I was actually excited about the entire adventure. But when the tasks are completed and there is nothing left to do but think, I find myself despairing over what I've done and the ramifications of my actions." Ashlynn nodded her understanding and Luella smiled at her briefly. "Where is your sister?"

"She sleeps below. It has been a long two weeks for her."

"You as well, I imagine."

Ashlynn shrugged. "I will rest when I feel the need. Have you seen Elas?"

Luella nodded and glanced down at the ocean below. "I see him every so often, speeding about like some sort of fish." Everyone was safe and accounted for and Luella gave a soft sigh, thoughts returning to Ashlynn's question. "I think of my mother and all that she's been through in these past few years. She has suffered so much loss and now with my absence I fear for the status of her mind."

Ashlynn frowned. "Do you think she would harm herself?"

"She has tried before." This obviously surprised the fairer girl, but Luella nodded her confirmation. "When the castle was attacked not long ago, she lost a child. Now my father is dead and both of her living children are gone from her sight..." An expression of regret turned Ashlynn's eyes down toward the water. Luella saw this and covered one of Ashlynn's hands with her own. "This was my choice, Ashlynn. Do not take my burdens upon yourself, save the one part we share in, if you choose to be burdened by it."

"But I don't," Ashlynn replied, "and I think that is why I feel as I do. I have taken a man's life and feel no shame, though my prayers are very much with your mother." Luella gave her hand a squeeze before settling back on the wooden railing. "Luella, you still haven't told me why you're helping us. Why would you risk everything, knowing in the end that..."

She trailed off and Luella supplied the rest. "That I am forever a hunted exile or my brother must lose his life?" She grimaced. "I would sooner sacrifice myself than see this world torn apart by constant warring. Laidley wants to be just like Tadhg - no, he wants to be worse - and if stopping him from doing so results in his death, then the rule will be to me once my mother is gone or simply passes it on to me, and we shall finally know peace."

"And what of you? What if the sacrifice demanded is your own life? We sail for Siness, not to simply go home, Luella. We go to prepare for war."

"I know." Her voice was so soft it was almost lost in the wind. "If my life is the price that must be paid it will not have been for nothing." She turned her head to look fully at Ashlynn. "Because of you and thanks to Elas, we know more about Tadhg's ultimate goal, or what we think it may have been. Ashlynn, we're sisters now in a way that I could never be a sister to Laidley. He must not be allowed to be our children's Tadhg. We have to put an end to this before his hatred is too broadly bred."

For a long moment the girls simply looked at each other. When the silence between them was broken it was by Ashlynn, still with a trace of remorse in her voice. "We will do all we can to protect you. You have my word."

"I do not fear for my life. When Laidley realizes I'm with you it will only add to his determination to kill you. He will save me for last and it will pain him, but he will try to kill me."

The hardness Ashlynn was known for was finally returning as thoughts of a battle with Laidley forced softer emotions away. "Let him come. We will find the others and end his reign before it can even begin. I will not let him be the king of war he so wishes to be."

~*~*~*~

The sound of footsteps above deck the next morning made Kenayde open her eyes. Her rest had been fitful and even though shards of sunlight filtered down through the floorboards, she felt too exhausted to believe it could really be time to rise. She turned her head on her swinging cot to look over and see Ashlynn and Luella still asleep, both in identical hanging hammocks, Luella's below Ashlynn's. Making as little noise as possible, Kenayde sat up and swung her feet around, almost falling out of her bed as it swayed with her motion. With feet firmly on the floor she ran a hand over her blonde mane. Panic crossed her face when she realized how wild she must look. She wet her hands with her tongue and tried to tame what she could, still plaiting her messy curls by the time she was dressed and climbing above deck.

The sun was not yet very high at her back, but it was brilliant and fresh as only a new day can provide. Kenayde enjoyed the heat of it and smiled as she walked across the deck. In the distance was the silhouette of land. No one had to tell her that she was seeing the outline of her homeland. Something just felt right inside her at the sight; she was more at peace than before. The Isles had that effect on many people. It was not that they were untroubled by conflict (the Isles had seen their fair share of warring), but the very air seemed to breathe peace and hope into a person's soul.

"Where will we be docking?" Kenayde asked the captain, finding him at the command.

"Ain't got much to deliver this time so I planned on porting in Marl."

Kenayde grinned with excitement. Marl was just a small fishing village, but it was on the island of Siness and fairly close to Altaine. Grabbing the older man by his face, Kenayde kissed his cheek with great enthusiasm. He grumbled to put on a show as Kenayde ran off, but there was the smallest hint of a smile in his eyes.

"Lynnie! Lynnie, wake up!"

Ashlynn opened her eyes in time to see Kenayde rushing down the stairs from above. There was no panic in her voice, otherwise the older sister would have been up and on her feet immediately. As it was, she simply grunted a "What?" rolled over and pulled her blanket up over her head.

"Is everything all right?" Luella asked, yawning her question.

"We're almost home!" Kenayde answered, grabbing Ashlynn's blanket and yanking it from the bunk.

"Hey!"

"Get up! We're almost to Marl! I need you to fix my hair. Look at it!"

"Is there breakfast somewhere?" Ashlynn grumbled. She finally rolled over to get a good look at her sister and blinked. Despite the braid, untamed wisps of blonde hair stuck out all over the place. "What did you do in your sleep?"

Luella giggled and Kenayde looked exasperated. "I know! I need your help!"

"All right, all right. Calm down." Careful not to kick Luella, Ashlynn swung her legs over the edge and jumped down. "How did you sleep, Luella?"

"Fine, thank you." The princess watched as Ashlynn dug out a brush and pins from the things they had purchased in town. She turned Kenayde around and undid the braid to brush it out. "Actually," said Luella, "this was more comfortable than my bed at home."

"I slept terribly," Kenayde complained. "The constant swaying kept waking me up."

"Well, you will be able to sleep in a bed of your own tonight," Ashlynn consoled.

"I know! Even though Siness is more your home than mine, Lynnie, it will be nice to simply have a bed again!" Kenayde was so excited that it was as if the events of the past few days had not even happened.

"What's our plan once we get there?" Luella pushed her blanket back and sat up in her hammock. "Should Elas and I wait in Marl until you feel it is the right time for us to join you?"

Ashlynn shook her head, already taming Kenayde's hair into several small braids she was draping across the crown of her head and wrapping around the hair that was left unbound. "No, both of you should come with us. We will need to call council immediately and there is no need to waste time. No one will know you unless they've been to Montania and I doubt there will be many, if any at all, who have."

Luella grimaced. "I suppose that is one of the benefits of having lived such

64

a sheltered life."

"Lynnie, let me do your hair," Kenayde said as her sister finished. She looked at Luella with a timid smile. "I can do yours as well, Luella. If you'd like."

The smile Luella returned was one of gratitude, truly touched by the offer. "I would enjoy that, Kenayde. Thank you."

"Come, we should go up into the sunlight." Luella went first, then Ashlynn with Kenayde following. The older sister stopped halfway up the stairs and turned to give Kenayde's chin a gentle pinch. "What?"

"Thank you for being as sweet as you are." Ashlynn smiled affectionately and brushed aside some of Kenayde's bangs. "The Giver must have known what a brute I would be and put you on this earth to even things out a bit."

"I love you too, Lynnie." Kenayde smiled and went to join Luella above. The princess was at the bow of the ship peering out across the ocean at the land they approached. "Have you ever been to the Isles, Luella?" Kenayde grabbed a wooden crate to stand on while she brushed Ashlynn's hair out.

Luella shook her head, expression placid. "No, I was rarely allowed outside the castle walls." She saw the pitying look Kenayde gave as she wound Ashlynn's hair into a twist, and Luella smiled. "My father was always afraid that if my mother or I ever left we would somehow be captured and used as leverage against him."

"He was right to think that," said Ashlynn, touching her hair gently once the twisted knot was fastened at the base of her neck. "That was an option we once entertained." There was no apology in her tone, just the simplicity of stating a fact. "Your father was not ignorant of the fact that he had many enemies."

"No, he reveled in it."

Kenayde lifted her brush to signal she was ready to to start on Luella's hair and the princess moved to where Ashlynn had been standing, facing the land that was getting closer by the second.

"Luella," Kenayde ventured as Ashlynn disappeared to find them all something to eat. "I cannot even begin to understand why you don't hate us for what we have done, but I am very glad you're here with us."

Looking down toward the sea Luella smiled sadly. "I would be lying if I said I never hated you. My family has seen so much heartache that the world has never known about. To lose my father, especially like that, was a blow that none of us were expecting. He was an evil man to his very core...but he was still the only father I ever knew." She felt Kenayde's fingers rake through the hair at the left side of her face, pulling strands up and brushing them before pinning them back in small sections. "I mourned him for as long as I could," she continued, raising her eyes to the land ahead of them. "But as soon as I heard Laidley speaking the way he was, I knew my grieving had to wait and that I had to act. My plan was flawed, however." Luella sighed. "I didn't think ahead and acted on impulse. I knew I had to find you and warn you, but I did not think about what I would do after." She laughed softly. "Though had I thought ahead I would never have imagined myself joining you."

Kenayde smiled and wrapped her arms around Luella's shoulders from behind in an embrace. The older woman stiffened at the unfamiliar show of affection, but Kenayde was hardly deterred. "I'm glad you did," she whispered in Luella's ear. "I thank the Giver for your friendship and for a new sister."

Despite her discomfort, Luella was touched by the show of affection. She lifted her hands to rest them on Kenayde's arms and gave her a gentle squeeze in return. "Thank you, Kenayde. I am thankful for you as well."

Still smiling, Kenayde kissed Luella's cheek and let her go. "Your hair is done, Princess."

"And just in time." Ashlynn carried three round loaves of bread, some cheese, and a pitcher of warm milk on a board used for a tray. "Breakfast, anyone?"

"I'm starved!" Kenayde hopped down and took one of the loaves before Ashlynn even had a chance to set the food down. Luella smiled her thanks and took some cheese with her bread. "What about Elas?" Kenayde asked once she'd swallowed the big chunk she'd bitten from her loaf.

"He is quite full, I assure you." Ashlynn took some of the milk. "It has been a long time since he's had fresh fish."

The girls chuckled. "You spoke with him then?" asked Luella. "He must be exhausted, swimming all this time."

Ashlynn shook her head, swallowing the sweet milk. "He crept aboard last night and slept below deck with us."

"I knew I saw him!" Kenayde exclaimed. "I thought I was dreaming."

Luella smirked. "Where is he now?"

"Swimming somewhere ahead of us. The closer we get to the Isles, the more anxious he becomes."

"Why?" Luella asked.

"He's afraid of being rejected," Kenayde explained, sympathy in her tone. "He fears being turned away because of the way he looks, like he was when he was a boy."

"Which I just told him a few moments ago was ridiculous." Ashlynn brushed bread crumbs from her bodice. "We are not going to Ibays, at least we have no plans to at this moment. The people of Siness will think nothing of it."

Kenayde frowned. "But it's not as easy as that, Lynnie. You know that if you're born with the Celts you don't belong to just one country. We all belong to the Isles. You should be more sympathetic to his reservations."

"I know," Ashlynn replied quietly.

There was a soft smile on Luella's lips, almost sad. "What a beautiful relationship. I never realized there was such a kinship among the different nations."

Kenayde nodded. "We are not Siness, or Ibays, or Cieria, or any one of the seven nations. We are Celts."

By the time breakfast was finished and taken care of the ship was only moments away from docking. Kenayde was practically bouncing with excitement, Luella was silent and reserved, and Ashlynn had a look of determination on her face. Her eyes scanned the fields before them as if searching for something unspoken.

Marl was just a small village with less than a dozen tiny homes scattered among the gentle hills and fields. The grass was green and lush, flowers of purple and white dotting the vibrant landscape and sending sweet wafts on the cool breeze. The girls thanked the captain before leaving the boat, and Ashlynn was already thinking about what the next step would be.

"Luella, would you summon Elas? Nadie, you stay with Luella in case he needs someone else to coax him."

"What are you going to do?" Kenayde asked.

"I am going to talk to the villagers and see if Briac has somehow made it home before us."

Ahead of them was a little girl holding a basket of freshly shorn wool, staring. As soon as Ashlynn turned and met her gaze, the little girl shrieked and dropped her basket, running a short distance to the little house behind her. "Mama! Mama, she's home!" The door opened and a woman stepped out.

"Quiet! You're going to wake the baby!"

The little girl grabbed her mother's apron and tugged, pointing down toward the docks. "Look, Mama! It's the queen! High Queen Ashlynn has come home!"

"What are you..." The woman stopped mid-sentence as she raised her gaze and saw Ashlynn approaching. She inhaled sharply and clutched at her heart, bowing deeply. "Oh, thank the Giver! Oh, Your Majesty!"

Ashlynn smiled at the woman, then at the little girl as she stooped to pick up what had been dropped. "Good morning. Please stand."

The woman rose at Ashlynn's beckoning, beaming. "Praise be to the Giver that you've come home safe to us." She smiled thankfully as Ashlynn handed her the basket. "And Princess Kenayde?"

"She is safe as well. She is with two of our new friends at the docks at this moment. Tell me, have any other ships come through here since yesterday morning?"

The woman shook her head. "No, Your Majesty. None."

67

Ashlynn frowned slightly. This was not what she had wanted to hear, but it was not terrible news. There were many other ports throughout Siness that were close enough to the capital. "Thank you. Will you..." Her voice trailed off as her eyes caught a flash of silvery white farther off in the fields disappearing into the forest. Forgetting what she was doing, Ashlynn walked past the house with eyes on the lush tree line in the distance. Putting her lips together curiously she whistled a little tune.

Elas was already out of the water and shifted into his human form when they all heard the whistle. Kenayde's head jerked up, surprise in her eyes that quickly melted into excitement. "Suule," she said softly. Gathering her skirts in her hands she took off running in the direction of her sister. "Come on!" she yelled to the other two.

Upon hearing the whistle, something in the trees paused a moment, walking slowly between thick trunks looking ghostly. Ashlynn grinned and whistled again. The creature hesitated only a moment before breaking through the trees and thundering across the field on heavy hooves.

"Suule!" Kenayde exclaimed, reaching her sister. Luella and Elas joined them in time to see the sun catch the gleaming coat of the horse racing toward them, giving it an ethereal glow. It neighed a powerful cry and as it neared, they saw this was no normal horse.

From its head protruded a horn of twisted silver and colorful opal. Its long mane was white and full of waves that reached down almost to its knee. On the side of the unicorn that the mane left exposed, black fur that formed an impossibly intricate rope of knots ran up his leg from the opalescent hoof, exploding into a web of knots on his neck that faded into his mane line and came together just behind his eye.

"Oh, Suule!" The unicorn lowered his head as soon as he was close so that Kenayde could throw her arms around his powerful neck. Ashlynn approached to stroke the soft velvety fur of his nose and he whinnied softly, nudging her so that she almost fell back.

"Cormain lindua ele lle, mellonamin." She stepped forward again and kissed his nose.

"A unicorn," Luella breathed. "I didn't think they existed anymore."

"They barely do," Ashlynn said, smiling as she watched the wonder and gentility with which the princess held out her hand. Suule touched his nose to her open palm in greeting and Luella's eyes filled. "That is his way of saying hello," Ashlynn told her.

"Hello," Luella laughed, tone uneven with emotion. She pet his cheek. "If I ever doubted there was beauty left in the world, I doubt it no longer."

"Suule is one of very few unicorns left," Kenayde explained, running her fingers through his silky mane. "They are hunted on the other continents but here they are free and protected."

"Like the dragons." Elas also stared at the unicorn. "The Celtique Isles truly remain the last safe haven for all that is magical and pure."

"That will never change if I have anything to say about it." Ashlynn turned her eyes to the unicorn. "Atua kwentra sen lye mar." She kissed his muzzle and Kenayde let him go, understanding what had been said. Suule snorted and pawed the ground, dipping his head as if in a nod. They all took a step back as the magical beast reared up with a joyous cry. He tossed his mane as he landed with a thud and turned, running from them as fast as he had approached.

"He is so beautiful," Luella said in awe. Looking at Ashlynn, she seemed to have a permanent expression of elation on her face. "Was that Gaelic you spoke to him in?"

"Elvish." It was Kenayde to answer. "Unicorns only respond to the old elfin tongue. They refuse to learn English."

Elas laughed, disbelieving. "Refuse?"

With a roll of her eyes, Ashlynn shook her head. "You have no idea how stubborn a unicorn can be." She turned back to the mother and daughter behind them. "My apologies."

The older woman smiled. "Nothing to apologize for, My Queen. Can I make you all some tea?"

"Thank you for your kindness, but we must reach the castle as soon as possible." Ashlynn's smile had faded and was replaced with an air of a ruler that merited respect without having to ask for it.

The woman nodded slowly, a wrinkle of worry creasing her brow. "Has the time come?"

A frown pulled the corners of Ashlynn's mouth down but only momentarily. "It approaches, yes, but do not fear. Everything will be well at hand." Bidding mother and daughter farewell, the four began their trek across the fields.

~*~*~*~

Soft grass brushed a welcome against the bare skin of hands and legs as they marveled at the colors and textures around them. Closer to the edge of the forest, bursts of color showed among leaves too stubborn to change for the season. Despite living in one of the Celtique nations during his childhood, Elas had forgotten how captivating it could be. Not just what his eyes could see, but the very air itself seemed somehow different. An inhale brought life to his soul and the deadened parts of his spirit. He flinched as fingers ran gently across his human cheek. Blinking, he turned to see Kenayde walking beside him with a tender smile.

69

"Welcome home, Elas." She slipped her hand into his, her serenity almost tangible.

Just to their left walked Luella. She, too, was in a state of wonderful muteness as everything was being taken in. Something stirred in her that she could not explain and her cheeks were growing weary from a smile that would not disappear. Even Ashlynn, glancing over her shoulder to see the clasped hands of Elas and her baby sister, felt she could walk on air. The world did not feel so grim anymore. She had optimistically held the hope of winning this war; now she felt it was impossible for them to lose.

It took them most of the day to cross the fields, and with the forest still sheltering them from the harshest of winds to their left, they finally climbed the side of a steep and grassy hill. At the crest, all four stopped, speechless and appreciative, to take in the vastness before them. The land went on for miles, much farther than anyone could guess at first glance. Fields and hills, some gentle and some not, boasted acres of land for farmers and livestock. Shadows moved in ghostly dapples as thick and fluffy clouds passed overhead in the fading light of day. Small houses, much like those in Marl, littered the countryside in small clusters of two or three where households shared the work of the gardens, the animals, and lived as their own little communities.

Farther away the houses grew in number and luxury, eventually joining together to form the shire of Altaine. From where they stood, it looked very much like a child's playset of village homes, with people and things so tiny that none could see them. Directly in the middle was a small mountain, atop which stood the pride of Siness, the castle Altaine. Tall dark spires reached skyward with flags streaming in the wind, looking majestic and perfectly set against everything surrounding it.

Kenayde was beside Ashlynn now, face lifted to the colorful sky and eyes closed as the wind tossed stray strands of hair about her face. "Listen," she breathed. Ashlynn closed her eyes, Luella and Elas doing the same. With the beautiful scenery below them no longer a distraction, what they were listening for was not hard to be found.

"Pipes," Kenayde said, her voice almost lost to the wind. The sound of the bagpipes was faint, even as it seemed to be all around them, a haunting echo bouncing off every gentle slope to come back in musical whispers.

"I have heard tales of this place," said Luella after a long moment, eyes still closed. "They speak of it in ballads and bedtime stories."

Giggling, Kenayde opened her eyes. "This is not Heaven, Luella. But it is close, I should think." She looked at the castle far below, gaze specifically focused on the flags atop the spires and turrets. "Suule has already been to the castle. Look!" She squealed in clear excitement and started running down the hill. No one else seemed to have noticed the familiar unicorn waiting for them just a ways down, or the man next to him. He had brown hair that brushed his shoulders and carefully maintained scruff on his face. His clothing was worn and what they would see more of as they approached the town; a kilt of graying brown to suggest the long life it had seen, a long sleeved Jacobite shirt and leather boots on his feet. As soon as she reached him, Kenayde jumped up to embrace the man. He was grinning as his strong arms caught her, winding around her waist as he lifted her and twirled around. When she was set down, words were exchanged that the others were too far away to hear.

"Who is that?" Luella asked, pushing windblown hair from her face.

Ashlynn's expression was a soft one as she looked fondly upon her sister and the tall man she was so happy to see. "Jaryn," she answered with a small smile. The two turned to look uphill to see what was taking so long for the others to get down to them, and Ashlynn's smile grew. Jaryn met her halfway before she could make it down and they immediately fell into a tight and intimate embrace. One hand went around her waist, the other cradling her head as she buried her face in his shoulder.

It was fascinating to see this tender and very vulnerable side of Ashlynn. As much as Elas and Luella thought they should look away and give them a moment, it was hard to. Jaryn was very gentle with Ashlynn, as though she were made of the thinnest glass. The girl they had come to know over the past few days was much stronger than that.

Ashlynn finally lifted her face, relief in every bit of her expression. "It's all right," Jaryn said, his accent much thicker than either of the sisters'. His hands now cupped her face, a smile on his lips and bright hazel eyes sparkling. "You're home now, love."

"I was beginning to think I would never see you again," Ashlynn confessed, drawing a frown from Jaryn.

"Do you really think I'd ever let that happen?" Ashlynn only smiled and closed her eyes, leaning her forehead against his chin. The two of them seemed to have forgotten anyone else was there until Jaryn glanced to his right and saw three faces turned in their direction. "Come on," he prodded gently. "Let me meet your friends." Ashlynn nodded and felt him brush a kiss against her brow before reluctantly letting her go.

As Ashlynn collected herself, Kenayde took the opportunity to get another hug in, bringing Jaryn's wide grin back with ease. "Ah, I've missed you, Pickle."

"Pickle?" Elas asked with a smirk at Kenayde.

"It's a long story," she replied, blushing.

"I'd be happy to share it," Jaryn offered, slinging his arm across Kenayde's shoulders in a brotherly way.

She blanched. "No, thank you."

"One time she had this..."

"No thank you!" Kenayde raised widened eyes to his face.

Ashlynn chuckled. "Jaryn, let me introduce you to our two new friends."

Names were exchanged and Jaryn removed his arm from Kenayde's shoulders. He stepped forward to firmly clasp forearms with Elas, never blinking twice at the way Elas looked, then took Luella's hand and raised it to his lips. "Jaryn will be at council tonight," Ashlynn explained, "and integral to what we plan to do afterward."

He grinned, looking almost feral for a moment. "Aye. Nobody goes to war without me."

"Can we get going now?" Kenayde asked, a slight whine in her voice. "I would very much like to bathe and change before the business of running a country finds us to welcome us home as well."

Jaryn nodded in agreement. "The sooner we get to the castle, the better. Tasarin will be more than happy to return the throne to you."

As the group continued its descent, Ashlynn shook her head. "If he didn't want to do it, he should not have become my regent."

Not at all interested in talking politics, Kenayde fell back with Luella and Elas. "You are about to see a very different side of my sister."

"Another different side," corrected Elas. Luella nodded in accord. "We've already seen several different sides of her."

"That is how it must be when you are a ruler," Luella explained. "You quickly learn to be all things at once is a liability. You cannot be a parent or a lover when engaged in battle, just as you cannot be a warrior with no heart to your beloved or your children. You learn to change your role when your company changes. Not because you want to but out of necessity."

Looking at Luella oddly, Kenayde asked, "Are you all right?"

The question seemed to surprise the older girl. "Of course. Why do you ask?"

Kenayde briefly pursed her lips. "Unicorns are very sensitive to a person's feelings. They are born with the gift of empathy and know very well how we humans feel if they're close enough to us." She glanced meaningfully over Luella's shoulder. "Suule has not left your side since we reunited."

Looking, Luella saw the unicorn had indeed been somewhat beside her, just out of range of her peripheral vision. He was so big and loud on his hooves before that to know he could be so silent when walking startled her. She smiled at the unicorn and slowed her steps so they could be side by side. "How do you say hello?"

"Vedui'."

Luella ran a hand down his neck, smiling. "Vedui', Suule." The unicorn gave a small whinny and gently shook his mane, though Luella didn't remove her hand from his neck. "He knows how I am feeling?" Kenayde nodded and

Luella's smile revealed some of her sadness. "Perhaps he could tell me how I feel because I am not quite certain myself."

"Are you worried for your family?" asked Elas.

Luella thought on it a moment and eventually shook her head. "Perhaps, though I think it is more than that. I know why we have come here and I know that I found you to prevent more needless killing. Now we speak of going to war and I do not know the side I should stand on. I have all but banished myself from Caedia, but I'm not of these Isles. Where am I to go?"

Her answer came, but not from the person she was expecting. This time it was Elas who spoke up. "Firstly, do not be under the illusion that I have any great knowledge. While the three of you were on that ship, I was alone in the water and had space to think. I, too, was feeling as you do now; I still am to a small extent. Ibays has not been my home for many years. The tunnels under the monastery were my home, yes, but I was not really of Caedia." He shook his head, looking ahead as Jaryn and Ashlynn stopped their conversation and joined the others. "I was anxious when my feet first hit the soil, but it lasted no longer than a fleeting thought. I am Gaelic by nature, the blood of the ancient Celts running through me like fire in a way I have not felt in a long time until today. I may never go home to Ibays again, but the Isles are not just Ibays, and these Isles are my home." This brought a smile of camaraderie to Kenayde's lips that Elas saw as he looked over at Luella. "I saw your face when we were walking back there. Can you tell me you didn't feel these hills sing to you? And the pipes? What did you feel when you heard them?"

Luella didn't answer right away. Her fingers played with the hair of Suule's mane. "I felt," she answered at length, hesitant as though her answer might be wrong. "I felt like I was where I belong. Where I was home."

"And so you are." The look on Ashlynn's face was of gentle authority. "Caedia was supposed to be part of the Celtique nations, according to our history. In fact it was for a very long time, until some generations ago. Their king decided his country didn't need to be part of any sort of kinship with another."

Jaryn was frowning. "Forgive me, but may I ask a question?" His tongue swept over his lips and he stroked the scruff on his chin. "I know that you wish to remain anonymous, but what is the harm in the people knowing who you are?" Every gaze was now upon him and Jaryn shrugged. "I've been to Caedia. I've even performed inside the castle and I recognized you as soon as I saw you. Want to know what my first thought was?" When no one said anything, he continued. "Thank the Giver! We've turned one over to our side!" Luella chuckled, but Jaryn was serious. "It's the truth."

"You did not think me here as a spy, or a rogue agent for my kingdom?"

Now Jaryn chuckled. "With all due respect, my lady, you are a woman."

Ashlynn took a playful swing at him and Kenayde pelted him with a flower. "Sorry," Jaryn grinned, ducking as Kenayde threw another flower at him. "Things were getting a little too serious for me. I had to lighten the mood somehow. In all honesty, I believe the people would appreciate your openness and your trust in them."

"But how can I know they will trust me?"

"You can't," Kenayde answered honestly. "You just have to have faith."

"It is not a decision you need make right now," said Ashlynn. "We will speak with Tasarin as soon as we are inside. Let us all get washed up and into proper clothing. Then we will get down to business." She had her chin held high, ready and more than willing for the burden she was about to bear. "Prepare yourselves," she said to all around her. "This is going to be a very long week."

CHAPTER SEVEN

The small group turned toward the river that ran between the town and directly under the mountain instead of going straight for the main gate. This less public entrance would allow them to bypass all the citizens hoping to personally wish them a warm welcome home; there would be time for that later. Right now calling council was top priority.

The tunnels and stairways beneath the castle were no place for a unicorn so they bid farewell to Suule, though not before Ashlynn gave him a hastily written note to carry and orders for delivery. He was to make haste for the keeps scattered across Siness that housed representatives from the five other nations that were part of the Isles. They needed to be at Altaine as soon as possible. Suule was only too glad for this mission and left as the others headed into the damp darkness under the mountain.

By the time they neared the top of the secret entryway and saw light coming from under a door above them, everyone was wet, dirty, and exhausted. "This is not how I pictured my homecoming," Kenayde muttered as she wiped her slimy hands on her skirt. Jaryn pushed the stone door open, letting light spill out. "Can we not do this anymore?" Kenayde asked, blinking. "I have seen enough underground tunnels, thank you."

"I felt quite at home," Elas grinned. Kenayde stuck her tongue out at him, even as he helped her up the last few steps and into the light. They had come into a cell, a large room with thick stone walls and another stone door before them. There were beds enough for four grown men, and a chamber pot, though they were only for appearances. The real law breakers were further back in the dungeon so as to keep this room's true identity a secret.

Ashlynn went to the door and pulled it open, shocking the guard in the hall into speechlessness for a moment. When he saw the dirty face of his queen he recovered quickly, bowing his head and bringing his right fist up to rest on his heart. "Majesties," he greeted.

With a quick nod Ashlynn led the way out of the dungeons. The others followed silently, though Kenayde paused to thank the man by name. Jaryn, last to exit the cell, thumped the guard on the shoulder and the man straightened, closing the cell door behind them.

Ashlynn was walking so quickly now that Kenayde was almost running to keep up. Up the stairs and out into the hall, courtiers gasped and moved aside in shock to see Ashlynn for the first time in so long, then slowly formed a gathering parade behind her. The courtiers who had been waiting in the great hall to welcome Ashlynn home had not yet realized she was already there and so it was the stragglers that were late to the gathering to find her on her way through the castle.

Following the lavish red and gold carpet along the stone corridor, Ashlynn payed no heed to the long familiar portraits and paintings on the walls, or the vases overflowing with flowers at every turn. Tall wooden doors with iron embellishments swung open as Ashlynn followed the wave of whispers rippling through the castle that further announced her return and soon, the crowd following her had nearly tripled.

At the entrance hall a double staircase framed the enormous room, lit by torches and high windows of clear glass. There was a set of doors on the first floor in the direct center of the room with another set above it on the second floor. Carefully maintained ivy wound itself around and through cracks in the stone of the upper balcony wall. Flowers of white, cream, and pink stood out brightly where they bloomed and breathed their perfume into the air. The group took the stairs closest to them, Jaryn shooing the curious and chatting courtiers away. Pushing the heavy wooden throne room doors open with both hands, Ashlynn's entrance may not have been grand, but it was effective.

Every guard, four on each side of the room and two flanking the royal thrones, dropped to one knee with bowed heads, bringing their fists up to their hearts as the guard in the dungeon had. A reflection of the rest of the castle, the red and gold carpet covered the floor here, too. The light from the torches and sunlight streaming in from the windows made the room seem as it if had no roof at all.

In the brilliant light of the setting sun, a figure rose from the small seat beside the ruler's throne. He had long hair striped with the colors of honey and gold, and wore floor length robes of mossy green and white. Stepping closer, his eyes were so pale a gray that they seemed unnatural, and his ears were pointed at the tips, the tell-tale ears of an elf.

"Tasarin," Ashlynn greeted with relief in her tone. They met in the middle of the room, joining hands with joyful smiles. "Oio naa elealla alasse'."

Tasarin dipped his head gracefully. "Nae saian luum', arwenamin." He kissed her hands before letting them go. "I was most pleased when Suule told me of your return."

"I'm certain," Ashlynn smiled. "May I introduce my companions: Elas McGee of Ibays and Luella Ellison of Caedia. This is Tasarin Blackwood, my chief adviser, regent, and long trusted friend." Tasarin bowed his head again, every movement graceful. His smile was warm to the two strangers before turning brighter as he looked at Kenayde. "It does my heart well to see you safe, Princess."

"Thank you, Tasarin. It is good to be home. Well...sort of home."

"Now," said Ashlynn, turning back to the elf, "is there anything pressing I should know about before retiring to my quarters for a bath and clean clothes?"

"Suule has just delivered your letter to an Ibayish emissary as we speak. As for matters of the kingdom, none that need be reported before you rest. A box was delivered for you yesterday, a crate brought over on a shipping freight. Directions were given that you and you alone open it." Ashlynn quirked a brow and Tasarin nodded once. "I suggest it be opened in your presence but to have another open it for you."

"Right." Ashlynn nodded. "We will reconvene in the morning once I have slept and have my head on straight. Let the people know that I am truly in the castle and will give them audience soon. Tell them nothing of our journey, but do tell them we will be having many guests these next few days. I expect nothing less than absolute hospitality and kinship, from my people as well as those visiting."

"Yes, Your Grace."

"I know they will wish to celebrate and I believe they should do so. We will proceed as normal until a decision is made, for or against war."

"Of course."

"Let the kitchen know we will be having guests, and how many there will be as soon as you know."

Tasarin frowned ever so slightly. "I can only see what Suule sees. I cannot hear what is being communicated around or to him."

Ashlynn looked at the elf a moment before relaxing her tense face. "Of course, Tasarin. Forgive me. My thoughts are trying to run faster than I can keep up with."

A smile touched the smooth corners of Tasarin's lips. "You are forgiven. If I may speak as a friend?" Ashlynn nodded. "Go and rest yourselves for now, and do not rush. I have been acting regent for more than a year. To add another day to that will not harm me."

Jaryn coughed and there was a quick flash of irritation in the elf's otherwise serene expression. "Sorry," Jaryn apologized. "Dry throat." His grin was innocent. "Ashlynn, may I suggest taking two of these men and seeing about that crate?"

"I want to know what it is," piped Kenayde.

"No, Nadie." Ashlynn spoke now with the authority of a sister and not a ruler. "Go rest. You may see it later." A young servant girl was passing by the open throne room doors and Ashlynn called to her. "Please see to it that one of my gowns be brought to Lady Luella's quarters." She glanced at Jaryn, who nodded to say he'd already taken care of seeing their guests had rooms before coming to greet them. "And send two of my girls in to aid her in anything she may need."

"Yes, Your Majesty."

Jaryn looked at Elas. "I have some things that should fit you."

"Anything else?" asked Ashlynn as the girl led Elas and Luella away to their rooms. No one said anything and Ashlynn took that to mean their small meeting was adjourned. "Tomorrow morning," she reminded them all. As Kenayde stalked off to her room, pouting, Jaryn pointed to the two closest guards to tell them they were appointed as crate openers and followed Ashlynn down the corridor toward her quarters.

"Any idea what this delivery may be?"

Jaryn shook his head, frowning. "I've not a clue. Whoever sent it wanted you to open it, though..."

"I know." Ashlynn was bothered by that as well. "That was the reason I didn't want Nadie to be here. It is impossible to know the danger that could be inside."

Ashlynn's quarters consisted of a sitting room, a large bedroom, and her own bathing room. Both the bedroom and sitting room were decorated in tapestries of black and silver. The handwoven rugs covering the stone floor were thick and lush, spanning from under her four poster bed close to the fireplace in the sitting room. There, high backed chairs faced the fire that had already been lit. Between them was a small table littered with candles and her favorite book. It was just as she had left it, except for the wooden crate by the window.

It wasn't very big, as small as two of the wooden boxes milk was delivered in to the villagers. Ashlynn stepped into the room and her nose wrinkled. There was a foul odor in the air and, looking at the men with her, it was clear they smelled it too. Jaryn gently grabbed Ashlynn by the arm as she started forward again. He looked at one of the guards and motioned to the window with a lift of his chin. As soon as it was opened, a fresh breeze of cool air moved through the room. It helped take the terrible smell away but did nothing for the knots in Ashlynn's stomach.

"Open it," she commanded evenly. The two men moved to do as told. They had to slide a poker from the fireplace between the nails to loosen it before either of them could get a tight enough grip to pull the top off. The smell worsened, but Ashlynn took a step forward to see inside. All that was visible was a bloody brown robe. Briac's robe. And it was clearly wrapped around something.

"Ashlynn," Jaryn said softly behind her.

"Unwind it." She was amazed at how steady her voice was since she was feeling anything but steady.

"You don't have to do this," Jaryn pleaded. "You know what you will find."

Neither guard had moved and Ashlynn tore her gaze away from the bloody robe to look at her men. "Unwind it," she commanded again firmly. With no outward show of emotion, one of the men stooped and pulled out the robe. He held it carefully as the other pulled the loose edges back. Prince Laidley had done a cruel thing by making a mockery of them, disrespecting all of the Isles by not sending Briac's body and only his head.

Ashlynn felt her knees buckle, but Jaryn was right there. He held her firmly, turning her around so her face was to his chest. "Get it out of here," he ordered quickly. The men acted swiftly, putting the robe back in the crate and carrying it from the room.

As the doors closed, Jaryn held Ashlynn tightly. Her breathing was rapid and she trembled in his embrace, but she did not cry - either strength or stubbornness wouldn't allow it. Her hands, clutched together at her chest, now moved to take hold of the front of Jaryn's shirt. She clung to him in desperation. "I should have stayed behind." Ashlynn turned her head to look at absolutely nothing. "I would have had a better chance against them than Briac."

"You don't know that," Jaryn soothed, rubbing a hand over her back. "There was a reason Briac was the one to stay. If he hadn't, they would have had you or Kenayde and it would have been worse than what was done to Briac. The Giver would not..."

"Oh, curse the Giver!" Ashlynn pushed away from Jaryn, looking up at him with unbridled anger. "Curse Him!"

Jaryn watched somewhat helplessly as she stomped past him into her bedroom. "Ashlynn, you're hurting. You don't know what you're saying."

"I know very well what I am saying. Do not tell me the Giver made Briac choose to stay behind." She turned to face Jaryn, eyes almost emerald with rage. "For what? To be slaughtered like a farm hen? How can someone who only takes away be called Giver? What has He ever given me, that I should choose to follow Him and trust in Him? What!?

She was on the brink of losing it now and Jaryn proceeded carefully. "What has He given you?" Jaryn repeated gently. "Emiline and Wessely."

"After taking my parents away," Ashlynn countered.

79

"Kenayde."

"To look after all this time!"

He moved into the room now, closer but not too close. When he spoke again his voice was tender, almost wounded. "And what of me? He gave me to you."

Ashlynn stared at him, glaring for a long suffering moment. When it seemed as though she would not move or speak again, her gaze suddenly went to the floor. Her shoulders sagged and she shook her head. This prompted Jaryn to take a daring step closer. He reached out to gently take her chin in his hand and make her look at him. "I have never been more serious, Ashlynn. Do you not realize we were created for one another, and no one else? Before we were even born, we were being designed for one another, having things set in our path that would lead us and bring us together. You have been and always will be the most precious gift He has given me. And what of you?"

"What about me?" she whispered. Tears that now filled her eyes had to be blinked away.

"Stubborn, hard-headed, unforgiving on the worst of days and yes, I'll say it...even a little aggressive at times. How many sought to have your hand?" She scoffed and tried to turn away, but Jaryn wouldn't let her return to her grief without a valiant attempt at distraction. "I am being quite serious. How many?"

"I don't know."

"So many you lost count, then. What made me stand out? What was it about me?"

Warm tears slid down her cheeks. "You only wanted one thing."

"And what was that?"

"To see me smile."

Jaryn nodded, brushing her tears away. "All the others sought to woo you and I would have been happy with one real smile."

"But one was not enough," Ashlynn corrected, sniffling.

"Well of course not." Now that her defenses were down, Jaryn took the one last step that would close the distance between them. She didn't resist his arms going around her and buried her face in his shirt. "One smile is simply not enough," he continued as she cried. "It will never be enough. So I kept right on making a fool of myself, all just to get your attention. You see? The Giver made me a fool just for you."

"You are a fool," Ashlynn mumbled, "to love me as you do."

Dipping his head, Jaryn kissed her hair. "And I do so love you."

"Briac was a good man. He did not deserve to die." Ashlynn lifted her face, cheeks tear stained and reddened. "How can you believe, Jaryn? How can you trust the Giver is there so faithfully when things like this happen?"

With a slight shrug of his shoulder, Jaryn gave a small smile. "How can you know the people you know, see the beauty of your homeland day after day and not?" She said nothing but turned to rest her cheek against his chest. "I have seen miracles, Ashlynn. I have tried to believe He is not there, especially in the hard times, but my soul knows He is."

"I wish I could have the certainty you do. I wish I could so easily believe."

"You can," Jaryn told her. "You've just got to stop fighting Him so hard, love. He wants to be with you. He wants you to love him as He loves you. He wants you to need Him."

"I just don't know how." Her voice was thick with emotion and Jaryn's arms held her tighter.

"I will help you. We'll do this together. We will do all of it together."

She nodded, lifting a hand to dry her face of the newly shed tears. With a deep breath in she was collecting herself, reconstructing the wall she was always hiding behind. "I need to get things ready for tomorrow." She also needed time alone to properly grieve. Briac's death was her fault and no matter how Jaryn tried to distract her with loving words, the weight of that settled on her shoulders like lead.

Jaryn nodded, slowly letting her go. "What would you like done with the crate?"

On this, Ashlynn had already come to a decision. "We will send word to his family and have a service for him tomorrow tonight." Jaryn nodded and Ashlynn looked at him. "Please say nothing of this to Kenayde. I should be the one to tell her."

"Of course." Jaryn offered a smile of encouragement. "I'll let you alone and go fetch some clean clothes for Elas." Ashlynn nodded, gaze slowly falling in the way of someone lost in thought. "Ashlynn?"

Her head lifted. "Hmm?"

"I love you."

Her questioning expression gave way to a soft and genuine smile. "I love you, too."

~*~*~*~

The atmosphere at Altaine the next day was one of grief and anger. Once Kenayde had been told of Briac's death, the news quickly spread. Where there had been celebration of the sisters' return, there was now mourning. Inside the long rectangular room that was the conference hall, Ashlynn was speaking quietly with Tasarin about the service that would be held for her fallen friend that night. She wanted to make sure that everything was taken care of for the ceremony and was somewhat cold and rigid, hiding her true emotions.

Kenayde sat at the head table of the three that made an open rectangle, completely silent with the exception of a sniffle now and then. Luella was with her, holding her hand for comfort and unsure of what else could be done. Her unease prompted her to try to name the countries from the different banners hanging from the ceiling around the room.

The doors opened and Jaryn and Elas entered. Both men were cleaned up and in new clothes, a simple black shirt and a kilt of the Altaine tartan of red with stripes and crossings of blue, white, yellow and black. As soon as they were close enough, Kenayde stood and went to Jaryn. He gave her a strong embrace and let her cry on his shoulder.

"How are they?" Elas asked Luella softly, standing by her and giving Kenayde and Jaryn space.

Luella stood and shook her head. "Ashlynn has been stoic and Kenayde has been silent." They both turned to watch Tasarin leave through a side exit.

"Suule has returned," Jaryn announced somberly. His brotherly embrace still held Kenayde. "I suspect that was the reason for Tasarin's departure."

Ashlynn nodded, eyes glazed and unfocused for a moment. "Yes. He said not everyone is here yet."

"Good." Jaryn gently pulled Kenayde from him so he could see her face. "That gives you all time to eat something."

Ashlynn looked at him and Kenayde's brows came together as though she were angry at the suggestion. "I'm not hungry."

"You have to eat," Jaryn admonished. "You have to keep your strength up. I know you're grieving, little sister, but when was the last time you had anything substantial in your stomach?"

"He's right." Ashlynn looked drained as she sat at the head table. "There will be a feast tonight, but for now we need something small."

"Go sit down." Jaryn nodded, smiling with gentle encouragement at Kenayde. She was scowling as she made her way back to her seat. Looking at Elas, Jaryn asked, "Would you be willing to help me?" Elas nodded, squeezing Kenayde's shoulder before leaving with the other man.

"What will happen now?" Elas asked as the pair walked down the hall. They were heading for the kitchen and he was following Jaryn's lead.

"At council or the service tonight?"

"Both."

Jaryn took a breath in before wetting his lips. "Council is nothing more than a bunch of formality and pretense. Ashlynn will give her report of this past year, someone will ask her if she realizes the consequences, though it is clearly beyond that point. She'll get haughty and ill-tempered, which is always fun to see, by the way. That is, unless you happen to be on the receiving end."

"A year?" Elas was surprised. "I didn't realize they had been away from home for so long."

Jaryn nodded. "Over a year actually, but not by much - perhaps a couple of months. Before that she was here for two years from Oceana, working to root out all of Tadhg's men still here, sympathizers to his crown. During those two years she met me, the handsome slightly-older rogue that I am, and the plan for Tadhg's assassination began to quietly take shape. They were tense times. She was only fifteen, Kenayde thirteen, when they left us to go to Caedia with Briac. Siness felt very uncertain and vulnerable. It was not a good year for us. Tonight should be interesting, though. Mark my word, council will not close tonight before someone accuses someone else of being out of line, overstepping their boundaries, or saying that something was uncalled for. And there will be at least a dozen, 'If I may,' moments in there as well." He grinned. "We should keep count and compare afterward. It will keep us from falling asleep."

Elas couldn't tell if Jaryn was joking or not. "Are you serious?"

"Of course I am. You have no idea how tiresome these council meetings can be."

The kitchen staff was well underway with preparations for the celebration that night. As the two men weaved in and out of the busy moving bodies in search of sustenance, it looked something like a circus act. An elbow to the ribs, a broken pitcher and several annoyed glares later, the two made their way back out into the hall. Jaryn had somehow managed to grab some mugs to carry apples and dried meat in while Elas carried a pitcher of warm tea. "They haven't been this excited in awhile."

Glancing over his shoulder, Elas didn't see the kitchen as excited but very busy. "They're preparing for tonight?"

"Yes. There will likely be a service for Briac first - something small as a way to say goodbye. Then the celebration will begin." There was mischief in Jaryn's smile. "Food, dancing, singing, stories...we have a very good time."

"So it would seem," agreed Elas. "Did you know Briac?"

"Not really. He was Ashlynn's contact. I met him once before they left for Caedia, but that was it. You?"

Elas shook his head. "No. I met Ashlynn and Kenayde just after they had left him. I'm afraid I wasn't very welcoming to either of them."

Shrugging, Jaryn waved a hand. "Ashlynn gives it out all the time. She can get some back every once in awhile. It's good for her."

Glancing over at Jaryn, there was curiosity in Elas' expression. "May I ask...about you and Ashlynn?"

This caused a grin to spread across the younger man's face. "We are to be married. Actually, we were supposed to be married at Samhain last year but that didn't happen for obvious reasons."

"I'm unfamiliar."

"It's the night the harvest ends and the beginning of the new year." Jaryn

83

scratched the scruff on his chin. "If you ask the elves and the older humans, they believe it's the time when the barrier between the living and the dead is the thinnest, making communication between worlds easiest."

Elas raised an eyebrow. "That doesn't sound particularly romantic."

"It's not meant to be," Jaryn laughed. "I don't believe in it myself. I go by what I hear in church and read in the scriptures, but Ashlynn wanted our ceremony to be on Samhain so she could feel her parents were there. I understand that, even if I don't agree with it."

"You seem complete opposites."

"Oh, we are." Humor was etched into every smile line. "We are nothing alike. But it's why we fit so well together. She is everything I am not, and I am everything she is not. Apart we're only half a person but together we're whole."

Elas smiled slightly. "Will you marry now? Before there is war?"

"That depends," Jaryn replied, growing more serious, "on what happens at council tonight."

CHAPTER EIGHT

It had been a long time since the last time the conference hall had been so full. Every seat was spoken for, and even then there would be people that were left standing. Everyone wanted their chance to weigh in with their own thoughts and opinions. Ashlynn was not completely surprised that representatives alone had not come, but actual leaders. This was pleasing to see. They all wanted to hear her report and employed every possible tactic to get to Altaine in time to have their say in what was to happen next. She also knew that with so many people there to hear what she had to say, word of her bragging would get back to Laidley and no doubt incense him. It was for this reason she smiled to herself as she watched the empty seats slowly fill.

Kenayde was not yet there, but Ashlynn had never left the room. Beside her sat Tasarin to act as moderator for the night, and just behind were Jaryn and Luella with an extra chair for Elas if he decided to attend.

Ashlynn looked around the room at all the different nations being represented. Though she wanted to get up and greet them all, this was her home and it was customary for each group to present themselves to her before sitting down. There would be time for real socialization later.

So far there had been familiar faces, but none Ashlynn truly recognized with friendship. The hall was nearly halfway full when Kenayde slipped through a side entrance, Elas right behind her. Ashlynn nearly scolded her sister for her tardiness, but Tasarin touched her arm and said, "Your Grace." She swallowed whatever it was she was going to say to Kenayde and turned a placid smile to those who approached.

"Your Majesty." A young woman bowed low, a long brown braid falling over the shoulder of her simple gown. "May I present High King of Ibays, Donnchadh McKane."

"Welcome, High King Donnchadh. You will forgive my surprise. I did not expect to see anyone other than your representative, Cailin, here in Siness."

"Highness. It is a pleasure to be in your beautiful country again." Donnchadh was an older man with red hair that was fading to gold at his temples. As he knelt, Ashlynn admired his sterling armor and the circlet on his head. With the greeting over, the small group from Ibays went to find their spot among the nations, Cailin and Ashlynn sharing a quick secret smile before following Donnchadh. Another group was already entering, making Ashlynn sit up just a bit straighter. She had not anticipated seeing the winged creatures walking down the center to greet her, either. The one to kneel first with a bowed head had shaggy blonde hair and the white wings of a dove. "Nóe." Ashlynn's tone gave away her surprise. "I did not expect to see any of the Volar here, least of all their high king."

Nóe raised his head, a warm smile on his face and a sparkle in his deep blue eyes. "We wouldn't have missed this for anything."

The reflecting smile Ashlynn gave was genuine. "Thank you for coming, and please accept my congratulations. I was told you recently married."

It seemed impossible that the king's smile could get any brighter, but it did just that. "Yes, not long after your departure last year. May I present my wife, Nuala."

"Your Grace." The small woman beside him had long golden hair and eyes the color of turquoise. Like her new husband, she also had wings. Though not at all alike in looks, her wings were the kind that would have been found on the ever elusive Phoenix. They were long strands of feathers that went from crimson red, to orange, to gold, and finally a pale yellow. Bowing her head, she was somewhat timid by appearance, though it was clear by the look on Nóe's face how much he loved her.

"A pleasure," said Ashlynn. Nóe nodded once more before moving on to find seating.

Jaryn leaned forward to say, "She looks a lot like you."

Ashlynn smirked. "Except for the gorgeous eyes and wings."

"Too shy," Kenayde added.

"Well, if you cannot have the original," teased Jaryn further, "you do with what you can."

Ashlynn shook her head with amusement. Her eyes followed Nóe, watching how he pulled out the chair for his new bride and held her hand when they were both seated. Even their gazes upon each other were caressing. Though she'd never admit it out loud, there was a small part of Ashlynn that was jealous. She and Nóe believed they would marry some years ago, but it was not in the Giver's plans. She loved Jaryn dearly, and very glad Nóe had found someone to make him glow as he did now.

The next group to enter had both Kenayde and Ashlynn speechless. The sisters glanced at each other as three men entered the room wearing the long brown robes of a familiar order. "The brethren," breathed Kenayde. "Briac did say they were sailing to the Isles."

"Blessings, sister." All three bowed their heads slightly. "We are glad to see you again."

"You as well," replied Ashlynn, recovering from her shock. "This is a pleasant surprise."

The smile the monk in front gave was grim. "What is decided here tonight will effect our world as well."

"Of course."

"We were very sorry to hear of brother Briac. Our deepest sympathies."

Ashlynn swallowed the lump in her throat. "Thank you." As the small group left, Ashlynn turned to Tasarin. "Remind me to speak with Suule later. He did far more than I asked of him, and with impossible speed. My thanks and perhaps some sugar are due."

Tasarin smiled. "Yes, your highness." His gray eyes had been scanning the room to see how many were left to join them. "It would seem there are only two seats left unclaimed."

Kenayde bit her lip. "Lynnie, I forgot to tell you something."

It didn't matter what Kenayde was saying now. The last couple was there and walking forward. Both wore serene smiles and bowed as all the others before them had. When the man lifted his head, there was a deep love on his face. "Do not cry, little Lynnie. It wouldn't bode well for your reputation."

"Papa." Ashlynn blinked as Wessely and Emiline blurred in her vision. She looked at Kenayde. "You knew?"

She nodded sheepishly. "I saw them before. It was why Elas and I were late."

Returning her attention to her parents, Ashlynn shook her head. "But how did you know? How could you have known to be here now? Oceana is almost a week of travel away."

There was an odd little smile on Wessely's lips and he glanced over his shoulder. "We had a little help."

Ashlynn followed his gaze to see Nóe watching them, a humble look upon his face. Ashlynn struggled with wanting to get up and go to him. She took her eyes off the winged man to focus on Wessely. "You had Nóe watching us?"

"Not Nóe," Emiline corrected in her soft voice.

"Unlike some rulers," added Wessely, "Nóe is a king that recognizes the need to delegate."

Tasarin leaned in. "With all due respect, Your Majesties..."

Wessely nodded his understanding. They could all talk more once council was dismissed. He and Emiline bowed once more before going to the last two available seats.

"Did you know?" Ashlynn asked Kenayde in a hurried whisper.

Kenayde blinked. "About one of the Volar watching us? I had no idea." Frowning, Ashlynn sat back in her seat as Tasarin rose from his.

"Now that we are all here..." The incessant chattering in the room went from a soft buzz to silence. Tasarin smiled when he had the attention of everyone in the room. "As I was saying, now that we are all together let us give a word of thanks." All around the room heads bowed. Even if a person did not believe in the Giver, or any higher power, the beliefs of the host kingdom were to be respected and followed. "Blessed Giver," said Tasarin, "we thank You for all the friends gathered here tonight and ask that You bless this meeting and our time together. Help us to think with calm minds and speak with loving tongues. Govern us in this time when we need You most. Dear Giver, we thank You for bringing Their Majesties, Queen Ashlynn and Princess Kenayde, back safe to us." There were several murmurs and whispered exclamations of agreement. "Tonight we mourn the loss of a dear friend and brother. Help us to rejoice in the knowledge that he is with You now, and to reflect only on the good and not the dark. We ask these things in Your name." The entire room spoke an "Amen" in a unified chorus.

As eyes opened and heads raised, Tasarin sat and Ashlynn gained all the attention. "Welcome. Please accept my apologies for requesting your presence so swiftly, but I am certain you will recognize the necessity of it by the time we are through. My sister, Briac of Cieria, and myself left the Isles over a year ago, vowing to return only when the Red King was no longer on his throne." She smiled with dark pride and traces of sadness over the loss of her friend. "As you can see, we have returned."

Cheers of victory went up around the room, while some stayed sober and silent, awaiting the consequences of this win for their nations. When the room quieted, Ashlynn began her recount of events. She spoke of the monastery in which they stayed and gave mention to the three monks there with them now. She spoke of Briac convincing the order to let him go along each time Tadhg requested spiritual counsel. It was the only way they would have had any knowledge of what the interior of the castle looked like.

Kenayde had been responsible for researching methods of disposal since she loved to read and learn about anything she could get her hands on. It was she who discovered the Rabis plant in one of the old books within the church, as well as the recipe for the Rabia powder.

At that time, Ashlynn began riding into the village of Montania with any travelers or suppliers that passed by the church on their way. Dressed as a boy, she offered to help when and where she could. She visited so frequently that, over time, the villagers recognized her as someone familiar. Every so often she had the opportunity to ride into the castle itself. She would manage to steal away on several occasions to mentally map out the route Briac described to her up to Tadhg's chambers. From there she could also make sure she knew well her route of escape.

As soon as Kenayde felt she had perfected the powder, it was tested on Briac. In a minuscule dose it would make him as sick as though he'd been drinking the entire previous day. Within hours of consumption, the desired reaction was observed and a final plan of attack was set in motion. It was at that time, before the testing on Briac began, that the order left the monastery. All the while the monks had stayed purposely ignorant of what was going on. They had ideas; by not intervening but choosing to leave, they had given their approval while showing they wanted no part of it. The church could have no blame if things went wrong, and the three taking shelter there understood perfectly.

It was three days before anyone passed by, and Ashlynn was more than happy to travel with the wagon full of textiles, especially when she saw they were extravagant enough for only those within the castle. She helped unload as usual, but with an excuse of an upset stomach, left to creep through the halls to make her way up to where Tadhg was getting ready for his day. In her hand was the pouch containing the deadly powder she would have to somehow slip him. It was luck that placed a maid in her path, carrying a tray of food and a pitcher. Knowing she had to be bold, Ashlynn discreetly called the maid over to ask where she was going. When the maid revealed she was on her way to the king with his breakfast, Ashlynn told her it would not do to serve him with her shoes laced up so hastily. They were uneven and sloppy, and could cost her employment. While the girl re-laced her shoes, Ashlynn balanced the tray against her chest with one hand and dumped the entire contents of the pouch into the pitcher with the other, praying it had already passed the inspection of a taster. The powder dissolved before the girl was even finished with her shoes.

Once the tray was handed over, Ashlynn quickly headed out of the castle through a lesser used exit she'd found months before. Out into the village as a rain was quickly picking up, she kept her head low and hands in her pockets as she blended in with the villagers. At the gate, after making sure no one was paying attention, she gave the watchman a wineskin of drugged mead. He collapsed and she dragged him into the bushes to leave him there while she took up his post.

From there, she went on to recount what had happened with Merrik, the escape, Briac's sacrifice, the underground tunnels, and meeting Elas. As speculative gazes fell upon him, he dipped his head slightly in acknowledgment. When it was time to discuss how they'd met Luella, Ashlynn paused. She couldn't simply turn around to speak with the princess and ask what her decision had been about her identity. Thinking quickly, she directed her thoughts at Elas.

What does Luella want me to say about her?

There was no answer for a moment and Ashlynn bought herself some time by taking a sip of the goblet of wine before her. *She has a very strong wall up,* Elas finally answered. *Either she cannot hear me, or simply won't answer.*

Setting the cup down, Ashlynn made the decision for herself. "When we surfaced, we met Luella. She was eager to aid in any way she was able, and secured us passage on a ship that was leaving Amme that afternoon."

"Tell them."

It had been spoken so low that Ashlynn wasn't sure she had actually heard anything at all. Kenayde was turning her head to look behind them, an expression of sorrow and guilt on her face. "Luella..." she said softly.

"Tell them," Luella repeated, a little louder and more demanding. Ashlynn hardly had to turn around to imagine the look on her new friend's face; her tone gave it all away.

Ashlynn kept her veneer neutral and hid the deep breath she took before speaking. "Luella was so willing to help because she knew what we had done before she even found us." Frowns of bewilderment stared back at her, but Ashlynn continued. "She sought us out, knowing if we were found by Prince Laidley, successor to Tadhg's throne, he would kill us. Her heart wanted no more needless death. By joining us she disavowed herself from the kingdom, and is as much a criminal as we are."

"Tell them *everything.*"

Some faithfully paid attention to Ashlynn while others tried to discreetly look past her. Ashlynn wet her lips and looked at the table for a moment. She could almost feel the hurt and anger in Luella. This was not a time to introduce someone, not when they were feeling that way. But slowly, Ashlynn lifted her head. Her eyes went from Nóe to her parents, and back again as she spoke. They sat opposite of each other and she knew neither would overreact. "Luella is now as hunted as we are, not simply for betraying her kingdom, but also her family. Tadhg was not her father by birth, but High Queen Finola is her mother and Prince Laidley, her brother. Luella is of the House of Tadhg Ellison."

The room became a flurry of commotion in an instant. Some stood to look with anger at Luella, and even at Ashlynn. Some, like Wessely and Emiline, stayed perfectly calm and only conversed with each other quietly. Precious few looked surprised but hopeful, like Nóe and most of his companions. Ashlynn looked at him as though asking for help, but his only answer was an encouraging smile. His eyes moved past her and Ashlynn could hear the scrape of a chair. Luella hastened from the room, taking the exit Elas and Kenayde had come in not long ago.

"I told her to go," Jaryn said quickly, seeing the concern on his beloved's face. "None of that was easy to hear, Ashlynn."

90

"I know." She turned back around to see her calm and organized council in a state of disarray. People were arguing now, nation to nation and even amongst themselves. Ashlynn looked at Tasarin and nodded, causing him to rise.

"If you would all be so kind as to find your seats." The serene elf spoke so evenly that it was hard to believe anyone would hear him. Perhaps it was a gift, or perhaps all knew that when Tasarin stood, their time to speak was over and they needed to listen. Arguments cooled and even those farthest away from the head table slowly sat. When the room was quieted and he was content with the result of his request, Tasarin sat as well.

"Do you have any idea what you have done?" The demanding question came from a young woman with dark skin and black curls. She, along with the four with her, had different tattoos all over her body of different shapes and sizes marking them as from the Nagin tribes from the southern nation of Alybaen. "Bringing her here is the same as inviting the prince here himself."

"Did you not see the look of rage on her face?" A male dwarf with a baby face and big eyes spoke up from the table across the room. "She was seething the entire time the queen spoke."

An older man with graying blonde hair shook his head, a thoughtful frown on his face. "She wanted us to know who she was. If she came to seek out information to send back to her brother she would have chosen to stay anonymous, to hide in plain sight."

"And of course she leaves before we are able to question her," scoffed someone from Ibays.

"If I may," said Nóe with a frown. "I do not believe the report to be finished." His gaze swept the room before landing on Ashlynn. "Am I correct?"

"You are. Luella was instrumental in our escape. It was she who found us a ship and she who paid the captain to let us go with him. Without her aid, as well as that of Elas, I have no doubt in my mind that we would have been caught and a crate would have been sent home with three heads inside instead of one."

The woman with the black curls shook her head. "With all due respect, it was not within your rights to bring her to the Isles and potentially endanger us all the more."

"What would you propose I should have done?" Ashlynn asked coolly. "Send Kenayde home to get a vote from the council while I stayed with our two rescuers, awaiting a decision on their fate? Forgive me for being impulsive, but I was not going to leave anyone else to die; not on my behalf."

As further arguments were presented, Elas glanced over at Jaryn. He could see the love and the pride on his new friend's face each time Ashlynn responded and held her own. Once he saw Kenayde open her mouth as if about to speak, but Ashlynn's stronger voice won out over hers. Leaning forward while someone else spoke, Elas tapped Kenayde's shoulder and whispered, "Give me your

91

hand." She obliged without looking at him. With a bowed head and closed eyes, Elas appeared to simply be praying. No one could see the contact he had with Kenayde.

Why don't you speak? he asked, his voice in her head causing her to flinch.

Ashlynn says all that I want to say, but with better articulation.

Elas squeezed Kenayde's hand lightly. *But you are of this kingdom as well. Don't they seek answers from the both of you?*

I am not exclusive to Siness and Altaine. I was born here, yes...but I will go back to live in Caedia at Oceana. Besides, Ashlynn is the ruler here, the first born of their last high king. I am not the heir here, only the spare.

Not to me.

Ashlynn's lips were drawn into a tight frown. The question presented to her was about Luella, or rather, the true Luella. What if this woman had been a plant while the real princess was being prepared for battle, or the right time to switch places and tear them apart from the inside? None of them had ever seen the real princess, so how could they know?

"This is bloody absurd," Jaryn mumbled. He rose and lifted his hands momentarily to draw everyone's attention. "I have seen the princess before, several years ago." The room quieted and paid him full attention. "As some of you know, I was a professional traveler before coming to Siness, doing what I could, where I could, to make a living. Five times I was inside the Castle Montania, and twice I saw the princess. *This* princess."

"And how do we know it is not a maid that happens to look like her?"

Jaryn did not bother trying to hide his annoyance. "A maid who looks that much like her? Besides, a servant could fake the poise, but not the education."

"A very good point, Jaryn." Wessely nodded his agreement. "Unless they had been planning to use a false princess against us all along, it would be impossible to have someone so conditioned and ready to make a switch that quickly. How soon after Tadhg was killed did you meet her?"

"Almost a week," Ashlynn answered.

"And," Nóe added, "if they knew where to place a false princess so she would end up in your path, why not simply capture you directly?"

"Because they want a war." Again, it was the darker skinned woman. "This is a family that thrives on carnage and drawn out executions. To kill them all in one fell swoop would take away the hunt and the game. It would be over too quickly to satisfy."

One of the elves from the island nation of Mirasean, a group that had said nothing to this point, lifted her chin. "Forgive me for interrupting," she interjected. Her voice was as soft and soothing as Tasarin's, somehow still demanding respect and attention. "I feel as though we are wasting time by arguing over a woman already here. Was not the point of this council to decide what happens now? Unless someone has discovered how to travel back in time, none of us can change her being here. I believe our energies would be better spent deciding on the next best course of action." She leaned forward to turn her steely eyes on everyone scowling back at her. "Let us turn our focus to what needs to be done now, and not what we cannot change."

There was a heavy silence in the room that seemed impenetrable. Everyone stared at everyone else, practically daring someone to speak first with their gazes.

"Well, I should think it rather obvious," grumbled the baby-faced dwarf at length. "The prince will not fail to attack Altaine when he realizes you aren't coming for him in retaliation for the death of your friend, nor will he hesitate to try to knock down a few more of our strongholds while he's here. I say we fight for our lands!" Dutifully, he looked at Ashlynn. "We protect our own. Always."

Ashlynn nodded, offering a thankful smile. Nóe was quick to add his support. "The Volar stand with you as well."

"As does Oceana." Wessely added.

The laden silence came back only for a moment before High King Donnchadh nodded. "As does Ibays."

"We are with you as well," said the elfin maiden. Echoes of the same slowly made their way around the hall. Ashlynn appeared grim, but was satisfied in knowing Siness would not be alone in her fight.

"Very well," she replied when no one else spoke for a few moments. "I will meet with my tactical advisers in the morning. I urge as many of you to be there as is possible. For those that can stay, you will have rooms here at Altaine and are welcome to join our celebration tonight." Wetting her lips, she leaned forward and brought her hands together atop the table. "We mourn the loss of Briac as well as celebrate his life. Let us share a night of joy before we are thrust into dark and dangerous times once more."

Around the room were reflected many emotions and Ashlynn felt as though she were feeling every single one of them. "My home is your home. As you go, my sincerest thanks for your presence tonight." She glanced at the two men at the doors. A nod from her had them opened. "This council is now closed. Go in peace."

One by one, the room cleared of visitors. When most had gone, Ashlynn rubbed her eyes. "I need to find Luella. I feel terrible."

"There is no need," Tasarin told her, a slight look of concentration on his face. "She is with Suule."

"She finds comfort in him," Kenayde observed. "It was the same in the fields yesterday." She stretched her arms over her head. "We have not had a council that long for awhile."

"Or as loud and interesting," added Jaryn. "You held yourself perfectly, my love."

Ashlynn gave a weary smile over her shoulder to him. "You know how I love a good debate."

With a nod, Elas admitted, "That was quite impressive."

"Thank you." Ashlynn turned in her seat so as to get a better look at the young water dragon. "Now that you see no one wants to condemn you, will we see more of that fighting spirit I did so love when we first met?"

He grinned. "Perhaps."

"Excellent." Standing, Ashlynn cracked her spine. "I will try to speak with Luella before tonight. Nadie, Mama and Papa are staying, right?"

"As far as I know." Side by side, Kenayde and Elas left the room to go in their own direction, Tasarin disappearing down a side staircase. Ashlynn slid her hand into Jaryn's as they left the room as well, slow in their gait. They came out the end of the corridor and turned to head to Ashlynn's quarters. To get there, they had to pass the throne room and the landing above the entrance hall. Here they paused to look over the balcony at the faces below. Some were exploring the castle, others retiring to their rooms before the feast, while some were enjoying new company early.

"So many unfamiliar faces," Ashlynn commented quietly. She was watching an older man with salt and pepper hair converse with a dwarven man. Beside her, Jaryn leaned on the balcony and shrugged. His attention was captured by a man of the Volar, one of the many stationed across the nations as messengers by the look of his clothing. He was tall and muscular with the soft green filmy wings of a lunar moth on his back. He was holding conversation with a female elf and a bald man from the Nagin. Like the others of the Nagin tribe, his tattoos were numerous, running down the length of his arms, across his neck, and even an impressive knotted star on his skull.

"Maybe I should get a skull tattoo," Jaryn commented, grinning in mischief as he pointed the man out to Ashlynn. As she admired the man's designs, something beyond her caught Jaryn's attention and his smile went from teasing to warm and welcoming.

Curious, Ashlynn turned to see Emiline and Wessely approaching. Now that they were through with council and away from all the formality demanded from such a meeting, she was free to greet them however she chose. Her embrace with the two was long and comforting. "I cannot tell you how surprised I was to see the both of you."

"I think we may have some idea," said Emiline with amusement.

"You must tell me everything," Ashlynn begged, holding on to Emiline's hand. "Everything from the day we left until now."

"There is little to tell," Wessely admitted. "When you left for Siness, we were still seeing Nóe regularly. It was his offer to send his people to watch over you when you made up your mind to leave the Isles. As soon as Kenayde had perfected her recipe, one of the two Volar watching over you flew to Oceana to tell us. We left that very same day to sail for Siness, as I'm sure did many others. We have all been anticipating this moment for some time now."

Jaryn was nodding. "Very well played, Your Majesty."

Wessely smirked. "I would thank you if it had been my plan." He stepped forward and gave Jaryn a tight embrace. "It is good to see you, Jaryn."

"You as well."

Emiline embraced him next before asking, "Am I correct in assuming it may yet be another year before the two of you are finally wed?"

Jaryn frowned, but Ashlynn appeared thoughtful. "Perhaps not." She looked at Jaryn with narrowed eyes. "I was thinking in my quarters earlier. Laidley sent what was left or Briac home in hopes of igniting a harsh and immediate retaliation. He wants us to be so furious that we immediately prepare ourselves for war and sail once more for Caedia." She took a breath. "Tonight we have a service for Briac," she said evenly. "A sad thing and one that would drive any normal ruler to madness and an immediate and harsh reply. But after the service we will be celebrating, not fighting! Who celebrates on the verge of war?"

"Lunatics," Jaryn answered with a proud grin.

Ashlynn smirked. "We are also rather close to Samhain. That is an important night for the Celts, and one we did not get to celebrate last year."

It was clear her parents were still with her and listening, though Jaryn seemed confused. "You still want to have Samhain?"

Turning to him, Ashlynn took his face in her hands. "I still want to marry you. I want to go into battle knowing I fight beside my husband and my king."

His hands rested on her arms. "And that means..."

She nodded, knowing the rest of his unspoken question. "We will have a crowning as well. My people have waited long enough to recognize me. They call me 'Queen' now as it is. Why not make it official?"

"In the meantime," Wessely interjected, "Laidley will be prepared for a war that isn't coming."

"Exactly." Ashlynn turned around to meet her father's gaze with excitement. "Laidley will be so prepared for our outrage over Briac that he will no doubt be assembled for battle. In fact, he is probably meeting with his own advisers as we speak so as to be ready for a quick attack from us. But when we don't come, he will probably send someone here as a spy to report back to him. He'll be told we are living life as normal and not as any who would be going to war. He will be forced to come to us, and it is here where we will defeat him, as planned. Tadhg's reign of savagery will not continue into the next generation. We end it when we end Laidley."

CHAPTER NINE

The hill was well lit with candles, and a moon not quite full lent its light for further illumination. A small cairn had been built up with rocks and stones of every different shape, size, and color to cover the spot where Briac's crate was buried. Beside the cairn stood two torches, tall and unlit. There was no wind to make the flames of the candles dance, no breeze to rustle the tree branches surrounding them. It was almost as though nature - the Giver - was also mourning and could not bear to let anything disrupt this service.

Wessely and Emiline were there, as well as Nóe and Nuala. The winged king had also been friends with the old man and wanted to pay his respects. There were many from the village, including those who brought instruments to play softly as others came and joined in the ceremony. They were there out of respect for what Briac had sacrificed for them. Each person in attendance held their own candle and laid a new stone on the cairn. Briac's family sent their thanks for his service but were not in attendance. They didn't agree with the choice he'd made to take part in Tadhg's assassination, but they would mourn the loss of him. The three monks who had accepted him as a brother, however, were there in the family's stead.

By the time it was Kenayde and Ashlynn's turn to go up, the pile of stones was so colorful that it was unusually beautiful in the moonlight. Knowing what it covered took some of that beauty away.

Kenayde was sniffling through her tears as she put a dark gray rock with glittering mica among the others. When she was done, she kissed her fingers and touched them to the stone before going to stand with her parents.

Finally Ashlynn approached. She was downcast but not teary. Holding her sandstone before the pile, she hesitated. Her eyes swept over the faces of all who had known Briac and had been touched by him in some way. "Briac was a good

96

man," she told them, standing by the cairn. "He was someone who enjoyed life and everything about it, even the trials. In the darkest of moments, he could find the light. He was so strong when Kenayde and I felt weak...so faithful." She laughed softly. "Slightly unorthodox, but he loved the Giver. Briac was sweet, kind, caring, and extremely stubborn." She was silent for a moment and when she spoke again, her voice broke. "And I loved him dearly." Ashlynn kissed her stone before adding it to the others. "Be at peace, my dear sweet friend."

Stepping back to stand with Jaryn, a soft breeze began to play around them and silence settled over the group for a long moment. Then someone started humming softly. It was a song of loss that was old and easy to recognize. As Ashlynn closed her eyes, she started singing the words.

Someone began to beat the rhythm on a bodhrán, and a fiddle was played softly as well. With a deep breath in, Ashlynn opened her eyes to look at the dark cairn. A single thought had it ablaze in brilliant blue and gold flames; this was Briac's send-off. As Ashlynn opened her mouth to sing again, more voices joined in.

Though it was a sad moment, there was an undeniable electric current of excitement in the air. Briac was gone from this life to be with the Giver forevermore. It was a time to celebrate, not to mourn. As the song came to its last verse, the tempo of the music picked up, and the feeling in the gathered crowd was something more joyful. Everyone watching joined in to sing, even the teary-eyed Kenayde. Their voices were loud, numerous, and beautiful, and as they walked in one large procession away from the valley and into the streets of Altaine Shire, a general feeling of levity rushed through the crowd as the festivities of the evening began.

The capital of Siness was similar to Amme, without the arrogance of its people. Those who resided in the shadow of Castle Altaine were kind and caring, putting others before themselves and ever loyal to Kenayde and Ashlynn. Like any other town there were disagreements and scuffles, but for the most part it was a place of peace and unity. On a usual evening there would be little movement about the place, though it was never perfectly still and quiet. Tonight, Altaine was bustling with activity. Shops were still open, lanterns were lit in every corner, and the tavern was practically bursting at the seams for all the patrons inside. Out farther from the town was the fairground where fires were going, music was being played, and laughter was hanging in the air like a song. Sweet scents of honey glazed nuts mixed with the salty aroma of roasting meats caused empty mouths to water.

Long past her preferred bedtime, Ashlynn felt like she had been greeted by every individual in her kingdom, as well as those from others as she'd passed through the crowds. Some would walk by her with a smile and a greeting and the gestures would be returned. Some from the jousting arena even cajoled, trying to get her to join in on their fun and games. At present, she sat on the gentle sloping hill on one side of the bustling contest grounds, watching the celebration going on inside of it. She had been able to let Briac go, along with a portion of her sadness; all Celts learned at an early age that death was not an end to weep over, but a new beginning to celebrate. It was the guilt that was reluctant to leave.

Looking away from the games being played inside the arena, Ashlynn lifted her gaze to the sky. There were no clouds overhead and the millions of stars burned brightly with cold light. She traced familiar patterns with her eyes, amused at the thought of those who read fortunes by starlight and imagining Briac already trying to rearrange them just to confuse people. The simple thought of it made her smirk to herself even as someone sat down beside her.

"I was wondering if I would get to see that smile again."

Ashlynn lowered her gaze from above to rest on Nóe's face. She looked warmly upon him, affection swelling her heart. There was something about this white winged man that brought the tenderness out in people. He was always smiling and optimistic, gentle and peaceful. It made even the angriest person want to be around him all the time. "What is your gift, Nóe?"

He looked at her serenely, lips curved upward slightly. "If I have one, I do not know what it is."

"You must have one; all Volarim do. It is directly connected to your spirit creature."

Nóe laughed quietly. "Mine is but a bird; a dove with no magical powers."

Thoughtfully, Ashlynn lifted a hand to run her fingers over Nóe's wings as only one privileged with a close friendship could. She felt the hard spine of each feather and the silky threads of the plumage. "I do not believe you a simple bird."

He raised an eyebrow, amused. "Oh no?"

Frowning, Ashlynn shook her head. She retracted her hand and met Nóe's eyes. "You calm people with just your presence. You fill a person with peace and hope."

His skeptic look dissipated as Nóe laughed once more. "How much mead have you had tonight?"

"Not nearly enough," she promised, darkness entering her expression for the quickest moment before taking its leave. "And don't laugh. I am quite serious. No one can instantly calm me and lift my spirits as you do, not even Jaryn. Though you may not see it, I believe that to be your gift."

"Now you are embarrassing me," Nóe said softly. "I am a simple man, Lile. You think too highly of me if you think me more than that."

Ashlynn sobered some. *Lile.* That was a name she had not heard for a very long time. It was something only Nóe called her, meaning lily in another tongue.

Just hearing it brought on a flood of memories and emotions that had been put away long ago. She could see the two of them, several years younger, running over the sandy beach at the foot of Oceana. Nóe chased her, his wings still soft with the down of a hatchling and Ashlynn running and laughing with flowers in her hair. It was a time after the sadness of losing her father had passed, and before the reality of life had a chance to set in.

"Forgive me," Nóe ventured after a moment of silence between them. "It came out before I could stop it."

Ashlynn shook her head, her smile nostalgic and sad. "Do not apologize, Nóe. When you call someone something for so long it is hard to change." As memories of childhood played in her mind, she felt a tumult of emotion. A look at Nóe told her he had been thinking of some of the same memories they shared, like the day he'd asked her to marry him and she summarily turned him down with a claim that she would never marry. "I saw you less and less after that day."

Nóe nodded, his downcast eyes unreadable but clearly understanding which day she spoke of. "It hurt too much to see you every day. So I began to distance myself."

"Until one day you never came back." Ashlynn looked at him sadly. "It wasn't fair to leave me like that, Nóe."

"You cannot refuse me and speak of fairness."

Ashlynn's brows came together. "I did not refuse you."

"Not directly, perhaps." Nóe looked at her. "It would not have been fair for you to expect me to see you every day as we were both so used to. Not after that."

Her expression softened. "I never meant to hurt you."

"We never mean to hurt anyone, Ashlynn. It just happens." He took a breath in and let it out slowly. "It would seem the Giver had other plans for us to begin with."

"Yes, He did." Ashlynn let her gaze sweep the faces inside the arena. She was surprised not to see Jaryn there once the games had gotten underway and shouts of cheering and cursing began. Team sports were his favorite games. "I would never wish things to be different than they are now. I am truly happy with Jaryn and love him deeply. I do not regret choosing him. If there is any benefit to being orphaned so young and swept away to a tiny kingdom I would never rule, it is that I am free to choose my mate and not worry about silly infancy betrothals."

"He suits you well," Nóe commented, his smile returning. "I have never met anyone quite like him."

Ashlynn laughed. "I have heard that before."

"That does not surprise me."

Across the arena on the other side of the wall, some of the Volarim had come to watch the games. They seemed amused at the simplicity of them, making comments to themselves about the poor grounded humans, no doubt. Nuala was among them, though she was the exception to the joking. She stood close to the wall and watched with genuine interest. "Nuala seems lovely," Ashlynn said as she spied her. "Very sweet."

"She is," agreed Nóe. He saw her as well and looked on her with adoring eyes. "Though do not let your initial meeting fool you. She has quite the spirit about her. Not nearly as demure as she appears to be once familiar with someone." As though sensing she were the subject of discussion somewhere, Nuala looked away from the games and eventually found the two sitting on the hillside. Nóe waved her over. With the grace befitting her status, she left the small group of her kindred to make her way over to her husband. Her gait was slow with her head turned toward the field. The long white dress she wore brushed the ground as she walked, the trails of her colorful feathers like streams of fire behind her.

"How are you finding the celebration, my love?" Nóe rose to greet her with a kiss on the lips.

"Much to my delight." She dipped her head to Ashlynn. "Your Grace."

"Please," Ashlynn argued. "We are no longer in council and have no need of formalities. You may call me by my name if I am free to call you by yours."

"Of course." With a shy smile, Nuala sat in the place Nóe had been, while he sat on the other side of her. "I feel as though I already know you," Nuala confessed. "Nóe has spoken so much about you."

"How unfair that you should know so much of me when I know so little of you." Ashlynn looked past Nuala to narrow her eyes at Nóe. "What have you been gossiping about?"

"Not gossip," assured his bride. "My husband thinks very highly of you."

"And I him. Nóe is like a brother to me now." Upon saying "now," Ashlynn glanced at Nóe.

"She knows." His hand found Nuala's and their fingers intertwined. "She knows everything."

Ashlynn smirked. "And would be my friend the same."

Nuala looked at Nóe, love in her turquoise eyes. "He was meant for me," she said with certainty. Nóe's free hand brushed her cheek. "He was my gift from the Giver."

There it was again. Ashlynn looked away from the couple, thoughts turning back to what Jaryn had said earlier. He said they had been made for each other, designed by the Giver Himself to fit perfectly together. Here, even Nuala expressed her belief in Him. Why was it so hard for Ashlynn?

"I saw you watching the games," Nóe said with amusement. "Would you like to learn how to play?"

Nuala bit her lip and nodded. "I think I would." They looked at Ashlynn as though asking permission to be excused. When she realized as much, she smiled an apology. "Of course! Go! Have fun! Watch out for the old man with the blue trousers, though. He takes his games very seriously."

The pair stood, grinning. "Thank you for the warning." Nóe bent to kiss the top of Ashlynn's head. "Whatever that shadow is lurking behind your smile, I suggest you speak to Jaryn about it. There is a reason he is called your partner."

They were sage words, and though Ashlynn expected no less from Nóe, she wrinkled her nose at him. She stayed a little longer to watch the pair be introduced to the games. When someone told them there was no flying allowed, their wings disappeared completely in a shimmer of golden white light. Nóe, having spent much of his time growing up with humans as a squire to Wessely at Oceana, was familiar with the rules. Since Nuala was not, she was allowed a practice hit and run at Stool Ball. Her paddle made good contact when the ball was thrown to her. It went sailing and Nuala ran. She squealed in glee as she rounded the base and headed back to home. Running straight for Nóe who was cheering her on behind it, she made it back before anyone had tagged the base. Nóe caught her and lifted her off the ground in a victorious twirl. Ashlynn could not help but smile. Yes, it would seem the two truly had been made for each other. She was glad to see Nóe so happy, with such a sweet and loving wife.

Now standing, she brushed herself off and left the arena to find Jaryn, her ever-present guards trailing behind her. Everywhere people were gathered in crowds of varying sizes. Some were outside, some were filling homes when there was no more room in the tavern. Fire pits were lit everywhere, including the large one near the heart of the town where music filtered in on the wind. In her search for Jaryn, she found her sister and Elas, as well as Wessely and Emiline, sitting around one of the sporadic fire pits, listening to a young bard with several of the villagers.

"Ashlynn!"

The high voice that called to her with familiarity and a thick Ibayish accent had her frowning, turning to see who would be so bold as to call her by her name. Seeing the young woman rushing toward her lessened the sternness in her expression, though not before it was seen.

"Forgive me, Your Majesty."

"Cailin." Ashlynn greeted her friend by grabbing her hands and squeezing them, stopping the younger woman from bowing. "I am so happy to see you here."

Cailin's lips curved upward; she was practically glowing. "I had to come. When we were told you were sailing back for Siness and preparations were being made to come here, I begged to come along. I knew it wasn't necessary for the representative to go since the high king himself was going, but I had to see you."

It was impossible not to smile despite the leftover heaviness from her conversation with Nóe, and Ashlynn shook her head. "You have come a long way from a kitchen maid at Oceana."

"All thanks to you. In fact, did you know I'm one of the few women in the castle not of noble birth who can read? If you hadn't taught me how or put in a good word with the king's sheriff, I never would have been more than a servant. I'm so thankful."

"You were my very best friend in that castle, Cai. It was the least I could do. I am very pleased to see you thriving in an environment that suits you."

Cailin nodded with a grin. "The same for you. Being the head of a nation suits you, even if it's not official yet." Her smile dimmed slightly. "I'm sorry about the loss of your friend."

"Thank you." Ashlynn's throat tightened. "I apologize for having to cut our conversation short, but I was looking for Jaryn. Have you seen him?"

"Can't say that I have, but that's not too surprising with so many people moving about." Cailin gave a little bow of her head and let go of Ashlynn's hands. "Don't let me keep you. We'll talk again soon."

"I would like that very much." Ashlynn watched her friend leave, another wave of nostalgia washing over her and adding to the weight in her chest. Determined now, she pushed her way through crowds of people and avoided eye contact in hopes of preventing being held up even more.

After searching most of the places she expected to find him, Ashlynn was beginning to feel as though she'd walked the entire maze of the city streets without finding Jaryn. She was about to give up and go back to her family when the sound of dice rolling on a wooden table caught her attention. Jaryn was too social a creature to be sitting at a simple board game, and yet that was exactly where she found him.

At a table outside of a quaint little home there were six of them in total, quietly conversing over dice and cards. Three of them were elves, one male and two female, one pale skinned Nagin man, a man from the village, and Jaryn. He appeared to be to game master, dealing out cards as they were needed. At present, it appeared they were speaking in elvish. They were the majority at the table and such was custom as long as everyone else could speak the language as well.

Standing far enough away so as not to be easily spotted, but close enough to listen, Ashlynn watched her beloved. Something the Nagina said, too quietly for Ashlynn to hear, had them all chuckling. She was hypnotized, not for the first time, by Jaryn's smile. He lit up the entire area with his laugh and his energy. Ashlynn knew it was intimate moments like this that would make him a great king and why there had been less contest than expected at her engagement to the wandering bard. He was personable, accessible, and someone the people would willingly look to for leadership. Conversing back, he was careful at choosing his words so as not to say the wrong ones, or use an incorrect dialect. He had traveled to a variety of places and learned so many different languages, much more than Ashlynn knew herself. It was easy to understand why he was so careful. Sometimes she found it hard to imagine that he had once been a young boy, moving from place to place, singing songs of history, great romance, and epic tragedy. It had been a long time since she'd heard him sing, and now she had a sudden longing ache for his voice.

One of the female elves rolled the dice. Whatever came up had the others groaning and cringing while she looked victorious. Jaryn complimented her luck and the elfin maiden blushed in the lamplight. It made Ashlynn smile. For all Jaryn teased her about the men who had been, and were occasionally still, after her affection, he had his own admirers. He was just oblivious to them because his eyes always remained on Ashlynn.

A lump formed in her throat, though she couldn't understand why. Stepping into the shadows of an unlit alley, Ashlynn leaned against the side of the house and looked skyward. She searched the darkness for answers to unspoken questions, afraid to let her mind form words that her mouth refused to speak. She didn't understand the sudden hollowness, or the almost violent need for something - or someone - she did not quite understand.

Because she was so skilled in her own magic, Ashlynn did not need to see Jaryn to let him know she was there, or that she needed him. The flames in the lanterns suddenly changed color, the blue and gold coloring giving off more of an ethereal light than usual. Everyone at the table blinked their surprise, shying away from the foreign flames. Except for Jaryn; he handed the deck of cards to the familiar villager and stood with a bow of his head. "My lords and ladies, it has been a pleasure." As soon as he was away from the table, the flames turned back to normal.

Not knowing where she was, only that Ashlynn was near, Jaryn would have walked right past the alley if she hadn't reached out and grabbed his arm. He was startled and appeared even more so when he saw her troubled expression. He began to speak, but Ashlynn put a finger to her lips. With her hand in his, she led Jaryn down the alley and through a series of several more. They passed through the outskirts of the village and made their way out into the open fields beyond. For the way it looked, everyone was in the heart of the village and no one was at home.

"Permission to speak, Your Majesty." He was joking, thinking she had pulled him away so they could be alone. As she turned to him now, however, he could see how troubled she really was. "What is it?"

"I don't know," she whispered. "I don't know what is wrong with me."

"There is nothing wrong with you," Jaryn offered quickly. He moved to take her other hand, but Ashlynn backed away as though not wanting to be touched. She clutched at her neckline, a panic rising.

"Yes, there is. I feel like...I don't know. I feel like I am missing a part of myself."

Thinking he understood, Jaryn nodded. "Of course you do, love. You saw Briac every day for..." He trailed off as Ashlynn shook her head.

"That's not it," she whimpered. "I wish it was, because then I could name it. I could identify it and figure out how to address it, to make it better, and to move on."

"Then what is it?"

"I don't know," she answered helplessly. Turning away from Jaryn, Ashlynn ran her hands over her face. "It started when you told me I was your gift. It was the raw, gnawing feeling. Then when I was speaking with Nóe and Nuala. She said the same thing, that Nóe was her gift from the Giver. The Giver and the Deliverer. They pop up everywhere in every day, normal conversation. So I started wondering what it was that was so appealing about this God we all claim to love and trust, and I realized that no one was *claiming* anything but me. Everyone else truly loves and believes."

Jaryn nodded again. "Yes, we do."

"I started looking at everyone, thinking, trying to figure out what the difference was between you - all of you - and me. What made you stand out once you were a true believer?"

"And what conclusion did you come to?"

Now Ashlynn turned around. She looked like a child who could not find her parents. "You are at peace all the time."

"Not all the time," Jaryn argued gently.

"But you are." She moved toward him, placing open palms on his chest. "You get upset, you get flustered, you are conflicted...and yet there is peace." Ashlynn shook her head. "I feel all of those things and I appear to remain calm, but on the inside I am tormented."

"I know," was his soft answer. "Ashlynn, it used to be the same for me. I was a much different person before you knew me, before I came to the Deliverer."

"Tell me," she pleaded quietly. "Tell me everything. Tell me anything you can to make this feeling go away."

"I will tell you, but you must understand that the choice to fill the emptiness is yours. Nothing I say or do will be your remedy, my love." She nodded, though it was hard to tell if she really understood. "Come with me."

Jaryn took her by the hand, feeling how chilly her fingers were. He led her to a cold ring of stones, the communal fire ring for the few houses nearby.

Ashlynn lit it with her own fyre and sat before it. Her emotions were erratic and strong, and the flames moved in the same manor. One moment they would be dull, the next they would be so strong and high it was as though they were trying to burn the very stars. Sitting beside Ashlynn, Jaryn held her hands and rubbed them to try and get them warm again.

"When I was a boy, I was always getting into trouble. My parents, bless them, never knew what a new day would bring. I would come home with black eyes and split lips. I stole and cheated, and had no care for anyone that was not me. I was born with the need to be the best at everything and to prove that I needed no one." He smirked, though there was shame in his eyes. "By the time I reached my eighth birthday, my mother had passed and my poor father had no idea what to do with me. It was a bard just passing through who took special interest in me. He happened to be present when I was in the middle of a scuffle. When the fight was broken up he offered to be the one to take me home. On the way I spoke almost nothing to him, but he had no problem filling the silence between us with his own voice. He told me of how he saw much of himself in me and by the time we reached my home, had offered to take me with him when he left."

"Dollen," Ashlynn said quietly. "Your mentor. I remember you telling me of him."

Jaryn nodded. "Dollen was such a gentle and peaceful man, and his tales of travel seduced me easily. I wasn't happy at home and I knew I could sing. To go with him seemed the natural choice."

"How did your father feel?"

"Relieved." Jaryn laughed. "Dollen and I left just a few days later and so began my life as a bard. It didn't take me long to love the man as I never loved or respected my father. He treated me with more kindness and patience than my own father ever had and that started my change. When someone believes you're better than you are, you strive to prove you can be that noble. Besides, he was hardly ever crooked or offensive and people flocked to him in a way I had never seen before. It would not do for his apprentice to be seen as a dirty-mouthed little urchin. Dollen was not the best singer; he wasn't terrible, but I have heard better. Yet everywhere we went he made friends and never grew weary or chose to keep company with the fair over the foul.

"I can't remember what prompted me to do so, but one day I asked what kept him so positive and happy. He said if I wanted to know, I would wake up early the next morning and go with him. I was to ask no questions, pass no judgments, and make no comments until they were asked for."

"Where did he take you?"

"To the most beautiful place I have ever seen." There was a soft glow of nostalgia about Jaryn as he spoke, a light shone in his gaze that could not be

105

ignored. The very way he sat changed, as though he had particular pride in this part of his tale. "To tell the truth, there was nothing all that spectacular about the old building. It was falling apart in places and desperately needed architectural attention. Inside there was no place to sit, save the benches along the wall for the weak and the weary. I didn't understand what the reason could be for going to such an odd place, or why it would be as filled with people as it was. My first thought was that there was going to be a performance - some kind of show from which Dollen drew his inspiration."

"But it was not as you expected," Ashlynn supplied. This was a tale she had heard a few times before, but now it was taking on a new meaning. Once it had been about the bard and the kindness he'd expressed to her beloved. Now she understood more of the motivation behind such kindness. Somehow, it made the familiar story new.

"They opened with a long spell of singing, such singing as I had never heard before. The talent behind the notes mattered little; no one was listening to anyone else. With eyes closed and faces and hands lifted to the broken roof above them, people were *praising*. Though I didn't fully understand it at that exact moment, I could most certainly appreciate it. Dollen had spoken of the Giver before, many times. It was simply a subject I'd learned to tune out or ignore. But to see this grown man...my *teacher*...weeping for all the love and devotion he could not contain...it was enough to make me pay attention."

Ashlynn tilted her head. "You never told me that part."

Jaryn looked at her briefly. "I never felt led to. You have never been receptive enough to truly hear."

In a whisper she replied, "Please go on."

"The praises and the worship went on for a long time. Even when the old priest spoke, some still sang quietly or hummed to themselves. Normally the speaking is where anyone of interest would have lost me, but I could not stop listening, even if I had wanted to. It was as though the words he had chosen were meant to speak directly to me. He was speaking of the Deliverer, a being I'd never even heard of before, and how he was the son of the Giver but also the Giver in flesh, sent to Earth to walk among us, to be with us and, ultimately, to die for us."

The lump in Ashlynn's throat, vanished for a time, was threatening to return. She wanted to ask Jaryn to tell the story he was told. This, too, was not new, but its meaning was now entirely different. Her tongue swept over her lips, but she did not speak for fear of that terrible lump turning into tears.

"The priest said He knew, the Giver did, of all the terrible things that would happen in this world. All the lies we would tell, the crimes to be committed, all of our sins. He knew all of mine before I did, knows all of the sins of my children though they are not even born yet. He sent His son to lead us and to teach us that the only way to eternal life is through Him. But we humans are not so eager to listen when we are told we are doing things wrong. We are even less eager when we are told we should start following one God and praising Him alone.

"This man, this Deliverer, was different from all the tyrants seeking power. He was kind, gentle, soft-spoken, and loving, though his wrath could be terrible when it was shown. People started calling him Lord, Chosen One, and Messiah, and there were other men of power who did not approve. They told the Deliverer to rebuke his followers, with their titles and devotions. Yet he would not. It didn't take long after that for men such as they to secretly plot his death."

"Because he had followers?" Ashlynn shook her head, confusion on her face. "He was kind and caring. Why is that so terrible, especially in a world as harsh as this one? Would they rather the people follow someone with ill intentions?"

"They would rather the people follow them."

Ashlynn nodded her understanding, even if she did not agree with it. "Go on."

Jaryn was silent for a moment and his eyes remained closed. Watching him, somehow Ashlynn knew he was praying. He was struggling with emotion, with finding the right words. As his eyes slowly opened, she instinctively reached for his hand. He was teary and pulled her close. "Tell me the rest," she whispered. "Please tell me the rest."

"The Deliverer asked his Father to spare him, though he knew what he had to do, and would do so out of obedience to his Father and love for us. He prayed so diligently and powerfully that he even began to sweat blood. It was on that mountain that the soldiers came upon him. They took him and he suffered a long night of beatings and provocations.

"At daybreak, all the elders of the people assembled, including the leading priests and teachers of the religious law. The Deliverer was led before the high council, and they said, 'Tell us, are you the Messiah?' But he remained silent and did not answer them."

"But why?" Ashlynn looked at Jaryn. "Why did he not speak up, proclaim who he was and make them see the truth?"

Jaryn's expression was sorrowful. "The truth is only truth to someone open enough to receive it. He could have spoken all day and still they would not have believed. Their minds had already been made up." Ashlynn looked into the flames with a quiet sigh, falling silent once more.

"The governor decided to have the Deliverer beaten with clubs and whips of nails, and sharp rocks and metal pieces. He thought if the man was beaten severely, the crowd would be pleased and satisfied enough to let him go. Even with all the blood spilled, the crowd still wanted him dead. The governor, not understanding their hatred, washed his hands of the matter and turned the Deliverer over to the people to do what they would. They fastened him a crown of thorns and bore it upon his brow with such force that it made him bleed.

"They nailed him to a large tree and by his hands and feet, the Deliverer hung, broken and bleeding, while people mocked and played games at his feet." Beside him, Jaryn could hear Ashlynn crying, though he did not look at her. Instead, he continued with his story. "They said if he was the Chosen One he could save himself. Even as they said such hateful things to him, he was loving them and praying for them. He hung there for six hours before crying out and releasing his spirit to the Giver."

No more words were spoken for some time, the only sound in the night being the fyre and Ashlynn's tears. Even the sounds from the village-wide celebration had somehow been muted. "I don't understand," she wept. "Why did he not save himself? Why would he let them hurt him so?"

Now Jaryn reached out to comfort her. "Because then we would not be saved. His blood was shed to cover us, my love. To cover you. He let all of those terrible things happen, knowing they were going to happen, to save us. Do you understand that? Do you believe it?"

"I do," she said emphatically, "but I don't understand why. Why save us? Why save me?"

Jaryn's voice was very soft as he got on his knees before her. "Because we are his children. You are his cherished one. We are all his cherished ones, and he was protecting us from a life of pain and separation. Would you not die to protect Kenayde? Would you not suffer terrible things so that she wouldn't have to? It's the same way with the Deliverer, only his love is so much more powerful than we could ever imagine."

"But he died for me," Ashlynn sobbed. "I didn't want or ask him to. Never would I want anyone to die in my stead."

"You didn't have to ask him." Jaryn lovingly ran a hand over her hair. "He did it because he wanted to. Ashlynn, he did it so that you would come to him with this broken heart and accept him."

"I do," she cried, "I do. Oh, forgive me for not believing sooner."

Jaryn took her hands in his, pressing them gently as she joined him on her knees on the ground. Bowing his head, he closed his eyes. "Dear Father in Heaven...how we love You and how our hearts break for the sacrifice You gave for us. Lord, I thank You for your unfathomable love, and Your willingness to forgive each one of our many sins. I praise You for Your hand of mercy on my life, and thank You for Dollen. Without him, I don't know if I would be as faithful to You as I am today. I ask You now to be with Ashlynn. Fill her, surround her with Your glory, Your might, and Your strength. Show her how much You love her and cherish her, now that she can truly see. I thank You so much for her, Father. Thank You for bringing her into my life. Thank You for the opportunity to share You with her tonight. Thank You for the right words because I know they did not come from me, but from You."

"Thank You," Ashlynn echoed, her own eyes closed and head bowed. "Thank You for dying for me, and loving me, even when I didn't think of or love You." She trembled from her own powerful emotions, but forced herself to go on through her weeping. "Deliverer, forgive me for not knowing You sooner, for not seeking You earlier. Forgive me for all the wrong I have done and help me to do right by Your name."

The pair was silent for some time. Jaryn only continued when he was certain Ashlynn had nothing else to say out loud. "Be with us in these coming days, that we may honor You in all that we do. Thank You for your grace in our lives, Lord. We love You so much. In Your name we pray...Amen." Ashlynn echoed the closing sentiment, and they both stayed with their heads bowed and hands clasped for some time. Eventually, Ashlynn opened her red and tired eyes to look at Jaryn.

"What about three days later?"

The question seemed to surprise him at first, but surprise gave way to a grin. "So you didn't completely tune out all of your lessons as a child."

"Not all of them," she confirmed sheepishly.

"Three days later the tomb was empty. The Deliverer was gone, in Heaven with his Father."

"I like happy endings," Ashlynn admitted.

"But it's not over yet." Jaryn brushed the hair from her face. "There is so much more to come."

Using the hem of her sleeve, Ashlynn dried her eyes. "What became of Dollen?"

Jaryn smiled again, wistfully. "After the service, he and I had a conversation much like this one, only I was the one in tears. I had so many questions that he was willing and patient enough to answer. We had communion and did something that was rather symbolic." He frowned in thought. "I have neither bread nor wine, but we can certainly do the second part." Getting up, Jaryn jogged to one of the houses and searched by their wood piles. When he came back he had two small branches in his hand. As Ashlynn stood, he gave one to her.

"What is this for?"

"The Deliverer was crucified on a tree. He took all of our sins upon himself so that we might be free of them. This branch is a part of that tree. Symbolically, of course. Throwing it into the fyre to watch it burn is more of a tangible way of watching our sins be taken from us. We confess and ask for forgiveness, and then throw them into the fire. Our sins are turned to ashes, and we are no longer yesterday's men."

"Yesterday's men?"

"Aye. The men we were yesterday." Jaryn smiled gently and gave a nod. "Throw it into the fyre, and speak your heart with him." Ashlynn stared at the flames a moment before tossing her branch in. Jaryn did the same and they were quiet, each lost in their own private conversation with the Deliverer.

After a time, Ashlynn took a deep breath. "Ready to go back?" Jaryn asked gently. He moved closer to her, wrapping his arms around her.

"No," she admitted. "I think I want to take some time by myself for now."

"I can understand that." Dipping his head, he gently kissed her lips. "If you have any questions about anything, come find me. Or your parents. Someone. Just don't be afraid to ask."

Ashlynn nodded, smiling her answer. Jaryn let her go and started back to the village. He turned around in time to watch a transformation he had missed seeing the past year. Ashlynn's small frame grew, turning from human to dragon with the ease of a skilled shifter. The pain still came upon her, but she had been doing it long enough now that she knew how to ignore it. She was beautiful in the moonlight, shimmering golden scales and massive wings that extended well over the length of any normal jousting arena. Turning to look back at Jaryn, her green eyes were filled with a peace he had never seen. Her strong legs pushed away from the ground as her wings felt the air around them. Jaryn had to hold an arm across his face to keep debris from getting into his eyes. When the wind had died and he was able to look, she was gone.

Flying had always been freeing for Ashlynn. The air was familiar to her in a way she could not describe. She could feel the changing currents and drafts, knowing when to bank and use the wind, and when to use her wings to move herself. Tonight the air was cold and crisp, and the sky was clear from clouds. Ashlynn flew high, exalting in the freedom of the air and marveling at how different everything looked to her now. She saw everything with a new beauty and as a gift. Even her city, far below with labyrinthine streets carefully woven around Altaine to make an intricate knotted design that could only be seen by flyers, seemed magical to her. Tears came to her again, but not the tears of someone broken. These were tears of someone filled with love and joy; someone becoming whole.

On the streets of the capital, every face turned skyward as a trumpeting cry rang above them. They could see the golden dragon soaring among the stars, turning circles and truly enjoying her flight. Many knew the dragon and smiled at seeing it. Gaels with the ability to fly soon shifted as well, joining her in the sky. Even the Volar, with their wings of many different shapes and colors, joined the dragons. It was not long before the stars were blotted out by magical beasts, a perfect ending to a night that had held so many emotions for them all.

CHAPTER TEN

Laidley could hear his mother weeping in the next room. The sound of it was driving him mad. It was not his duty to console his mother; it was not his job, not when she was like this. It was Luella's responsibility and she was nowhere to be found. The sobbing continued and Laidley slumped in his throne. His head was propped in one hand while his mind frantically searched for something else to focus on: the breeze through the window, the people coming in and out of the open throne room, the smell of the old metal crown on his head, the hardness of the unforgiving throne he was in. Yet still, she sobbed.

"Stop it," he hissed to no one. It was worse than a constant drip and finally drove him to his feet. "Stop it! You weak and irritating woman!" His harsh words echoed all around him, and when they faded away there was no other sound. Courtiers, hanging by the doorways in hopes of catching Laidley in a talkative mood, jumped and shied away from his angry gaze.

She had finally stopped crying. Laidley's squire moved forward in tiny hesitant steps when Laidley did not sit back down. With slight trepidation, the squire bowed. "Is there something you require, my Lord?"

Laidley looked at the boy with misdirected anger. "No! Leave me! All of you! Get out! Find Merrik!" The squire scrambled and left the room quickly, the courtiers awaiting an audience with the prince quick to follow. It was not long at all before Merrik was there, bowing as the squire had.

"Your Grace."

"Have you found my sister?" The few moments of absolute silence had calmed him some and Laidley was sitting once more.

"No, Your Majesty, however, I have been told by an informant that she was seen boarding a ship bound for the Isles."

Laidley looked alarmed, worried. "She was taken prisoner?"

"I do not believe so," answered Merrik. "It appears she went peacefully,

111

even...willingly." Laidley stared at him but said nothing. It was as though the young prince could not fathom what he was being told, and when he remained silent, Merrik continued. "If I may remind you, the princess did not agree with seeking out your father's murderers." Laidley flinched and the anger began to return. "She begged you to leave them alone. She wanted to let them live, despite what they had taken from you. Your father's body was not yet cold, and your sister was willing to let those filthy Celts live." He held Laidley's gaze and saw betrayal there. "It would appear she has chosen their lives over retribution."

Merrik's tone had not changed from its ever even tenor, but his chosen words had Laidley angrier by the second. "She let them go, my lord. She helped them escape your wrath and your justice." Laidley was practically writhing in anger, unable to sit still in his throne. "Your sister wanted them to live, despite the life they had taken, the life of the father you both loved so well. They got away because of her." He paused to watch the effect he was having on Laidley, and when he spoke again his voice was almost a purr. "All but one." He could not keep the smugness from entering his eyes. "You found that one, and you disposed of him."

Laidley settled some, his expression softening. "The monk," he said in gentle remembrance. "He paid for his crimes."

"You watched him die," Merrik goaded. "You saw the blood run from his body as my blade slid along his throat. You saw the ground stained crimson as he breathed his last breath. How did that feel?"

Lifting his head, Laidley looked clearly through his anger at Merrik. "Hollow."

The honesty in both the answer and Laidley's expression would have been rattling to a lesser man. Merrik only replied with, "Next time it will be your kill. Then it won't feel so hollow. It will become a hunger - an insatiable need that can only be met with blood." Laidley nodded, looking away from Merrik in thought. "What will be done about your sister?" asked the older man. The soft question was exactly the right one to bring back the deepening rage in Laidley.

"She has betrayed me," he growled.

Merrik nodded. "She has betrayed you, this kingdom, and your father's memory. She is now a sympathizer to the enemy."

"That makes her an enemy," Laidley seethed. "She has denounced me and I will not tolerate deserters to my throne."

"Of course not, your Majesty. Shall we then treat her the same as the others we hunt?"

"Yes..." A sound caught his ears and Laidley turned his head, tilting it like a curious bird. Finola had started crying again. It was enough to make him twitch. "I cannot stand this!" Laidley raged. "See to it that my mother is taken care of, Merrik! Do it now, before I kill myself only to be rid of the sound of her weeping. And do it quickly. I am assembling the Privy Council."

Merrik's brows twitched together. "My Prince?"

"They led my father through many a siege and slaughter. With what was sent to the capital of Siness I am expecting quick reply. I will not be vulnerable."

"No," Merrik agreed quickly, though there was confusion behind his gaze. "Forgive my impertinence, but how are we to know these children have the following or the funding to begin a war with Caedia? There is no High rule there, only a regent. Surely he wouldn't be foolish enough to take a country that's not even his into battle."

"He's been regent for many years, Merrik since Nir was killed. Why wouldn't he take this opportunity? Conquering Caedia, as obscure a possibility as that may be, would give him fair argument to become the true ruler Siness is missing." Laidley smirked seeing the surprise on Merrik's face. "It would be a disservice to yourself, Merrik, to believe me too young and incompetent to think these things through."

The older man dipped his head. "Yes, Your Majesty."

"Now go." Finola's wailings were beginning to sound like that of a trapped spirit. The louder she wept, the more Laidley entertained the idea of driving spikes into his own temples. It was keeping him from thinking clearly and sparking a temper that should have long been cooled. "See to my mother. Quickly."

"As you command, My Prince."

Merrik left the throne room to let Laidley soak in his anger and cursed the daily duties that kept him from Laidley's side. The young man was neither stupid nor too sick with grief that he could not see through the haze and rule his kingdom. Merrik needed him to be livid, to be so malleable under his command that there would be no hesitation or question. He had to do something quickly, or he would lose his opportunity to gain control.

He took the familiar path down a hallway that would lead him to where the queen sat in mourning. Tadhg's robes lay on a stone table inside an ante-chamber off of one of the meeting halls, his body long since burned in the funeral pyre. It was here that Merrik found Finola. The queen looked up from the robes she wept into when the heavy door was pushed open. "My Queen," Merrik greeted softly.

The torchlight was severely low in the windowless room and the smell was thick and pungent. All he could see was the silhouette of Finola as she sat slumped on the floor. "Merrik?" she questioned faintly. "Please...I do not wish to be disturbed."

"Your Majesty, your son worries for you." As his eyes adjusted to the dim light, Merrik could see the ashen skin of his queen. She'd not left this room

113

since the day after Tadhg burned, not to bathe, not to use her own private chamber pot. In the corner of the room Merrik could see the one she'd been using and found a small pile of food that went unfinished. It was disgusting.

"My son worries for no one but himself," Finola argued bitterly. "He is his father's son and will soon be as lost to me as my husband."

Merrik stood beside the queen, the flickering and dying light of the torches hiding his expression in shadow. "Your daughter is gone from you as well. She has left for the Isles with the fugitives."

This news did not seem to surprise the queen as she nodded slowly. "That is well. It is where she belongs; she would have found her way there eventually. Would that I had gone with her."

"Your Majesty?" Her words made no sense. Why would Luella ever desire to leave Montania, let alone go to the Isles? It could have been her grief speaking, but she seemed more present now than she had in a very long time.

Finola waved her hand dismissively. "It does not matter, Merrik. None of it matters anymore." She began to weep again and Merrik took another step closer.

"Your heart must be broken. Perhaps I may help to ease your pain." There was no chance for Finola to ask what he meant. Not a breath was passed before he was behind her with his dagger. As the sharp blade ran across her neck and blood poured from the gash, Merrik had no thought or feeling for what he was doing. She tried to scream but choked on her own blood, resulting in nothing more than a drowning, sputtering sound. Stepping back, Merrik stood patiently to watch as his task was completed. Finola slumped over into Tadhg's robes, lifeless and immobile.

After several long moments he moved forward again, placing the hilt of his dagger in her hand. "Your Majesty, no!" As predicted, heavy feet sounded only moments later. The door was thrown open by three knights to find Merrik against the wall, slouched on the floor. He looked stunned. "She took my dagger from me," he explained as their gazes found Finola. "I had no chance to stop her."

The three men stood perfectly still, only their eyes moving to one another for the briefest of moments. Whether they believed Merrik or not, none had the desire to question the older man for fear of repercussion. Instead, Merrik was helped to his feet by one of the guards, while the other two checked on the queen. "Shall we tell the prince?" asked the man who helped Merrik stand.

"No," he replied gravely. "Let me. Take care of the queen. See that she is cleaned up so he doesn't have to see her this way."

Laidley was in the same place Merrik had left him, almost in the exact same position. As Merrik entered the throne room it was not with the same confident flourish that was his constant. This time his steps were slower and heavier. He had Laidley's attention before he even had a chance to bow. "What

114

is it?" Laidley asked darkly.

Merrik kept his head bowed. "I...I haven't the heart to tell you."

Laidley turned himself so as to sit properly in his seat, dark brows knit together. "Merrik, what is it?"

With a deep breath in, the older man answered in a sorrowful tone. "The Queen...your mother...forgive me, Your Majesty, but I could not stop her."

Leaning forward, Laidley now demanded, "Out with it, Merrik! What has happened?"

"She took my dagger. It was at her throat before I knew what to do."

There was a long interminable silence as Laidley just stared at Merrik. When he broke the silence at last, there was no emotion in his voice, though the corners of his lips turned up at the edges as though he had been let in on a secret. "She slit her own throat." Merrik nodded and said nothing, and Laidley relaxed. "Did she know of Luella?"

"She asked of her, Your Majesty. I could not lie to her."

"Of course not," Laidley agreed distractedly.

Merrik wet his lips. "She did say that it came as no great shock your sister had gone, or where she had gone to. Why might that be?"

Laidley shook his head. "My mother was mentally unstable. She said many things that made no sense." He cursed quietly. "Relight the flame in the mourning tower. We will burn her tonight and I will be made king." There was a weight in his words that was not of sadness, but responsibility. "I am truly all that Caedia has left now."

"Do not forget, My Prince, you are not alone."

With a slow nod, Laidley gave the older man a tight smile. "You are a true and most valuable friend. You served my father well and I have no doubt you will do the same for me." Merrik bowed but said nothing. "Thank you, Merrik. Please see to the arrangements for this afternoon. Find me when it is done and I am to be crowned."

"You do not wish to be present at your mothers' burning?"

Laidley shook his head. "I need to make ready my council. My mother gave me nothing in life. I owe her nothing in death."

~*~*~*~

The Privy Council was made up of several important men from Caedia's lesser kingdoms: Duke Terrance Brooks and Sir Robert Drakken, Marquess DeSwitt, Count Alayra, and a small handful of others closer to the capital. These men were from different kingdoms but came to court when called for and lived inside Montania for weeks at a time with their families. They were well versed in the politics that were involved in running a country and had been Tadhg's trusted council for many years. Laidley himself knew enough of politics to be confident, but told Merrik he would be leaning heavily on his knowledge if moments of uncertainty should arise.

The men all stood when Merrik and Laidley entered and sat only when Laidley had seated himself. "Your Grace," began DeSwitt, "I am deeply sorry for..."

Laidley waved a hand. "There will be time enough for that later. Gentlemen, I have assembled you now, before the coronation, so that we may discuss the matter of war. Though it is not yet upon us, I cannot help but feel it will be fast approaching. The murder of my father was just the beginning." He shot Merrik a glance, unreadable. "My Captain tells me it is a small matter to worry over, that it is only two girls that have slipped through our fingers; but they're of Siness and I fear they'll find themselves confident with such a high profile assassination."

"Siness has no high ruler," said Brooks. "Surely they would not carry out such a plan under the order of a regent."

Alayra scowled. "You would choose to believe two little girls and an old monk acted of their own accord? Castle security is constantly on high alert. Our threats come at us from every angle. I find it hard to believe that an action such as the murder of a high king could have been conceived by these few minds."

"Men with armies behind them have tried to storm Montania before," added DeSwitt. "It is not a thing easily done, getting inside unnoticed like that."

"But that is the beauty of a small vigilante group," Drakken countered. "There are fewer numbers to worry about. They would have time to plan on their own and perfect what they needed to before any action was ever taken."

Laidley sat back and let the men argue with each other, listening very carefully. He was beginning to feel more like himself, the young man who observed before reacting, who thought before commanding. This would be Montania's defining reign. He would be the king people remembered for avenging the stolen life of his father, for smiting the enemy, and finally bringing things to order.

"We are but one small nation," Alayra was saying. "Not even with all the men in Caedia could we overthrow the Celtique peoples."

"It was what Tadhg was trying to do," Merrik offered, finally breaking his stoic silence with the deep cadence of his voice. The others quieted and looked to him, Laidley doing the same. "He was not warring just for war's sake. It was a slow takeover of all six Celtique nations. In the beginning at least. Near the end it was his love of death that drove him, but the goal was never far from sight. The Celtique lands are the only places left in the world where the Gaels can live without fear. Tadhg was after the fabled Elementals, believing them to be hiding among these different nations. He knew by defeating the nations and

116

bringing them under his rule, even from afar, he would eventually find these exceedingly powerful Gaels."

"Caedia was once part of those nations," DeSwitt reminded sagely. "It was Tadhg's father who made us an independent nation. It was he who made hunting the Gaels into a sport and killed every one he came across."

"Caedia was once many things," Laidley said evenly. "We are greater now than we have ever been before." He looked at Merrik. "Find me a map of all seven nations." Merrik nodded curtly and left the room, biting back his anger at being sent on an errand like a page boy.

"No other nation rivals us in military numbers," continued Laidley after a moment. "My father's attacks were too quick to allow any real threat to develop. No kingdom, not even the higher ones, ever had the time enough to amass the numbers and the skill to be any real opponent. Ibays has been all but destroyed and handed over to us from the very first year of my father's reign. Where can they go in this world that they're not looked upon as a fallen people? They are nothing and that was because of my father. Their island may be large but their heart is no longer beating. They will never be a threat to anyone again."

Merrik was back quickly and spread the large map across the length of the table with the help of a squire. Caedia, Ibays, Alybaen, Cieria, Mirasean, and Braemar were each colored different from surrounding nations, given a green tinge to show them in unison even though they did not touch each other. Laidley stood and went around the chairs to put a finger on Siness. "The people of Siness have been without a leader for so long I do not wonder that they should be too disorganized to do much of anything right now."

"Cieria could be a problem," said Drakken with a scowl. "They are known for their warriors."

"If we left them for last they would rather surrender than fight," said Brooks. He had been born in Cieria and knew their fighting spirit only so went deep.

"Which leaves the Nagin and dwarf tribes in Alybaen, and the Volarim in Braemar."

Here Laidley frowned. The winged creatures of the Volarim were valuable as messengers. They could be defeated, but at what expense? He knew it was better to have someone in his employ willingly than as a slave, especially a creature who could so quickly disappear to other lands. "The dwarves and the Nagin can be dealt with easily enough. They're savages in their own ways, forgetful of the way the world works outside their lands. It's the Volarim I pause at."

"Do they still think of themselves as part of the Celtique nations?" Alayra asked.

"I don't know," Laidley answered honestly. "You, squire. Send in Ories."

The boy left immediately and Merrik stood closer to the table to look at the map. "You forget the elves on Mirasean."

"Hardly." There was no mistaking the humor in Laidley's voice as he looked at the tiny island amid the much larger nations. "The elves are not warriors. They would sooner jump into the ocean and drown themselves than fight all of Caedia."

Brooks looked at the men surrounding the table, brows elevated. "Is that the plan then? Are we going to attack the nations as a whole? Wipe out the Celts?"

Laidley raised steely eyes from the map to Brooks' face. "The world would be better off without them."

"Your Majesty," began Alayra tentatively, "we do not have the men to fight four nations at once."

"I do not plan on spreading the men so thin," replied Laidley. He went back to his chair at the head of the table and sat. "These girls from Siness, the ones who share the same surname as their former high king, will not stay silent when they receive the gift that was sent to them. If they are Nir's children they will have a quiet army behind them by now."

Drakken's brows raised. "You believe Siness will fight to restore its freedom from Caedia? Your father had us believe Siness had no heir to the high throne."

"My father hoped but never knew for certain." Laidley shook his head. "I have no doubt of their retaliation at this point. They will come here for a fight and fail without question. And we will make an example out of them here where we are strongest."

Before anyone could question Laidley the door opened and pulled everyone's attention from the discussion at hand. A tall man wearing dark, loose fitting clothing entered the room. His skin was a golden brown and his long black hair hung loose, hiding half of his face and the patch he wore over his left eye. Wings of onyx rested upon his back and when he entered, he bowed his head respectfully to the entire room. "You sent for me, Your Highness." His voice was quiet and his tone low.

"Yes," said Laidley. "Do the Volarim count themselves among the Celtique peoples still?"

Ories turned one dark blue eye to the prince and gave a slight shake of his head. "No, my lord. We are an independent nation, answering to no order but our own high king and queen, and that of the hosting kingdom messengers are sent to."

"You see?" Laidley's attention went back to the other men. "That leaves Siness, Cieria, the dwarves, and the Nagina. One has no real ruler, one will bend easily to a stronger will, and two are made up of savages. When they see my

118

father's murderer strung up for the birds to feed from and her paltry little army lying bleeding at her feet, they'll fall before us and beg for mercy to be spared the same fate." He waved a hand at Ories to send him off, and the winged man gave a slight bow before exiting. Laidley looked across the room to Merrik once Ories was gone, a brow raised in challenge. "Well, Merrik? What do you think of the princeling now?"

Merrik hesitated only to return a wolfish grin. "I think it is time for the princeling to be a prince no more." He looked pointedly out the window to the midday sun. "We will go to war. But first, there is a coronation you must prepare for."

~*~*~*~

Rain and darkness would have been more appropriate than a day of sunshine. Laidley stood on the parapet of the castle wall, eyes fixed on the fire lighting one of the turrets like a giant blazing torch. The body of his mother was still burning, and the people of the village were not quite sure what to do with themselves. When a ruler died, it was customary to have some sort of service. If the ruler had been well liked, there would have been fanfare and deep mourning. If he had not been held in high esteem, there would have been time to pay respects and then life would go on as normal. Word quickly spread that Finola had killed herself, and though this came as no great surprise, the proceedings afterward were unnatural. The prince could be seen where he stood, and there was the understanding he would be crowned later that day. The expression he wore as he gazed up at the tower was a mixture of disgust and irritation. Could one man truly have so much hatred for his own parents?

Merrik joined him, mirroring Laidley's stance with legs slightly spread and arms crossed in an almost defensive position. "It will not be long now," the older man reported. "Preparations are being made in the Great Hall for your coronation."

"No." Laidley didn't bother to look away from the turret. "I want it outside in the courtyard. Double the guards if you have to, but I want everyone to see who now sits in the king's chair."

There was a flicker of a smile, quick and elusive as Merrik nodded. "As you wish."

"I want it done now." To lend authority to his words, Laidley looked at Merrik with a stern scowl. "I want the fire at my back when I am made king."

Merrik remained expressionless. "You realize such an act is as good as spitting on the grave of your parents." Laidley said nothing, only looked at the older man with the same hard expression. Once again, Merrik bowed his head. "It will be done." He hesitated a moment, obviously wanting to say more, but stopping himself from doing so. This had the desired effect when Laidley lifted an eyebrow to give him the permission to continue. "It troubles me to know, My Prince, that you are the last of your bloodline fit to rule, especially with what we have planned. I fear that there will be those that would seek to kill you only to try and claim the throne for themselves to try and stop the war."

"And what would you have me do?" asked Laidley, bemused. "You worry too much, Merrik. With you by my side, I fear nothing. Besides, I will be taking care of that very worry soon."

"Yes, of course. Forgive me. I only wish to keep you aware of the potential dangers. If that is all, I will see to the arrangements for the ceremony and have them moved to the courtyard, as you request." Turning, Merrik strode away with a small smile on his face.

Within the hour, Laidley was dressed in the finest garments in all of Montania, clothed in a doublet of gold with black trimmings, black pants and boots. He wore the jewels of his father, and a long formal cape of gold with white trim at the edges. The crier had been sent to tell the people of the village that their attendance was not requested but required. This meant that whatever they were doing, no matter the importance, it needed to be put on hold so they could dress themselves as well as they could to be present as their new king was crowned. The air of confusion had not left and as families gathered, they whispered among themselves at the oddity of the entire thing. Gazes went to the fire still burning in the highest turret, all knowing it meant Finola was still not quite gone. If this was a sign of what was to come under Laidley's rule, it was not a good omen.

Even with so little time to prepare, the ceremony was boisterous. There were musicians scattered throughout the crowds along with fools that juggled and told jokes. There were maidens peddling roses and men selling mead. They may have all been confused at the timing, but for the residents of Montania village, a chance to play and relax with drinking was an opportunity to be taken. As the crowd was drawn in by laughter and levity, Laidley looked down on them from a high window in his chambers. They would love him. He would protect them from the rest of the world, and they would love him.

Trumpets blared, announcing the ceremony was about to begin. Nervous, giddy, drunk or not, the crowds gathered around the stone platform the prince would walk out on to receive the crown of his father. The priest was already there, standing patiently at the end of the long red carpet. Beside him stood a young boy holding the golden crown on a white velvet pillow. Merrik appeared first, walking to stand on the other side of the priest, then Laidley filled the entryway. All chatter stopped and every person turned to watch him. There was a quiet excitement on his face as he walked forward, his long cape trailing behind him. As he reached the priest, he knelt down on one knee and bowed his head.

"Laidley," said the elderly man, "son of Tadhg, long ruler of the Castle Montania: by the blood in your veins, you are charged with leadership in the tragic death of your father and the sudden passing of your mother. As the eldest child, this right passes to you by generations of tradition. You are required to rule this land with gentility and fairness. Do you accept this responsibility?"

With head still bowed, Laidley replied with a level, "Yes."

"You will govern your people and your household with truth and justice. You will hold no other kingdom above your own, save that of the Giver in Heaven above. Do you accept this?"

"Yes."

"You will give your very life for the protection of your kingdom, for a king is no greater than the one he serves by ruling. Do you accept this?"

"Yes."

The priest turned to take the crown from the pillow. It was heavy with jewels of garnet and onyx and as it was placed on Laidley's head, the priest appeared indifferent to what was happening. "Rise now, Laidley, prince no longer, but High King!"

The cheers that erupted as Laidley stood were artificial, given only because no one knew anything different. Though to some, with another nervous glance at the turret above, cheering was the last thing they wanted to do. Laidley swept an unreadable gaze over his people, seeing faces without truly looking at them. He was aware of the fear in every one of them; it was palpable and it was feeding him. They feared him now, but soon they would revere him. As he pulled out the sword from the scabbard at his side, the cheering abruptly stopped and everyone stared at him in confusion and surprise.

"My first act as King." His voice was strong and carried far without much effort. Turning to look at Merrik, he said, "Kneel before me." Merrik wore no expression and showed no hesitance in doing what was commanded of him. "Merrik, most trusted adviser and friend to my father, now to me, his son. As I have been charged with the protection of this land, so shall you be charged as well." He laid his sword, broadside flat, against Merrik's shoulder. "Should anything happen to me before I have an heir, your rule will be the next this kingdom sees." As the sword was lifted and moved to touch Merrik's other shoulder, the surrounding crowd was absolutely silent. No one was so naive as to think Tadhg had come up with all his dark plans alone. The delight the captain of guards drew from bringing pain to other people was no secret. If he ever became ruler, their lives would truly be over. Now their best hope was in Laidley, a prince who had once been a sweet boy, now turned into a young reflection of his father.

Lifting his head, Merrik looked humbly at Laidley. "It is an honor you

121

bestow upon me, My King. Let us pray it is a thing we will never need worry about." After sheathing his sword, Laidley offered a hand to Merrik. He pulled the older man to his feet and the two embraced. As the villagers stayed silent, Laidley broke the embrace and glared out at them. The applause was a soft pattering at first but grew in decibel for fear of repercussions.

"Now," said the new king to Merrik, "let us go have ourselves a drink in celebration!"

Tables filled the great hall where food was piled high, steaming and filling the air with rich delicious scents. The courtiers, always loyal to whomever took the royal throne, laughed and danced, jovial as they ate and conversed. Laidley felt comfortable in his skin for the first time in a very long time. He found his own laughter came easily and a weight had been lifted from his shoulders. Men came to bow before him and pledge fealty; women flirted, some from afar and some bold enough to be close.

Afternoon came quickly and evening pressed in soon after. Still, there was no sign that the party would end. Laidley was celebrating not only his new position, but a sure victory against the Celtique Nations. He and his men raised glasses to one another and shared secret smiles and unspoken congratulations. Merrik appeared to be the only one in the entire castle to be ill at ease. He stood off to the side, his expression hinting at irritation though he was trying very hard to hide it. As Laidley walked across the wide hall to speak to him, the crowds parted to let their new king through.

"Merrik, you look as if your favorite cat has been killed. It would not hurt to smile." Laidley stood beside the older man and grinned out at the people. Glancing at Merrik, his brows rose. "Or perhaps it would."

"Forgive me, Your Majesty."

His words were tightly spoken and Laidley's brow furrowed. "What is it?" Merrik glanced at Laidley as if weighing the effects of freely speaking. Laidley gave an impatient nod and said, "Well, out with it!"

"I do not wish to spoil the evening."

"If I was worried about you spoiling my evening, Merrik, I would not have even bothered to come this way." The new king looked across the room to a group of young females. When they noticed him looking in their direction they turned to each other in peals of giggles. It made Laidley grin. "Nothing you say can ruin my evening. trust me."

"I fear we may be celebrating prematurely."

Laidley's grin only dimmed a fraction. "Ah, but that is your job, isn't it? To be the voice of reason?" The younger man sighed and crossed his arms. "Do you know I have never heard music like this in these halls? It transforms the entire castle into something completely different."

"Indeed it does, Your Highness."

Ready to get back to more uplifting guests, Laidley clapped Merrik on the shoulder. "Relax, my friend. Eat, dance. Take a woman or two back to your quarters and have a good night." He glanced at the group of young women again, a wicked smile on his lips. "I know I will."

Merrik stayed where he was and watched as Laidley crossed back across the hall to be greeted hungrily by the waiting females. The older man hid his disgust well. It wasn't Laidley's lechery so much as the lack of control Merrik had over the younger man. He needed counsel now himself, and it would not be found here.

With one more quick look at Laidley to make sure he was completely preoccupied, Merrik left the feasting and the dancing behind to head for the dungeons. Everyone was too drunk to ever notice him gone.

D. E. Morris

CHAPTER ELEVEN

The morning dawned brightly and the air was chilly. Each day that passed brought the winter season closer and made the land colorful in preparation for the change. Trees were on fire in leafy cloaks of orange, red, and yellow. By mid-morning the bright sun would be so high that the brilliant azure of the surrounding sky would be a soothing contrast. In the still early morning hours, Altaine woke up under a blanket of thick fog. It hung low to cling to rooftops and familiar paths and walkways. Far above, the castle Altaine was free of the mist and shone like a beacon in the rising sun. Luella looked up at it with no discernible expression. She sat outside the tavern at one of the many tables scattered about the town left out overnight.

"I know what you are thinking."

A mug of hot mulled wine was placed before her and Luella wrapped her hands around it. The heat seeped into her fingertips and palms, burning a trail down her throat as she swallowed a sip. It felt as good as it tasted. Smirking, Luella looked at her companion as she set her mug down. "Really?"

"I am not reading your mind, if that is what you suspect," replied Tasarin. He sat across from her with his own mug.

"Can you read minds?"

The elf shook his head, tasting his wine. "No. Some elves can. Some can see the future, some can cast spells with old magic. There are many varied gifts among my kind."

"And yours is the spirit-link with Suule?" Tasarin nodded before Luella asked another question. "Can you have more than one gift?"

"Yes," he answered thoughtfully, "though it does not happen very often and has only happened once, that I am aware of, in my lifetime."

Luella's eyes narrowed in mischievous amusement. "How old are you?"

He said nothing for a moment, his mossy gray eyes sparkling with unexpressed laughter. He even took a slow sip of wine while Luella watched him impatiently. "I am a few short years away from two hundred fifty."

For a moment Luella looked shocked, though she quickly recovered. "Wow. The world must have been such a different place when you were a child."

"I have seen many changes," he agreed. "With the Giver's blessing, I will see many more."

Luella gave a small smile, raising her mug in agreement to his statement before drinking. In her turmoil last night, she had fled council and made her way outside of the castle. Suule found her on the road down the mountain and going into town. With persistent encouragement from the unicorn, she'd climbed onto his back and wrapped her arms around his strong neck. The speed with which he ran down the mountain and through the streets of Altaine was exhilarating. It almost felt like flying, or what she assumed flying felt like. There had never been any opportunity or freedom to use her own wings before.

Suule sped past surprised and awed villagers out into the open fields far past the outskirts of Altaine. Luella didn't know how long they kept up the breakneck pace, and couldn't even remember where the unicorn had taken her, but when they stopped running they appeared to be in the middle of nowhere. There were no houses to be seen, no trees. Not even the tallest spire of Altaine was outlined in the dark. They were surrounded by lush green grass and a cloudless night sky above them.

When Luella's feet hit the ground her legs were sore and unsteady from the long hard ride. She fell to her knees and Suule was right there, nudging her to make sure she was all right. Despite the weakness, she was laughing. She'd never felt so carefree. Her hands went to Suule's cheeks and her forehead rested against his muzzle. "I am fine," she told him through her laughter. He whinnied softly, making it sound as though he was laughing as well. "Thank you, Suule." She pet his velvety face, still resting against him with her head. "I know I am not speaking elvish but somehow, I think you understand me." He nibbled at her ear and she shrieked, giggling and shying away from his whiskers tickling her face.

They were out in the fields for a long time. Luella lay in the grass while Suule rolled beside her. Sometimes he was still, sometimes he stood to eat, twice he even left her though Luella didn't worry. She had no fear that he would leave her for too long. She took the time alone to stare upward, count the stars, and think of happier times from her childhood.

It was impossible to tell the hour at which Tasarin found her, only that it was late. He came with Suule, walking beside the unicorn to whom he was so connected. "Suule told me you were together, though I did not expect to have to travel so far to find you."

"Oh!" Luella sat up at hearing the gentle voice. Even quick hands could not completely tame her windblown hair or find all the grass and leaves stuck within. She started to get up, but Tasarin held up a hand.

"Please do not rise on my behalf." The elf pet his unicorn, speaking something quietly in elvish. Suule pawed the ground lightly and whinnied, causing his companion to smile. Bringing his attention back to Luella he asked, "May I sit with you?"

"Yes, of course." Suddenly she was overly self-conscious. As Tasarin sat beside her she smoothed the skirt of her gown over her legs. She looked around awkwardly, searching for something to say. When she looked back at him, his smile was genuine even though hers was crooked and half-hearted. A thought struck and Luella pursed her lips briefly. "Have you come to tell me that Ashlynn is displeased with my actions?"

"Hmm?" Tasarin blinked "Oh, no, not at all. I simply came to make sure you were all right. Suule told me you were, and though I trust his judgment above that of any other, I wanted to see for myself." His pale eyes flickered to her hair, lips curving upward. "Forgive me." He reached over and pulled a blade of dead grass free. Luella blushed furiously upon seeing it, thankful darkness hid her coloring. She ran a hand over her hair, feeling for debris.

"You said Suule told you I was fine?" She wanted attention elsewhere, but Tasarin pulled another bit of grass from her hair. "How did he tell you? Do you speak telepathically?"

"Suule cannot actually speak," he explained, taking the last leaf from Luella's tangled mess. "He understands the common tongue, will almost always respond to elvish, but cannot verbally communicate himself. However, because we are spirit-linked, he can speak to me through pictures."

Luella looked at the elf strangely, running a hand over her hair one final time. "I do not understand."

"Everything he sees, I can see. Everything he feels, I can feel. Even the feelings he absorbs from others, those too, to an extent. Right now I can see your face from his point of view, feel his feelings for you, and feel some of your nervousness."

"I'm not nervous," she defended quickly.

Tasarin gave a gracious smile. "Sometimes the feelings of others can be misread. Forgive me."

Luella looked over at the unicorn standing only a few feet away. He blinked lazily. "What does he feel about me?" she wanted to know. "How does he see me?"

There was a brief moment of silence as Tasarin gathered his information. "He sees you much the way I do, though there is an odd tint of lilac about you - perhaps because of the lack of light. As for his feelings about you, he is very fond of you. Protective."

Her heart melted, and Luella felt warmth all over. "He's protective of me?"

Tasarin nodded. "You are emotionally vulnerable and he wishes to correct that. It seems he liked you from the moment you met." His brows came together slightly. "You said he was beautiful?" Luella nodded, causing Tasarin to smile. "That explains it. Unicorns are very vain creatures and are attracted to those who find them as beautiful as they find themselves."

Luella laughed and Suule snorted dispassionately. "Oh Suule, I cannot believe you that superficial." Tucking her hair behind her ear, she looked at Tasarin. "How did you realize your special link with him?"

"It is something of an odd story," the elf said with a slow smirk. "I did not realize I had the gift of spirit-linking until late in my childhood. Suule found me in the woods one evening. I was on a scouting expedition and saw him moving through an opening in the trees. He was not even half his present size at the time, and shone so brilliantly in contrast to the dark surroundings, I thought him a spirit. In fact, that is what Suule means in my language - spirit. Not understanding what I was truly seeing, I broke from my assignment to follow him. Suule, being the intelligent creature he is, gave in to a great chase. I now know how playful his kind are. He stayed well ahead of me, too far to see what he truly was but close enough to taunt me.

"All at once, he was gone. I tried to track him but for all the prints I found, he had simply disappeared. I am still uncertain of how long he let me look. Eventually he appeared directly behind me, soundless, as I was turning around. His stealth startled me more than anything and I stumbled back. As an elf, I have senses enhanced far beyond that of a normal human; I had never had anyone sneak up on me like that - at least not successfully."

Suule neighed, an obvious laugh. "He is amused by this?" Luella guessed with a giggle.

Tasarin looked to his unicorn with a wry smile. "He is greatly amused, yes. It would seem he had been tracking me since I was a child. Staying close and always watching me."

"How did he know you were the one he would be linked to?"

"They say the unicorns are born knowing, though I cannot say for certain if that is true. All I truly understand is that they are born on the same day as their linked, and will die in the same way."

Luella wrinkled her brow. "What do you mean?"

"If Suule were to die with his heart pierced by an arrow, a wound would open itself in my own heart and we would pass from this life together. In the same way, if I were to have my bones broken and my final breath stolen, Suule would surely stumble and find his end." Tasarin looked at Suule, seriousness in his gaze. "To lose a linked is as crippling as any fatal wound. It is worse than losing a spouse or a child. It is losing yourself. Your soul loses its will to

127

continue."

"That is so sad...and beautiful at the same time." Luella looked down, wondering what it must feel like to be so connected to another living being. "Forgive me, your story went in another direction."

Tasarin shook his head lightly. "No need to apologize. Most know the legend of the spirit-linked. It is refreshing to tell it to someone unfamiliar. Now, where were we?" He took a breath. "Suule startled me and I stumbled. As I stepped back, a brier scratched my face, causing it to bleed. Suule immediately stepped forward and touched his short little horn to my wound. It was healed instantaneously and at that very same moment I saw myself in my mind, though clearly from Suule's point of view and not my own."

"Did it frighten you?"

"No," the elf admitted. "I had been told of the spirit-linked by then and quickly realized what was happening. It excited me more than anything, to be perfectly honest. By that age, most would have come into their natural born gifts. I was assuming that I would be among those who would possess no extra abilities. Meeting Suule was thrilling. We were quick in learning how best to communicate with each other, quite literally gaining new perspectives on things. The part that took the most adjustment was the emotions. Suddenly I had the most intense feelings for people and creatures I had never even met."

Luella's nose wrinkled in slight amusement. "That must have been very strange."

"It was," Tasarin nodded. "The affection was not the problem, nor even the rare faces of loathing...but the pain was not something I was expecting." Suule approached them now. Close to them, he went down on his front knees, tucking his legs under his body as he lowered himself to the grass. "We have both lost friends and family," the elf continued. "To share anguish like that is paralyzing at times." He was silent for a few breaths, solemn and thoughtful. Luella could think of nothing helpful to say and was surprised when Tasarin turned his head to give her an encouraging smile. "But the good will always far outweigh the bad."

For the rest of the night, the pair spoke of childhood memories - things they would never forget and the times they wished they could. It was easy conversation and deeply meaningful. By the time the sun began to lighten up the sky, Luella felt as though she had known Tasarin for years. He was gentle, caring, and easy to talk to and trust. There was nothing about him that seemed foul and though she was exhausted, Luella was reluctant to return to the castle to seek rest.

Now in the hazy morning light she drank the rest of her wine and gazed across the table at her companion. "You never told me what I was thinking."

Sensing a challenge, Tasarin raised an eyebrow. He didn't answer her right away, but instead spent a moment examining all the little scratches on his mug, rotating it on the table to see every chip taken from the pottery in its many uses. "At the moment," he answered finally, "it appears as though you are regretting your decision about coming to Siness."

"For a moment I was," she admitted with a frown. "I was feeling sorry for myself, thinking no matter what my decision had been, I would have regretted my choice."

"And what good does that type of circular thinking do you?"

Luella grimaced. "None at all."

"And so naturally, you changed your mind."

"Naturally," she laughed. "Being with you helps."

This brought a smile to his face and Tasarin dipped his head in thanks of her words. "You flatter me," he replied humbly. "I have very much enjoyed my time with you as well."

Curious and playful, Luella quirked a brow. "How is it that you've been alive for so many years and yet you have no wife, no children?" She blinked, a sudden thought occurring to her. "Or have you and they live elsewhere?"

Tasarin laughed briefly. "No, I have no family in that manner of the word. When you are linked, it is like a marriage. You are always with one another to an extent. Finding someone we both can agree on would be a bit of a challenge. I am content in my life at the moment and choose not to seek out a mate. If I am meant to be with someone, only the Giver will know how to organize and orchestrate it." He looked at her oddly then, almost fondly, and Luella felt her cheeks grow warm. Tasarin noticed and looked down. "Forgive me. Suule is very fond of you."

"As you said last night," Luella replied softly. "Does that make you fond of me as well?"

"It does," he admitted. "Though I cannot say for certain it all comes simply from him."

Luella smiled. "You were kind to come to me last night and even kinder to stay. I have not felt so comfortable just being myself before." She sat back in her chair and it creaked with the movement. "No one has ever really cared to speak to me of worldly things, or of anything with substantial meaning. After the way I left council like a sulking child, I was certain it would be the end of the alliance between Ashlynn and myself."

"Have more faith in her," Tasarin prodded gently. "She tried to protect you last night."

Luella nodded, ashamed. "I know she did. But to hear of all the planning and the work that went in to the infiltration of the castle, of the actual murder of my father..."

With a frown, Tasarin leaned forward to touch her arm across the small tabletop. "Luella, I do not know anyone that would have reacted any differently. You must know that no one finds fault in your actions."

"I just think I could have reacted better."

"When you left, many people came to your defense."

The comment raised her eyes to his face. "Really?"

"The high king of the Volar, as well as Ashlynn's own parents."

Luella bit the inside of her bottom lip, truly regretting her reaction. "I need to apologize."

"I believe that would take some of the weight from Ashlynn's shoulders." Tasarin pulled his hand back to his wine. "For all the toughness she presents, when something hits her she is wounded deeply and carries everything with her. She felt dreadful when you had gone."

"I would not want her to feel badly." Luella looked up at the castle again. They were all on the verge of something great and terrible. To be separated by something that was so easily mendable would be foolish. There was no more time to play at being on either side. She knew it was time to choose and to commit to her decision. "It is hard to remember why this whole thing even started. I sometimes forget that Ashlynn and Kenayde lost their birth parents to an act of warring led by my own father."

"If it was not her to stop Tadhg, it would have been someone else. Forgive me if this sounds callous, but the results may not have been as clean had it been another to assault the king."

Luella nodded solemnly. "I know, and you are right in that. Many others would have simply attacked the castle, as they have before." There were years of hurt and sorrow beneath her surface. Her expression sometimes gave it away.

"Luella." She looked at him as he leaned forward to bring his hands together atop the table. "You are not alone anymore. There is nothing you will be asked to shoulder by yourself. Please remember that. In times of joy as well as those of heartache, there are those that would have you lean on them to share in your feelings. I would ask that you think of me as one of them."

A smile came to her lips, shy and slow. "Thank you, Tasarin. I will remember and try to let myself depend on others when I need to. It's not something I have done before so forgive me if I sometimes forget."

"Of course." He stood, his smile mirroring hers. Offering his hand, he suggested, "Perhaps it is best to head back to the castle. The meeting to discuss tactics will be beginning shortly. Will you be joining us?"

Luella pursed her lips briefly. "Do I need to?"

"No, though I believe it will show great support for Ashlynn if you did. It is important to show unity now."

She nodded slowly. "Then I need to apologize to her first. Is there time?"

"There is always time for an apology."

CHAPTER TWELVE

The war room was unlike any other room in Altaine. It was completely round with no windows, save for the glass roof above them. Seating consisted of wooden benches and tables that encircled the room. Built in tiers to be stadium seating, there was enough space for five times the company that had been at council the night before. No seat held more importance than any other, meaning the royal family of the castle had no more power within that room than any other in attendance. Above the third and last row of seats, the walls were covered in maps. Every known continent was covered in one painting or another. Some were clearly older than others, their age more evident in the yellowing of the paper and the curling of the edges. Just being in the room was enough to give a person a sense of purpose. Things happened in this room. Plans were born and details were seen to. More than anything, lives were changed. Not only those in attendance, but those whose lives would be touched by the decisions made.

"I had forgotten how impressive this place was," said Wessely, entering with Nóe. There was no one else assembled yet. The two had been walking the halls, catching up, and simply decided to make their way to the assembly early. "This room brings back many fond memories."

Nóe looked around, his arms crossed over his chest. "Fond memories?"

Wessely smirked, eyes on one of the enormous maps high above. "The whole castle, really. But yes, the war room especially. Nir and I spent many hours in here when we were young." The king moved behind one of the small wooden tables to sit at the bench behind it. "We were blessed enough to grow in an age that knew very little turmoil. This room was used once for real tactics meetings, but it was used many times by my brother and me. We pretended to be great rulers, always warring with one another, of course." Wessely's brows came together in seriousness and mock displeasure. "We would yell and curse at each

131

other as ill-tempered old men are wont to do in times of battle." His expression smoothed, replaced by a small smile. "Those are some of my favorite memories."

Nóe traced his eyes over the many places for people to sit. "Has this room ever needed so many stations?"

"Oh, yes." Wessely's lips curved into a frown. "The council my father held in here, as well as the one directly before Tadhg invaded and killed Nir."

Footfalls out in the hallways would not have distracted either of the men, but for the fact that they came closer to the war room and eventually entered it. Both saw the unusual blue hair before they could see the human side of Elas' face. He looked around before seeing he was not alone and offered a quick bow. "Forgive me, Majesties. I didn't mean to intrude. Obviously I'm early." He started to back out, but Wessely shook his head.

"You intrude on nothing, Elas. Please, come and sit with us. We have not had the chance to truly speak." Upon the young man's obvious hesitance, Wessely nodded. "I should like to know more about the man who helped my daughters to safety and there is still time yet before others will arrive."

Elas dipped his head once more. "Of course." He made his way over to sit beside Wessely, then felt awkward about his face and wondered if it would have been a better decision to sit on the other side of the two men. Fidgeting a bit, he tried to turn enough so that they were peering more at the human side of his face.

Wessely, sensing the feeling of intimidation in the young water dragon, simply sat back in his seat and gave an obvious look at the scales. "Quite remarkable," he said in an awed sort of tone. "My daughter told me of your tale but did not mention what it was you were attacked by."

"Wolves, Your Highness."

Nóe furrowed his brow. "That must have been quite the ambush to leave you unable to fully be human."

"It was," agreed Elas. "There were five of them. Had I not already been in the process of shifting and had greater strength to defend myself in my dragon form, I have no doubt they would have killed me."

"Remarkable indeed," said Wessely. "And so, with your family rejecting you, you fled and lived on your own for many years, and at such a young age. You have a strong character, Elas."

"Thank you, Your Grace."

Jaryn appeared in the doorway with a small group of people. "Ah," he said, pleasure on his face. "It would seem we are right on time. Please, ladies and gentlemen, sit wherever you like." As his group moved to find seats, Jaryn went to the three men. "I see how it is, having a secret meeting without me."

"Nonsense," Wessely laughed. "Nóe and I happened by here early and decided to wait. Elas only joined us a moment ago."

"Could anything secret be kept from you?" Nóe wondered.

Jaryn thought a moment before shaking his head and grinning. "Doubtful, since I am the one to need the secrecy most of the time." His grin of mischief turned hopeful as he looked at Wessely. "Have you spoken with your eldest since last night?"

"I have," answered Wessely, elation on his face. "She came to Emiline and me this morning. Thank you, Jaryn."

With a shake of his head, Jaryn waved off the thanks. "I was only there to guide her and answer her questions. The thanks does not belong to me."

"Indeed." Wessely rose to step around his table and embrace his future son. "There is no one I would want more for Ashlynn's husband, Jaryn. You truly are a match designed in the heavens."

"I've told her that before," Jaryn agreed. "Wonder if she'll believe me now." As they chuckled, more people came into the room. "Speaking of my betrothed, I wonder where she could be. It's not like her to be late."

Ashlynn would have been there before any of them, in fact, had she not opened the door from her quarters and found Luella standing there. The older princess looked as though she hadn't slept all night and was wearing the same blue gown lent to her the previous day. Her hair was unbrushed, and there were dark circles under her big blue eyes. "Luella?"

"I came to ask your forgiveness for the way I acted last night."

"Luella, there is nothing..."

"But there is." Despite her disheveled appearance, there was something very noble in the way Luella stood, the way she looked at Ashlynn and held her chin high amid the lowly act of offering a sincere apology. "I acted the way a child does when they are displeased with their circumstances. I am not a child, and should not have responded the way I did. You spoke of my father and the amount of time and planning that went into your actions, and it unsettled me. It would appear I do not deal well with being unsettled. This does not excuse my actions, but it does explain them." Now she bowed her head, submissive. "Please forgive me. I am here to fight on the side of you and your people. Such a thing will never happen again."

Looking at Luella with her head bowed and her hands clasped before her, Ashlynn drew in a slow breath. There were several things she wanted to say, but knew her thoughts needed to be organized before she spoke. Instead of standing on the threshold, she pressed her back to the door and motioned for Luella to enter. When she did, Ashlynn followed her to the sitting room where they each took a chair.

"I feel it is I who must ask forgiveness." Luella looked up, somewhat startled and confused by the statement but said nothing as Ashlynn continued.

133

"You expressed your uncertainties about being in council last night from the very moment I mentioned the meeting. Had I been listening as a friend and not thinking solely as a ruler, I would have seen it would have been better for you to be elsewhere. I caused you pain when it was unnecessary. That does not sit well with me."

Luella shook her head. "Ashlynn, you may not yet understand this about me as we are still new friends, but there is nothing you could make me do, had I no desire of my own to do it. Queen in this country or not, I would have been there even if you had commanded otherwise."

Ashlynn nodded in understanding and rested her hands in her lap with a sigh. "Tell me you are still my friend and all will be forgiven?"

"Of course I am still your friend. And there is nothing for me to forgive." Her head tilted. "What has happened to you? There's something different."

"I don't quite know. Perhaps a re-birthing of my spirit. It's still too new to speak of. I fear putting it into words will make it disappear."

"Then don't speak of it." Luella leaned forward, smiling and extending her hands to Ashlynn. When they were joined, Luella said, "Whatever it is, I see a new light to you." Ashlynn grinned. "Now, tell me how I may be of service to you this morning."

Ashlynn smirked, giving Luella's hands a squeeze. "Please know I mean nothing cruel by this, but I believe the greatest service you could offer me would be letting one of my girls get you changed and ready for the day."

Letting go, Luella sat up and looked at herself. She ran a hand over her hair and grinned sheepishly. "I suppose that would be the best thing to do."

"What happened to you last night, after you left?" Now concerned for her friend, Ashlynn realized the look of not sleeping was more than just appearance. Luella had to have been up for most, if not all, of the night.

"Suule took me for a ride. I can't tell you where he took me, but he appeared out of nowhere and convinced me to go with him." She gave a peaceful sigh. "I couldn't think of anything when I was with him. It was all about feeling his strong muscles under me, the pound of earth against hoof, the wind blowing over us as though we were fighting against the current. The place he took me was peaceful, far away from the village and the castle. There was nothing to see but nature around us and brilliant stars above us."

"That sounds lovely."

"It was," she agreed. "Tasarin joined us after a time, and he and I spent the night in conversation." Her tone was quieted some, as though she were embarrassed to be telling that part of her story. "The elves are a very kind people, gentle, and far from judgment."

"Aye." Ashlynn did not smile too largely for fear of further embarrassing her friend. "I chose Tasarin as my second because of his very character. Much of it is bred into him, but some is of Tasarin alone." Luella listened now, looking as though she wanted to ask for more but was too shy. "He has been here at the castle since my great grandsire built Altaine. Back then he was a counselor. He knew my father and my uncle when they were born, watched them grow to manhood. When my father took the throne, Tasarin was a fixture in the castle. He stayed a counselor, but also became my father's most trusted friend. It was he who laid the foundation plans for our escape the day Altaine was invaded."

Luella's brows had slowly drawn themselves together. She blinked, curious and distraught. "I have heard small pieces of your story, but not the whole thing. I would very much like to hear it sometime."

"Of course. I would tell it to you now, were I not expected in the war room."

"Do I have time to dress?"

Ashlynn bobbed her head. "I will buy you the time." The women stood and shared an embrace. "Thank you for coming to me, Luella. I would not have been able to think properly with the idea of losing a friend weighing on my thoughts."

"There is no danger there," Luella replied, breaking the embrace. "We are sisters now, remember?"

"I do." Walking to the door, Ashlynn opened it and called for her maid. "Please follow the princess back to her quarters and assist her in anything she needs. Her presence is required in the war room in no more than thirty minutes."

No more than a half an hour later, Ashlynn entered the war room to find it already full of people. In fact, she was informed as she found a seat beside Jaryn, she was the last to arrive. Green eyes scanned the room while everyone talked, finding Luella and Tasarin in the second row across from them next to the Nagin with the crescent and star skull tattoo. The women met gazes and Luella flushed. Ashlynn grinned before looking at Tasarin. He wore a smile as he gave a polite bow of the head, and Ashlynn shook hers. "All right, what did I miss?" Jaryn was following her gaze and was clearly confused.

"I'm not sure what *I* missed." She smiled lovingly and took his hand, moving her eyes to his face. Last night had changed so many things inside of her. She used to think she couldn't love Jaryn more, but looking at him now, the feelings seemed new and stronger. The sudden rush of emotion was almost overwhelming. "Marry me?"

"Today if you'd let me."

Wessely leaned forward to look around Jaryn at his daughter. "Shall we begin, then?"

Ashlynn nodded. "The floor is yours, Papa."

Clearing his throat, Wessely stood and chatter began to quiet. "My Lords and Ladies, it is a pleasure to see all the familiar faces from last night in attendance today, as well as those whom with I have yet to become acquainted.

135

Please understand that the things we discuss today are not light-hearted and that it may indeed take a very long time to come to completion. As with any meeting of a great variety of groups, we cannot expect to all leave this room of one mind. Not everyone will agree upon the decisions which will be made. Best to accept it now and save yourself the illusion of complete unity. I do not say this to be cruel or pessimistic, but to be honest and realistic."

"He's very good," Jaryn whispered.

Ashlynn squeezed his hand. "I have parchment if you would like to take notes." She smirked and glanced over at him before returning her full attention to her father.

"As your leaders informed you last night, I am certain, an unavoidable war is close at hand. Our goal for today is to speak of tactics..."

It was a long day, indeed. By the time people were leaving the war room, Ashlynn had a headache large enough to make her stomach queasy. There was a plan in place and most everyone agreed upon it. In the morning, many would be leaving, headed home to gather the armies of their people, though tonight they would all feast together as one. It would only be a matter of time before someone under Laidley's rule was sent to Siness to investigate. Their best hope now was for a report to be sent back to the young prince, now high king according to one of the Volarim scouts, that the Celts were going on about life as though there was nothing they feared.

"I am not surprised he has already taken the crown," Luella said with a frown. The room was clear of practically everyone now. Emiline and Wessely remained, as well as Nóe and Nuala. Elas, Tasarin, Jaryn, and Kenayde had stayed behind also. "I was afraid of what my mother would do."

Ashlynn touched her hand. "You cannot take her actions upon yourself, Luella."

"How can I not help but feel guilty?"

"By thinking of the lives you have saved," supplied Tasarin. "Had you stayed and done nothing, Ashlynn and Kenayde would not be alive now. Then it would only have been a matter of time before your brother set his sights on this kingdom." Luella bowed her head but said nothing.

After a moment, Elas ventured to speak. "I wanted to tell you, Ashlynn, about some information I was able to gather last night." Attention turned to him. "In the tavern there was a bard. He was taking requests from the patrons and I was doing my best not to listen to him, trying to glean what I could from the conversations at different tables. It was getting late and with nothing too valuable to report, I decided to head back to the castle. But a man in a long green cloak, darker skinned with black around his eyes and jewels about his neck, spoke up to request a song. His voice was deep, like the sound from the bottom of a well. The song he requested was one I had not heard before." His blue eyes were intense with excitement. "It was a song about the Elementals."

"What?" Requesting such a song was not completely odd; bards wrote songs taken from scriptures, old legends, even personal experiences. They were often revered as historians, for every word they wrote and sang was something remembered and passed down to generation after generation; the surrounding circumstances made it strange. Songs of the Elementals were not lighthearted tunes to drink and laugh to. They told of sadness, betrayal, and war. To ask for a song on the eve of a new war was either bold or careless.

"Was this man one of the Nagin?" Jaryn asked, considering the description of the man.

Elas shook his head. "I can't be sure, but he didn't seem to be one of them. Though I could only glimpse his face, there were no tattoos. There was a certain air about him, like old blood."

Wessely's brows came together. "I do not remember someone fitting that description at council last night."

Ashlynn wore the same thoughtful expression as her father. "Neither do I. Is it possible he could be here as one of Laidley's men?"

"Already?" Kenayde questioned. "That would be awfully fast."

"Too fast," agreed Luella. "He will still be awaiting an outraged army darkening his door. To send a spy so quickly would be a misuse of resources."

Ashlynn frowned. Looking at Elas with narrowed eyes, she asked, "Can you show me?" His expression was one of confusion so Ashlynn continued. "Show me. It's like mind-speak but instead of sharing words you are sharing memories. Have you never done it before?"

"Only once, with Luella when we were under the monastery."

Ashlynn nodded, remembering. With a look of encouragement, she repeated, "Show me."

With a deep breath in, Elas focused all of his attention on Ashlynn. He pulled up the vision of the man, concentrating on his clothes, his face, and especially his eyes. When he tried to summon the memory of his voice, Elas felt things go fuzzy and he swayed slightly.

"That's enough," Ashlynn whispered, feeling his dizziness. "Don't try that yet. You need more practice."

"Did you see the man?" Luella asked.

Ashlynn nodded, frowning once more. Unsure of what to make of it, she looked at Wessely. "He's a Badarian."

Again, the group was in a surprised silence. "Badarian," said Wessely. "What would he be doing all the way up here? The Sandlands are several months' travel from here."

"From the great sands," Nóe said softly. "They do not travel this far north for pleasure. We are too cold and wet for them on our best days."

"I agree with Elas," Ashlynn stated. "There was something very old about him." She could still see the man in her mind. His eyes were golden and outlined in black, dark as pitch, and his skin the color of rich honey. The long green robe hid his hulking figure well enough, but there was strength in his face that betrayed the strength of body he was trying to conceal. "He wasn't here today. There were many new faces, but his was not among them." Looking at Elas, she asked, "Which ballad was sung? Which one did this man ask for?"

"The one about the conjuncture of the Elementals. I have only heard it once before and it was not recited in civilized company."

"That is because the song was written by a bard who was later found guilty of organizing and leading a movement to overthrow the church," said Jaryn. "They say that particular ballad is blasphemy."

Ashlynn wet her lips. "I do not know the ballad. Sing it for me."

Jaryn blinked. "What? Here? I have no instrument."

"You have your voice," she told him in all seriousness. "Please, Jaryn. I need to hear it."

He sighed, casting a dark look at her and clearing his throat. The song was one he had not heard in a very long time, and the words came out slowly. His voice was loud, strong, and perfectly clear – a baritone of great training. Ashlynn closed her eyes, trying to listen to the words and not just his voice. It would be too easy to get lost in the melody and forget the reason behind it.

The song told of a time before humans, when dragons had complete control of the earth. How they were charged, eight of them, to protect and to serve, not only the Giver, but those He would create to be His children. The story continued to tell of the Deliverer, his birth and death. It then spoke of the world falling into chaos and darkness. Both the Deliverer and the Giver turned their backs to the world because the gift of life was not accepted and even ridiculed. The eight dragons, still present but changed, were the key to getting back to the light. If the scattered dragons were brought back together, unified in a common goal, the world would see a new hope. Should the dragons never be together again, all would be lost.

"What a depressing song," Luella said softly, once Jaryn had finished. The mood was felt by everyone. "Do you really think it's as black and white as that? Either we live in paradise or are cast into darkness forever?"

"According to scriptures," Jaryn told her somberly. "I can see why the song was banned. It makes the dragons out to be the gods and our true God something like an extra piece of cake at the party."

"Do you think there's any truth to it?" Ashlynn asked.

138

"About the dragons being the real gods?"

"About bringing them together. These songs are not written from nothing. There has to be some fact to it."

"I have never heard that particular telling of the story," Nuala interrupted. "When I was young I lived much farther east of the Isles. This tale is known there as well, though the ending is somewhat different." She looked first at Ashlynn and then her husband as if judging whether or not she had permission to continue. When no one seemed to object, she spoke again. "Our legend tells of twelve dragons. One each for the six elements, one each for the seasons, and two to govern the good and the evil in the world. As you sang, Jaryn, they were commanded to protect the disciples of the Deliverer and to represent and teach the law of the Giver. He watched over us, He and His son. He was hurt when we turned our backs on Him, not the other way around. The Giver would never do that, according to my own personal beliefs. Since we wouldn't accept the generous gift of His son, the dragons became the key to staying connected to the Giver. They represented Him and what he was, but they weren't gods. They sinned as easily as we do; they stole, they cheated, they lied. It was the people who elevated them to the godly status, countering what their mission was in the first place. Eventually they were scattered, by choice in some cases, by force in others. Some were imprisoned for the things they taught, some fled for fear of reproach, some tried to spread the Giver's word until their final breath."

"But what of them coming together?" Jaryn asked. "If they died, how did their abilities pass on to the next generation?"

"Their children," answered Ashlynn. She looked pointedly at Elas. "That is what you were told as a child, right?"

Elas nodded, his blue eyes going to Nuala. "The first born of an Elemental receives the power as well as the responsibility."

Nuala nodded in agreement. "Precisely. The day the parent dies the abilities awaken within the eldest child, as well as the purpose. As the generations passed, the Elementals grew further apart and the original charge left to them was all but forgotten. The Elementals themselves became more of a myth, a legend of fantasy more than history and reality." She took a breath. "If they are brought together, according to what I was taught as a child, there would be a new hope, yes, but it did not mean the return of the Giver. It simply meant a new chapter."

The room was silent as everyone sifted through this new information. Different legends from different lands, but with many common threads. This only further convinced Ashlynn that it had to be real, at least some of it. Her lips pursed, wishing to know more. "What does the Badarian signify, then?" she questioned softly. "Why would he be here and why would he ask for that specific song?" She turned her thoughtful scowl to Elas once again. "I must ask

139

a favor of you."

"Name it."

"I need you to find him."

Elas bowed his head. "I'll go at once."

"I will go with you," Kenayde added. She smiled at him. "Two pairs of eyes are better than one, right? Can you show me his face?"

"No," he replied, "since you're not a Gael, though I should be glad of your company." Returning his attention to Ashlynn, he asked, "What shall we do with him once we find him?"

"Bring him here. I have many questions for him."

"Understood." Standing, Elas offered a hand to Kenayde to help her to her feet. Once they had gone, the others looked to Ashlynn for any further orders.

"Nóe, your people come from all over the globe, don't they?"

"They do," he agreed.

"I want as many versions of this legend as you can find. Will you and Nuala see to that tonight?"

"We will."

"Tasarin, I would like you to speak with Suule. Have him run the perimeter and to stay on watch. If this stranger got in so easily, I do not wish to see anyone else slip in or out unnoticed." The elf nodded in acceptance, then left the room as well. "The rest of you shall accompany me to the feast. Let's try to relax while we can. Something tells me we won't have many more moments like this for a very long time."

CHAPTER THIRTEEN

The streets of the capital were not nearly as crowded as they had been the previous night. The festivities had left the town in disarray at daybreak, but now all was as it had been before. Houses were lit with candles, lanterns, and warm hearth fires. Doors still stood open as neighbors went back and forth in visitations and sharing of meals and conversation. The sounds of laughter and voices were comforting to Kenayde, though Elas seemed too determined in his mission to notice or care. She wondered if she wasn't being serious enough and tried to focus. They were looking for a Badarian man; someone tall with sun darkened skin and a deep rumbling voice. There was a good possibility that he wore a long cloak as well. Almost every guest of the kingdom was inside the walls of the castle and no one residing in the village had skin that was very dark. In theory, this man should not be too difficult to find.

The tavern came into view, light spilling onto the street from the open entrance, smoke making an ethereal haze about the door. Kenayde wrinkled her nose, repelled at the thought of going inside. Still, she followed Elas as he headed in. There was no reason to question Ashlynn or Kenayde in the streets of the town, but to see the young princess inside the tavern was a completely different story. Conversations fell to a whisper before stopping, drinks waited in between being raised and set down. The only person to keep moving was the tender standing behind the wide bar at the left of the room. He finished filling a mug of ale as Elas and Kenayde approached him and looked at the pair, curious and cautious but nothing more. "Your sister's been in here a time or two," he said to Kenayde. "Never expected to see you here though."

"We are looking for someone," she told him, feeling slightly uneasy at all the attention. "Someone who was here last night."

The tender grimaced and leaned his hands on the bar. "No offense,

Majesty, but there were a lot of people in here last night. Can you be a little more specific?"

"A man," supplied Elas, his voice a bit more solid and commanding than Kenayde. "We think he may be a Badarian. He was up front, close to the bard." The tender's expression was blank and Elas added, "He requested the last song of the night."

A light of recognition washed the tender's face. "Yeah, I know who you're talking about. I haven't seen him in here all day."

"Do you know where he may have gone last night?" Kenayde asked. Since everyone was paying attention to them, listening closely, Kenayde turned around to scan the room. "Does anyone know where he might be?" There was a long silence in which Kenayde begged silently. Elas scowled at the room, a growl low in his throat.

"If anyone has any knowledge of where this man might be, it would be best to come forth now." When still there was silence, he turned back to the tender. "If you see him, you are to inform someone at the castle immediately. Not after you serve him a drink, not after he leaves. Immediately. Do you understand?"

"Sure." It was a casual answer, but the tender was clearly taken aback by the dominance of the young man before him.

With a gentle guiding hand at the small of her back, Elas led Kenayde out into the night. She shivered, but not because of the cold. "Did you see the color drain from his face?" she whispered as they walked. "He was afraid."

"I know." Elas frowned. "But of what?"

"Do you think the Badarian is hostile? Do you think he is here under an ill will?"

Elas shook his head. "I don't know. Kenayde, I don't think that I want you here with me, looking for this man. If he is the cause of the tender's fear, I don't want you in danger."

Kenayde look worried. "Do you really think he's a person to fear?"

"I don't know," Elas repeated, "but I don't like the idea of risking your safety." They continued walking, asking people they passed on the street for any information. Elas intended to walk Kenayde up to the castle and then return to continue on in his search. The reaction in the tavern when the Badarian was mentioned was more than enough to make Kenayde not want to be there when he was found. She did, however, suggest he take Jaryn and Tasarin with him. "We don't want to look like a hunting party," Elas argued softly. "We only wish to speak with him, not make him think we're after him."

"But you are." Kenayde frowned. "I don't like the fear I saw. Will you at least take Jaryn with you? If only for my benefit? I would worry more about you meeting this Badarian in a dark alley if you were by yourself."

"*This* Badarian?"

They had just passed the edge of the village and were crossing onto the tree-lined road that would lead them up to the castle. The voice behind them sounded like it had come from the very center of the earth itself, so deep the tone. A thrill of fear ran down Kenayde's spine, but in a breath Elas had her behind him and a hidden dagger drawn. The voice had no figure to be seen and this made Elas shift his gaze to every shadow that seemed to move. "Show yourself!" he demanded.

"Sheathe your blade," was the counter demand, though the voice from the darkness was far more calm.

"This isn't your land, Badarian. You don't give orders here."

"It doesn't sound like this is your land either." A figure, hulking and dark against the darker night, stepped onto the path. "No one gives me orders." The man didn't move a muscle, but suddenly the dagger Elas held erupted into fierce blue and gold flames. The young water dragon yelped, dropping it almost instantly. His arms flew back as though he could encompass Kenayde to shield her, eyes darting to where the man stood only to find him gone. Shuffling around and keeping Kenayde behind him, Elas looked for the Badarian.

"Coward!" he challenged.

"A coward is someone who relies on weapons instead of his natural born instinct to defend himself." The voice seemed to be everywhere and nowhere at once. The flames on the dagger died, though the man did not show himself. "Who are you, that you think a little butter knife could cut me down?"

"Elas," Kenayde hissed, close behind him. "The flames. Did you see the color of the flames?"

"Yes," he answered just as quietly. "He's an Elemental."

"At least your wits are quicker than your moves."

Kenayde screamed when she felt a finger run down her jawline. Both she and Elas jerked to the side in time to see the cloaked figure smile wickedly, moving just out of arms reach. "I like it when they scream," he admitted, using the same deep and gritty amused tone.

"Touch her again and die."

The Badarian shifted his gaze to Elas, light from the moon high overhead catching his eyes and making them gleam golden. "Is that really your challenge?" he laughed. "Clearly, fighting is not your strong suit." He paused to get a good look at Elas. "That face of yours must make life rather interesting."

Elas went to lunge at him, but Kenayde gripped his arm. "No!" she cried, blue eyes locked on the stranger.

"Best listen to her," said the stranger. "Unless you just can't help yourself. Nothing like fighting to protect the honor of a woman." Reaching up, he pulled the hood of his cloak down before removing it completely and tossing it aside.

With the light shining down on him, his skin was a golden brown, curving over every muscle in his arms, his thick neck, and bald head. His eyes were rimmed in black and golden snakes with jade eyes wove around his left bicep. He wore a sleeveless tunic and trousers with no weapon evident and the sandals on his feet left no room for a hidden dagger.

Letting his arms fall to his side, Elas lifted his chin and threw his shoulders back before snarling and launching himself forward. His fist flew to the side of the Badarian's face, but the other man was too quick for the hit to find its mark. He grabbed Elas by his extended wrist and twisted, bringing Elas to his knees with a cry. Adrenaline made Elas twist his body, bringing his wrist and the Badarian's hand up over his head. He was on his feet in a flash and swinging a leg out to kick his opponent's feet out from under him. But the Badarian jumped, Elas being a second too slow. A fist found the center of Elas' spine and he was on his hands and knees with another outcry.

"Is that really all you've got?" the Badarian questioned, disappointment in his voice. "I'm not even out of breath."

Elas growled, throwing himself at the other man and wrapping his arms around his strong torso. They moved back, the Badarian staggering out of surprise. He hadn't expected Elas to recover so quickly, but he recovered swiftly as well. Bending, he wrapped his arms around Elas and lifted, attempting to throw Elas over his shoulder. Elas let go when he felt himself leave the ground but, preparing himself for the fall, landed on his feet instead of in the heap the Badarian was hoping for.

"Stop it!" Kenayde yelled, but neither man was listening.

Elas jumped to land on the Badarian's back, but his face was met with a fist and he was sent flying backward. He landed with a thump on the ground. A distinct copper taste teased his tongue from a bloody nose, but he would not stay down. As he braced himself for the impact, there was a look on the Badarian's face that said he was clearly impressed by the way Elas was not giving up. They met with a dull thud and fell to the ground with appendages flying. Elas managed to get a good swing in and the Badarian's voice was heard in the night when the fist connected with his jaw.

By the time she heard movement behind her, Kenayde was so distraught that she didn't know whether to get angry or to cry. She turned to see soldiers from the castle coming down the path at a run and a Volar scout flying overhead with the wings of a bat. The two men had to be torn from each other, though Elas was putting up more of a fight than the Badarian. He was bleeding from cuts to his face, but the Badarian smiled at his smaller opponent. It was a smile of pure elation. Elas did not mirror the expression and struggled out of the soldiers' grasp.

Spitting blood at the man's feet, Elas ordered, "Bring him to Ashlynn."

The stranger could have escaped the men if he wanted being that his size and strength were so much greater, but he went along without a fight. As they pushed him past Kenayde, he looked her over with a hungry eye.

"Are you hurt?" Elas had his hands on her shoulders and Kenayde tore her gaze from the stranger to look up into the familiar face. "No." She glanced quickly over her shoulder, frowning when she returned her attention to Elas. "No, but you are." Her brows came together with worry as she gently touched the human side of his face. He winced and she bit her lip. "You should not have fought him like that."

"He shouldn't have touched you." He raised his hand, pausing before touching her cheek. Decidedly, Elas tugged at one of her curls instead. "At least half of me is still in one piece."

Despite the situation, Kenayde gave way to a smile and a small laugh. Side by side, they started up the path with the Volar scout overhead to keep watch.

Dinner was over and Ashlynn was waiting in the throne room when the doors were pushed open. Two guards entered first, then the two holding the Badarian, and finally Elas and Kenayde. Upon seeing the blood on both men, Ashlynn was on her feet and scowling. She looked to the blue-haired man beside her sister and demanded, "What happened?"

"The Badarian surprised us," Elas told her. "He threatened and I attacked."

Surprise registered on Ashlynn's face and she looked at Kenayde as if asking if Elas spoke the truth. "Elas was bringing me back to the castle and the Badarian came out of the shadows behind us. Elas drew his dagger to protect me and the Badarian set it on fyre." Ashlynn's eyes widened and she glanced at the man. Kenayde nodded confirmation before continuing. "He then came around behind us and startled me. It ended with a fight between the two of them."

Ashlynn shifted her gaze from her sister to the stranger kneeling on her throne room floor and looked down on him with a cold expression. "It would appear you took as much of a beating as you offered."

The Badarian smirked, lifting his eyes to her face. "It would appear that way, wouldn't it?" For a moment the humor slid from his face. He started at Ashlynn the way someone might stare at a spirit. It made Ashlynn uncomfortable.

"What is your name?" she demanded evenly.

"Cavalon Amenti." He bowed his head, not completely in mockery, but hardly out of genuine respect.

"Cavalon, if I let you up so that my healer may take a look at you, I expect you to remain exactly where you are. Is that understood?"

"Sure." Looking at her, it was easy to see she was not satisfied with his answer. He rolled his eyes. "I won't move."

A nod from Ashlynn had the two guards releasing him and stepping to the side of the room. Tasarin came forward from a chair at the side of Ashlynn's throne and looked Cavalon over. He moved a hand over the wounds and bruises, speaking very softly in a language the Badarian did not understand. He did understand the warmth flooding his body, though, and knew the elf had healed him. Before he could even get so much as a nod of thanks, Tasarin moved to Elas for the same healing process.

Ashlynn stepped back to sit on her throne. "My sister says you came out of the shadows. Am I correct in assuming it was an intentional surprise on your part?"

With a better view of his surroundings, Cavalon saw the man seated beside the queen, as well as several other faces in the room. When his attention was back on Ashlynn, he looked at her without apology. "It was very much intentional. I had a few opportunities to show myself but decided to wait for that perfect moment."

"Now why would that be?"

"Seems to me when people are talking about forming a search party for someone they don't even know, they wouldn't be looking for him just to welcome him to the kingdom."

A smile, quick and without humor, twitched at the corners of her mouth. "Perhaps not. Yet something tells me this is the exact reaction you were looking for when you requested a certain ballad last night." Cavalon said nothing and Ashlynn lifted an eyebrow. "Judging by your lack of expression, I would say that I am not far off. Why are you here?"

"I heard the mead was good. I had some last night and really wasn't all that impressed."

Clearly he was looking for something in her reaction, but she refused to give him what he sought. "Perhaps the wording of my question was too vague. Let me try from this angle. It would be very much in your best interest for you to tell me why you are here. I do not take kindly to abrasive strangers in my land, especially when they make it very clear they are not here to make friends." The guards that brought him in had their hands on the hilts of their swords. "I know what you are, Badarian. That does not mean I must treat you differently than any other that would antagonize my house."

Cavalon smirked, nonplussed by the thinly veiled threat. "Abrasive, huh? Well, I've been called worse." Again his expression changed dramatically, irritation replacing levity. "If you really knew who I was you'd have a little more respect for who you were talking to."

"And if you knew who I was, you would know I give respect only to those that earn it, not to those who feel entitled to it." Her patience with this war of words was gone. Ashlynn lifted a hand with an annoyed scowl. "Take him below. You can stew there until you learn some manners." She kept her eyes on

146

him as he was flanked again by guards and finally led out of the room. When he was gone and the doors were closed, she muttered, "The nerve."

"What was all that about?" Jaryn asked, looking confused beside her. "The way he looked at you when he was brought in, and then his tongue? What in the world would have made him come here with such a superior attitude?"

"He certainly acted superior, didn't he?" Wessely had been off to the side of the room with Emiline and Luella. "I have never known a Badarian to behave in such a way."

"Savages," grumbled Ashlynn.

"Not all of them," her father argued. "I have met several in my years and none have ever acted quite like that."

"He can still get out," said Kenayde. "You thought of that, right?"

Luella looked from one sister to the other. "How can he get out?"

"He is an Elemental, and Elementals can travel through their own fyre," supplied Ashlynn. "There is still much you have to learn about who you are, Luella. Yes, Nadie, I did think of that. I would like to see if he does leave on his own or if he will wait. There's a reason he's here and if he wanted to go on a killing spree, I have no doubt he could have had you two very easily. I mean nothing by it, Elas. He is simply twice your size and who knows how big in his draconic form."

"I hit him a few times," Elas argued.

"He hit you a few times more," countered Tasarin.

"He is here for a reason and I would very much like to know what that reason is. If only he weren't so caustic. What gives him the right to come into my kingdom and disrespect me and mine in that way?" Ashlynn stood now, scowling. "I have half a mind to go stand at his cell door and berate him until he speaks."

"Let us pray the other half of your mind is thinking more reasonably," said Wessely.

Ashlynn's scowl deepened some. "It is. Unfortunately."

"Your majesty." The doors had opened and a young squire was shown in by one of the guards. In his hands was a scroll.

Ashlynn looked at the boy with a frown. "Yes?"

"Dani." Luella's eyes were wide as she looked the young man over. "He is one of Laidley's squires."

The boy looked frightened, though there was a slight relief when he saw a familiar face. "We're not going to eat you, if that's what you are afraid of," snapped Ashlynn. "What are you doing in Siness?"

"I come with a message from my king."

"Well go on then, read it."

Dani unrolled the parchment, casting a glance at Luella. She nodded and he read. "To the Witch Queen. I trust you have received your gift by now and hope it has found you well. By the time you read this letter, I will be king. My father was not known for his generosity and I do hope to leave a better legacy than his. That is why I am giving you until Samhain, that pagan holiday of yours, to surrender yourselves to me. If you have not done so by then, I will be forced to assume you seek less civil manners of resolving this situation and the appropriate actions will be taken against you. Please understand I am aware that my sister is with you and that this altercation goes far beyond one kingdom to another. My father was murdered in the midst of a quest and I intend to see his goal reached. My victory over you and the rest of your cursed nations will be pleasant and serve as a much needed boost in morale for my own kingdom. Most sincere and best wishes, Laidley, High King of Caedia."

The squire was trembling as he finished. His hands lowered to roll the parchment and he could see Ashlynn's anger from as far away as his spot at the doors. "That doesn't give us much time," Jaryn said softly. He rested a hand on top of Ashlynn's. "It is not the boy's fault, my love."

"I know." Yet still, she glared at him. "You will take a message back to your king. Write it down later if you must, but for now, listen very carefully and remember. To *High King* Laidley. Due to certain pre-engagements, a Samhain surrender simply does not fit into our schedule. Therefore, we look forward to seeing you in Siness. Your greeting will be one you shall never live to forget." She stared hard at the boy. "Now go, before I decide to rid myself of you and have one of my own people deliver my message." Dani did not need to be told twice and scampered from the throne room. Ashlynn cursed under her breath.

"What do we do now?" Kenayde worried.

"We begin preparations," Jaryn answered. "Samhain is less than three weeks away. Luella, how true to his word is your brother? Will he come sooner or could this be a bluff?"

Luella shook her head. "It is no bluff. My brother doesn't make threats unless he plans to follow through on them. Especially with Merrik there to goad him on."

"We will issue a call to arms," Jaryn decided. "We will ready underground basements and storage houses where the weaker or unable can be hidden. They will be safe." He looked at Wessely and Emiline. "I cannot ask you to stay. This is not your land."

Wessely stepped forward, offering a hand of camaraderie to Jaryn. As they clasped forearms, Wessely looked at him sternly. "You need not ask anything. This was once the land of my brother, and our father before that. Now it belongs to my daughter, soon to you as well, Jaryn. I will stay and I will fight to protect this land as much as I protect its legacy."

Jaryn nodded, thanking Wessely as he embraced him. It was a great risk he was taking in deciding to stay. With the very real threat of death before him, Wessely put Oceana in danger of having no heir should he and Kenayde perish.

Jaryn looked at Emiline, who smiled knowingly. "I am not a fighter." She stepped forward and gave his hands a squeeze. "Though I will not go home, not until all of this is settled; I will stay here to help with the wounded, if you permit."

"We would be honored to have you stay, Your Majesty."

It felt odd to let Jaryn take over, but Ashlynn knew anything she had to say would not be helpful. She simply sat and thought, taking a mental inventory of all the possible ways into and out of the kingdom. They would need to dig in and fight to protect themselves. All the nations of the Isles, the nations of the Celts would have to come together to protect their own. This was not a single kingdom attacking another with the aid of its allies. This was a war against a people. A people who would not stand to be easily defeated, by any measure.

"I will stay and fight as well." It was Elas who spoke, a clear determination in his eyes. "I can find others of my kind, the water dragons. We can slow them down, maybe even stop some of them all together."

"I want to stay, too." Kenayde looked around, afraid of the reaction she would get. Ashlynn started to speak, but Kenayde took a step forward, fists clenching her skirts. "Don't say it, Lynnie. I know I cannot fight as well as you can, but I can help with the wounded. I can use a bow and I can learn to use a sword. I'm not useless and I do not want to be shut away as if I were."

Ashlynn offered a patient smile. "I know you're not useless, Nadie. I just have to keep reminding myself you're not as helpless as I am too frequently thinking you to be." Looking at Tasarin, she raised an eyebrow in question.

"Are you asking me if I am willing to stay?" he questioned. "The elves are a gentle people. We do not enjoy taking the lives of others, even when there is merit."

"This is a heavy thing we ask of you, Tasarin," said Jaryn. "If you do not wish to be a part of it, no one here will fault you."

"Speak for yourself," Ashlynn quipped.

Tasarin grimaced. "Long before either of you were ever born, I pledged my fealty to this kingdom. I take no pleasure in the role I must play in this war, but play it I will." He lifted his fist to his chest and bowed his head. "I will fight by your side as long as I am able to draw breath."

Everyone in the room had declared where they would stand, all but one. Attention now turning to her, Luella wore a slight frown. "I know what you would like for me to say," she began, "but what I will say is quite different. I will stay and fight. I feel it is my duty now, as an Elemental, to protect this place. All I ask is that I am away from the heart of the battle. I do not wish to see my brother slain. Though I know what he is slowly becoming he is still my

149

brother and I should like to keep the fonder memories close, instead of the foul."

Placement had not yet even come to her mind, but Ashlynn and Jaryn nodded together. "Of course," said Ashlynn. "Luella, you must know this brings me no pleasure."

Luella nodded somberly. "I do, but that does not make my position any easier."

"In order to fight," Tasarin inserted, "you must truly understand what you are and what you have to fight with."

This made Ashlynn frown. "We will work hard, Luella and I."

"I was not only speaking of Luella."

The frown Ashlynn wore directed itself at Tasarin. "I know all I need to know about what we can do. Surely you're not suggesting I seek counsel from the Badarian."

"He is an Elemental," the elf reminded.

"I know that," she said acidly. "We still have no idea why he is even here."

Tasarin looked at her patiently. "It is something we must find out. His aid would mean a great deal, and if he is an enemy, to know it now would be better than to find out later. I must agree with Elas; there is something about the Badarian that speaks of age."

"Could he be older than you?" Kenayde asked.

When Tasarin only shrugged a brow, Ashlynn cursed for the second time that night. She sighed heavily. "I will go down and speak with him myself."

"Not alone," Jaryn said with concern.

"Luella will come with me. As will Tasarin."

Now Jaryn frowned, albeit briefly and before he touched his lips to Ashlynn's. "Then I shall see to meeting with the heads of state still here. Plans have changed quickly and we'll need to begin preparations immediately. Your Majesty, will you accompany me?"

Wessely nodded. "Yes, of course."

"Elas, I think now is a good time to find others of your kin." The water dragon nodded at Jaryn's order. "Kenayde, if you and your mother could look for High King Nóe and his bride, I'm certain any information they've found can be helpful as well." Jaryn looked around, pleased at the orders given. "Right. See to it, then." Emiline and Kenayde left together with Elas right behind them. Ashlynn turned to join Luella and Tasarin, but Jaryn grabbed her hand. "In less than three weeks we will be making war. Just because the time draws closer doesn't mean I feel any differently. I want to be your husband when I go to battle."

Softness made her features less harsh. She reached up to touch his cheek. "I want that, too."

"Tomorrow, then," he replied softly, covering her hand with his own.

"Tomorrow, marry me."

"Then this country will finally have the king and queen they have waited for."

Jaryn pressed his lips to hers once more, taking a small step back only when Wessely cleared his throat. Ashlynn grinned up at her beloved. "Time to go to work." With a smirk in her father's direction, she left the throne room with Luella, Tasarin, and her constant company of guards in tow.

CHAPTER FOURTEEN

"What do we know about the Badarians?" Ashlynn asked her chief adviser.

"They are a hearty people," answered Tasarin as they walked. "Like our own Nagin tribes, they live off the earth; they hunt only for meat and pelts for clothing. The richer of them enjoy expensive jewels."

"Do they live longer than humans?"

"I have never heard they have, though I cannot say I have ever heard anything about their lifespans at all."

"You are a well of information, Tasarin."

They were greeted at the mouth of the dungeon by a guard who quickly moved aside upon seeing who was coming. Ashlynn walked with clear purpose down the long corridor that split to the left and right. To Tasarin's credit, most of the cells were empty. He had done a good job as regent in her stead. The few that were occupied received not so much as a passing glance from Ashlynn as she made her way to the cell farthest back on the left. It was from this cell that she could hear the deep rumbling voice of Cavalon as he conversed with a guard. As soon as their footsteps were heard the guard stood at attention. Ashlynn glanced in at Cavalon before looking sternly at the man in her employ.

"What is your name?" His face was unfamiliar to her. "How long have you been working this station?"

"Treval, Your Majesty. This is my fourth week training as a guard. Two days will make a month."

"How terrible it is that you shall not see that month," Ashlynn replied without pity. "You are not given wages to speak with those in detention. Having been here for more than four *minutes* should have taught you that, never mind four weeks."

"But he said..."

"I care very little about what he said," she interrupted. "Is it he whose castle you are supposed to guard?"

"No, Your Grace."

"And is he, being behind metal bars, a person of quality whose statements and opinions can be trusted over a direct order from myself?"

"N...no, Your Grace."

Ashlynn smiled deceptively. "And it is for those correct answers that you will receive my mercy. No longer are you to work at this station, do you understand? If you wish to remain in the employ of this castle, you will report immediately to the stables. If you manage to do your work correctly there, we may reassess the situation after a time." With nothing else to say, she simply stared at the man until he realized he was free to go. Before he was even gone, Cavalon was chuckling.

"You made that poor kid wet himself. Does urine rust metal armor?" His golden eyes lifted to Ashlynn's face as she turned to look at him sitting on the cell floor. "I'm not too proud to admit that I didn't think you a woman that had the spine to be a leader."

"And are you too proud to admit you were wrong?"

"Not at all." Standing now, Cavalon wrapped his enormous hands around the iron bars, towering over Ashlynn.

Ashlynn folded her hands together as she peered up into his face. "What did you tell him?"

Cavalon shrugged. "I told him you sent me down here because I was a bad boy. Then I told him I could just get out anytime I wanted, showed him my pretty fyre, and a conversation began." He pushed his face closer to the bars, closer to her. "I know you'd like nothing better than to take a bite out of me. How about you show me the more..." His eyes ran over her body, "beastly side of you, and..." He didn't get to finish. Tasarin grabbed a heavy torch in a flash of movement and smashed Cavalon's fingers against the bars. The Badarian leaped back from the cell door. "I was willing to play nice," he growled, looking darkly at the elf.

"Were you?" Ashlynn laughed. "Pity, I'm not in the mood for games tonight." Despite the way Cavalon was conducting himself, she took a step closer to the cell. "Why not do away with all this silly bantering, hmm? Can we perhaps speak to one another as civil adults?"

"Can you keep your guard elf down?"

Instead of answering, Ashlynn reached through the bars, a hand extended in a truce. Cavalon eyed her a moment before moving his injured hand to grab hers. A flare of blue and gold flames surrounded them both and when they died, Ashlynn was in the cell with Cavalon and the stone floor was scorched where she had been standing. Tasarin was already searching his ring of keys for the correct one to unlock the door, but Ashlynn stopped him. "Not exactly what I had in mind," she admitted, shaking her head at Tasarin. "He got me in here easily and he knows I can get myself out just as quickly."

"I'm not going to hurt you," Cavalon promised, letting go of her hand. "I may be a lot of things, but I am not a man who would strike a woman... unprovoked."

Ashlynn shook her head, eyes narrowed. "Who are you? Why are you in my kingdom?"

"I believe we already established who I am, and from things I have overheard this isn't exactly your kingdom." If he was looking to get a rise out of Ashlynn, he was disappointed. It showed when he sighed, crossed his arms and leaned back against the cell wall. "I am King of the Light Dragons." As he announced this, he extended a hand to show skin turning into scales in a ripple that started at his fingers and ran up his arm. They were white, shimmering with an iridescent pink, blue, and purple before turning back to human skin.

"You *are* an Elemental," breathed Luella.

Cavalon looked at her with amusement. "Welcome to the conversation."

"Keep your attention on me," Ashlynn snapped.

"That's not too terrible of a request."

"*Why are you here?*" she asked again, slowly.

For a moment it appeared as though he wasn't going to answer. Eventually, his eyes slid once again to Luella, his expression blank. "*She* called me."

Now they were all looking at Luella and she blinked in obvious surprise. "I did no such thing. I wouldn't even know how."

Using his shoulder, Cavalon pushed himself from the wall to peer through the bars at Luella. He completely ignored the way Tasarin stood close to her, protective. "How old are you, princess?" He asked in a way that was almost condescending, and they all knew his name for her was not a recognition of her title.

"Twenty." She didn't seem afraid of Cavalon, but she was certainly curious.

"Then you wouldn't have felt it. You're still a baby."

"I am not!" she objected hotly.

"Easy," Cavalon chuckled. "The last thing we need is for you to shift and kill us all." He glanced over his shoulder. "Is she always so easily offended?"

Ashlynn ignored his question, returning with her own. "What do you mean she called you?"

"You're Darkness, right?" he asked Luella.

"Yes, but I have only shifted a few times and have used my fyre twice. I hardly know how to-"

"So it still hurts when you do it." Cavalon leaned heavily on the bars, captivating her with his unusual eyes. "Pain still rips through every fiber of your being and makes you feel like your soul is being taken from your body." She nodded slowly, a light in her expression showing his words touched something inside of her. "It gets better," he promised, "but not for awhile yet. You need more practice." Hearing Ashlynn clear her throat, he nodded to Luella. "You're the Elemental of Darkness. Not even two weeks ago I was walking along the beach in my homeland and I felt you shift. I had felt it before, like the ground was coming out from under me. Yet somehow, this last time was different. There was a feeling of purpose behind it."

"I am Darkness and you are Light," Luella replied quietly, awed.

"I'm your elder and your opposite," he continued. "I felt you because I've been waiting for you since your father died."

She searched his eyes. "You knew my father?"

"Mortagh was a good man. Not as pious as an Elemental is supposed to be if he had an affair with a married woman, but he was still a good man. He would have done better by you than Tadhg ever did."

"That is enough." Tasarin stepped between the cell door and Luella when he saw her eyes fill. "How do we know you speak the truth and are not just saying what it is we want to hear?"

Cavalon sized the elf up then returned to leaning against the cell wall, unimpressed. "I guess you're just going to have to trust me."

"Because you have offered so much good of yourself that trust should come so easily," countered Ashlynn. She was growing more annoyed by the moment. "Can we agree to play nice and leave this dungeon? Cavalon, despite my instant dislike of you, I feel what you can share with us would be of great value. We have an approaching war on our hands..."

"So I've heard."

"...and if you are here you will either be with us or against us. Being what you are, I would much rather have you on our side than have to destroy a kindred Elemental."

For a moment it looked as if he were going to laugh. Whether it was the seriousness of Ashlynn's expression or his clear lack of options, Cavalon decided to control himself and hide his amusement. "You're small but you're not timid, are you?" Ashlynn's answer was a simple tilt of her head to indicate she awaited his answer. "All right," he conceded. "I'll behave." Bending, he picked his cloak up off the ground. "Can I have something hot to drink while we talk? It's so cold in this place!"

~*~*~*~

Ashlynn waited with tempered impatience as her summoned companions slowly joined her for a private meeting. They all gathered where council had

155

been the previous night, seated around one of the long rectangular tables with hot mulled wine to warm the chill away, and bread with butter and honey. Cavalon was not shy about helping himself to anything and ignored the mixed stares from everyone at the table. Only Luella watched with a bit of awe in her eyes.

"What did he say to her?" Jaryn asked Ashlynn quietly, reading her irritation and glancing at Luella.

"He said he knew her father."

Jaryn frowned. "Wonderful." With a shake of his head, he looked at Cavalon. "Listen friend, as much as I'm glad to see you enjoying our hospitality, I do believe you were brought up here to talk and not just eat."

Cavalon stuck some of the honey covered bread in his mouth and looked at Jaryn as he chewed. Jaryn crossed his arms and Cavalon swallowed, then took a sip of his wine.

"Civility," Ashlynn reminded.

"I was being civil," Cavalon argued. "I didn't want to speak with food hanging off my teeth." He even took the time to wipe his mouth before pushing his plate away. "All right, where do you want me to start?"

"How old are you?"

"One thousand, two hundred twenty years old." No one said anything for a moment and for the first time, Cavalon looked uncertain. "I tell the truth. I've seen the peoples of two different millennia and haven't been impressed with either."

"You saw the continents split?" asked Kenayde, awed.

"They were already split when I was born." He looked at her, smiling slightly with that same haunted look in his eyes as when he'd looked upon her sister. "My mother lived when they were one, but not me."

"How is it you have lived so long?" Tasarin questioned with suspicion.

Cavalon lifted his hands in a shrug, sitting back in his chair with great amusement. "I'm an Elemental."

"That doesn't make you a god," countered Jaryn.

"Close enough," the Badarian laughed.

"Shall we cut you to prove you can bleed?" Elas seemed all to eager to make good on his offer.

Cavalon's smile slid effortlessly into a sneer. "I think you've seen enough of my blood, Water Dragon."

Elas was on his feet on an instant. "Don't speak to me as though you're my superior!"

Laughing and satisfied with the reaction he was receiving, Cavalon locked his hands on top of his head. "Oh, but I am."

Ashlynn reached over and slapped Cavalon upside the back of his head.

"Hey!" he growled.

"Elas, sit down. Cavalon, be quiet unless you have something useful to say!"

"I was asked a question."

"Which you never answered." Ashlynn's eyes were narrowed and full of something that was getting dangerously close to anger. "You will answer the questions asked of you without sarcasm or snide remarks, and you will not turn this into a one-man show where we all play to your amusement and whim. If you cannot control your very loose tongue, you will be sent back to your own country with it cut from your head so that you may still live but you will not be able to ridicule another person for as long as you happen to be alive. Do we have an understanding?" Cavalon simply looked at her, causing Ashlynn to lean over to bring her heated gaze even closer. She repeated herself, slower and softer. "Do we have an understanding?"

It was very clear the Badarian was having a war within himself. He obviously considered himself superior to everyone else in the room, if not the world. He also recognized how dangerous the wrath of a woman could be, especially a woman of great power. With a deep breath in and a slow release, he gave in. "All right. I'll play by your rules now, but when it comes down to the battle, I go by my own rules."

"It still remains to be seen whose side you are on." It was Wessely to speak up this time. "You need to respect my daughter, not only because she is the ruler this land recognizes, but also because she is a lady. That, in the very least, should be enough to quiet you when you wish to be glib."

Cavalon looked at Wessely but said nothing. Instead, he seemed to pull into himself some, as though he were resigning himself to the fact that some of the things he wanted to say would not be acceptable. Eventually he looked at Tasarin. "Elementals can't die of old age, in answer to your question. Our bodies mature to optimal health and then just stop. We're like your people in that."

"You can die in battle?" asked the elf.

"Yes, though we're much harder to kill than you. Each species of dragon has their own spot of vulnerability. Our scales are invulnerable to human weapons, making us almost impossible to kill in our shifted state."

"So you stay dragon most of the time?" Ashlynn asked.

Cavalon shook his head, smirking. "No, I'm just very careful not to make enemies." The collective expression around the room was one of apparent disbelief. "Usually," he added in an undertone.

"Did you really know my father?" Cavalon was watched closely by all to see how he would respond to Luella, if he would latch on to her vulnerability and exploit it. His reaction was actually quite surprising. Everything about him seemed to soften at once, from the lines in his face, to the rigidity of his shoulders, to the sarcasm that seemed permanently etched into his gaze.

"For many years. He was my brother as an Elemental, but also a fellow Badarian."

Luella blinked slowly, connecting things in her mind that never fit before but now suddenly did. "That explains why my skin has always been so much darker."

"The blue eyes must have come from your mother," Cavalon observed. "Mortagh had eyes the color of wheat in the noon sun. But he had long, thick black hair like you, like most of the clans. Same nose, same curious way of tilting his head when he was listening to someone." Upon realizing she was, in fact, tilting her head, Luella straightened herself and Cavalon chuckled. "Did your mother ever tell you about him?"

She shook her head. "No. My mother never even told me I did not belong to Tadhg. I made that deduction for myself the first time I shifted."

"Smart girl," the Badarian complimented. "Perhaps later we can talk more about him. I would very much like to share some stories with you and learn more about the daughter of a friend."

The corners of Luella's mouth lifted hopefully. "I would like that very much."

"You said you felt it when she shifted," reminded Ashlynn as soon there was a break in the conversation. "Explain that."

Remembering there were other people in the room, Cavalon looked over at his questioner. "I'm linked to her as her opposite element. As the elder of the two, she affects me more than I affect her. I now know the rumors about you being an Elemental are true since you survived my fyre. Which one are you?"

"Earth," she answered matter-of-factly.

The Badarian frowned in thought. "I hadn't realized Siobhán had passed, though I noticed the resemblance the moment I saw you."

"You're going to tell me you knew my mother, as well as Luella's father?"

He looked truly offended. "I've known all of them. I am and have been the oldest Elemental for generations."

The room fell silent momentarily, no one quite knowing how to reply. After a moment, Nóe asked, "Who is Ashlynn's opposite? Would they know of her as you knew of Luella?"

Cavalon looked at the winged king. "Mei Xing is her opposite, the Elemental of Air. I couldn't say if she knows of you or not." Returning his attention to Ashlynn he asked, "The last time you shifted, what was the reason behind it?"

Ashlynn shrugged. "I wanted to fly, to feel the air around me. I was emotional but also happy at the same time."

Again, Cavalon frowned. "And the time before that?"

"I hadn't shifted in over a year before that."

"Then she wouldn't know. She would have felt you, but not with the urgency I felt with Luella's last shifting."

"Well, do you know where we can find her?" Elas asked, still holding onto his contempt of the man.

Cavalon shook his head. "I haven't seen her for nearly three hundred years. She could be anywhere."

"What about the others?" Ashlynn asked.

"Could be anywhere as well. Listen, I don't stay with too many people for any great length of time. I like my solitude. Obviously it's been awhile since I've sought out any other of my kind if I didn't even know Siobhán was gone. That pains me to hear, whether you want to believe it or not. She was the best of us. You have a strong legacy to live up to." It was strange to see the brokenness in his expression, especially with the way he had been dealing with all of them from the very beginning. But the sheer vulnerability of it was what made Ashlynn more inclined to believe him. She had questions about her mother but refused to get teary-eyed and sentimental like Luella. She simply didn't have time for it. Still, when she spoke again, her voice held a gentler tone.

"Cavalon, we have a lot of questions. About who we are, what we can do...what we're supposed to do. Nothing would be greater than to have you come along side us, to be our mentor and to teach us things we may never learn on our own." It was a humbling thing to ask someone for help, especially when nearly everything inside was screaming that it was the wrong thing to do. "In less than three weeks we will be facing battle. I can teach Luella all I know, but I do not know everything. You have hundreds of years on both of us and can teach us so much more. I am asking you as your Elemental kinswoman. Please help us."

Cavalon kept his gaze downward for a moment, lips pursed as he thought over her request. Eventually he nodded, his expression blank. "We'll start in the morning but only Ashlynn and Luella. I don't want an audience."

~*~*~*~

The morning came entirely too early, at least for Cavalon. He woke to the sound of persistent knocking on his door and walked to answer it with sleep in his eyes and no clothing on his body. The young maid on the other side flushed and kept her eyes locked on his face. "Her Majesty requests your presence in the training room."

Cavalon yawned and rubbed a hand over his head, ignorant of the girl's embarrassment. "Tell Her Majesty that I'll be down in a half hour." With nothing more to say, he closed the door in the maid's face and went back to bed.

Down below in the castle training room, Ashlynn had decided to get Luella

159

started while they waited. Both girls wore simple tunics and trousers, making Luella slightly uncomfortable since she was used to her expensive court gowns. While Ashlynn took a moment to gather the things she needed, Luella took a look around the long room they were in. Unlike the rooms upstairs, everything was stone with no fancy decorations to make it pretty. Along one wall stood straw figures for practice. Shields were hung as well as swords, maces, and other weapons she had never seen before. There were trophies and favors, and the marks of men who must have died in combat over the years.

"This is amazing," she admitted, turning to Ashlynn. "Our training room looks nothing like this. We have the straw people, the chests of weapons...but you have pride in your men here."

"And women." Ashlynn held a long flamberge in her hand, a wave-bladed sword. She nodded with a crooked smile. "I grew up wanting to be a knight and always knew there were other girls, other women out there that wished to serve in that manner as well. I would not be the one to tell them that they weren't allowed."

Though she heard what Ashlynn was saying, Luella's attention was on the blade in her hands. "What are you going to do with that?"

"You said you had some sword skill. I would like to see the extent of it, if you please." Ashlynn lifted her chin toward the weapons laid out at the side of the room. "Pick whatever you would like."

With a concentrated look, Luella did as she was asked. Blue eyes scanned over the swords, daggers and things, trying to decide before settling on a basket-hilted, two-handed broadsword. Ashlynn watched her carefully, smirking at the unease with which her friend moved, then startled when Luella dropped her rouse of uncertainty and rushed at her, causing Ashlynn to lift her own blade in a block. She quickly brought her blade down to swipe at Luella's legs but she jumped, swinging at Ashlynn's midsection as her feet were leaving the ground. Ashlynn felt the graze of the blade tip against her clothing despite her slight bend to be out of the way of it. Using the momentum of her own swing, she spun to aim for Luella's neck but was met with the loud clang of steel on steel.

The sound of it reached Cavalon's ears as he was coming down the steps into the ante-chamber of the training room. He could also hear their feral yells and grunts as they battled one another. As he approached the door that would take him inside, he waited and leaned against the frame, crossing his arms to watch. Like the two women, he wore trousers and a tunic, though his had no sleeves to cover his arms. On his belt were two blades and three daggers. He continued to watch for a moment before unclipping the sheath of one sword to set it down. Drawing the other, he threw himself into the match.

To watch would have been witnessing a dance of the finest choreography. Cavalon was relentless even though the girls tired before he was even short of breath. The hilt of Luella's sword hit Ashlynn in the face, scratching her cheek and leaving her to bleed. She backed herself out then, pressing fingers to the wound to see how bad she was bleeding. It was nothing that wouldn't heal and she allowed herself to lean on her sword to watch, catching her breath as she did. The match was over quickly when Cavalon caught the broadsword in a downswing and had Luella unarmed with a simple follow-through, dislodging the weapon from her hand and sending it clattering to the floor.

Ashlynn watched carefully, seeing the concentration on Cavalon's face as he waited to see what Luella would do. What she did was highly unexpected; she started to laugh. He rolled his eyes and relaxed his stature, lowering his sword. "A word of advice? Don't do that on the battlefield."

"Sorry," she giggled, though she sounded anything but. She raked the hair from her face, her eyes dancing with sheer joy. "That was so much fun!"

"Fun?" Cavalon asked.

Ashlynn grinned. "See how it feels to play with sharp objects?"

"I've never fought that hard," Luella admitted, ignoring Cavalon for a moment and looking at Ashlynn. "It felt like I wasn't even myself. It was as though I was letting the sword tell me where to swing and my body tell me how to move."

"Because fighting is organic," Cavalon replied. "It doesn't matter your size or gender."

"Oh, I hurt you!"

"You did," Ashlynn laughed, touching the mark again and pulling her hand away to find it had already stopped bleeding, "but as you can see it is just a scratch. You were amazing!"

"Why did you back out?" Cavalon pointed his blade at her as if it were a finger. "You fight like you've been trained whereas she fights to survive."

"I have a wedding on the horizon," Ashlynn answered, grinning. "Anything more than this and Jaryn would never forgive me."

"There's a difference?" Luella turned to Cavalon, questioning his comment.

"Of course there's a difference," he told her, sheathing his sword. "Both have their pros and cons. Fighting with pure instinct gives you more freedom, but it also has the ability to give you too much. You can lose your focus easier and end up just wanting blood on your sword."

This startled the smile away. "Oh...I would never do that."

"You're half dragon. You don't have the knowledge of yourself yet that's required to say what you would or wouldn't do." She looked down quickly as a rush of heat went to her face, and Cavalon walked past her. "I brought you something."

"Me?" Luella turned around to watch him, casting a glance at Ashlynn.

161

Just as clueless, Ashlynn watched as well, silent. The Badarian picked up the second sword he'd brought, still in the sheath. Turning, he presented it to Luella, hilt first. She looked at him with question.

"Pull it out."

Slowly, she grasped the black leather bound hilt and pulled. The blade that followed had her gasping and Ashlynn stepped forward to examine the weapon closer. The sword was two-handed with a simple cross-hilt design with downsloping arms that ended in spatulate swellings of a rose design. A bigger rose rested in the center where the arms met the hilt. The blade itself, hammered thin and sharp, had also been etched in a design of roses and thorns that ran from tip to hilt on both sides. There were no scratches on the blade, nor any marks that had suggested it had ever seen battle.

"Gorgeous," Ashlynn breathed. She looked at Cavalon with curiosity. "Who made this for you?"

"No one made it for me," he answered deeply, enjoying the look of awe on Luella's face. "This was forged over sixty years ago." Now both women looked at him and he nodded. "It's true. This sword was made by an old magician for your grandsire, Luella. He gave it to your father and the last time I saw him, he gave it to me for safe keeping. Since he never came back and I knew you had his Element, I brought it up here with me to give to you. It belongs to you now."

For once, Ashlynn was shocked into silence. She watched as Luella took the sword and backed away, giving it a swing and a spin to see how it felt in her grip. "It feels so different than what I am used to...so heavy."

"You'll get used to it," Cavalon promised. He watched her maneuver, smiling his approval. "You look good with it. Keep it close. It's done your family well and I have no doubt it will treat you with the same loyalty."

"Thank you, Cavalon." Luella smiled at him, truly touched.

"You're welcome. Now, since it's clear we have no need to talk of swordplay, shall I begin the lesson of the Elements themselves?"

"Yes, please," said Luella eagerly. She took the scabbard from Cavalon to put her sword away.

His lesson began with mostly talk. He told them of the powers of each Element, both glad they already knew at least that much. The dragon of Fire could burn with a touch, his fire colored scales more heated than the white-hot center of a flame. His opposite, the Water Dragon, was much as Ashlynn remembered her father telling her years ago. She had only vestigial wings and a snake-like body with four short legs, and blue and black scales. She lived where it was damp and wooded, and ate anything she could catch that was low to the ground and easy prey. As Elas demonstrated when they had been below ground, she could transport herself through water.

Looking expressly at Ashlynn, Cavalon told her of how she could hide herself, shifting her shape not only into a dragon, but anything organic as well while retaining her draconic figure. She could disguise herself as a bush of roses, her scales turning to the same colors and textures. "In a sense, you're like a chameleon. You'll have to really experiment with it yourself to truly understand it. It isn't something I can explain with words and you'll fully grasp."

Ashlynn was amazed. "So you're telling me that if I was in my dragon form and I clung to the wall of the castle, I could blend in and no one would see me?"

"Correct," Cavalon answered. "If someone was looking hard for you and had amazingly strong vision it would be possible to see you, but otherwise you would just be part of the architecture."

"That would have been so helpful to know earlier." Her attack against Tadhg, running from Merrik and his men in the woods. So many things would have been different. But, she reminded herself, they were this way for a reason. "What of Air? I want to know more about her. What was her name again?"

"Mei Xing, that is, if she's still alive." She was gentle, as Cavalon recalled. She had a long serpentine body like the water dragon, white with a blue iridescence, and no wings to fly on. Yet she could still soar through the air, being able to use the currents like humans used the solid ground to walk. She was always gentle and kind, and if there was a time she was angered, storms would rage to reflect her mood. Like her counterpart, she, too could shift, but not into anything solid. She could take on the form of clouds, drifting, and sometimes communicate to others with the shapes she would make.

The dragon of Darkness, Luella, was a dragon that could move through fyre, but also through shadows. Entering the shadow of a chair in one room could take her to the shadow of a willow tree in another country. There was nothing she could shift into, but hidden in the darkness she was all but invisible.

Cavalon, as Light, could do the exact same thing, but through large natural sources of light. If a sunbeam fell in a pool in the woods, he could step into it and reappear anywhere else there was light to be found. "In terms of travel, Luella is the strongest of us and the most powerful. There is always darkness, no matter how much light may be shining." Looking at Luella, he said, "You will never be stranded or be kept too confined. There will always be a place for you to go. But we both have to be careful - light and shadow can change and if we're careless, if we become too complacent in our gifts, we could very well lose ourselves."

"Is that how you got here?" Ashlynn guessed.

Cavalon nodded. "It is. And that was no small task. The sun sets on my country before it sets here. It took very careful planning."

"The ballad you asked for the other night..." she continued.

"The song of the Conjuncture? Yes, it had eight dragons in it."

"And we have heard elsewhere that there were twelve in total."

Cavalon took a deep breath in, lines in his brow deepening as he nodded. "There used to be twelve, then four of them disappeared. The eight were alive for a long time, but like the four before them, two of them turned into the myths people believed them to be. If someone tells you that you don't exist for long enough, you start to believe it yourself."

Luella tilted her head. "They simply disappeared? Does that mean there are truly only six left, or can we...summon them somehow? What were they?"

Cavalon shook his head. "They simply disappeared. They are now more a part of this earth than anything else and won't return. Four controlled the seasons, and two, the will of humans."

Ashlynn, a little quicker than Luella, said something first. "The will of humans and still opposites? Good and Evil. Just as Nuala said."

The Badarian nodded. "They weren't part of my time, but I did hear that the world had much more evil back then."

"I find that hard to believe," Ashlynn argued softly. "There is still much evil now, it is just not as easy to recognize." She crossed her arms. "So now what of this conjuncture? What is supposed to happen when all the dragons are together again? We have heard everything from a single new dragon coming to life with the powers of all of them, the return of the Deliverer, right down to the very end of life itself. What is the true version?"

Cavalon shrugged and it was a bit of a let-down to both women. "I couldn't say. That part is as much of a mystery to me as it is to you. But there are three of us here. I'd like to see what would happen if the other three joined us." He started walking to the door, nodding for them to follow him. "This war you're so worried about would be over before it had its chance to begin if all six Elementals were on one side."

They headed up, going outside to the large inner courtyard so there would be room for all three of them to move. "I hadn't thought of that," Ashlynn mused quietly, eyes squinted against the brightness of the sun. A cold breeze brushed over them and she shivered. "What if not all six would be on this side? What if they were loyal to Laidley?"

Luella shook her head, strands of black hair blowing about her face. "My father hunted the dragons. If they were in their right mind, they would have nothing to do with him even after he is gone."

"We'll look for them." They both looked at Cavalon, not fully understanding what he was saying. "Luella and I will look for them. We can move about faster and have no country to run. It'll also give her more practice in the usage of her abilities."

Ashlynn looked at Luella, expecting to find the older woman shocked. Instead she seemed excited. "Luella?"

"He's right, Ashlynn." Luella looked at her with wide eyes. "It makes the most sense. We can go search for the others, try and convince them to come back here with us. I know you want to help, but you have a country to run and a war to plan." She stepped forward to take Ashlynn's hands.

Ashlynn sighed softly. "I know, and you're right. I just worry."

"I hope you're not worrying about me." The girls parted and looked at Cavalon. His expression was defensive. "I know I came off as an ass, but I won't let anything happen to her. She's safer with me than anywhere else."

Ashlynn looked at him, stern and searching. "How can I believe that? We only met you yesterday and the first thing you did was molest my sister and bloody my friend."

"I didn't molest her," he protested. "It was barely a touch. As far as Elas goes...I don't make friends easily."

"I can't imagine why."

"Listen, her father, your mother...they were my friends. They were family to me. I'm going to do everything in my power to make sure nothing happens to either of you." Cavalon shrugged. "If you don't want to believe I would do it for you, believe I would do it for them."

Ashlynn didn't want to see sincerity in his eyes. She didn't want to see that he very much meant his words because she would feel obligated to trust him. But the sincerity was there, along with the same strange softness he'd had the night before when talking about Siobhán and Mortagh. "If anything happens to her..."

"The Element of Darkness would be lost forever," Cavalon supplied. "Do you really think I want that?"

Ashlynn's lips were pursed. "I don't know what you want. All the same, I am entrusting her to you."

There was the briefest flash of victory in Cavalon's expression, but it disappeared quickly as he stepped back. "We'll leave tonight then, after we eat." Luella opened her mouth to argue, but Cavalon cut her off. "Right now I want to see what you really look like." He didn't wait for questions or quizzical expressions. Backed far enough away from them, Cavalon was already beginning the transformation from human to dragon. White scales rippled up his body, fingers turning to talons and face into a snout. They watched him grow as white wings, long and powerful shot forth from his back to complete the transformation. The girls gaped. In his dragon form, Cavalon took up almost the entire space of the courtyard; he was bigger than any dragon they had seen. With a whipping beat of his wings, he was up in the air and sending strong currents of wind to chill them. Luella shook her head, dazzled.

"Beautiful."

Ashlynn snorted. "Don't say that to him." Stepping away from her friend,

Ashlynn followed suit. Her golden scales reflected the sunlight with such intensity that Luella had to look away. She could only look again when the two dragons were above her, flying around each other and looking as though they were playing. She wanted to join them. With a deep breath in, Luella let herself relax enough to begin her own shifting process. The pain Cavalon so knowingly mentioned ran down her spine like a knife. Above her, the white dragon trumpeted, letting her know he felt it. Somehow knowing she wasn't alone made it easier. Her transformation took longer than the other two, but she eventually rose to join them. Her size was much smaller in comparison to Cavalon, and her color such a stark contrast.

Below, Jaryn came into the courtyard with Tasarin just in time to see the three of them rise higher and fly away. "Did you see the size of him?" Jaryn asked, staring after their dark spots in the sky.

Tasarin frowned and did not answer. Instead, he turned around and went back inside without a word.

CHAPTER FIFTEEN

Laidley stood at the window of his throne room, watching the darkening sky. He was not overly thrilled with the idea of waiting to launch an attack, but Merrik was convinced it was the best thing to do. Tadhg had not been known for his patience and upon giving anyone a time limit to surrender, would then attack almost immediately. Those on the Isles would be expecting the very same thing, no doubt. They would gather themselves and their resources, call in any favors owed to them, and be prepared for war immediately. Prepared for a war that was still three weeks away. When the time actually came they would be disheartened and probably close to turning against one another for making each person wait so long. Laidley's men, with Merrik and himself leading them, would swoop in for a quick and easy victory. It was not ideal in the young man's eyes, but as Merrik reminded him, Laidley did not want to fight a hard war when still so young a king. There would be further opportunities to prove himself in battle. This was simply about justice.

"Has Dani returned yet?"

Merrik shook his head even though Laidley had his back to him. "No, my King. It is likely he will not return before sunset tomorrow."

"And Ories?"

"Should be back any moment. It was wise of you to send one of the Volar. I think no one else would have been able to blend in as easily."

Laidley turned around, a smirk for the captain of guards on his face as he moved to take his throne. "I may be young, Merrik, but I'm not stupid."

Merrik returned the small smile. "I would never presume to say such a thing, my liege."

"You didn't have to say it out loud for me to know you were thinking it. Your very way of speaking to me is coddling."

"I did not mean to offend..."

"You haven't offended." The younger man watched the older with a blank expression. Merrik had been disappearing often and when pressed, would not reveal his secret reasons for being distracted. It was a good little mystery to keep Laidley's mind off of waiting. Sometimes when Merrik returned to Laidley's side he seemed lighter, sometimes quite the opposite. Right now was the first time in a few days that he appeared to be his usual self. "It has been part of your duty to watch over me like the child I was. A crown does not magically change that perspective."

"Perhaps it should. Forgive me. I will try and refrain from speaking when it is unnecessary."

Laidley laughed. "Now you pacify. Merrik, if I held no value for what you said or felt, and thought you were speaking out of turn, don't you think I would have said something before now? I very much value your vision on things. You have many more years at this game of war than I, and I have nothing but complete trust that you won't lead me astray."

"I will do everything in my ability to make certain Caedia's new high king will have a long and prosperous reign."

"I have no doubt about that."

Both men looked up upon hearing footsteps drawing close to the great hall. Recognition of the approaching winged man had the young king leaning forward in anticipation. "Ories," said Laidley, motioning for the man to draw closer. "Your ears must be ringing."

"No, Your Majesty, they are not." The Volar scout approached the throne and stood beside Merrik, humorless and looking more at the wall than at Laidley. "I have come to report my findings and collect my fee."

Laidley waved a hand. "On with it, then."

"The young princess and her sister are indeed at their home castle of Altaine in Siness. Your sister is with them, a willing comrade and not a hostage. I was unable to attend the council meeting as High King Nóe had already selected companions to accompany him. I was, however, able to explore the castle once permission was given by Ashlynn herself. All the guests were allowed to move freely and I took great advantage of that."

"Were you able to hear anything that might be useful from Ashlynn herself?" Merrik asked, and Ories nodded.

"The next morning there was a meeting for tactics, rather informal and unstructured. You were correct in your assumptions of her heritage. She is Nir's daughter, though both she and her sister were fostered at Oceana here in Caedia. Are you aware this girl is not yet queen of her country?"

"Yes, I was," Laidley answered. "We would have heard news of it if Siness had a high ruler once again."

"She is very clearly the one in charge. No one questions her orders and the

168

people of the Isles, even the ones not from her lands directly, revere her as High Queen there."

Laidley was thoughtful. "Interesting. Continue."

"There is going to be a coronation and a wedding."

"Is there anything else?"

The scout finally looked at Laidley. "No, your Highness."

Laidley stared at the winged man, searching the return gaze to see if there was anything being withheld from him. When it appeared he was satisfied, the young king nodded. "Very well. Your payment will be waiting for you at the door."

This satisfied Ories and he nodded curtly. "Thank you, You Grace." With one more bow of his head, he left the throne room.

Laidley waited until the Volarim was gone from the room before turning his attention to Merrik. "Thoughts?"

For a moment Merrik didn't speak. His lips were pursed into a thin line of concentration for the longest time, and when Laidley was close to asking again, the older man gave a small sigh. "We must look at this from every possible aspect. It would be folly to rush to war with this report alone."

Laidley scowled, impatient. "Then what do you suggest? You heard Ories. We are not even a concern of theirs at the moment. That girl, the one who killed my father, isn't afraid of a battle. She is getting *married!*"

"Which is precisely my concern. She is young, yes, but she is not foolish." Merrik rubbed his chin. "It *would* be foolish to not be worried and to carry about as usual."

"Stop speaking around the meat of it, man! What are you trying to tell me?"

"Only that it might prove prudent to wait for your squire to return. Hear his report before making a decision on the next course of action."

Laidley growled impatiently. "Fine. Then I will be in my chambers planning the best way to cut down these pests for once and for all."

~*~*~*~

The dark was cool in a way that was unexpected, like jumping into a pool of water on a warm day. Luella was enjoying playing with her new-found ability. After Cavalon revealed it was something she could do in her human form, she had been doing it all day, disappearing into the shadows of one room only to appear in another and frighten anyone who might not have been expecting her. At first, she apologized profusely for startling people. Then she started to enjoy it. Cavalon watched her for a little while, then decided to make a game of it, telling her to find a place where he couldn't follow. This was a challenge to her, one she was taking on with great enthusiasm.

Upon entering a shadow, everything would get fuzzy in her vision, almost like she was blind. This was disconcerting at first and when she told Cavalon about it, he told her not to use her eyes. If she could forget about her sense of sight when in the darkness, she would be able to better feel where she was allowed to go and where there would be no room for her to enter into the more physical world. After trying that, after closing her eyes in her world of darkness, she immediately knew what Cavalon meant. It was like a swimmer knowing which way was up without having to actually look to find it.

Luella was laughing, jumping from one shadow to the next with Cavalon close behind, using natural sources of light to move with her. She jumped into a room and stopped, knowing she had found the place Cavalon could not enter by his gift alone. The room she stood in was completely dark with no source of light at all. Even a light from under the door was blotted out somehow. Blinking several times, Luella was amazed by the way her vision adjusted. Before knowing exactly what she was she'd always thought her eyesight was simply better in the dark. Knowing now that it was true, and the reason why, it all made sense.

The blackness began to ebb and she could make out shapes and forms. Some article of clothing had been shoved against the door to block out the light on purpose; the room was darkened for a reason. Panic rose in Luella's throat, wondering if this was some sort of a trap. She looked around preparing to leave, when she saw a figure in a chair. Instinct made her take a step back, pressing her spine against the wall.

"Why are you afraid?"

The voice was familiar, cool and soft. She stepped away from the wall, a hand over her heart. "Tasarin, you nearly frightened me to death."

He laughed in the blackness. She could now see his face clearer and that he smiled at her. "That was not my intent." Luella marveled at how she could even see the lighter bits of his hair fall over his shoulders as he walked to her. She smiled now as well, reaching to touch what looked so different in the dark. "I knew this was the only way to catch your attention."

She let go of his hair and looked up into his face, confused. "If you wanted to speak with me, all you had to do was ask."

The smile Tasarin wore faded. "I could speak to you anytime I like, but you would not be alone." The elf looked to the door. "Even now, I know that he is out there, waiting to feel you move so he can follow you again."

Luella laughed softly. "We're playing a game. He told me to find a room where he could not go..."

"...and you have found it." Tasarin stepped closer and Luella found herself against the wall again. "Luella, do not go with him."

170

His forwardness was unexpected and made her shake her head. "I have to. Tasarin, we need to find the others."

"He can do it on his own. He came all the way up here without a companion and found two Elementals without any help."

"He found two because he was lucky to find Ashlynn and I in the same company." Luella breathed softly. "He only knew where I was to start because he felt me call to him."

Tasarin frowned and backed away. "A call you did not even know you put out."

"You do not trust him." It was an observation more than a question.

"He has not given any of us reason to."

"Tasarin." Luella moved to stand in front of him, looking up into his somewhat blurry face. "If Ashlynn hadn't trusted Elas on a good feeling, or even me, things would be very different right now."

"I do not argue that. Ashlynn knew what she was doing when she made her decisions. Not to mention that she was bringing you both back here, to her home, where she would have stronger security around her. She was not leaving for foreign lands where no familiar help would be available to her."

It was hard to keep herself from smiling. Tasarin's concern was touching. "I am not so helpless myself."

"I did not mean that." He pulled her to him and wrapped his arms around her. "The thought of you being somewhere where neither Suule or I can see and protect you..."

Luella rested her head against his chest and and closed her eyes. "When there is a threat upon your home, sometimes you must put yourself in danger to protect it. It may be foolish to leave with Cavalon, but I am neither frightened nor worried. There is little I feel I can do here while you and Ashlynn prepare for war. I feel useless."

"But you are not." Tasarin insisted, his chin sitting lightly atop her head. She smiled against him. There was a complete comfort there in his embrace, and a desire to stay there as long as she could, but a knock came to the door.

"I know you're still in there," came Cavalon's muffled voice. "Are you all right?"

"Fine," Luella called, breaking Tasarin's embrace. "I will be right out." She looked up in time to see Tasarin trying to hide a frown. She lifted her hands, taking his face into her gentle grasp. "Do not trust him if you feel that you cannot. But trust me. I will be safe, and I will return."

"I do trust you," he answered, voice just above a whisper. His hands covered hers. "But when you return, will you be returning to me, or will you be returning with him?" Tasarin sighed softly in the darkness. "I care for you, Luella, Perhaps more than I should because of Suule...but I care for you."

171

She blushed, glad he couldn't see her. "I care for you as well, Tasarin. We shared more than stories and memories the other night. I have not felt a bond like that before and I have no unicorn to blame my feelings on."

"I was not blaming..."

"I know. I was teasing."

She felt him relax against her before he whispered, "Stay here with me. I will keep you safe."

Luella let go of him, his words causing irrational annoyance to spark within her. "I can keep myself safe. I am quite skilled with a sword, you know. Unless the danger you wish to keep me from is really Cavalon."

"We know very little about him."

"And yet it was you who suggested to Ashlynn that we seek his guidance in our abilities." Luella shook her head. "Tasarin, he will not harm me. It is in his best interest as an Elemental to keep me safe, keep me alive."

"He is attracted to you."

A heavy silence fell between them for a quick moment, but Luella broke it with a chuckle of disbelief. "What?"

"You spent one night with me. Now you will spend two weeks with him."

Luella suddenly understood and felt the heat of anger burn in her face. "Is that what this is all really about? You fear more about losing my hand than me losing myself?"

"No, I did not mean..."

"Yes, you did. Tasarin, we have known each other very little in the grand scheme of things, but long enough to have formed a strong bond. I am going with Cavalon for the good of this country and this war. As one who has had the throne for the last year and has acted as the leader of a nation even in proxy, you should understand that matters of the heart come last when it comes to saving lives." Calming herself, Luella took a step away from Tasarin and reached for the door. "You can either choose to trust me, or to simply let me go." She pulled the door open and let light spill in. Cavalon stood there with a grin for her, then a confused look inside the room when he saw the irritation on her face.

"I win," she told Cavalon, brushing past him. "No more games. I need to get ready. There is a wedding to attend."

~*~*~*~

There were three girls inside Ashlynn's quarters, helping her with everything she might need before it was time to go down to the beach for her wedding. After the early morning sparring and then flight, she'd needed a nice long soak in a very hot bath. Oils had been added to the water so as she washed her tired muscles, soothing perfumes seeped into her skin making it soft and sweet smelling. Once the water started to turn cold, she'd put on a long robe and had her hair set in fire warmed rods to give it some curl. One thing she had always admired about Kenayde was the natural wave she had to her hair. Ashlynn's hair had always been straight as a pin. As her hair dried, one of the girls worked on her face. Dyed powders were used to smooth her complexion, add color to her eyelids, and give her cheeks a blushing tint.

When her hair was dry, the rods were unraveled to reveal long spirals. Skillful fingers were run through once all of the rods were removed, loosening the tight curls to form rivers of gold running over her shoulders and down her back. All three girls busied themselves with pinning back small sections of hair from close to her face. Most of it was left down with white orange blossoms giving her a look of delicacy.

With everything done but getting dressed, Ashlynn looked at herself in the mirror and took a deep breath. She hadn't expected to be so nervous. There was a knot in her stomach and a lump in her throat that she simply couldn't explain away. When a knock came to her door, she jumped and laughed at herself. It was Emiline, come to see how things were progressing and if she could be of any help. She looked stunning in a simple gown of red and gold. It was strange for Ashlynn to feel the tears sting her eyes. "Mama."

Emiline was there in a breath, dabbing at Ashlynn's eyes with her own handkerchief. "No crying yet, heartling," she soothed. "You look absolutely lovely. Don't ruin it before Jaryn even gets to see you." Ashlynn laughed thickly and reached up a hand to cover Emiline's. "You're trembling," the older woman observed.

"I know. I can't seem to help it. Were you this nervous on your wedding day?"

Emiline nodded and sat back when her daughter's face was dry. "So nervous that I almost ran away."

"Really?"

"Really."

Ashlynn took a steadying breath, trying to relax. "How did you calm yourself?"

"I didn't. I simply told myself that I loved Wessely and would rather face life with him than without him. I was shaking and almost in tears the entire time. As soon as I saw him though..." She trailed off, a far away smile on her face as she remembered her own wedding day. "I knew it was silly to be afraid. I knew everything was going to be just fine and that I could never love another man as much as I loved him. Still love him." Touching her daughter's hair, Emiline's expression turned sad. "I wish your parents could have seen you grow up. You have been such a joy to me."

It was hard not to tear up again at those words. "I wish they could be here too, but..." She shook her head and sniffled. "Kenayde and I could not have asked for a better mother or father in their stead. And I couldn't love you any more, were you the one to give me life." Openly crying now, the two women embraced tightly. It had been a very long time since she and Emiline had been together like this. She was as strong and independent growing up as she was now. There were only a few times she could specifically remember going to Emiline for this type of comfort. She had always been closer to Wessely, whereas Kenayde was the one who turned to Emiline first. This moment was one they both would cherish forever.

Sitting back on her heels, Emiline wiped her own eyes before offering over her kerchief. "So much for keeping it together." They both laughed and held hands while the girls went back to work on Ashlynn's face.

"How are Kenayde and Luella?"

Emiline nodded. "Ready. As is the beach, for what Luella told me. She said it looks lovely."

Ashlynn smiled even though her lips were being painted. "I can't wait to see it."

"You are done, Your Grace. Shall we get you into your gown now?"

She took another deep breath, locking eyes with her mother. "Yes."

The gown had been hanging inside her wardrobe and was now taken down so Ashlynn could get into it. A deep sapphire blue, the color of purity, the dress was made of silk, with flowing sleeves and layers over the skirt. The boned bodice hugged her frame as it was laced up, leaving her shoulders and neck exposed and framing both her waist and neckline in alternating soft scoops and points. There was lacing in the front as well as the back, more for decoration than true purpose. Flowers, the same orange blossoms that were in her hair, had been made out of snow white linen and sewn onto the sides of the bodice where it held the laces. The full skirt had swaths of darker blue silk flowing over it to make it look full and indulgent. This by itself was gathered in delicate dips with the same sewn flowers on the bodice. The train, once it was attached, trailed behind her a yard in length. As a final touch, a sash of the tartan of her clan was draped across her, held in place by a silver Stuart clan pin.

Almost completely ready, Ashlynn turned to see her reflection in the mirror. Her hands went to her stomach, resting on the flat surface of the bodice. Her own image took the words from her mouth. It was a daily process, getting dressed and ready for the day in big, elaborately decorated gowns. But this dress, this wedding dress, was so simple and so elegant, she felt for the first time that she was as beautiful as the thing she wore.

"Lift up your left foot, Lynnie," Emiline stepped beside her daughter to meet her reflected eyes. Ashlynn did as she was told, watching one of the girls slip a boot on her foot and lace it up. As her other boot was put on, Emiline lowered a golden circlet onto Ashlynn's head, the ornate knotting dipping low to hang a sapphire tear just between her brows. "There," Emiline finally breathed. "Now you are ready."

~*~*~*~

Down on the beach a slight wind had picked up. The fragrance of the blue and white flowers filled the air like a light blanket, and chatter among the guests was just a little louder than the whispering rush of waves on the shore. Everyone gathered mirrored the fallen leaves closer to the forest line, colors ranging in bright vibrant green, to a deep crimson red. Women wore their best dresses, all brightly colored brocades and silk. The men wore kilts or breeches and hose with doublets of matching colors. Everyone stood awaiting the bride and groom. A long runner of blue ran down the beach and ended under a trellis decorated with a blue and white tent of silk. There stood a man of the cloth, speaking quietly with Jaryn.

The groom wore a doublet of the same deep sapphire of Ashlynn's gown with a white tunic underneath. Around his waist and reaching down to his knees was a kilt of his clan. The colors were of rich blue and green, with thin crossings of a dull black and even thinner stitched lines of a bright red. Around his waist was a silver chain that held his foxhead sporran in place.

A carriage pulled by two black horses with blue and gold dressings came close to the beach and two women began to play a soft slow melody, one on a small lap harp and the other on a flute. Accepting the hand of the driver for assistance, Ashlynn stepped down from the solid floor of the carriage onto the soft sandy beach. All faces turned in her direction and her eyes left the driver to find the face of her beloved. He saw her just as she looked upon him, and Jaryn's breath hitched in his throat. She smiled at him, already weepy as she walked down the center aisle. He had never seen her as lovely as she was at that moment. The breeze played with stray curls as she walked, giving her the uncanny ability to look untamed even in her elegance. Ashlynn approached to stand beside him with the minister and it was all he could do not to touch her face, to take her in his arms and press her against him. It felt as though his heart could burst at any moment, and by the way Ashlynn looked at him as a tear ran down her cheek, it was obvious she felt it too. Her smile was genuine, even if it was hard to hold on to as Kenayde stepped forward from the crowd and wrapped a long white ribbon of silk around their joined hands to bind them together.

"Dearly beloved," began the minister. "We are gathered together here in the sight of the Giver to join together this man and this woman in holy Matrimony, which is an honorable union, instituted by the Giver in Paradise, and into which holy estate these two come now to be joined." They cast a look at each other and shared the same smile. "Therefore if any man can show just cause as to why they may not lawfully be joined together, let him now speak, or else hereafter forever hold his peace."

Turning, Ashlynn scanned the faces of the gathered, wearing an expression that said if anyone spoke up, they would pay a high price. This brought out a ripple of laughter among the witnesses. There was no one present that was not pleased with this union. It was something they all had been looking forward to for a long time now. Everyone was smiling, or in the case of a few women, crying. All except Cavalon. The look he wore suggested he was uncomfortable, maybe even in pain. Ashlynn ignored him and turned around to face the minister once more.

He looked first to Jaryn, then to Ashlynn. "Before your vows are charged to you, take this moment to face each other and speak from the love you pledge this day."

Ashlynn and Jaryn turned to look at one another once more. "My love," Jaryn began, practically sighing the words. "How long have I waited for this day. From the very moment I saw you, all blonde tangles and untamed temper, I knew you were the one the Giver had been saving me for. Created me for. You had my heart the moment you told me where it was I could stick the lute I had strapped to my back." Everyone laughed again. Even Cavalon seemed amused by what he heard. "I never knew I could love someone as feisty, ill-tempered, stubborn, and hard-headed as you." She grinned. "I never knew I could love so deeply," he continued, "until you. I pledge to be loyal to you and to be the kind of man you deserve. I promise to pick up after myself, to let you win every other argument...and to kiss you before we sleep each night, even if I would rather be sleeping in the stables because of how angry you are with me."

His vows were whimsical, but it was exactly what she had been expecting from Jaryn. By nature, his outlook was lighthearted and sometimes even silly. If he had said anything too serious, Ashlynn would have been shocked. Knowing it was now her turn, she took a deep breath. All the work her girls had done was probably for nothing as tears rolled down her cheeks, but she still wanted to avoid smudging colors all over her face if it was at all possible. She started to speak but had to stop, feeling as though she would sob instead of form any intelligible words.

"It's all right," Jaryn said softly, lowering his head to press his forehead to hers. "Take your time, love. I'm not going anywhere."

"I can do this," she whispered.

"I know you can."

With one more deep breath in, Ashlynn steadied herself so that she could say what she wanted to and Jaryn straightened. "Never has a man annoyed me and held me captive before as you did on the day we met. I remember saying that I wished you had never wandered into this country, yet secretly hoped you would never go. While many would run from a woman who spoke exactly what was on her mind, you stayed and even let yourself be drawn by it. You won my heart in so many ways that it was impossible not to love you. You support me and hold me steady when I would sway. Like now." Jaryn chuckled and squeezed her hands. "I will love you when you sing out of tune and when you have terrible morning breath. I promise to always seek your counsel and to be honest and truthful in everything. Above all else, I promise to love you until I can no longer feel love."

The minister waited a moment to be sure neither bride nor groom had anything else to say. When they only stared at each other with smiles, he assumed it safe to continue. Looking to Jaryn, he said, "Will you have this woman to be your wedded wife, to live together after the Giver's ordinance in the holy estate of Matrimony? Will you love her, comfort her, honor, and keep her, in sickness and in health, and forsaking all others, keep only unto her, so long as you both shall live?"

Jaryn nodded, never taking his eyes from Ashlynn's face. "I will."

"Will you have this man to be your wedded husband, to live together after the Giver's ordinance in the holy estate of Matrimony? Will you obey him, and serve him, love, honor, and keep him in sickness and in health, and, forsaking all others, keep only unto him, so long as you both shall live?"

Sniffling, Ashlynn nodded as well. "I will."

As Kenayde freed their hands from the ribbon, the minister took the small parcel from his pocket. He waited while Jaryn removed his clan pin from his sash and pinned it to the one Ashlynn wore, just above her own clan pin. Now the minister unwound the parcel and produced two silver bands. Each ring had an overlay of golden knotwork running around its entirety. "Like the knot of our beloved Isles and the circle of these rings, there is no beginning and no end. Let your love be like that of our Father above, unending. By giving these rings to one another you therefore intertwine your lives and become one with each other, a knot of beautiful design. Yet like the knot, you will each have your own path that makes it complete. Share each other's burdens and help each other when you stumble. That is your charge. If this is acceptable to you, please take these rings and present them to each other with a willing heart."

Both took their rings from the minister. Jaryn slid his onto Ashlynn's hand before Ashlynn did the same in return. The minister smiled and looked past the couple into the crowd of onlookers. "By witness of the men and women present, and by the authority of the Giver above, I declare this man and woman, husband and wife."

"Can I kiss her now?" Jaryn asked eagerly.

The minister laughed and nodded his head. "Yes, you may kiss..." But before he even had the chance to finish, Jaryn had pulled Ashlynn to him and kissed her without reservation. Ashlynn wrapped her arms around him as everyone clapped and cheered. When they finally parted, Jaryn wound his arms around her and Ashlynn folded herself into his strong embrace. There was no moment she could recall that equated to the sheer joy she was feeling. Now all the butterflies and the nervousness beforehand seemed silly. As Jaryn released her to thread his fingers with hers, she gave a silent word of thanks to the Giver for the man beaming down at her.

"Since we are all here," said the minister, "I believe there is another matter to attend to." Behind him on white velvet cushions were two crowns. Facing the minister again, Ashlynn and Jaryn held hands and knelt before him with bowed heads. "Just as you are charged to love and protect one another, your blood and your bond have charged you with the same vow for the people of this land. As High King and Queen, you are sworn to rule with a just hand and a fair heart. The people of this nation need only lift their voices to lend their support to your appointment."

There was not even the space of a breath between the minister's words and a loud cheer from everyone gathered. This brought a smile to the old man's face. He carefully took the circlet from Ashlynn's head and exchanged it for a silver crown of delicate knot work. Placing it on her head he said, "This crown was worn by your mother and your father's mother before her. With this crown comes a legacy and a past that will aid you in becoming the ruler you are meant to be."

Next he took the larger and heavier crown to place it atop Jaryn's head. "This crown was worn by Nir and his father before him. With this crown comes a legacy and a past that will aid you in becoming the ruler you are meant to be. Predestined by the Giver, you will reign in this land for as long as you shall live. Arise, High King Jaryn and High Queen Ashlynn." The couple stood while everyone clapped and cheered for a second time, elation warming the chilly autumn air.

As the couple walked down the aisle to climb into the carriage, Tasarin let Kenayde tuck her arm into his and they joined in the procession that would walk back to the castle for the reception feast. "You look positively radiant," he commented, his other hand resting on hers.

"Thank you," Kenayde answered softly. "You clean up nicely as well."

Tasarin's laugh was warm and hearty. "And they say Ashlynn is the one with the quick wit." Kenayde grinned up at him but the elf was looking to the side, distracted. "Elas," he greeted. "Could you see from where you were standing?"

Elas nodded, drawing up to them. He only glanced at Tasarin before looking at Kenayde. "Yes, I could see perfectly. It was a perfect ceremony. The weather was...perfect."

With a small smile and tactful grace, Tasarin removed Kenayde's arm from his. "Elas, would you do me the favor of escorting Kenayde back to the castle? There are some people I wish to greet."

"Of course." Elas took Tasarin's place, realizing a little too late that Kenayde would be stuck talking to the scaled side of his face. With a slight frown, he took Kenayde's arm and looked down as they walked.

Kenayde glanced sideways, her brow wrinkling. "Why do you do that?"

Elas blinked at her. "Do what?"

"You look away from people when they're on this side of you. You almost look disgusted."

His mouth curved downward as his gaze fell back to their path. "I don't want to offend anyone."

Kenayde's lips pursed. "You offend me by assuming I'm offended."

After a moment of walking in silence he hesitantly turned his attention to her. "I'm not sure how to respond."

"Elas, have I ever shied away from you? Have I ever averted my eyes when you've looked at me or spoken to me?"

"No."

"Then why should you think I would be offended?"

He was always assuming he was offending people with his face. How could he not? He didn't look natural with one side of his face all covered in blue scales and an odd white eye looking about. He hated his own face, why should anyone else feel any differently? "I'm..." He frowned for the third time as his voice quieted to finish his statement. "...ugly."

Kenayde stopped in her tracks, making Elas stop as well since they were still connected. Around them people pressed forward like a stream splitting at a rock in its current. Her smile, forced as it was, was formal and sweet enough to keep the crowd moving. No one stopped to see if there was anything the matter, not even Wessely and Emiline. Her father cast her a questioning look over his shoulder but Kenayde only smiled wider. "We will be right behind you." She watched her father nod and when they were well enough behind the crowd, Kenayde withdrew her arm and folded her hands together as she looked at Elas.

"You look like your sister when you do that."

"What happened to the dragon we met under the monastery?" His comment went unanswered. "You were rude, and quick, and cared nothing for what we thought of you. The man standing before me at this very moment could not possibly be that same dragon."

"I don't expect you to understand," Elas growled in reply, looking away from her as his defenses went up.

Kenayde, having a stubborn streak in her by default, moved to stand directly in his line of vision. "Make me understand," she challenged.

It was all he could do not to snarl. "That was my home. I was comfortable there. I could be myself there. Do you know how long it had been since the last time I was in this human form? Do you think I enjoy wearing these clothes and being land-bound for so long? Every morning I have to get up and see this ugly face in the mirror. It's not who I am. It's a mockery of *what* I am and I hate it."

"There it is," Kenayde replied softly. "That is the honesty I was looking for."

"You want honesty?" Elas snapped, feeling a sudden surge of anger rush through him. "Sometimes I feel so unworthy to be near you that it takes everything in me not to run to the sea and never return. When you come into a room, you fill it with a light that is pure and beautiful. When I'm with you, your light is tainted by my very presence. I draw all the attention."

"I never liked being the center of attention anyway."

Elas made another low sound like a growl in his throat. "You mock me."

Kenayde flinched. "I do no such thing."

"What do you want from me?"

Taking a step forward, Kenayde put her hands on his face. "I want you to see yourself as I see you."

Jerking away from her touch, Elas took a step back and shook his head. "It will never happen. And even if it did, to what avail? I would be the joke of your kingdom, entertainment for guests of the castle." The beast was only ever loved by the fair maiden in the stories told to children in their youth. Nothing like that ever really happened. He knew that. "I've overstayed my welcome as it is. After Laidley is dealt with, I'll return to my home."

Kenayde looked for a moment like she would cry. "No," she pleaded softly.

In a quick motion, Elas had her by the arms with his face close to hers. His tone was deep and feral when he demanded again, "What do you want from me?"

Clearly shaken by this sudden turn in his temper, tears rushed to Kenayde's eyes. Her hands were balled into fists, but she didn't try to escape his grasp or look away. "I want you to trust me enough to let me in." She whimpered. "You're hurting me."

Letting go immediately, Elas backed away several steps and ran a hand over his face. After a moment he said, "I do trust you, Kenayde. It's myself I can't trust." He looked at her, his expression so blank that it was impossible to glean anything from it. Even his voice had fallen flat. "You've been kind to me in more ways and more often than someone like me could ever hope. I think it would be best if I kept my distance from now on."

Kenayde clasped her hands together under her chin. She didn't understand what was happening. Moments ago, she was sharing in a beautiful wedding and feeling the lightest she had felt in a very long time. Now, she felt like her heart was being torn to pieces. "Elas, please..."

"I'm not a gentleman and never will be one." With one last look at Kenayde, there was only coldness in his gaze. She was helpless to watch him walk away, unbuttoning his doublet as he went. She knew he meant to take to the water. It was his comfort zone and a place where no one could reach him.

A sob caught in her throat as she watched him shed the doublet and tunic like a snake with his skin. Tears spilled from her eyes and she turned away to walk back to the castle.

CHAPTER SIXTEEN

The great hall of Castle Altaine was brimming with activity. Nearly everyone that was present at the ceremony was seated, talking with others, laughing, and watching the newly wedded couple as they smiled at each other and held hands. Each table was decorated with white and blue flowers, and laden with food. Roasted meats, gilded and slivered calves' heads, fish, cheeses, nuts, fresh fruits, oysters steamed in almond milk, ale-flavored bread, stewed cabbage, tarts and custards, fresh fruit preserves and spicy mulled wine were all served and partaken of as soon as a blessing was given.

Luella looked sideways at Cavalon. It was entirely possible for that he had half the food right there on his very own plate. He ate without ceremony and with no care to who might be around and watching him. With delicacy, Luella ate a slice of the warm, cinnamon glazed apple on her plate. Looking up, she caught a glance from Tasarin as he seated himself beside Jaryn. The gaze they shared across the room was timid and Luella looked away quickly. Noticing the chair beside Ashlynn unoccupied, her brow wrinkled and she returned her attention to Tasarin. He, too, noticed it empty, and together they looked around the great hall. Kenayde was nowhere to be seen, and neither was Elas. Despite just having sat, Tasarin rose to make his way over to Wessely and Emiline, Luella watching him discreetly. The elf bent close to Wessely's ear and when he straightened, Luella saw the king shake his head.

"Kenayde isn't here," Luella muttered.

"What?"

She looked at Cavalon who had just filled his mouth with goose and dates. There was a brief moment of disgust that she tried to push down. "Kenayde should be here, sitting at the table beside her sister. She and Elas should both be here and neither of them are."

Cavalon swallowed, casting a quick glance around the room. "Maybe they decided to stay behind and stop pretending they're not attracted to each other."

Luella frowned. "Have you ever been to a wedding? Tasarin sees to Jaryn's needs and Kenayde should be doing the same for her sister. It's tradition and she wouldn't abandon her duties like that."

Finishing chewing what was in his mouth, Cavalon's expression turned cold and his attention went back to his plate. "I've been to a wedding before." He motioned his head toward Luella's plate. "Eat while you can and as much as you can. We have a long flight ahead of us. And eat more than that sickeningly sweet fruit." He took some of the meat on his own plate into his hand and dropped it onto Luella's plate. "Meats and breads would be better." All she could do was blink and look at the food now before her. "Eat," Cavalon encouraged, taking his own advice and tearing into a piece of bread with his teeth.

Tasarin was about to go look for Kenayde himself when one of the heavy doors to the great hall opened. The elf watched her slip inside before closing the door after herself. He made his way over and gently took her arm. "Are you all right?" he asked, concern in his face.

"Perfectly so," she answered with a hesitant smile. "Forgive me for straggling. Have I missed much?"

"No." The way Tasarin looked down at her made it obvious that he didn't believe her. "Where is Elas? I left you with him."

For a moment Kenayde's composure wavered, though she was quick to fix it. "He was feeling a bit anxious and needed to feel the water. I don't think he has been for a swim since we landed."

"Kenayde..."

Looking up at him, Kenayde smiled again, this time with more strength. "Come, we have newlyweds to attend to."

"Kenayde."

"Tasarin, please."

Despite her efforts, there was sadness in her eyes. Slowly, the elf nodded, giving her a small smile. "Yes, we have newlyweds to attend to." He extended a hand, letting her go first and following close behind. As she reached the head table where her sister and new brother sat, she wrapped her arms around Ashlynn from behind and surprised her. Ashlynn closed her eyes, smiling warmly and resting her hands atop Kenayde's arms.

"I love you, little sister."

Kenayde kissed Ashlynn's cheek. "And I, you, big sister." She unwrapped her arms and moved to kiss Jaryn's cheek. "I suppose you want some affection as well."

"If you're giving it away freely." Jaryn stood to fully embrace Kenayde, too engulfed in his own happiness to notice anything wrong with her.

"I guess there really will be no getting rid of you now, will there?"

Jaryn grinned. "Absolutely not."

~*~*~*~

The meal lasted well over three hours. By the time plates were being taken away, everyone was feeling the effects of a full stomach. Even the minstrels seemed to be dragging. The sun had fully set, though the night was still early. Sensing the exhaustion in the room, Wessely went to the small band of musicians in the corner and suggested a tune. They all nodded slowly, tiredly, and began to play. The flute piped quickly with a fast beat from the bodhrán drum to keep it in pace. The lute added a nice twang, and people started to come alive. It was slow at first, but eventually people began to stand and clap. Some even danced right where they stood. As more and more people abandoned their seats to move farther back in the room where there was still a great wide open space, the kitchen staff filed in to clear the tables.

Within minutes only a few were still left sitting, choosing to watch the excitement rather than partake of it. Cavalon was one of the few and sat in his chair with his arms crossed and a scowl etched deep into his face. His eyes took everything in with an air of disapproval and he sat back. He watched Luella stand off to the side with a few people, laughing and clapping. Letting his gaze wander, he found Kenayde sitting in her chair, turned and watching but not participating. He wiped his mouth on a napkin of cloth before standing and making his way over to her. "Not in the mood to party?" he asked, his deep voice startling her.

Kenayde looked up at him, feeling very small with the way he towered over her. "No," was her quiet reply. It seemed an answer was all Cavalon needed for an invitation to sit. He took the seat beside her and turned it around so he could face the rambunctious crowd. "What about you?" she asked, glancing at him. "You strike me as the kind of man that would enjoy a chance like this."

"A chance like what?" he chuckled. "To drink myself stupid and make a fool of myself?" He shook his head, his small smirk settling in place. "I do enough of that when I'm sober, thank you very much."

With a quizzical expression, Kenayde looked at Cavalon's profile. There was something different about him. He didn't look at her in the same way he had before, like her very presence was unexpected. Now there was this cold complacency in its stead. She didn't know which she liked better or if she was bold enough to ask him about it. For now, she mirrored him and simply sat watching the dance. It was hard not to smile when someone moved in a funny way, or took an unexpected partner and began dancing around the room. It looked fun, but not the kind of fun Kenayde felt she could actively participate in.

She preferred to just observe at the moment.

"When do you leave?" she asked once another song had begun.

"Soon," Cavalon answered, crossing his arms. "Why?" He didn't even turn to look at her when he asked, "Eager to get rid of me?"

"No." Kenayde's brows came together as she finally turned to him. "I was simply curious. Are you eager to be away from Altaine? It seems you would rather be anywhere but here."

A great huff of air was expelled and Cavalon pursed his lips. He frowned, watching Ashlynn dancing and laughing with Jaryn. "I don't like weddings."

Kenayde shook her head in obvious disbelief. "There has to be more to it than that."

"Why? Do you think I'm a complex man? Trust me, I'm not."

"I think you are." She narrowed her eyes as though trying to see something hidden in his face. "Why don't you like weddings? They represent happiness and new beginnings. They are love in visual form. What is there to dislike, unless you dislike love."

Cavalon tossed his head back and rolled his eyes. "Is this the part where you tell me that maybe I don't understand love because I was never loved myself?" He sat up right again and shook his head at Kenayde. "Let me stop you right there, little one. I've seen *too much* love in my life. That's why I don't like weddings."

"How can someone see *too* much love? Is there such a thing?"

For a long minute, Cavalon didn't respond. He looked angry, but by the time he spoke, the cold distance had returned. "I don't want to ruin this day for you or your sister."

"Ashlynn is not here speaking with us, is she? As for me, my day has already been blemished."

"You're not going to like what I have to say."

Kenayde raised an eyebrow in challenge and the Badarian wet his lips. "I've been married thirteen times." Kenayde blinked her surprise, but Cavalon continued. "I've had more children than I can count and only one of them is still alive. If you stood us next to each other, he would look like he was my father and not the other way around."

"Oh," Kenayde breathed in sad understanding. "Because you're an Elemental. You are practically immortal." Cavalon looked at her long and hard before the realization hit. She clutched at her heart, her gaze going to her sister. "Oh," she whispered.

"Elementals could live forever if we stayed out of trouble. Humans are another story."

"Oh, Lynnie..."

"This will be the happiest time of her life, and nothing she ever experiences will come close to this. Eventually Jaryn will die. Your parents will die...you'll die, and she'll be left with nothing and no one familiar to her."

It was a harsh reality that stung worse than her exchange with Elas on the beach. Looking at her sister now, Ashlynn was practically shining with joy. She kissed her husband and their love was evident in the exchange. There was not a day Kenayde could recall that Ashlynn had been so happy before Jaryn. To imagine him aging like a mortal and then dying while Ashlynn stayed frozen in time was painful. "But that's not fair," she managed.

"No," Cavalon agreed solemnly. "It's anything but fair, but it's the truth." He was kind enough to hand Kenayde a clean napkin to dry her eyes on. "I've known others that have killed themselves once their lover is dead. They couldn't face a world that didn't have their beloved in it. Thankfully, they all had at least one child so their gifts were not lost."

"What happens if she is childless?" It was impossible not to think of what was coming. If Ashlynn was killed in the fighting...it was something Kenayde did not want to think about, but she had to know.

"Most likely you would be next in line."

She nodded, wiping her face dry. The evening was not going the way she'd imagined it. There was supposed to be nothing but elation today, yet here she was, crying for the second time. How terrible it would be to live through love and death, generation after generation. As much as it pained Kenayde to think of Ashlynn suffering that kind of fate, it gave her more empathy for Cavalon. When her tears stopped and her face dried once more, her head dipped in heavy sorrow. "I am so sorry, Cavalon."

When he looked at her he was clearly confused. "Why are you sorry?"

"I cannot imagine what it must be like to live so long and lose so many people you care about."

"There's a reason why I don't get close to people." His voice was low with the honest admission, and for once there was a real vulnerability to him. "There's no point in making attachments when you know they're only going to last a few short years."

Kenayde bit back the urge to argue. For herself, even if she knew she would outlive almost everyone she knew it would be unbearable to be alone forever just to avoid heartache. It was part of life, every much a part of it as the love and joy in the world. "Will you excuse me, please?" Cavalon looked up as Kenayde rose, watching her leave the room before sighing and going back to being an observer.

Out of the great hall the air was noticeably cooler and felt fresh when Kenayde breathed in deeply. She pressed her back to the wall and felt the uneven texture of the stone against the bare skin above her collar. There was no one about, save the ever-present guards, and she felt a fresh sob catch in her throat. Cavalon's information was too heavy for her, too much to shoulder. It wasn't something she wanted to share with Ashlynn, but it would almost feel like lying if she withheld it. Lifting her hands, Kenayde hid her face and let herself weep. Not the controlled crying she did on the beach or the tears she allowed herself to shed inside. She broke and didn't bother trying to stop it. Looks of concern passed between the castle guards as she doubled over, but just when she felt herself starting to sink to the floor, strong hands were around her and pulling her close.

She could still smell the ocean on him, the briny salt and the sweetness of the cool autumn air. Elas wrapped his arms around her and Kenayde buried her face in his doublet. His hand stroked her hair as he tried to soothe her, telling her he was sorry. Kenayde lifted her tear stained face to look at him in confusion. She couldn't understand why he was apologizing for the quickest moment, then remembered their argument. "No," she managed with a shake of her head. "It's not that."

"What is it?" His hand cupped her face, worry now in his gaze.

Kenayde closed her eyes. She tried to take a deep breath and shuddered with the effort. "I don't know how to say it."

Elas furrowed his brow. "Just tell me. Kenayde, tell me." She was trembling and each second made his worry deepen. "Is someone hurt? Are you hurt?"

"No." She was desperate to convey everything in one word. "Cavalon..."

The worry quickly turned to anger. Elas had a clear vision in his mind of the way the Badarian had first looked at Kenayde. "What did he do?" he growled.

"Nothing." With another deep breath in, Kenayde tried to steady herself, to remind herself that no one was going to die right now and that this worry of hers was not even relevant for the day in which they stood. "I... I just need to breathe for a minute."

"Okay." Taking her by the hand, Elas led Kenayde down the long staircase saying nothing even as they stepped out into the cold night air in the open courtyard. She shivered, and when he would have removed his doublet to drape it around her shoulders, she stopped him with a soft shake of her head.

"It feels good." She wrapped her arms around herself and took a few steps away from the doors, breathing deeply. The cold was enough to shock some sense into her and the feeling of air going in and out of her lungs gave her a center. She lifted her face, looking at the inky black above her. Time must have passed a lot quicker than she realized. Pin pricks of light twinkled in stars above her. "Another clear night," she commented idly, feeling herself calm some.

"They say it will frost tonight." Elas stood with his arms hanging loosely at his sides. "Winter is coming."

Kenayde nodded mutely. The first snow had been a joy of hers for years. A blanket of white drifting down from Heaven to cover everything and make it new again felt like a rebirth. It was symbolic of a fresh beginning. Everything was white and clean. This year the white would be stained with rivers of red. The very thought gave her another shudder, and this time Elas stepped forward. He put his hands on her arms to try and rub some warmth back into her chilly skin.

"Can you tell me now?"

One more deep breath and Kenayde nodded as she turned to face him. "Cavalon and I were talking while everyone else was dancing. He reminded me that Elementals are nearly immortal and that Ashlynn will watch us all die." She saw the anger in his eyes. "I asked to hear it, Elas. I wanted to know why he was always so indifferent to everyone and everything. He told me the truth and I wasn't prepared to hear it."

Still, Elas frowned. "You know that is nothing you have to worry about for a very long time, right?"

"The war..."

"Will not be her end." He stopped rubbing her arms but kept his hands on her shoulders. "Your sister is strong. She knows exactly what she is capable of."

Kenayde nodded with some reluctance. "She also has a fierce love of this land, Elas. She would give her life to save it." She felt the bubble of emotion in her chest but worked to push it down. "What do I do? Do I tell her of our conversation? I feel like I have to."

"Why?"

"Because she is my sister and the person I tell everything to."

Elas looked past her in a moment of thought. "Sometimes it is better to keep some secrets." Kenayde opened her mouth to argue, but Elas looked at her and quickly cut her off. "What would Ashlynn gain from knowing that Jaryn will die and that she will have to continue life without him?"

Kenayde was all but pouting, her eyes large. "Nothing."

"How would you feel if you were her? If you knew without a doubt that your future would hold such a crippling pain?"

"I would feel like now is worthless if it couldn't last forever."

Elas gave her a small sad smile. "Exactly." He lifted a hand to brush the hair from her face. "Look at what it has done to you. It would only be worse for her."

"I know you're right," Kenayde whispered, looking down. "This knowledge just feels like such a burden."

"You do not carry it alone." His reminder was gentle. "I am here, and I will help you if you let me." She looked up again, heavyhearted, and he held her gaze as he continued. "I *am* sorry. Sorry that you have this knowledge, sorry that it hurts you so much. And I am sorry for drawing the first blood."

"It was my fault."

"No," he argued in a quiet tone. "I've been feeling all out of sorts for days and my humanity level simply broke today. As I walked away from you, I didn't feel bad for hurting you. In fact, I felt nothing. I was numb. But as soon as I was in the water, as soon as I felt the currents washing over my body, I felt like I was alive again. For a few moments I felt such elation. Then I was crushed with the knowledge of the way I acted toward you and the things I said." He looked at the ground briefly. "Nothing I said was a lie. You have to know that. It simply could have been said differently, if it needed to be said at all."

Kenayde inclined her head to the side. "You really feel unworthy around me?"

"Yes." It looked like the admission physically pained him. "I feel unworthy because I feel so much...and deep down I know that you deserve so much better than what I have to offer."

"I always thought that was for me to decide."

It was with hesitation that Elas met Kenayde's gaze. "I love you, Kenayde. I think I loved you the moment I saw you fall off that ladder and into the water."

"Y...you saw that?" It was hard to decide which revelation was more shocking. She was soaked through with hair all wet and clinging in clumps around her face. Yet he was telling her that he loved her. No one had ever said that to her before, outside of family. She was just Ashlynn's little sister. It was the older sister who always got the attention and the suitors. Ashlynn would be queen of a large kingdom with a rich history. Kenayde would only be queen of Oceana some day in the far off future, a tiny kingdom with a small castle on top of a cliff. In comparison, who could blame anyone for overlooking her? "You love me?" Her question was almost unheard, her voice so quiet.

"I do." He looked downcast at the admission, confusing Kenayde.

"Does that make you sad?"

This drew a quiet laugh from him. "No, and in a way...yes."

"Why?"

"What can I offer you? I have no family, no money. I live in a tunnel underneath an old monastery and most of the time, I'm a dragon."

Kenayde frowned, searching his eyes. "Is that all love is to you, what you can offer someone? Is a dowry so important?"

"No, but..." He stopped, not because she was going to interrupt him, but because of how large her eyes grew and how excited she suddenly seemed. "What?"

"Elas! Do you know where I live?"

He shook his head. "Aren't we standing before it?"

"No!" She was no longer smiling, but grinning. "I mean...sometimes. But

189

remember what I told you the other night? My real home is at Oceana. I live on top of a cliff that is right on the *ocean*!"

Elas looked down, pieces falling into place as realization hit him. "You will have your own kingdom."

"On the ocean!"

Elas dropped his arms and his gaze, backing away from Kenayde slightly. He shook his head as he replayed her words. "You have your own kingdom. Kenayde, some day you will be a queen."

"Yes." She couldn't understand why she was the only one excited. In fact, Elas looked a little worried. When he looked at her again, her suspicions were confirmed. "Why? What is it?"

"Kenayde..." The way he said her name made it sound like she should understand completely what was running through his mind. She was going to be queen and if he stayed with her the way he wanted to, if Wessely even allowed it, Elas would be king. No kingdom should have a king they couldn't even look at. There was a hurt there that Kenayde was slow to interpret, but when she did, her excitement completely vanished.

"I feel like we are back on the beach."

"Not everyone sees me the way you do."

"Does everyone else matter as much as I do?" It was a question that had no good answer. She closed the distance between them and took his face in her hands. "When I look at you I see a man with passion, conviction, and a strong sense of duty. I see someone beautiful and courageous."

"What about when you look at the other side of me?"

Kenayde looked into both of his eyes, different as they were, and settled into a determined expression. "I see no other side of you. What I see is all of you. I *love* all of you. Is that not enough?"

For a long moment all he could do was stare back into her eyes. They had been his ocean when he was on dry land. Now, the shade of their blue was so deep and so intense he felt he might drown in them. It was such a foreign sensation, but one he wanted to hold on to for the rest of his life if it was at all possible. The passion Kenayde spoke of was what gave him the push to take her in his arms and cover her mouth with his. Kenayde startled at first, but soon wound her arms around his neck and gave in to the kiss.

When they parted, Kenayde gazed up at him with a smile, running her fingers through the damp blue hair at the base of his neck. "I have never felt like this before. This day has taken me from high to low, to even lower, to right back to where I started." She sighed heavily, though never losing her smile. "I am exhausted."

"I know how to cure that," Elas offered quietly.

"You do?"

He grinned, looking like a prince and a strange monster all at once. Grabbing Kenayde by the hand, he headed back inside. By the time they reached the great hall, only Cavalon was seated and the room was heated with people dancing. Elas spun Kenayde once, grinning at her before they joined in with the large group to enjoy the music and each other.

~*~*~*~

It was very late when Cavalon and Luella prepared to set off. Both were full of food and ready for the journey that lay ahead. The wind was fierce and biting as Cavalon, in his enormous dragon form, beat his wings to give himself elevation. Since Luella was still testing out her abilities, they would travel by air to begin, then when their destinations would be closer together, they would travel through their elements.

Luella stood with Ashlynn and Jaryn on the parapet. Kenayde, Elas, and Tasarin had all come to see the pair off. She and Ashlynn were embracing one last time. "I am so very happy for you," Luella told her friend.

"Thank you for staying," replied Ashlynn. Breaking the embrace, she held Luella's hands a moment. "Be safe, my sister. Do what you must, but try not to stay away too long. I fear I have grown so used to seeing you here that I will feel the lack of your presence too greatly."

Luella grinned and looked over Ashlynn's shoulder at Jaryn. "Something tells me you will not have time to worry about that."

Cavalon trumpeted above them, causing them all to look skyward. His hulking white figure soared high overhead in impatience. Trying to hurry, Luella said a quick goodbye to Jaryn, Kenayde, and Elas. When it came time to bid farewell to Tasarin, she hesitated before him. "Please be safe." He was the first to break the silence between them, and Luella nodded her head.

"I will. Tasarin..."

The elf gave her a small smile when she did not continue. "It is forgotten."

She returned the smile, then threw her arms around his neck. "Keep them safe for me while I'm gone."

"You have my word."

"And you as well. Keep yourself safe." Giving him one final squeeze, she whispered, "I will come back to you," before letting him go.

As the group stepped back, they watched the transformation that made Luella wince in pain and change so drastically in shape. Soon she was in the sky, half Cavalon's size and almost invisible against the darkness. As the pair of dragons sped away, their friends watched, each praying for their safe journey and a speedy return.

D. E. Morris

CHAPTER SEVENTEEN

The bowels of the castle were dark and filled with stale air. It was not a place Merrik enjoyed visiting, even if he understood the necessity of it. If the dungeons were practically uninhabitable, this was even worse. He traveled downward on old stone steps, so far down that it felt as though he were moving into the center of the earth itself. With a torch in hand to help him see the way, Merrik was slick with sweat. No air circulated and the heat and stench of dead things was making him sick.

This was a place of which Laidley did not know. Tadhg hadn't even known this passageway existed. It was a pathway to the the very darkest part of the dungeon and a place many would run from.

"Seeker."

Merrik paused where he stood on the long curving staircase. He was not even to his destination, yet the voice had clearly spoken. "Seeker," it repeated when Merrik did not reply.

"My lord," he answered with a bow of his head. There was a moment of silence before, "Enter," echoed deeply around him. The wall began to glow as a door was carved into existence. It swung in heavily and Merrik entered. He never knew when the door would come or where it would lead, but he never hesitated in entering.

The room he walked into was nothing more than a cave. There was no distinct shape to the walls or the ceiling, only the floor was somewhat flat. There was nothing inside but scattered stones and boulders, no table or chairs, no windows. As an odd blue light filtered into the room from an undetectable source, a high elevated throne phased into existence. It was large and Gothic in style, the look of it mimicking a castle with its tall turrets and spires, gold and cushioned with black velvet. It was the most regal and terrifying thing Merrik had ever seen. Though no one was seated on the throne, he went down on one knee and bowed his head deeply.

"Seeker," said the unseen voice for a third time. "Too many days have passed since last you came to me."

"Forgive me," Merrik pleaded, fear an undercurrent to his quiet voice. "Laidley has been keeping me very busy."

"Ah, yes." The voice sighed and it felt like a soft breeze in the room. It stank of death. "The young king. He has had you bowing to him day in and day out. Now you bow to me. Do you not tire of bowing, Seeker?"

"Yes, my lord."

"Would you not prefer to be the one people bow to?"

"Yes, my lord." The hard stone floor was uncomfortable under his knee, but still he did not move. "Laidley has appointed me ruler, should he perish in battle."

"Then it is complete, as I have asked."

"Yes."

"Excellent." Again the voice sighed. "I grow weary, Seeker. It is time I leave this realm." The light flickered, reflecting the weakening of the voice. "Are you ready?"

Merrik lifted his head with a slight tremble. "Yes, my lord, I am ready."

"With this power you will have the world at your mercy and control. Fear not this battle quickly approaching. You will have an army beside you, vast in number and great in strength. The young king will die, but you will rise in his place. No matter the victor in this skirmish, it will not be the end. In you will grow a power so dark and fearful, you will be the true victor." Silence fell around him and for a moment Merrik wondered if it was over and he was dismissed. Just when he was about to stand the voice ordered, "Rise, Seeker."

Merrik rose to his feet, his gaze fixed on the throne as though the command came from the unoccupied space.

"The time grows close when the Deliverer will return. He will claim this world for His own, and we...we must prevent this from happening. We must destroy his emissaries and take their knowledge from them. With every transference of power, our knowledge, like theirs, grows. Our powers expand. Soon, we will be unstoppable."

"I understand."

"That remains to be seen. I watched Tadhg. He believed he understood as well. Now ashes are all that remain of him."

A light from below illuminated etchings Merrik had not seen, forming three circles around him in fluid lines and symbols glowing in a bloody light. The inner and outer circle turned slowly to the left while the middle spun to the right, all increasing in speed. He watched them, fear surging through him with the offer of the unknown before him. There was no turning back now and doubt filtered through his panicked thoughts. What had he just condemned himself to? Would there ever be a way out? With a spark of blinding light, the circles rose out of the floor like sentient beings, spinning so quickly that their light throbbed and pulsed around the room like a drum being beaten too fast and too hard. They stopped on their own but the throbbing did not, and then there was an explosion of light.

It felt like his eyes were being seared with hot pins and the very flesh of his body being torn away by greedy, uncaring hands. He felt the tightening of the muscles of his chest as he screamed but did not actually hear his own voice. Light swallowed him whole, then exploded from deep within him. It shot in beams from his eyes, his nose, his mouth, even his fingers. It lifted him wickedly, letting him hang like a puppet with tangled strings before throwing him down callously to the hard cavern floor. After a few minutes, Merrik managed to prop himself up on his hands, panting as though coming up from being underwater for too long.

"How does it feel?"

The voice sounded different now. There was a harsher rasp to it, something that sounded labored and too long used. Merrik lifted his head slowly and found the throne no longer empty. An old man sat draped between the arm rests like a blanket tossed there as an afterthought. His skin was sallow and thin, showing veins and bones where there was no fat to give him any weight. He wore robes that would have looked fine on a young, healthy king. On the old man, they overpowered him and looked to be crushing him with their very weight. "How does it feel?" he asked again.

Merrik couldn't be sure. For a brief moment he had felt he was going to die. Now, as the pain flowed away from him in waves, he felt stronger with each passing moment. Standing was an expected challenge, but he found himself able to get to his feet without difficulty. He looked at his hands and ran them down his chest as though making sure he was still there. "Strong," was his answer at length.

"Strong in what manner?"

"In every manner." There were thoughts, memories in his mind that did not belong to him. The things he recalled were too old to be his thoughts and Merrik understood better what came with this transference of power. "There is so much knowledge," he said, wonder in his voice. He saw what others before him had done with their power and excitement grew. Looking around, Merrik found a particularly large boulder and walked to it. Even wrapping his arms around it did not let his hands meet, yet the boulder was lifted as though it were no heavier than a cup of tea. With a mighty swing of his arms, he sent it sailing across the room, smashing into the opposite wall. Hundreds of stones fell to the cavern floor as a result, and Merrik took on the stature of a man with a great confidence in himself.

Atop the throne the withered old man gave a weary smile. "Yes, my son," he whispered. "Show me what other manner of gifts you now have in your possession. Call on those that would aid you in your fight against the Gaels and the Celts."

He didn't know how, but understood the knowledge he sought was somewhere inside of him now. Without knowing what it was he was truly doing or saying, Merrik looked at the ground and spoke words foreign to him as though they were demands. They were thick and heavy, sounding harsh in the way they started and ended. Even before he finished there was a change in the air. A thrill of fear ran up his spine, causing the old man to frown.

"Do not fear them. It is they who shall fear and obey you."

It seemed as though the shadows had taken on lives of their own. Eyes glowing red and yellow molded themselves into unrecognizable faces and shapes. Merrik felt the fear leave him as an incredible sense of power rippled through him. Each summoned being hovered at the edges of the cavern, some hulking, some small and shifty. There was a general air of disquiet among them. "They await your orders," wheezed the old man. "Living or dead, none of us likes the quiet before the raging storm."

"Is that what they are, then?" Merrik asked, unable to pull his gaze from the dark beings. "The dead?"

The old man gave a weak shrug. "Who is to say?" He peered at Merrik. "Does the unknown frighten you? Perhaps my choice in you was incorrect."

"No." Now Merrik looked at his sire. "No, I'm not afraid. Teach me what it is that I am now."

"There is no time." If it was at all possible, the old man looked worse than when he had first appeared. He looked to be decaying. "It is best to learn what it is you can do on your own." As he spoke, his form faded. "Perhaps it will be best to test your new abilities against your new charges."

Merrik nodded, fighting a frown. It would serve in letting him evaluate what he was capable of and would show these demons, if that's was what they were, who their new master was. A breeze ran through the room and without looking, Merrik knew the old man was gone. Spreading his feet to a bracing position, he decided not to draw his sword. He wanted to see what he was capable of with bare hands alone.

"Now then, who wants to show me what they can do?" The blue light in the room deepened and darkened as a surge of black rushed forward in one wave of motion.

Merrik grinned before he was consumed.

~*~*~*~

While the men and women of the Celtique Isles went ahead with preparations, so too was Laidley deep in the motions of preparing his people. It was daily that he began meeting with his Privy Council. Daily that reports would come in of what ships were sailing where and with how many. Merrik attended each meeting as he should, but as the days went by he began to almost hover over Laidley, whispering things in the younger man's ear when the other men were otherwise distracted or didn't appear to be paying attention.

There were rumors fluttering through court that Merrik was indeed the real force behind the war. And it was true that the commanding young prince who had decided on this course of action was changing in subtle ways day by day. Moments of insecurity had been there his first days as king; he was slow to give orders before thinking them through. Now he was becoming reckless, seemingly spitting out the first thing that came to mind when asked for direction. Oftentimes Merrik would suggest a course of action and Laidley would easily agree.

A call to arms was issued and men came in from a multitude of lesser kingdoms. There were long days filled with harsh training and unforgiving skirmishes. Merrik was far from soft and encouraging. He demanded the best from the best.

It was a week before they were to set sail for Siness that Merrik's men arrived. The weary knights stood in watch as the new fighters poured through the castle gates like black water. Hulking men with pale white faces and red eyes. Smaller men with seemingly no weight to them at all, men with misshapen hands or faces. They didn't talk but grunted and growled, moving with an alien elegance and flowing as though pushed by the current of the wind.

Some of them were not so terrifying to look at, though the others quickly realized they had the potential to be more dangerous than their uglier companions. They charmed with looks and whispered promises. And when a man was vulnerable enough he was laid out by a quick and sudden attack.

This army would not be easily defeated.

"Where did you find them?" Laidley asked. It was their last night of training and he was there to inspect as much as to observe.

"Your Highness." Robert Drakken approached Laidley and spared the older man from answering. There was something dark behind his gaze that instantly had Laidley's attention.

"What is it?"

"There is a storm approaching from the west. It will be here in two days at the earliest."

"What does it bring us?"

"Snow and freezing rain. It is of my opinion that we leave tonight."

Laidley frowned in thought. He really wanted to wait, to have the snow with them as they sailed into harbor. It would be a fantastic effect. "What if we leave the morning it will arrive?"

"I would advise against it." Both Drakken and Laidley looked at Merrik. "It is a fast moving storm and will beat us to Siness if we wait for morning." Merrik looked at Drakken with something close to a sneer. "I have also been receiving weather reports."

"Of course," Drakken replied tightly.

"We should leave tonight." Merrik turned his attention to Laidley. "Then we will sail in just ahead of the storm. If we sail in with it, our enemy will not be the only ones with decreased visibility."

Laidley's lips curved into another frown, clearly disappointed. He nodded to Drakken. "We will leave in three hours. Take care that we're not late."

"Your Majesty." Drakken bowed deeply, casting a dark glance at Merrik before leaving their company.

"What was that about?" Laidley asked. He turned from the men and began walking with Merrik.

"Your council members are jealous. They believe I have your favor."

"You do." He raised an eyebrow at Merrik. "This was never something I planned to hide or seek to change. You were most trusted among my father's court, why shouldn't you also be mine?"

Merrik tilted his head as he gave the young king a tight smile. "When power changes hands the opportunity for others to rise in ranks is also a possibility." He looked over his shoulder and lowered his voice. "You are young, Your Grace, and easily malleable. It is not uncommon for a new ruler as unseasoned in life as yourself to be swarmed with many men fashioning for positions of power. They believe to hold such a place in the king's court would be almost to rule themselves."

"Then they do themselves a disservice." They came up from the armory and into the castle itself. As they walked, the house staff scurried out of the way and Laidley's squire fell into step behind the two older men, awaiting an order. "I am not some lump of clay," Laidley continued in a heated undertone. "I will not be shaped by any hand that can get a grasp on me. Young though I may be, I am not incompetent."

"It will be a long night," said Merrik, smoothly transitioning into a different subject. "Permit me to see to the final details while you find your chambers and rest."

It was the strangest thing; Laidley wasn't tired at all. In fact he was excited about their imminent departure and the coming battle. But at Merrik's suggestion of sleep, he felt as though his body were at least a hundred pounds heavier. A yawn passed his lips and Laidley's brow wrinkled. "I am tired," he said in quiet surprise. "I didn't realize it until you mentioned sleep. Perhaps it would be wise to take just a small nap."

"Try not to let worry of our journey keep you awake. I'll see that everything is taken care of."

"I have no worry of that with you around." With a clap on Merrik's shoulder, Laidley turned for his chambers and left the older man to his business.

Eight vessels were laden with supplies and crew members, dipping slowly left and right in the motion of the waves. Just before midnight, Laidley and Merrik stood on the shore watching crews bring crates off the ships while more carried on swords, pikes, and maces. It was the first time Laidley had been outside in days, having spent much of the time in strategical meetings. All his thoughts, all his plans from the council meeting, had been gently dismissed by Merrik. He had better ideas, better plans. And he told Laidley so often that the younger man now fully believed him. He was beginning to believe everything Merrik told him.

Laidley's sanity was leaving him in small streams as the days passed. The war, Merrik's promise of carnage, had him seeing only the battle and not what would happen after it was over. Laidley told him that he ached, almost physically, to feel his sword tear through the bodies of his enemies, and to return home to a people that would always fear and love him. His greatest wish was to be loved.

"We are almost ready to board." Merrik turned his gaze to the ships. Within moments, the crew had all but disappeared below decks and men started to board. He watched with dark interest.

"Merrik, you never did tell me where you found these others that are so willing to aid us."

The older man shifted, resting a hand atop the hilt of his sword for comfort. "They were ready to fight, my King, and answered the call. I thought their origins would be of little importance."

"True enough."

"They are skilled warriors, if that worries you." As though sensing they were being spoken of, several faces turned in the direction of the two men. Despite being so far away, their gaze on him sent a thrill of excitement up Merrik's spine. They looked first at Laidley before very plainly looking to Merrik as if awaiting an order. The nod of his head was imperceptible to anyone but them, and they continued in their assigned tasks.

Laidley had obvious discomfort in their presence, but Merrik was quick to whisper it away. He assured the young king that they obeyed Merrik and that was what truly mattered. With these strange fighters their numbers greatly increased and gave their army more of a confidence than before. Altaine was high and in the middle of a town; it wasn't built for war. They couldn't hold against great numbers for long, and despite the time they had to prepare, Merrik couldn't have been more sure of their victory.

"A full day and night of travel at sea," Laidley lamented. "We will be vulnerable."

"Only by appearance," promised Merrik. "I assure you, Your Majesty, we' will be well protected. Should anyone attempt an attack by air or by water, we are far from vulnerable."

Laidley raised a brow and looked at the older man. After a breath he clapped Merrik and said, "If you are confident, I am confident."

"Leave the worrying to me," Merrik said. As Laidley wandered away to find his quarters below deck, Merrik's fist tightened around the hilt of his sword. The young man was becoming a nuisance. This was Merrik's army, Merrik's war. The victory would be his. It behooved him to let Laidley play king for now, but if in the end he was still standing, Merrik would have to be the one to kill him. Weeks ago there would have been hesitance at the thought, even sorrow.

Now he practically longed for it.

D. E. Morris

CHAPTER EIGHTEEN

Ashlynn stood at the window of one of the castle's three tall watch towers and frowned, watching the preparations far below with a scowl on her face. The idea of losing her own people put a rock in her stomach. It was her fault this war was coming to their lands. Her fault that some of them would not see the peace that would come after the enemy was defeated. Though fighting in Siness had always been the plan, the ramifications of such a heavy battle were only now fully settling into her thoughts. It made her feel heavy and she let go of a breath that came out in a hot gush that fogged the window and her view.

"That was a very labored sigh."

Ashlynn turned her head to see Wessely coming up into the watch tower from the stairs below. She gave him a fleeting smile before returning her attention out the window. "I wish there was more I could do to protect them."

Wessely joined her with a nod. "It is never easy when you must choose a path that will take someone's life. They know what comes, heartling. They know why they fight."

"That hardly makes it easier." She watched the village and the small dots of people moving to and fro. "I feel like I have condemned them."

"It was their choice. You made that very clear."

Ashlynn looked up at Wessely with a wrinkled brow. "What would you say if your king asked you to fight? Would you hide with the women and children?"

Wessely shook his head. "No. I would fight for my king and my country."

"Why?"

"To run would mean cowardice."

"Precisely." Ashlynn shook her head. "We should have gone back as soon as that messenger was sent here. We should have attacked Laidley and not lain in wait for him to come here. This, what we are planning, what we

200

anticipate...this will be a slaughter."

Turning his body so that he completely faced Ashlynn, Wessely appeared frustrated, almost angry. "How can you say that? If you do not have faith that this battle will be in our favor, how can you expect your people to? You are their queen now, Ashlynn. As much as they held you as such before, they will look to you even more with that crown on your head."

"Is it my duty then, to pretend I do not fear for their lives?"

The frustration smoothed some giving way to an aged looked that Ashlynn had never really noticed about her father. "Yes," he said quietly. "I know it sounds callous, but in this situation it is the best thing you can do for them." His lips curled into a slight frown. "The term is not 'fearless leader' for nothing."

"But I am not fearless." She wrapped her arms around herself, as much to ward off the oncoming winter chill as to protect herself from what was coming. "I was never more afraid for someone else than I am now. Even when I was inside of Tadhg's castle and putting my very life at risk, I did not fear as I do now."

"Show that to me," Wessely offered, "not to them. Show it to Jaryn because he is now the other half of you. Show it to the Giver, love." Fatherly arms went around her and held her close; it didn't matter that she was now married and the ruler of her own land. As he kissed the top of her head, Ashlynn felt like she was still a little girl, seeking comfort and guidance from her father. "We are on the side of justice," Wessely reminded gently.

Ashlynn turned her head. "I took his life, Papa. Is that not a sin? Does it not say that we are not to kill and that vengeance is His?"

Wessely's chest rose and fell in a deep sigh. "It does indeed. Yet were Tadhg still alive there would be many more to fall at his hand, and with no real reason. What you did was for the good of many."

"Then as long as I am doing right by someone, doing wrong to someone else is justified?" Lifting her head, Ashlynn frowned. "I don't think that is exactly correct."

For a moment they stood together, drawing warmth from one another as they watched the village below. Ashlynn knew that Jaryn and the castle knights would be testing the warriors soon. Gender did not qualify one to be in battle - finesse, agility, skill, and the ability to keep a cool head did. Some of the men would be too old, too fat, or too slow. She could only hope there wouldn't be much trouble when they were told they'd go into hiding with most of the women and children.

"This feels different," she said at length. "Different than when I was in Caedia."

"How so?"

Ashlynn straightened but kept her arms around herself. "I had no care, no

201

thought or feeling for who would be hurt in the aftermath. I knew I was killing a man who had a wife and children. I knew, at least I assumed, he had people who genuinely cared for him and would feel the pain of his loss. Now...now I care very much. I feel for my people, but I also mourn for those families who will await the return of their loved ones, only to never see them again."

"Ashlynn..."

She stopped him with a look. "Don't tell me not to think on it, Papa. My people...even my enemies are still *people* to me. Lives that can be lost. They are not my pawns, so easy to let be captured in order to defeat the king."

"I was not going to argue, Lynnie. Your fierce protectiveness of your people may be the very thing that wins us this war." Resting his hands on the ledge, Wessely leaned forward. "You will think before you act because you want to spare lives. Even if you appear to be coldhearted, which I believe at times you must, it will only be in their best interest." His brow wrinkled. "It is a little like parenting."

Ashlynn quirked an eyebrow. "You now compare war craft to parenting? It is a wonder I turned out as well as I did."

"You have no idea."

~*~*~*~

By mid-day the tournament field was filled with weapons and men and women of every age. They were waiting their turn to try and best Jaryn and the men of the castle. Already several had passed the test and were being fitted by squires with armor that had seen its share of battles. Ashlynn, trading her court garments and crown for trousers and a loose braid, was at the other end of the field testing some of the men as well as some of the women who wanted to fight. So far only one woman had passed while the others, along with a small handful of pride-wounded men, were told they would have to stay where it was safe.

Kenayde was in a nearby field with a bow and quiver, practicing a craft she had not needed before but was thankful she was sufficient in. Alongside of her were many men and women who were more comfortable with the arrow than the sword. With a concentrated eye and a steady hand, Kenayde nocked an arrow, took aim, and hit her target more than thirty meters away.

An arrow shot past her head, making her jump. It found its mark in an old oak several meters back from Kenayde's own hit. She turned to see Sabari, the Nagin princess, grinning at her. Kenayde blinked, slowly melting into a matching smile. "That must have gone over fifty meters!" she exclaimed softly.

Sabari nodded, lowering her bow. "When you have to hunt for all your food, you get very good at distance shots. Sometimes you need to be a lot farther away from your target than you're normally comfortable with."

With another glance at the treeline, Kenayde asked, "What is your draw weight?"

"Sixty-five."

The surprise was quick and obvious on the younger girl's face. "Really?" Looking at Sabari's tattoos and bare arms, she could see the obvious strength there. "I'm only at a thirty-five."

Sabari offered her bow over in exchange for Kenayde's. She pulled the string back to test it before gently letting go to admire the wood. "This is beautiful. Is it willow?"

"Yes," Kenayde answered, looking over the bow she held. "Tasarin made it for me years ago. What is yours made of? It's so light."

"Ash," replied the Nagina. They traded back and Sabari gave Kenayde an encouraging smile. "The more you shoot, the stronger your pull will be. I bet by the time we're done with this war, a thirty-five will feel too light for you."

Kenayde smiled, managing to somehow look confused as well. "I'm not certain how that makes me feel."

There was no chance to respond, for suddenly the sky darkened with a rushing wind. Everyone on the archery field looked up; countless figures flew by overhead. Volarim with wings of every kind of bird, insect, and flying creature imaginable were so numerous that they could have been an army all on their own.

"Our numbers grow by the hour," Sabari commented idly.

Kenayde nodded, watching Nóe land first, followed by his people. "How are we going to feed everyone?"

Strapping her bow to her back, Sabari grinned once more. "That is where my people come in."

Ashlynn jogged past them to meet up with the Volarim and give them a personal greeting. "Is this everyone?" she asked Nóe, looking at the sea of faces before her. They all looked ethereal with their grace and lithe figures. In their light gold and silver armor, they also looked like deadly men and women with spears, swords, and weapons of great potential destruction.

"This is a good portion of us," Nóe confirmed. "My second in command will be here with the rest before nightfall." He looked with pride at his people. "All are well trained in hand to hand fighting, as well as areal combat."

"Excellent."

"Hear me," Nóe commanded. Every angelic and serene face turned to their king as he spoke. "From this moment out, you will take your orders from High Queen Ashlynn and her husband, High King Jaryn. Do not question or look to me for permission. For now, I am a warrior like you."

In one solid action, each Volarim soldier touched their fist to their heart and bowed to Ashlynn. "Thank you," said Ashlynn, moved by the show of loyalty. "Please see King Wessely in the tournament arena. He is keeping account of where everyone is and in what areas people are needed."

As the large group started to move, Ashlynn stopped Nóe from going with them by laying a hand on his arm. Both waited to speak, unmoving as the current of winged creatures flowed around them. When they saw the last one pass by the archery field, Ashlynn turned her head to look up into Nóe's face. "Thank you," she repeated softly. "I know the battle is for more than Siness now, but...thank you."

Nóe answered with a smile and a kiss to her hands. "Anything for you, Lile."

"Don't fight."

His smile did not fade. "Give me a good enough reason not to and I will promise to give it some thought."

She frowned, knowing her reasons wouldn't be acceptable. All she would offer were reasons as to why *she* shouldn't be fighting, and yet she was preparing herself for battle. "I fear losing you, Nóe. I couldn't live with myself if you died here – if Nuala was left to live without you."

A harsh gust of winter wind blew Ashlynn closer to Nóe. His magnificent white wings surrounded her to keep the biting chill away. "Do you feel the wind?" he asked her. "Even though I am trying to protect you from it, do you feel the wind?"

"Yes." There was question in her answer. She could still feel drafts above and below her.

"Like my wings protecting you, the Giver protects us in His wings. He holds us close and may not stop us from feeling the current or the chill, but He will do what is best for us if we let Him. We must not forget He is there, Ashlynn. We must not forget that He is on our side and fights with us. The moment we begin to believe we can do this on our own, without His help, we will lose this war."

As the wind slowed and died, Nóe looked around at the scattering of leaves. The sky held clouds promising rain, or worse, snow. "This is my choice," he told Ashlynn at length, pulling his wing in tight against his back. "Nuala and I know the possibilities. We are both accepting of them and choose to be here. We choose to fight and we choose to trust in the Giver's hand in all of this."

Ashlynn furrowed her brow. "We?"

"Yes. Nuala fights as well. She is not as delicate as she would appear."

Ashlynn placed her hands on her stomach. "I feel sick about this. All of it. I have for days now."

The winged man smiled in empathy. "Rest, Lile. All will be well if you put your trust in the the Giver. He knows what He is doing."

"I'm glad someone does."

Kenayde and Sabari approached, and Ashlynn looked at the darker woman and her bare arms and legs. "How are you not freezing?"

"I am cold," she admitted with a shrug, "but I am also used to the weather. If it would make you feel better, I will wear a cloak when I return."

Ashlynn looked at her with question. "Are you going somewhere?"

Sabari nodded. "With the arrival of the Volarim and the others on the way, plus the addition of my people, there is not enough food."

"I knew we would run into that problem sooner or later," Ashlynn sighed.

"I'll take some of my people and we will go hunting. Eat sparingly today and tonight we may feast."

Ashlynn nodded. "Thank you, Sabari. Your help is much appreciated." Sabari bowed her head in reply before turning to go gather her people. Kenayde started to go as well, but Ashlynn called after her. "Where are you going?"

Kenayde looked after Sabari. "Hunting." She spoke as if the answer should have been obvious.

Nóe and Ashlynn exchanged a humored glance before Ashlynn crossed her arms. "Since when do you hunt? You hate the idea of the cats in the castle killing the mice they catch."

"Well..." Kenayde shrugged her shoulders. "They catch them to play with them. We'll be hunting to feed ourselves. Besides, it will give me more practice with the bow."

It was a point Ashlynn couldn't argue with. "All right, but be careful. And take as many of our own archers with you as Sabari would allow. It would do them well to try hitting a moving target. And try not to come back with too many tattoos."

Kenayde narrowed her eyes and stuck out her tongue before running to catch up with Sabari. Ashlynn shook her head and gave a soft laugh. "It amazes me to see the people a war would bring together in alliance. I've known of the Nagin tribes for most of my life, but I never expected to be fighting alongside of them."

"Like the trees, they were just there," Nóe added, walking with Ashlynn back toward the tournament field. "It is alarming how much we overlook until there is a need."

Ashlynn looked skyward, the dark clouds making her uneasy. "The only people missing are the elves."

"And your friends."

She frowned, slowly turning her eyes from the sky to her companion. "It's been two weeks. I fear for them."

"You don't know where it was they had to travel to find the others." Nóe squeezed her shoulder. "They will return soon. Just remember to trust."

~*~*~*~

It was cold in this strange, unexplored part of the world. Everything was new. The trees and buildings were different, and the people...they were simply beautiful in their uniqueness. Luella had seen some of them before, travelers to her own country. It was another thing to see them in their homeland. She was following Cavalon, lead after lead, on the hunt for the woman called Mei Xing. When it was first established that the Elemental Dragon of Air still lived, they began the long road to finding her. Her lands covered an enormous region, sometimes too crowded with people to move through the light and shadows, or too thick with trees and forests to fly through, so walking was inevitable most of the time. They had been gone two weeks from the Celtique Isles and still had no trace of any of the three missing Elementals, only confirmation that one still lived.

"We are running out of time," Luella told Cavalon as they walked through the fading light of evening in a particularly dense forest. "My brother will be setting sail for the Isles soon and we have nothing to show for our journey."

Cavalon frowned under the hood of his cloak. It was even colder here and he made no effort to hide how miserable he was. They both had been counting the days since their flight from Altaine. He'd told her his hopes were high in finding the others quickly; with so much time gone and nothing to show for it, they were getting more discouraged by the hour. "If we still haven't found her by nightfall, we'll head for Badru's country."

"Badru?" Like Cavalon, Luella huddled under her cloak as she walked, the damp bothering her more than the cold. It settled somewhere deep inside, preventing her from ever feeling completely dry from all the rain they saw.

"Badru is Fire. His country is...well, the opposite of here. It's closer to my own homeland. If Nealie, the Water Elemental, is still alive, he'll be able to call her without us having to go searching for her."

Luella glanced at Cavalon but kept her gaze mainly on the broken path before them. This way had not been traversed in a very long time. Brambles and stones and roots of overgrown trees were carefully hidden among the fallen leaves and had already tripped them both a time or two. "Why couldn't we have had Ashlynn call Mei Xing?"

"Because I wasn't sure Mei Xing was even still alive. As Ashlynn is still so young in the knowledge of herself, she wouldn't know how to call Air even if I tried to talk her through it. It has to be organic, not forced."

"Perhaps it would have been a better idea to split up."

Looking sideways at her, Cavalon smirked. "Right. Because that would have helped you better understand your own abilities. Just throw you to the lions and hope for the best? Who's to say you'd even find whoever you were looking for?"

"Who is to say I wouldn't?" Luella argued. "We seem to be doing a smashing job together."

Cavalon stopped suddenly, an arm going out to prevent Luella from taking another step. His eyes lifted, scanning the treetops. Unsure of what he was looking for or what caused his alarm, Luella looked as well. She saw nothing but the dark outline of green against a white cloud covered sky. "We're being tracked," he said, his voice so low it came out as a rumble. "Draw your sword."

She reached up and pulled her Claymore from the sheathe on her back. Holding her sword in both hands, Luella moved to stand behind Cavalon, her back to his so there would be no chance of an ambush. Something like a rock being thrown or an acorn falling sounded to the left of them and they both looked that way quickly. Cavalon was slow in pulling down the hood of his cloak, as though any sudden movement would be folly. The sudden rush of wind was a poor indication that something was heading their way, but the Badarian closed his eyes and listened, catching a small arrow with a stone tip in one hand before it hit him straight between the eyes.

"Listen to me carefully." His voice was so deep that Luella could have sworn it came from the pits of the earth. "I want you to shift but not completely. Just your eyes. You'll be able to see better."

"How do I do that?" she hissed, staring at the small arrow he was now examining.

"Concentrate. Focus all of your energy into your eyes. Concentrate on the darkness of the shadows and think of nothing else."

"With arrows flying at us, that shouldn't be hard to do." Her sarcasm was thick, but Luella did as was asked of her. She picked a particularly long and black shadow to focus on as Cavalon moved behind her, keeping an eye out for another possible attempt at attack. Before she knew what was really happening her irises widened, taking up almost all of her eye in a brilliant blue, her pupil but a slim black slit in the center. "I did it," she whispered excitedly, seeing everything more clearly. It was a steep contrast to what she had just been seeing. Things in the shadows became as clear as if they were in the light, and things in the light appeared darkened.

"What do you see?" Cavalon asked, still scanning the area. "Do you see any movement?"

Luella ran her keen dragon-eyed gaze over every area of shadow in the forest. "No," she admitted after a moment. "I see nothing." She blinked, seeing movement as she'd spoken her last word. "Wait." There was something small and moving in the trees not too far off. "There is something over there."

"Come on then." With big hands balled into fists and still carrying the arrow, Cavalon started in the direction Luella indicated, irritation on his face. "You should know," he called ahead, "that this probably wouldn't have even broken my skin." As if to prove his point he snapped the arrow between two fingers and let it fall to the carpet of leaves they walked over.

Something whizzed past Luella's ear and sank into Cavalon's shoulder. He growled as Luella turned to see where a possible second assailant could be hiding. When she heard Cavalon hit the ground, her eyes widened and she crouched beside him.

"Cavalon?" She pulled two darts from his skin and scanned the trees with panic on her face. "Cavalon, can you hear me?"

"He cannot, lady," came a female voice from above. "Surrender yourself peacefully, else face the same fate as your oversized friend."

Deciding she would most certainly not go peacefully, Luella stood. A thought had blue and gold flames licking her feet and crawling up her body. "I forgive you your ignorance. You had no idea who you would meet this day."

Another dart flew quickly and found its mark in her neck. The flames died as she lost consciousness and fell to the forest floor beside Cavalon. "No, I did not," admitted the voice, "but at least I came prepared."

~*~*~*~

The smell in the air was what roused Luella from her deep sleep. It was smoky and warm, comforting even if a little more earthy than what she was used to. Blue eyes opened but felt too heavy to stay that way and quickly slid shut again. She was on a bed that felt and smelled of freshly cut straw. Turning her head slightly, she tried opening her eyes again and found Cavalon asleep beside her. The memory of what happened in the forest came back and Luella fought a little harder to stay awake.

"Cavalon." She lifted a hand and touched the side of his face. His skin felt like fire under her icy cold fingers. "Cavalon, can you hear me?"

He groaned, turning his face into her open palm. "Are we dead?"

She even gave a soft laugh. "No." Feeling more awake, she lifted herself up on one elbow. "I don't know where we are." The room they occupied seemed to be the only one in the small cabin. There was a table and a small kitchen area, and everything that decorated the interior had a homey feel to it. Hand knitted blankets were on the bed and two chairs by the wall. Glass baubles on the sill of the window caught the light and cast showers of colors on the ceiling. The smoky smell was coming from a lit fireplace near the bed. Before it, circled into a furry ball, was a sleeping black and white cat.

Cavalon sat up to look around as well. The blanket that had been draped over them was cast back and he got off the bed. As his boots hit the floor the cat looked up and blinked sleep from bright yellow eyes. "Did you get hit, too?" Cavalon asked Luella, helping her to her feet.

She nodded, a hand on her head. "I feel like I had too much to drink."

"Just take your time." He led her to one of the chairs and helped her sit. "Stay here. I'm going to go have a look around outside." After making sure Luella was all right, Cavalon walked out the open front door to explore.

The cat got to its feet and stretched, giving a tiny meow. Despite the dizziness, Luella smiled and pat her lap. "Come here, kitty." Indignant, the cat sat and simply blinked, wrapping her long tail around her feet. "Are you a shy kitty?"

"No, I am just not fond of being held by strangers."

Luella screamed and jumped to the bed, bringing Cavalon back inside at a run. "What is it? What happened? Are you okay?"

"She is fine," the cat answered. "I simply gave her a startle."

Cavalon blinked, taking a step closer to the feline and crouching. "A talking cat."

"Not a cat," she spat, her tail twitching in quiet irritation. "I am a shifter, a Bakeneko, for your information." Her small furry form grew and shifted into that of a female with long black hair and brown, almond shaped eyes. Her small body was wrapped in a silky purple and white kimono.

"Mei Xing?" Cavalon asked.

She shook her head, a flattered smile lighting her face. "I am Misuzu. Mei Xing is my mother."

Cavalon looked at her in awe. "You look just like her."

"Thank you." She looked him over, curious. "You are Cavalon. My mother has spoken of you. She will be glad to see you and know that you are alive and well."

"Where is she?"

Looking out the window and up into the hazy sky, her eyes narrowed. "She should be home soon. The sky darkens earlier with each passing day. She will not be out after dark." Misuzu offered a small smile. "Forgive me for frightening you and for darting you earlier. It is very rare that travelers pass through these woods. Rarer still that they are truly just travelers. More often than not, they are poachers that we need to confuse and send in the wrong direction." The statement was spoken with such distaste that it made the silent Luella curious enough to speak.

"Poachers?" she asked as she returned to her chair.

The girl nodded with a frown. "Yes. They do not hunt game, but my mother." She sighed. "My apologies, my lady. I do not know your name."

"Luella."

209

Misuzu's smile was warm. "It is a pleasure to meet you."

Cavalon crossed his arms. "So it's come to that, has it? They hunt the Elemental here?"

"Not just the Elemental." Misuzu added more wood to the fire, sending sparks up the chimney and bringing more of the sweet smoke into the room. "Dragons as a whole are being hunted. Every part of them grows in value by the day."

There was disgust on Cavalon's face. "What is this world turning into? I understand the necessity of the seclusion of this cabin."

Misuzu nodded. "We have been forced into hiding."

He looked at her. "How is it you're able to shift into a cat?"

The question made her grin. "I can shift into more than that. My father was a full Bakeneko – a feline shifter that was revered more as a demon than anything else, simply because the people did not understand what he was. My father was one of the rare good ones. He was a cat by birth and appearance, but he was many other things as well. I was born human and didn't know that I could shift until I was three." A soft breeze blew through the open door and Misuzu asked, "Why are you here? You have not seen my mother in many, many years, Cavalon. Why now? Is it to introduce this new Elemental?" She looked at Luella. "I saw your fyre. Which one are you, then?"

"Darkness."

Misuzu nodded. "Then I was incorrect. My mother said she knew Earth had passed awhile ago and I figured her child would come to meet their opposite. Forgive my assumptions." There was a soft worry on her face. "This is no friendly visit, is it?"

Cavalon frowned. "I wish I could say it was."

"Then please, tell us what brings such an old friend to this part of the world." The doorway was no longer empty. Mei Xing had made no sound in her approach, though now that he thought about it, Cavalon realized the soft breeze had probably been her approaching. She wore a long wine colored silk dress with patterns of white, gold, orange, and pink flowers. Her long dark hair was left flowing down her back and over her shoulders like liquid night. Smiling at her guests, she could have been Misuzu's twin.

Cavalon stood and crossed the room in two big steps. He wrapped his arms around Mei Xing's tiny body and pulled her into a bear hug. She giggled like a little girl, linking her arms around his neck when he lifted her off the floor in the embrace. "Mei Xing," he grinned. "You smell like the sky."

"My dear, sweet Cavalon." When her feet were back on the floor, she lifted delicate hands to frame his face in her grasp, her smile brilliant. "How I have missed this beautiful smile."

"No beauty compares to yours, àiren, except that of your daughter,

210

perhaps."

Mei Xing looked at Misuzu with pride, lowering her hands. "My daughter is beautiful. But who is this?" Her brown slanted eyes fell upon the face of Luella. "This is a woman of magic. A woman..." She turned her face up to Cavalon's, a wrinkle of question blemishing her brow. "...who is kindred to me?"

Luella stood, feeling disgustingly plain and dirty in her tunic and trousers. She bowed her head slightly. "I am Luella of Caedia. My father was Mortagh."

Mei Xing's eyes lit up, first in excitement and recognition, then turned back to Cavalon with sorrow. "I did not know..."

Cavalon nodded. "He died about twelve years ago."

"How?"

He glanced at Luella. She didn't even know how her true father had died. "He was killed in his sleep by someone seeking his fortune."

"That is terrible." Mei Xing's eyes glistened, showing how deeply she felt the pain of sudden loss. When she looked once again at Luella, she moved past Cavalon to enfold her in a warm and mothering embrace. "I am truly sorry for your loss, sweet child. Your father was one of the most honorable men I have ever known."

"Thank you." Luella felt a little odd about the physical show of affection, especially from a woman she did not know at all. Her own mother had never been a person who showed care with touching. "I am afraid you knew him better than I did." Mei Xing pulled back in confusion but kept her hands on Luella's shoulders. "I was born out of a secret affair. I never knew my real father."

"Oh." Mei Xing clutched a hand to her heart as though this pained her more than the news of Mortagh's death. "He was a wonderful man." Fully releasing Luella, Mei Xing's shoulders sagged with a sigh. "Why have you both come here?"

Misuzu stood before anyone could answer. "Mother, perhaps this would be best taken into the other room. I will get us all some tea."

"Other room?" Luella looked around the tiny cabin, but Mei Xing nodded. "Please follow me."

Mei Xing walked to the kitchen area and pulled aside a rainbow colored tapestry on the wall, revealing a hidden doorway. Luella and Cavalon followed her through and up baked clay stairs. The entire second floor of the cabin was one room devoted to entertaining company. There were plush pillows nearly everywhere, and a handwoven rug that covered the floor. Mei Xing moved toward a fireplace built into the wall and said, "Please, make yourselves comfortable. It will be warmer in here in just a moment."

"Here, let me." She smiled thankfully up at Cavalon as he started a fire, touching his arm tenderly. She found a spot near Luella and tucked her legs under her as she knelt and leaned back against one of the pillows.

"I prefer this fire to my own," Mei Xing explained. "They smell different with the wood. I do not know if you have noticed before."

"I have," Cavalon said, even as Luella shook her head to say she hadn't. "It smells earthy and more comforting somehow." With a fire growing, he now sat on the floor as well. "I didn't realize you were in hiding, Mei. Had I known as much, our search for you would have been quieter."

"Please, do not worry yourself over it." Mei Xing took Cavalon's hand in her own and squeezed. "There are much more important things that need to be discussed, correct? We have so much to talk about and I must get better acquainted with this lovely young lady as well. So much to be done!"

"Well, there should be plenty of time for that." His returning smile was not even half as bright as Mei Xing's. "There's a battle brewing."

"Is there a time when battle is not brewing?"

At this, Cavalon had to at least chuckle. "True. But this one is different. This battle is being brought to the Celtique Isles. A little over a month ago Tadhg was killed and his son, Laidley, is out for revenge."

Mei Xing tilted her head. "Why does he make war with the Celts?"

"Because, Ashlynn, Siobhán's eldest, was the one to give him the poison. It was also no secret Tadhg wanted to find and destroy all the Elementals. We believe Laidley may suspect her heritage and is picking up where his father left off."

In shock, Mei Xing's eyes widened. Her gaze flickered between her two guests. "But why?"

Misuzu came in with a tray as Cavalon told the story from the beginning, Luella correcting the bits he got wrong and filling in what was missing. At length, Mei Xing said, "I see." She took a dainty sip of her tea while she thought.

Misuzu looked at her mother and asked, "May I say something?"

"Of course, my daughter."

Misuzu looked at Cavalon and Luella. "You have joined in with this fight – one out of necessity and one out of loyalty to old blood. What is it you hope to gain, should you win? What will you lose if you don't?"

Luella took a breath and met Misuzu's eyes. "I believe we both want to fight for both of the reasons you mentioned. It is necessary to stop my brother, but I also have a deep love for Ashlynn and her country and people. I know my father – my real father – would have done the same, were he alive to do so."

Cavalon nodded in agreement. "Yes, he would have." Turning his gaze to Misuzu, he added to Luella's answer. "What we hope to gain is our freedom. If Laidley is killed, Caedia goes to Luella. That will make two out of the six Elementals in positions of high power."

"Power is not always the best thing," Mei Xing said sagely.

"Neither is being hunted," Cavalon argued. "Mei, you're hiding here in your own country and you're an Elemental!"

She remained placid, even with Cavalon's rising tone. "That does not make me better than anyone else, Cavalon. You have always felt it does, but it does not. If anything, it makes us more of a servant than a master."

"How do you figure?"

Now her expression was not serene. She looked at her friend, troubled, causing the wind outside to move through the trees with a heartbreaking wail. "Have you forgotten why it is we exist? We were not created to rule the world, but to help save it. We are here on mission. We are to bring the message of the Giver to every corner of the world; to every tongue and tribe as it says in the scriptures."

"I know that." His tone was much softer now. "But how can you do that holed up here like a scared animal? Unless we can get ourselves into a position where people *have* to listen to us, they won't listen at all."

Mei Xing shook her head. "There is a difference between a captive audience and an audience that is being held captive. You cannot force someone to believe water is wet when they know it as dry. They must be open to looking at things from a different point of view. They must be open and receptive to another way of thinking or you will be wasting your words. Or, perhaps, your leadership."

"So what are you saying?" he rumbled. "That we shouldn't fight Laidley? That we should let him win? He'll slaughter those people, Mei. He'll have no mercy on them, and then he'll come after us."

Mei Xing was quiet for a long moment, staring into her cup of tea. When she did finally look up there was a question in her eyes. "You care for them?"

Cavalon looked down as if ashamed. For a short moment his gaze went to Luella and he nodded. "Yes, I do care for them."

"You fight for more than power."

"I fight to protect them, so, yes, I fight for more than power."

"They are your family now." Mei Xing smiled ever so slightly. "I can see it in the way you will not meet my eyes. Do not feel shame, Cavalon. Love is not a vulnerability, but one of the greatest strengths in the world. You have not let yourself feel it for too many years. It is time to allow yourself that gift once more." Turning to Luella, she asked, "And you, young one? Do you care for them as well, these that have caused you pain?"

Luella nodded. "I do. I care for them very much. I will fight to protect them, or give my very last breath trying."

Mei Xing nodded, setting her cup down. "Very well, then." She stood, and Cavalon and Luella watched her with surprise.

213

"Very well, what?" he asked. "What does that mean?"

Misuzu started to gather the tea cups, and Mei Xing smiled. "It means, àiren, that I have seen a beautiful change to your soul. There is love there now. Love that cannot be ignored."

They got to their feet and Luella shook her head in question. "Does that mean you'll help us?"

Taking Luella's face in her hands, Mei Xing kissed her like a mother comforting a baby. "Of course, young one. Come! We must prepare to leave immediately!"

CHAPTER NINETEEN

It took two days to reach the lands where Badru lived. Where they could have simply been there in a matter of moments before, Luella and Cavalon were now slowed down by the addition of two new companions, one of which could not travel through fyre and left them having to fly south instead. Not entirely unlike the area Cavalon came from, it was hot and the air felt sticky, a drastic change from Mei Xing's homeland. The trees were tall and thick, heavy with fruit and flowers of different shapes, sizes, and textures. Birds called from unseen places, exotic voices Luella had never heard before. If searching for Mei Xing had not already proven as much, Luella was beginning to realize how much bigger the world was than she ever imagined. Finding Badru, the Elemental Dragon of Fire, was not as big of an ordeal as was expected. In these lands, the dragons were regarded as the kings of the beasts. They were respected and even worshiped. Upon hearing as much in one of the villages, Mei Xing clucked her tongue and tried to set the poor shop keeper straight. They would have likely still been there, had Cavalon and Misuzu not grabbed her and dragged her away.

After Luella was given precise directions to the place Badru lived they set out to find him. Their travels took them through wet and steamy jungles, walking over soft mossy grounds when the forests were too dense to allow flying. Misuzu was in heaven, a monkey swinging from tree to tree, screeching her enjoyment and occasionally returning with more directions. Luella walked beside Mei Xing, her sleeves rolled up and the legs of her trousers hiked up above her knees without shame. It was too muggy to be embarrassed about showing her legs.

"Tell me about Misuzu," she asked. "She told us some about what she is and what she can do, but I am still curious. Can she change into anything?"

"Anything that is living," said Mei Xing. Though most of her hair was pulled back into a knot, strands of black clung to her face and neck like a second skin. "She can only speak to us when she is in her human form, or that of the feline. This is because they are her true forms."

Luella looked up, watching the little spider monkey sail through the air and fall, catching a branch at the last minute. She smiled, amused. "What about her other forms? Like now, could she speak with another monkey if she came upon one?"

"She could." Mei Xing wiped the sweat from her brow with the back of her hand. "I believe she has and that is why she keeps coming back to throw things at us to get us going in a different direction."

Ahead of them, Cavalon smirked. "She reminds me a lot of you when you were younger, Mei."

This made Mei Xing beam. "Thank you, Cavalon. That is a wonderful compliment. It is true, I am not as playful, perhaps, as I used to be."

Cavalon turned to walk backward for a moment, grinning in a way that was impossible for the two women not to smile back. "You're still just as beautiful."

"You are still the charmer," Mei Xing accused with a laugh. "Have you married again, or shall I finally take you all for myself?" His only answer was a wink before he turned back around to walk on. She waited a few moments before speaking once more with Luella in a much quieter tone. "Or will it be you, young one?"

Luella's brows raised. "Will what be me?"

"To tame our Cavalon." Her gaze on him was fond. "He has found companionship many times in his life, but each time it has left him broken. I fear he will not let himself love again like he did with his first wife and their children, knowing they, too, will die." Her eyes slid to Luella's face. "And what of you, sweet girl? Is there someone who holds your affections?"

Luella nodded, a shy smile on her lips. "Yes. Though we did not part on the best of terms which worries me."

Mei Xing linked her arm with Luella's. "Love is a playful beast. It has no regard for who it tangles with and who may get hurt in the process. Try not to worry, àiren. Instead, tell me of Siobhán's daughter. I so very much look forward to meeting her!"

"There are two daughters, actually. Ashlynn is the eldest, newly wed and crowned. She is a great leader and her people look up to her and trust her implicitly. She has a bit of a temper."

"A bit?" Cavalon had stopped ahead, seeing the women trailing. He caught the last part of the conversation and smirked. "She's got a temper and a tongue on her as well."

"Ah," Mei Xing giggled. "Perhaps she takes more after her father?"

Cavalon nodded. "Without a doubt. Siobhán was much more of a lady than

Ashlynn. Kenayde, though...she reminds me a lot of Siobhán."

Luella blinked, connections being made in her head. "Is that why you kept looking at her the way you did?"

He frowned, not understanding. "What are you talking about?"

"Kenayde! You looked at her like you knew her."

"You will grow to understand," said Mei Xing. "When we have strong connections with someone, they do not diminish through time. Seeing them again, or even someone who looks or acts like them can be unsettling."

Misuzu swung from a nearby tree, shifting in mid-air to her human form and landing in a crouch in the gap between Cavalon and the women. She stood and flung her long hair over her shoulder, a wide grin on her face. "I like it here!"

"Have you found anything out?" asked Cavalon.

"Badru is ahead, maybe a mile at the most. If we follow the sounds of the waterfall we will find him. He lives behind it."

"Wait," said Luella, "the Elemental Dragon of Fire lives behind a waterfall?"

Cavalon shook his head. "He's never been the most sensible of us."

In the very heart of the wildness and the jungle all around them was a lagoon that was hidden from the rest of the world. Preceding its discovery was the fierce and beating sound of water cascading over a tall cliff. The trees buffered the sound well, keeping it in a protective circle from the rest of the jungle. Breaking through the treeline, the four travelers found themselves up on a high path overlooking the lagoon. Even as high as they were, they were nowhere near the top of the cliff where the waterfall started spilling down. This secret place looked like it was forgotten by the rest of the world, untouched by conflict or trouble.

"He's behind that?" Cavalon asked, pointing to the waterfall with raised brows.

"That is what I was told. The Fire Dragon lives behind the waterfall. But the locals say they have not seen him for a long time."

Mei Xing and Cavalon looked at each other. The Badarian frowned. "With our luck we'll find just a pile of bones and a note."

Despite the girlish giggle from Mei Xing, Luella's eyes widened. Only when Mei Xing shook her head did she realize he had been joking. Cavalon chuckled as he started down the narrow path that would eventually take them to the rocky cliff wall. The path was steep and unused, making it so narrow that they had to walk single file. Stones rolled at their feet rushing to beat them down into the lagoon. It wasn't easy to walk over the rough path and Cavalon went slowly so he could help the women when they needed it.

At the bottom, a stone walk waited for them. It was clearly man-made and hugged the cliff wall as it led behind the tumbling waters. When the path ended three feet above the wall, Cavalon jumped down, then turned to help the others. When they were standing as a group once more, Luella's eyes ran up the length of the towering cliff. There was power in the gravity pulling at the water and she did not enjoy the idea of having to go behind it. Even though it appeared the water fell away from the wall enough so as to let the stone walkway disappear behind, the thought still made her uneasy.

"Mother." Everyone looked at Misuzu who was staring out toward the middle of the lagoon. Suddenly there were bubbles, like someone was breathing just beneath the surface. As though one being, both Misuzu and Cavalon stepped in front of the others, prepared to protect and attack if necessary. Cavalon drew his sword as Misuzu nocked an arrow in her bow. The bubbles got bigger as the thing began to surface.

Surfacing like a mermaid from the depths was not the monster they were prepared to face, but a woman. Her back was to them, creamy bare skin covered by long red hair. She turned her head slowly, a wild animal well aware of being watched. "Is that any way to greet an old friend?"

Cavalon slowly lowered his sword, his free hand going out to lower Misuzu's arm. His expression was one of utter confusion. "Nealie?"

"Cavalon. Still traveling with a harem, I see." She grinned, her accent identical to Elas but almost too thick to understand. Reaching up, she pulled her long hair over one shoulder, showing even more skin. "Come to collect me and add to your numbers?"

His smile was slow and lazy. "In your dreams, precious. How about getting out of the water and putting some clothes on so we can chat?"

Nealie sighed, clearly not in favor of the request. She sank under the water and swam over to them. When she surfaced, she folded her arms atop the wall and rested her chin on top of them. She had eyes as green as emeralds and freckles all over her face, neck, and arms. As though realizing Cavalon was not the only one present, she took in the other faces. Her gaze was cold as it swept across Luella, but recognition gave her warmth when she noticed Mei Xing, and who could only have been Mei Xing's daughter. "Mei!" Nealie started to pull herself out of the water, but Cavalon stopped her with a hand.

"Hold on." He pulled his cloak from his pack and handed it to Nealie, who frowned up at him but took it anyway. He turned his back so she could pull herself up and wrap herself in the cloak. "Good?"

She shrugged under the heavy fabric, fully covered now. "That would be debatable." As Cavalon was turning back around, Nealie was throwing her arms around Mei Xing. "It's been ages, sister. How are you?" Stepping back, she looked at Misuzu before Mei Xing had a chance to answer. "You look just like your mother."

"My daughter, Misuzu."

Misuzu bowed ceremoniously. "It is my pleasure."

Cavalon looked injured. "I don't even get a hello?"

Nealie's deep red lips spread into a sweet smile that didn't reach her eyes. She kissed his cheek and said, "Hello, Cavalon. There, all better now?"

"Much," he rumbled sarcastically. "This is Luella."

"Is she with you?" Nealie raised an eyebrow, looking Luella over a little more acutely than she had to begin with.

It was surprising to feel self-conscious, but Luella couldn't deny that it was exactly how she felt as the redhead ran her gaze up and down her body. Still she held her chin high. "We are all together."

"Really?" Nealie's saccharine smile quickly disappeared when she spotted the hilt of a familiar sword strapped to Luella's back. Her movement was too fast for Luella to stop her and before she knew it, Nealie had Luella's own sword pointed at her. "Where did you get this?" the redhead demanded.

"Easy," barked Cavalon. He moved to take the sword back, but Nealie turned it toward him. With a sigh that was more like a growl, he stepped back and held up his hands defensively. "I gave it to her."

Nealie's eyes sparked with anger. "What? You gave her Mortagh's sword? It's not yours to give, sand rat! I demand answers, now!"

"I usually feel much more conversational when I don't have something sharp pointed at my throat." His stance was as nonthreatening as possible, and perhaps that was why Nealie didn't expect his big hand to shoot out and grab her by the wrist. Twisting her arm, she was forced to pivot. Though she was fast, she was no match for Cavalon's strength. The way her wrist was twisted made it so she had to turn her back to Cavalon to untwist it. He used this to his advantage, snaking his free arm around her waist and holding her securely, pressing the sword she was still holding up against her own neck with force. "Now," he said calmly into her ear, "are you going to play nice or do I need to throw you back into the water to cool off a bit?"

"Why does she have this sword?" Nealie demanded through clenched teeth.

"She has the sword because Mortagh told me to give it to her should something happen to him. She's his daughter." He felt her slacken in his grip but did not release her just yet. "I'm going to let go of you and you're going to let go of the sword. Deal?" His hand moved to the hilt of the sword as she nodded, and they both let go at the same time.

Spinning, Nealie trained her eyes on Luella once more. This time when she studied the younger girl it was apparent she was trying to find something of her old friend in the new face. "You have his coloring," she admitted, sounding pained and watching as Cavalon carefully re-sheathed the sword. Moving her gaze to Cavalon, Nealie wrapped her arms around herself. "What happened to him?"

"Ambushed and killed," Cavalon answered simply. "I'm sorry you have to find out this way. Do you know about Siobhán?"

"Aye...I think we all knew about Siobhán."

Cavalon frowned slightly. "Except for me." He shook his head. "What are you doing here? Where's Badru?"

Nealie sighed. "Off to see the birth of his newest grandchild. He left three days ago and I'm not certain when he'll be returning." She was reserved now, irritated without hope of being anything else for the time being. "Come inside. You must be starving." Though her offer was hospitable, her tone and her expression were anything but. Still, the suggestion of food had all of them ignoring her attitude. They followed as she walked the stone wall and disappeared behind the rushing waters. "Make yourselves at home," her voice echoed in the darkness. Torches lining the walls lit with sapphire and gold flames, letting everyone see exactly what type of place they were walking into.

Badru had made a home out of the hidden cave. They were standing in the entryway, a long hallway that led to a wooden door on the other end and opened up into a spacious sitting room. Off of that was a kitchen and several more doors leading to new rooms. The stone floor was broken up in places, covered in mats similar to the tatami mats Mei Xing was familiar with. The furniture was all carved out of a rich, maple colored wood. Sconces of black iron held torches and candles. It seemed impersonal.

Nealie waved a hand to the sitting room but said nothing as she opened one of the doors and closed it behind herself. With the four of them left standing there, Cavalon frowned and went to the kitchen.

"It is hard to believe Badru lives here," said Mei Xing, looking around. "It feels too cold."

"Maybe he's not home a lot." Cavalon brought some bread out to the table before going back for more.

Misuzu hopped over the back of one of the wooden couches and settled herself onto it, reaching to tear a hunk of bread from the loaf. "What do we do now? You said there is not much time, right?"

"Right." Now Cavalon had cheese, honey, figs, and dried meat. "I don't know. Babies aren't the most predictable things in the world." He turned back for the kitchen one more time, looking at Luella as he passed her. "Eat and pay no mind to Nealie. She'll warm up eventually." Luella nodded, giving him a thankful smile. With a pitcher of warm water and enough goblets in hand, Cavalon finally sat down to eat as well. "We may have to go back without him."

"Samhain is only a few days away," Luella said softly.

"Ashlynn must be very anxious," said Mei Xing, spreading honey on her bread. "We must get to Siness as soon as possible."

"We should spend the night here and set out before daybreak tomorrow. That way, it'll give Badru more time to show up, give us a chance to get some rest and still be back in time to be briefed on what's been going on and where we need to position ourselves."

Misuzu grinned as she chewed her figs. "I have never been to war before. I am excited."

This made Cavalon chuckle. "You won't be so excited when you're in it."

"I have known how to fight since I was a child but have never been able to put my skills to a real test."

"You'll get the opportunity soon enough," answered Cavalon. He looked up as the door opened and Nealie rejoined them. She wore a long simple gown of green that left her shoulders exposed and had gold stitched leaves around the hem. Her long red hair was pulled back just at the sides and she looked more like royalty, even in the simple gown, than a water nymph.

She picked up some of the cheese and figs. "So tell me, what brings this hunting party out for our brother?"

Luella looked at her, not at all surprised she chose not to sit with the rest of them but to stand and look down at them. She looked at Cavalon in hopes he would answer. He inhaled and turned toward Nealie. "You first. I asked you why you were here and you didn't even acknowledge the question."

"I needed a holiday," she said simply.

"Are you from Ibays?" Luella asked. "A good friend of mine has an accent almost like yours and that is where he was born."

Nealie looked at her, a cross between irritation and careful evaluation on her face. "Aye, born and raised."

"How long ago did you leave, if you don't mind my asking?"

Deciding to sit now, Nealie pursed her lips. "And what if I do mind?"

Cavalon looked at the ceiling in exasperation. "Will you just answer the question and stop being such an unwelcoming wench?"

Nealie looked daggers at him. "I left a little over three weeks ago."

Luella blinked. "Well then you must know of what draws closer to the Isles, even at this very minute."

"Of course I do." Nealie finished her small snack and crossed her arms. "Why do you think I left?"

Luella was unable to comprehend the meaning behind her words for the quickest second. "You...you knew war was coming and you left?"

"It's not my battle," replied Nealie casually.

"But you are a Gael, an Elemental. How can you leave your people when death is such a strong possibility?"

Nealie waved a dismissive hand. "If I concerned myself with every skirmish that involved Ibays or my kin I would be in battle every day of my life."

Frowning, Cavalon looked at her darkly. "Something tells me that you know this is no ordinary fight."

She sniffed. "Would it matter? It has nothing to do with me." Looking at Mei Xing she added, "Nothing to do with you or your daughter. And you, Cavalon. You have the least to gain from going into this war."

"How can you say that?" he argued. "We fight to protect the Isles and Siobhán's daughter."

"Siobhán's daughter," Nealie repeated. "*Her* daughter, Cavalon. Not yours."

The Badarian rose, frustration and anger in his eyes. "Nealie, they're after us. All of us Elementals. And even if they weren't, Ashlynn is one of us. It's our duty to protect her."

"Duty?" A bitter laugh passed her lips as she stood, glaring at Cavalon. "What makes it our duty? She brought this war upon herself. She is a *child*, Cavalon. A child! And as with any child, she should learn that there are serious and sometimes deadly consequences to her actions."

"If you think this is about the death of one man, you are deeply mistaken. Laidley isn't only after Ashlynn. She may have been the catalyst to this whole thing but..."

"Both of you stop!" Luella rose, hands lifted as if keeping Nealie and Cavalon from attacking each other. The torch light had been spitting and jumping, growing in reaction to the flaring tempers of two powerful Elementals. With Luella's sharp command they sputtered and shrank back to a calm and normal size.

"Nothing will be accomplished by screaming at each other. Both of you, please, sit." For a moment it looked as though neither of them would move. Finally, Mei Xing reached up to gently tug Nealie's hand and the redhead sat with obvious reluctance. Turning imploring eyes to Cavalon, Luella silently begged him to comply; he eventually conceded and sat. Turning to Nealie, her gaze hardened.

"Laidley, the king leading the attack against the Isles, is my brother – half brother. Details are probably required in order for you to have a better understanding, but at the moment I do not like you well enough to feel that you deserve them. His reason for war is the death of his father, yes, but there is so much more to it than that. He seeks to destroy what he does not understand and cannot control. The Isles, the nations of the ancients are bonding together and, in numbers, could defeat him. He will soon realize this, if he hasn't already, and seek to destroy these people one tribe at a time. Once they have been defeated he will then hunt the Elementals because conquering them would mean he is unstoppable. Being unstoppable and untouchable would make him better than his father. Killing the Elementals would make him immortal because no one would ever forget his name, and immortality is his goal whether he chooses to admit it or not.

"If you think that this has nothing to do with you, perhaps you should be teaching your eldest offspring what it is they will inherit when you die because the rest of us will not lie down and simply let ourselves be slain and the mission of our kindred be destroyed. Fight with us...or die alone."

Nealie stared at her, seething. A hard silence crept into the room that let Luella know the older woman would not be answering her any time soon. Shaking her head, all Luella could do was sigh. She turned and walked out of the room, needing the fresh air outside to cool what started to burn within her.

No one dared speak or move for the longest time. Eventually, Nealie's eyes slid to the floor and she stood again. "You're welcome to stay the night if you wish. You'll need your strength to make the flight back."

Cavalon looked at her. "Nealie..."

"I expect you to be gone when I wake in the morning." There was nothing left for her to say so she went to her room and closed the door behind her.

Misuzu looked between Cavalon and her mother. "What do we do now?"

Sensing the worry in her daughter, Mei Xing touched a hand to Misuzu's cheek. "Fear not, àiren."

Cavalon sighed. "We pray Badru decides to show up before we leave. I was hoping if I made her angry enough she'd shift and he'd come home."

"She knew that," said Mei Xing. "She was controlling herself. Nealie will not fight and wishes only to protect Badru from doing the same."

"She doesn't protect him by taking the choice away from him." Cavalon shook his head and got to his feet. "For a water dragon, you'd think she would have a cooler temper."

"Perhaps I may be able to speak with her." Setting her meal aside, Mei Xing looked to the closed door though which Nealie had disappeared, then to Cavalon. "You know how sensitive she can be."

The Badarian snorted. "That's not how I would put it." He shrugged. "Go ahead and try. Maybe you can get through to her."

With a nod, Mei Xing rose and went to Nealie's door, her knuckles rapping lightly on the old wood. "Nealie? May we speak privately, you and I?" There was no response for a moment, but then the sound of a lock being turned gave her unspoken permission to enter. Without so much as looking back at Cavalon and her daughter, Mei Xing entered the room and closed the door quietly behind herself.

The room was as sparsely decorated as the main area of the cave, though small touches told her this was definitely Badru's home. He had colorful pots on top of tables and shelves, books closed and stacked or open to different scientific methods and experiments. A sweet smile lit Mei Xing's face as she ran her fingertips over the pages of one such book. "He has always been the knowledge seeker of our family." Turning her head, she looked over at the large bed Nealie sat upon and the colorful patterned blanket she was idly playing with. "I have always admired his love of learning."

"But not his lack of housekeeping." Nealie's lips twitched upward in a slight smile. "Cluttered mind, cluttered home."

"Ah, but his mind has always been clear and organized, simply in a manner no one else understands."

The two women shared a quiet laugh, and whatever tension had been within the cave seemed to dissipate. Mei Xing moved to the bed and sat as well, touching Nealie's face in a motherly way. "You have changed so much. I can no longer say you are my little one; you are taller than I am."

Nealie looked down, her smile brightening. "It hardly seems fair how you have aged so little and I feel as though I have turned into an old woman."

"Not an old woman, but one who has let the world harden her." Mei Xing dropped her hand to rest it atop one of Nealie's hands. "Our gifts keep our bodies from aging only so much. If we let the harshness of life burden us, it will be reflected in the way we appear."

Nealie scowled. "How is it that Cavalon looks so young, then? I have never known anyone more jaded and callous in my entire life."

The question made Mei Xing giggle, a sparkle in her eye. "Perhaps he has a good moisturizer." This made them both laugh again, but while Nealie's smile faded, Mei Xing lost none of her lightness. "There is the young girl I remember."

Nealie pulled her hand away, her jaw setting. "Don't do that, Mei."

"What?"

"Don't try to soften me with your sweetness and your warmth. It may work on everyone else, but it won't work on me."

Mei Xing sighed quietly. "We need you, Nealie."

"No, you don't." Nealie turned back to Mei Xing, her expression pained. "What you need is to stay as far away from this battle as you can. Go back to your homelands, live a quiet and peaceful life."

"It has not been quiet or peaceful for a long time, I am afraid." Mei Xing shook her head. "I am hunted in my own country. Every day Gaels and dragons are captured and slaughtered simply because of what they are. My daughter's own father does not even know what I am, what Misuzu could someday become, because he hunts us as well. It is rare to find those sympathetic to the Gaels in my country, let alone one who would boldly take a stand for them."

"Mei...I didn't know."

224

"It is my duty to fight for the future of all Gaels. It is my duty to fight for a future for my daughter that is free of fear, one where she will not have to hide who she is." Mei Xing's brows came together. "Do you have a child?"

Nealie's gaze fell and she nodded. "One. My first."

"Then you have a duty as well." Mei Xing took Nealie's chin in her hand and made the younger woman look at her. "You must fight to keep your child safe."

"I have done that from the very day she was born." Nealie jerked her head free, anger in her eyes. "She is more protected than you and I are, were, or ever have been. I have seen to that." Standing, Nealie paced away from Mei Xing and crossed her arms. "How dare you try to use my child against me, to guilt me into a fighting in a war I want nothing to do with."

"Nealie, we need you."

"You need to leave." Nealie grasped the door and opened it, not even bothering to look out at the others. "I can't sleep with you in here, trying to make me feel things I don't want to feel."

There was sadness on Mei Xing's face as she stood, but her eyes didn't leave Nealie's face until she gave a polite bow. "As you wish." With grace and dignity, the older woman held her head high and left the room, not even flinching when the door was slammed shut behind her.

CHAPTER TWENTY

It was snowing when Ashlynn awoke. The sky was dark with heavy clouds that made her not want to even get out of bed. It was warm under the covers and safe, easy to pretend the rest of the world didn't exist. She whined, grabbing the heavy top blanket and pulling it back up over her shoulders as she rolled to her side. Jaryn still slept soundly. There were shadows of bruises on his face from days of hard training. He took as many hits as he gave and it was with pride that Ashlynn watched his combat skills grow. She traced a finger lightly over his cheek, feeling the rough stubble of his skin. Moving closer, Ashlynn kissed him and watched the slow smile that said he was awake. "Good morning, wife."

Ashlynn matched his smile as his eyes opened. "Are you going to say that every morning?" He had been greeting her the same way each morning since they'd woken up as a married couple.

"What if I do?" he growled playfully, wrapping his arms around her waist.

"I wouldn't mind in the slightest." She grinned into his lips as he kissed her. "Good morning, husband."

"Tell me something, love." Jaryn took a deep breath, exhaling slowly through his nose. He touched messy golden strands of her hair, brushing them from her face in an absent manner. "Have I been asleep for long? I had this terrible dream that we had a perfect wedding and our gift from another nation was the promise of war."

Ashlynn's grin turned into a sad smile. "No, my sweet...it was not a dream."

With a frown, Jaryn kissed her once more. "I thought not but felt it was worth asking." There was a knock at the door that had his brows knitting together. "Never a moment's peace, is there?"

"Lynnie?"

"Not when you are a king or queen." Ashlynn pulled herself up into a sitting position. "Come in, Nadie. We're both awake."

The door pushed further open and Kenayde walked in. She was already dressed in trousers and a winter tunic, her blonde curls pulled back from her face in a messy knot at the back of her head. On her face was an expression that had Ashlynn's heartbeat automatically accelerating.

"Sorry it's so early."

"It's all right," said Ashlynn quickly, searching her sister's face. "What's wrong?"

"Elas just came back from his scouting voyage. I think you should come down and talk to him."

"We'll be right down."

Kenayde nodded and withdrew from the room, Jaryn throwing the blankets back before the door was even closed all the way. "That can't be good."

"Not from the look on her face," agreed Ashlynn.

With heavy cloaks on, boots, and weapons strapped to their belts, the royal couple rushed outside within minutes of Kenayde's departure. As soon as the tall doors swung open and the cold air hit them, Jaryn groaned. "Snow?"

"It's early this year." Ashlynn was frowning as they came upon the tournament field. She could see Kenayde standing beside Elas, who was sitting on a wooden stool. Tasarin was tending to open wounds on his face, his arms, seemingly everywhere. "What happened?"

"He was attacked," Kenayde answered for him. "They were all attacked."

Now that Ashlynn and Jaryn looked around they could see the others, too many of them to count, bleeding and being tended to by healers. All of them, they both knew, were water dragons.

"We were swimming a wide perimeter," Elas said, wincing when Tasarin touched a particularly tender spot on his shoulder. "They were waters we'd been through before so we weren't expecting to be met with anything."

There was concern as well as curiosity as Ashlynn crouched before him. "What happened?" she asked again.

Elas shook his head in confusion. "It was as though we swam into a wall. There was nothing visually blocking us so we tried again. And when we tried for a third time they attacked us."

"Who attacked you?" His blue eyes were glassy and Ashlynn looked at Tasarin. "Can you do anything for the pain?"

"I am trying," the elf answered patiently. "These are not mere flesh wounds. There is magic to them."

Jaryn's brows came together. "What kind of magic?"

Tasarin shook his head. "None that I am familiar with." He signaled another healer and took a flask of wine from her which he gave to Elas and told him to drink. Stepping back, the elf wore a deep frown. "Ashlynn, my skills are sufficient. They are not extraordinary, but they should be able to heal him."

227

Looking down in thought, Ashlynn absently watched the way Kenayde's fingers moved soothingly over Elas' free hand. "It has to be Laidley," said the younger sister. "Right? I mean, who else...*what* else could it be?"

Ashlynn looked at Elas as he took a long pull from the flask. "Would he be in with darker forces? Even Tadhg didn't play with things like that. He was a barbarian, but he was intelligent enough to know that aligning himself with evil was the most foolish and dangerous thing to do."

"But is the son as smart as the father?" Tasarin asked. "What troubles me most is that the attack occurred when they were all shifted. A dragon should not come away from any battle with wounds like these."

"Elas." Ashlynn took his face in her hands and made him look at her. "I need you to tell me what attacked you."

He blinked some of the pain away, shuddering. "It was...they were black...small, like summer flies. They came at us through the barrier, speeding and shooting past us like double sided razors. The water turned murky with our blood and when we turned for home, they turned back for theirs as well."

Kenayde ran a hand through his blue hair as Tasarin went back to examining the wounds. "What do you think it was?" she asked.

Standing, Ashlynn shook her head. "Nothing I have knowledge of. Keep trying, Tasarin. I have faith in your skills."

The elf nodded as Jaryn and Ashlynn walked away. Jaryn looked at her. "What are you thinking, love?"

"I don't know," she answered quietly. "Tasarin's right, they shouldn't have been hurt. He is a skilled healer, no matter what he thinks of himself. If even he cannot help..."

Jaryn squinted as the wind shifted and blew small snowflakes in his face. "Can the Volarim fly in this weather? We could send scouts by air instead of water."

"And what if the same thing happens to them? Or worse?" Ashlynn shook her head. "I cannot send them out in good conscience."

"We should at least speak to Nóe about it," Jaryn argued amicably. "They're his people and he's commissioned them to be of aid."

"Whose command he relinquished to me." Her frown was beginning to feel permanent. "Us," she corrected. A deep breath was taken, the cold numbing her throat for a quick second. "If you think we should confer with him, then we shall. Just know my reservations on the matter."

"I do." They turned in the direction of the Volarim camp saying nothing.

Nóe was quick to agree that the danger was great but had no hesitance in sending out his own scouts. He saw the grim expression on Ashlynn's face as he gave his consent and met her steely gaze. "Would you send your own men out on foot if this attack had come by land?"

"I would have no other choice. We would need to know, to at least try and get a better understanding of what we would be up against."

"Precisely." Nóe took a cup of hot tea from Nuala as she joined them inside. "We are your army as well, Ashlynn. It would be irresponsible of you not to use us."

She shifted on her feet. "If your scouts are wounded and unable to fly home, they'll be lost."

"Then I will fly with them," said Nuala.

Ashlynn watched her kiss Nóe's cheek before making for her armor. "What?"

Nóe turned to assist his wife, helping her pull the leather straps tight while she adjusted the thin metal around her body. "Have no worries, Ashlynn. I'm skilled in combat and my healing abilities are unmatched by my kind. My warriors won't fall."

"Not with their queen by their side," Nóe agreed. He looked at Ashlynn and almost laughed. "Put your eyes back in your head, Lile. You're a warrior queen yourself."

"Yes, but..."

"Healing, you say?" Jaryn asked. "Perhaps before you leave you could take a look at the dragons."

"Already done." With her armor secured, Nuala's fiery Phoenix wings shimmered through the back plate to drape a feathery cape behind her. "I gave your Tasarin some of my feathers and he took a sample of my blood as well. He said he will get the alchemists working on a remedy immediately."

"Does he wish to reproduce your healing capability?" Ashlynn asked.

Nuala didn't know. "He will try making a salve first, I would assume." She hefted up a quiver full of black fletched arrows and picked up her bow as Nóe secured the quiver to her back. "We will return as quickly as we can. If anything I may offer will help I do not wish to be away for too long."

Nóe, as well as Jaryn and Ashlynn, followed Nuala out into the snow that was slowing in its descent. All the Volarim queen had to do was look into some of the faces in her camp and they moved to find their own armor. A dark warrior with long black hair to match the onyx of his wings moved to his queen's side. "My Queen."

"Ories." Nuala looked into the one crystalline blue eye not covered by a patch. "You have done much for us, acting as a spy for Laidley. I must ask more of you now."

"It shall be done."

She smiled. "You say that before you know what I ask."

"It matters not, Your Grace." Slowly, a smile turned up the corners of the dark man's lips. "I am my king's man, and at my queen's service, whatever she

229

asks of me."

"Then prepare your fastest fliers and your quickest archers. We know not what we fly into."

~*~*~*~

Within an hour Tasarin found Ashlynn having a cold breakfast of eggs and toast out in the open with the villagers. She looked up when he approached, watching as the elf sat beside her and helped himself to some food as well. "The plumage Nuala gave us was ground and mixed with herbs and warm water. When I applied the potion to Elas' wounds it was not an instant healing but a slow one, but he will be fine."

"And the others?" Ashlynn asked.

"We will use what we have on who we can until the queen returns. Once she is back, a complete healing for the party can be expected before nightfall."

With a nod, Ashlynn finished her breakfast. "Excellent. Well done, Tasarin."

He chewed his toast and washed it down with a mug of icy cold tea. "It was Nuala's idea, not mine."

"Your Grace!"

Green eyes lifted to see a man in leather training armor running in her direction. "Not even a buggering moment for breakfast?" she muttered. "What is it?" If Ashlynn had learned anything about her people in the past week, it was that a good portion of them panicked easily. Half the time it seemed they were struck with fear over things that could be handled with a cool head.

"Something approaches from the south," breathed the man, doubling over to rest his hands on his knees.

"Probably the Volar scouts," said Tasarin. "That was the direction they set off in."

"No," the man huffed. "What approaches is much larger than any Volar scout."

Ashlynn glanced at Tasarin with concern and they both rose. "Show me."

With a deep breath in for reserve, the man turned and led the two back across the field. Running past groups of weary people and out past the outer edges of their camps, he led them to a place where Jaryn already stood, Kenayde and Wessely at his side. "What is it?" Ashlynn asked, coming up beside her husband.

"I don't know," he confessed.

Tasarin's enhanced vision let him spot the cause for concern easily. Whatever he saw made his entire body relax. "They return," he said softly. "It is Luella and Cavalon."

Beside him, Kenayde let out a whoop. "We are saved!"

Ashlynn's eyes were narrowed, looking into the distance. "Who is with them?"

Shaking his head, Tasarin told her, "I do not know. It appears to be two more dragons."

"They must be the..." Kenayde's bottom lip stuck out as she calculated. "Wait, shouldn't there be three other dragons with them instead of two?"

Jaryn shrugged. "Perhaps it wasn't as easy to locate the other Elementals as Cavalon thought it would be."

Turning to the man who'd led them there, Ashlynn had specific orders in mind. "Go up to the castle and tell the kitchen to prepare a meal. Have my servants find clothes for them to change into and baths ready to be filled."

"Yes, Your Highness."

As the man left, Ashlynn put her hands on her hips and went back to watching the approaching dragons. "I was beginning to wonder if they were going to decide to come back or not."

"It is Cavalon," stated Tasarin flatly. "I am surprised he did not wait until we were at our end and then swoop in to save us all."

Jaryn grinned, crossing his arms over his chest. "Aye, that does sound like something he'd do."

"But not Luella." Ashlynn was absolutely certain of that. "She would be the one to direct them back here."

"Lynnie, do you think we can win without all the Elementals?"

"Of course." Moving to stand beside her sister, Ashlynn linked an arm with Kenayde's. Blue eyes met green and Ashlynn gave her a smile of confidence. "Fear not, little sister."

"From the west." Everyone looked in the direction Wessely was pointing. The Volar scouts had returned. "By my count," said the king, "all who left have also returned."

"Stay here," Jaryn told Ashlynn. "Your father and I will meet with Nuala and hear her report. You welcome back our weary friends." He kissed her before heading back toward the tournament fields with Wessely.

"I've missed Luella," Kenayde confessed.

"Cavalon," said Ashlynn, "not as much." Ashlynn and Tasarin shared a grin, but Kenayde was quick to give them a reprimanding frown.

"You do yourself a disservice, thinking him so one dimensional as to only be an annoyance."

Her words surprised both of them, though Tasarin spoke before Ashlynn could. "I saw you speaking with him during the wedding feast. Does this mean you have become friends with him?"

Kenayde gave a small shrug and returned her gaze to the sky. "Perhaps not friends, but not enemies. I understand him better now and find myself having sympathy for him."

"Sympathy?" scoffed Ashlynn. "For Cavalon?"

"He has walls," stated the younger sister quietly. "One can hardly blame him for them." Tasarin and Ashlynn shared another look, but said nothing more.

~*~*~*~

"Nuala."

The winged queen was being helped out of her armor as Jaryn and Wessely entered the camp. She and her companions looked no worse for the wear and there were no signs of any damage done to them. "We found nothing," she reported instantly. "Our perimeter was wide, as wide as Elas and his kin went, I believe. There was nothing to be seen above the water."

Wessely frowned. "Then you believe the threat comes from under the ocean?"

"I cannot say for certain." Her wings shimmered into nothingness so the back plate of her armor could be undone and taken off. "What I do know is that the wounds I saw on those men and women were real. Whatever it is that attacked them was real but isn't there anymore."

Jaryn looked at Wessely. "Ashlynn spoke of dark magics. Do you think it's really what we'll be fighting against?"

"It is hard to say," Wessely replied solemnly. "Nevertheless, we should prepare for the worst."

"We saw your friends," said Nuala. "We passed them on the way out. Since they were coming from a different direction it's possible they may have seen something."

Jaryn had already turned to run back to the others, but Wessely gave a small bow of his head. "Thank you, Majesty. Finding nothing doesn't mean your flight was not important."

"May I speak candidly for a moment?" asked the winged queen.

"Of course."

The smooth ivory skin above her brow wrinkled in thought. "The disappearance of this enemy could mean any number of things. Perhaps it is powerful magic that hides them from our sight or has taken them another direction. Either way, what approaches is not as simple as we thought."

Wessely nodded and followed her into the tent she shared with Nóe. The winged man looked up from a map he was reading as Wessely prompted, "Continue."

"Your daughter is prepared for battle as well as any true warrior could be. To be honest, I am amazed at how well she and Jaryn have brought things together." Nuala sat beside her husband and extended a hand for Wessely to sit across from them. When he did, she went on. "If our enemy was human, I have no doubt we would win this fight."

A frown created a crease between Wessely's brows. "But you believe it is not."

Nuala's nod was reluctant. "I spoke with Ories on the way home. He believes Laidley's captain, Merrik, is more powerful than even Laidley himself knows."

"Ories is keen in his observations," said Nóe grimly. "If he has reason to believe this, there is merit to it."

Wessely's gaze flickered between the two before him. "Speak plainly. Does your captain know for certain that Merrik has evil in his employ?"

"Not for certain," said Nuala quietly, "but I trust his instincts and if he believes Merrik is involved with magic, I must believe it as well."

For a moment Wessely said nothing. His eyes were on the ground and his expression blank. When he did speak, his tone was fairly neutral. "That is an area I am unfamiliar with. All the battles I have been in were men fighting men. I do not know how to combat a demon."

Nuala's smile was small and sympathetic. "I suggest we speak with Tasarin. His people know more about magic, good and evil, than any of us."

~*~*~*~

Cavalon was the first to land, his wings blowing stinging snowflakes into the faces of those waiting and watching. Luella was next, her black shimmering scales stark in contrast to the pearlescent white of the long, wingless and snake-like body of the dragon that glided to the ground just after her. Lastly came the fourth dragon, a beast just around Ashlynn's own draconic size and blue in color. When they had shifted into recognizable human forms Kenayde practically launched herself at Luella, the older woman smiling tenderly as she embraced her friend. "Hello, àiren."

"What does that mean?" Kenayde asked, letting Luella go.

"It means 'love' in Mei Xing's language." Blue eyes slid to the woman beside her, Mei Xing's face lighting up.

"Oh, sweet child!"

As Mei Xing embraced a surprised Kenayde, Cavalon and Jaryn gave each other a gentleman's greeting of clasping wrists. "We were beginning to wonder if you were coming back."

Cavalon smirked slightly. "So were we. Everybody, this is Mei Xing, her daughter Misuzu. Mei, wrong one."

Mei Xing held Kenayde at arms length, then found Ashlynn when she looked. She stared at both girls for a long moment before going to Ashlynn and taking her face in her hands. "Yes," she breathed. "Siobhán had eyes just like yours. How lovely it is to look into those eyes once more." Tears shimmered in Mei Xing's gaze. "You bless me." She embraced Ashlynn, the younger woman tentatively returning the gesture.

"You must be Water." Kenayde offered a deep bow to Misuzu, not taking into account that Cavalon had said she was Mei Xing's daughter. "I cannot wait for Elas to meet you."

Misuzu smiled at the girl before her, touched by the gesture but regret in her expression. "Water is not here." Kenayde straightened, confused. "You thought because of my color?" asked Misuzu. She shook her head. "No, it was just another shape to me. I had no real thought on the color."

"Misuzu is a shifter," said Cavalon. "We figured four dragons in the sky looked a lot more threatening than three dragons and a flying horse."

"But less pretty," lamented Misuzu. She looked at Kenayde once more. "Just the same, it is a pleasure to meet you."

"You as well," Kenayde responded, somewhat shy because of her mistake.

As the others talked and more formal introductions were made, Luella walked through the din of conversation to stand before Tasarin. The elf had been hanging back on purpose and as he locked eyes with Luella, everyone else seemed to fade away. She stood before him, close enough to touch. Lifting a hand, he cupped her cheek. No words were exchanged, but she folded herself into his willing embrace.

Nuala and Wessely joined the group as Cavalon was reporting the ships they had all seen. "There are three of them close to port down by the south-western side of the Isles."

"Beautiful ships," added Mei Xing. "Very old and ornate."

"The elves." Luella and Tasarin parted when the elf spoke up. "More to add to our numbers."

"Their timing could not be better." Nuala looked at Tasarin. "It is possible what attacked Elas was of magics darker than we're prepared to deal with."

"You found nothing then?"

The winged queen shook her head. "No ships, nothing in the sea....we found nothing that would have attacked them."

Cavalon looked between the two of them. "Wait, are you talking about the fleet going north?" Attention on him, his gaze was on Nuala. "We saw eight warships sailing north. They were close enough to Siness that you should have seen them."

"We saw nothing," Nuala repeated.

"Neither did I." Misuzu looked at Mei Xing. "You saw them when we stopped for a rest, I didn't."

Nuala and Cavalon still held each others gaze, both with eyes narrowed in thought. "Misuzu, you were human then."

"Perhaps human eyes cannot see through their cloak of invisibility." The revelation excited Nuala. "Of course! That makes perfect sense."

"You didn't think to shift?" Cavalon was surprised. "You were going to fly over enemy territory in a form that would be easily recognizable? They would have seen you and fired at you without a second look. Did you give any thought into the tactics of your little scouting trip before you went out, or were you just looking to be useful?"

Tasarin stepped forward, moving to stand in the space between Nuala and Cavalon. "Insulting the Queen's guest is an insult to the Queen herself."

"I'm pretty sure Ashlynn can take it."

Nuala looked serenely at Cavalon over Tasarin's shoulder. "Perhaps it was foolish, but our, *my* mistake, has shown us what we would have otherwise been missing."

Ashlynn nodded, expression unreadable. "That humans could be blind to their attacks." She felt a mild panic knot at her stomach. She looked at Jaryn, wishing they were in private so she could really say what she was feeling, that they were all in trouble. Instead she said, "Luella, take Cavalon and our new friends inside the castle. Meals have been prepared for you, as well as people ready to fill baths for you. I am afraid I can offer you no time for real rest with this new information before us. Let us all meet in two hours inside the war room. Nuala, please make sure Nóe is there, and Papa, please find Mama and bring her with you as well."

With the clear dismissal, people started to move. Nuala had her attention on Tasarin. "How are Elas and the others?"

Luella paused and looked up at Tasarin with concern. "What happened to Elas?"

"He and the other water dragons were attacked this morning on a scouting mission." Though his eyes seemed filled with trouble, nothing changed in his blank expression. "They are healing well, Your Majesty. Thank you."

Nuala nodded. "If I can be of any more assistance..."

"I will find you at once."

As the elf headed toward the castle with the others and only she, Jaryn, Wessely, and Nuala were left, Ashlynn visibly relaxed. Jaryn put an arm around her shoulders. "What are we going to do?" she asked dully.

"We will fight," began Wessely.

"And we will win," Nuala finished with confidence. "If the elves are porting to the south, how long do you think it will take them to get here?"

Ashlynn sighed, thinking. "That depends. On foot and with no rest? Ten days at the very least. On horseback and with the wind behind them, perhaps half that."

"Would they be open to alternate forms of transportation?" asked Jaryn. Ashlynn looked up at her husband. "What do you have in mind?"

~*~*~*~

Food was much needed and greatly appreciated. The dining hall was warm with a freshly lit fire, and food covered the top of the table they sat at. Cavalon ate his fill with hardly a word as conversation between the others flowed easily around him. When he was finished and rose to find his much needed bath, the others continued on as if he'd never even been there.

Luella, relishing the warmth of the hot mead in her hands, looked up from her mug in time to see Tasarin sitting across the table from himself. Had she not known he was truly beside her, the sight would have confused her. As it was, she managed a small smirk.

"Remarkable," said the real Tasarin. Misuzu's features shifted and colored, turning her into a twin of Luella. "There are those of my kind that have the shifting skill," said the elf, "though it is something like with the Gaels. There is a great deal of concentration put into it. Your transformations seem effortless."

Misuzu shifted again, now becoming a mirror image of one of the guards. "It is as natural as breathing to me," she said in her own voice.

"I imagine it must drain you."

"You would think so." Back in her own image again, Misuzu rested her chin in her hand. "I could sleep for days after multiple shifts, large or extended ones, but if I do not get it I can still function."

"Though her mother worries for her." Mei Xing tucked Misuzu's long hair behind her ear. "My daughter often forgets she has limits." Looking at Tasarin, she smiled. "You knew my Siobhán."

Tasarin nodded. "I did. Serving her was one of my greatest honors. Never have I known anyone like her, though Kenayde has much of the same spirit as her mother. Siobhán was the sharpest sword wrapped in the most comforting of velvets."

Mei Xing smiled and closed her eyes briefly. "How perfect a description. She was exactly that."

"Ashlynn is not her mother, but she is a good and competent leader."

"So Cavalon and Luella have told me."

Surprise lifted Tasarin's brows. "Cavalon? Really? It would seem all he said while he was here was either cutting or sarcastic. Are you certain his respect was genuine?"

"He is not merely the crass ·barbarian he likes everyone to think he is." Luella looked down at her plate. The words had come out before she could stop them and in a tone too biting.

Taking a breath, Mei Xing stood with a smile that said she was ignoring any tension that was now present in the room. "We will find our rooms now."

Tasarin stood out of courtesy and nodded. "It has been a pleasure speaking with you. Perhaps when this war is over we will have the opportunity again."

"Yes," agreed Mei Xing. "That would be lovely." As Misuzu left the room, Mei Xing went around the table and placed her hands on Luella's shoulders, bending to kiss her cheek. The younger woman reached up to cover the older woman's hand with her own for a brief moment. In the next, Tasarin and Luella were alone as Mei Xing swept from the room.

"She cares for you," said Tasarin as he sat. "The way she touches you and looks at you is the same as when she looks at or touches her own daughter."

"Mei Xing is a loving spirit," Luella agreed distractedly. She turned in her seat to look at Tasarin. "Forgive me for snapping. It has been a long journey and I am exhausted."

"There is no need for forgiveness. Clearly you know Cavalon better than I and take offense to my view of him."

"I spent every moment with him for the past two weeks, Tasarin."

He nodded. "I understand." There was a deep sadness in his tone and in his eyes when he lifted them to look at her. "Two weeks is not very long in the grand view of things, but it is enough time. Enough time to know someone better, to form a mother and daughter bond between strangers. Enough time to love someone that could seem like he did not want anyone in the world to love him."

She sighed deeply. "He is more complex than you know. There are things, people, he cares about deeply. I see that about him now and if you took the time to truly speak to him, you would see it as well." Finishing her mead, Luella rubbed her eyes. "You shouldn't be so quick to judge a man until you've spent time in his company." With a small sad smile, she rose, causing Tasarin to stand as well. "I need to lay down for awhile. Please excuse me."

Tasarin nodded only once, unsure of what to say and silent because of it. When Luella was gone, the elf sat and rested his chin in his hands. He had never let his heart get in the way of his logical thinking, yet it was his heart that ached over Luella's parting words. She was right. He should not be so quick to judge. There was just something about Cavalon that Tasarin didn't like, but with the approaching battle, it was something he was going to have to put aside. They were on the same team, after all. Matters of the heart aside, Tasarin knew the Badarian was a lucky ally to have. If only Cavalon didn't think of himself so highly.

~*~*~*~

237

The noon sun shone high, lending warmth to the crisp air of the early winter. Villagers and knights alike held swords, pikes, axes, and bows. Training didn't break for regular meals, rather people ate when they felt the need to and took times to rest on their own. With Ashlynn's own people, all winged variety of the Volarim, the Nagin tribes, and the dwarven kind, there was little room to be spared. At times the tournament field was filled with so many teams of combat that it turned into a full out melee. Jaryn watched one such battle with pride.

Men and women who had been soft and timid only weeks ago now swung their weapons, pivoted and turned, and took aim at their opponent without a moment of hesitation. Even those who had been wounded just that morning were back in the field and fighting. Elas, in the middle of it all, seemed to have found a fire and an anger in his injuries and this gave Jaryn a small hesitation. The older man could get careless in his quest for vengeance and it might lead to vulnerability. Calling out to him, Elas turned at the sound of his name and barely missed the flat side of a broadsword to his face. He arched, leaning back to let the sword slice the air above him. As he straightened he quickly doubled over and used the flat side of his own sword, smacking it into the back of his opponent's knees and sending him sprawling to the ground. Leaving the man there, Elas jogged through the chaos and joined Jaryn.

"You're doing a fine job out there," Jaryn commended, offering Elas a flask of water. He watched his friend drink and grinned. "I'd hate to come up against you in battle."

"That's the point, isn't it?" Elas gave the flask back and wiped his mouth with the back of his hand. "They've all shown some great improvement. You and Ashlynn have done well with them."

Jaryn shook his head. "It wasn't just us. She already had many fine knights in her employ, and the tribes that have joined us are skilled warriors as well." His gaze had gone back to the field but now returned to Elas. "How are your wounds?"

"Healed," Elas answered quickly, "but still sore."

"I saw you favoring your left shoulder a bit. That was the worst of it then, yeah?"

Elas gave Jaryn a frown. "I wasn't favoring anything."

Jaryn raised an eyebrow. "Aye, lad, you were. I've been standing here watching you."

"Lad?" challenged Elas. "Don't forget who's older."

"By what? A couple of years? You may be older but I know what I'm talking about."

"Really?" Elas picked up his sword and spread himself into a fighting stance. "Show me what it is you think I'm favoring."

Jaryn threw his head back in a laugh and when he righted again, Elas was still waiting. "You can't be serious."

"Afraid to take on an old man?" Now Elas was joking and it was apparent in his grin.

"Aye, I am afraid." Yet Jaryn drew his own sword. "Afraid I'll hurt you and we'll be less one skilled fighter." He lunged and was met with a blocking maneuver from Elas. Jaryn kicked out a leg to trip him, but Elas was quick and jumped to avoid him. One thrust while the other blocked in a violent back and forth that took them over the hill and back again. Jaryn lost ground while Elas gained, then one simple movement would turn the tables. When it seemed Jaryn would finally overtake Elas, Elas hunched himself and ran, left shoulder first, into Jaryn's torso and knocked them both to the ground. In the quickest second, Elas was back on his feet and had his sword pressed to Jaryn's neck.

Both had dirt caked to their faces and blood where punches and cuts had not been softly given. Jaryn's eyes were huge for a moment, but in the next both men were laughing. Elas helped him up and they both embraced. "Right," panted Jaryn as he reached for the water skin. "What was I saying about your left shoulder?"

"Can't remember," grinned Elas, taking the water when Jaryn was done. "But you've got yourself a nice imprint of it in your gut."

The sound of fighting was quieting around them, causing Jaryn to look. Behind him on the tournament field swords were lowering as faces were lifting to the sky. He looked up as well, shielding his eyes from the bright sun at the same time Elas chuckled. "Now I've seen everything."

The sky ahead of them was dark and growing darker still as a mass of bodies soared through the air. Dragons of various sizes and colors flew overhead, so numerous that they nearly blocked out the blue sky. Riding them were some of the most majestic beings to ever walk the earth. As the dragons landed where they could find room, elves dismounted and added to the growing numbers of the Celtique army.

"Wait," murmured Jaryn. Coming now through the sky were three dragons, each carrying two large carts in each claw, each cart filled with terrified horses.

Elas almost doubled over in laughter. "Okay," he corrected. "*Now* I've seen everything."

Much like Tasarin, the elves moved with a certain grace that made them almost ethereal. They wore robes of flowing earthy colors and silken textures. When the last of them were to the ground, the dragons shifted back into their human forms. Ashlynn was among them.

"Welcome to Altaine," she told the elves with a grin. "I hope you enjoyed your flight."

CHAPTER TWENTY-ONE

By the time early evening arrived, a scouting party had gone forth and since returned. Nuala, going with a few of her people and Cavalon, discovered the eight ships that were indeed heading north. Cavalon decided to boldly give the men a scare and, in his gigantic white dragon form, flew low over the ships. He was expecting terror but received no reaction at all. For all it appeared, no one on any of the ships could even see him. He circled the lead ship several times in lazy loops, eventually rejoining Nuala far above them. He didn't need the ability to speak to convey his confusion, for it was mirrored in her gaze upon him.

Testing a theory, she also flew over the fleet. In her majestic Phoenix form she even landed on the crow's nest of one of the ships. The man on lookout there didn't notice her. With the telescope to his eye he did see her companions however, waiting on the wing some distance off but not shifted completely into their spirit creature forms.

The man called out in a booming voice, alerting the archers. Men rushed onto deck like overflowing water, coming up from below in a steady stream. Nuala rose high into the air with a piercing scream; she may not have been seen, but she had definitely been heard. Merrik came on deck of the lead ship and looked around with narrowed eyes. "Drop the shields," he commanded. Nothing changed visibly, but Nuala knew the moment the invisible shields were gone. Merrik's eyes locked on her fiery figure in the sky and an arrow flew through the air without waiting for a command. It all happened so fast that she had no time to react and the arrow embedded itself in her shoulder, making it impossible to use her left wing. She cried again and started to fall.

A trumpeting call shook the sky as Cavalon came down from above and close to the lead ship. His clawed feet scraped the deck, tearing the sails with a slash of his tail. Speeding toward the ship with the archer that had fired upon

240

Nuala, he pulled the crow's nest free and dropped it on three archers readying to take aim at her descending body. As Nuala fell, she shifted into human form and Cavalon caught her on his back before she could hit the deck. The arrow stuck out from her shoulder and she winced as she tried to get a better hold on the back of the dragon. The tall main mast was ripped from the floor of the deck, crushed between Cavalon's powerful talons. Arrows from archers on several of the ships clattered against his scales without damage.

"Turn back," Nuala cried. "Turn back before we are killed."

Tossing down the splinters of the mast, Cavalon did as Nuala ordered and turned in the direction of home. She clung to his neck as his wings beat the air, immobilized by pain and the fear of falling off. He sped past her people, though they were quick to follow. When the ships were far enough behind them that they were no longer even a speck on the horizon, Cavalon found a tiny uninhabited island and landed. Nuala slid to the ground as Cavalon shifted.

He instructed the others to get behind her, each bracing a shoulder. "This is going to hurt," he told her. As he gripped the end of the arrow, he looked at her and was surprised to see her eyes open. Most people, women and men alike, squinted in the pain. Nuala impressed him by locking her eyes with his. "You ready?" She nodded, brow furrowed and breathing rapid. Cavalon took a breath and snapped the fletching off the arrow. She whimpered but did not cry out. "You all right? Are you breathing?"

She nodded again, preparing herself for what was going to come next. "Just do it quickly."

The scouts and Cavalon switched places. "I'm going to count to three." With a bracing hand on her shoulder and the other on what was left of the arrow, he counted, "One, two..." and pulled.

This time Nuala did cry out. Cavalon watched through the hole in her tunic as her wound healed over completely. "You said you were going to count to three," she growled, glaring at him as he walked around to face her again.

"And I thought you'd expect me to pull it at one. Two was a good compromise." He tossed the broken bloody arrow aside. "You heal pretty fast. Are you going to be all right flying home?"

"No, actually." Nuala rolled her shoulder and held it, wincing. "I could make the journey easily enough, but the wound is only healed on the surface. I would rather save my energy, if you do not mind."

"Carry you home?" She only looked at him and he shrugged. "Fine by me. Not like you weigh anything, anyway." He took a step away, making room for his shift, but turned back to Nuala with a puzzled expression. "You're a Phoenix, aren't you? Isn't healing kind of what you do? That, and burst into flames. How does that work for you, anyway?"

"I am half Phoenix. My mother was mortal so my abilities are not as a full blood Phoenix. I can completely heal if the damage isn't great; depending on the circumstances I can extend that to others as well. Most of the time I am simply a bandage to the bleeding. If I am killed, I will die in fire and be reborn."

Cavalon gave a thoughtful huff. "So you can't die at all? How does that work?"

Nuala mimicked Cavalon's casual shrug from a moment ago. "If I am injured beyond my normal healing capacity, I can have a rebirth at my choosing to do so. I will be reborn completely healed but it drains me considerably. I would need a few days to recover. If, at a time of disability, physical or mental, I choose to burn away and leave it at that, that is also my choice. As for being wounded to death, not so far. If I am killed by magic it may be different."

"Let's not see what happens, yeah?" Turning, he made his way down the shore a few more feet so he could shift. "Come on. Let's go home."

Siness had never seen so many faces. Standing on the parapet of castle Altaine, Ashlynn watched the movement in the town below with a calculating expression. There were easily over a thousand people preparing for war. At the moment it was quiet in a rare time of rest. This was the calm before the proverbial storm. The tension was high and no one was spared from exhaustion. The supply rooms were stocked with weapons and full quivers. Hidden basements were filled with enough food and water to keep the people it would shelter for almost two weeks. The thought of any battle lasting that long had Ashlynn cringing, but to have so much provision was a necessary precaution. She would rather have waste than want.

Emiline came out to drape a cloak around her daughter's shoulders, Nóe with her. "There are so many people down there," Ashlynn muttered, pulling the cloak tight around her neck. The wind was cold, unfeeling as it whipped around them.

Leaning his hands on the icy stone, Nóe looked down at the village and nodded. "All together we are ten different tribes and kingdoms."

"Ten?" Emiline looked as well, as though she could count from up so high. "Ten tribes from seven nations?"

"Yes," said Nóe. "My people, Sinessians, the Ibayish, the elves, the Nagin tribes, the dwarves, Caedia being represented by you and Luella, the Orient, and the Sandlands. Oh, and the nine other unicorns Suule rounded up."

"I didn't think there were that many still alive on all the Isles combined." The thought of it brought a weight to Ashlynn's spirit. "Ten unicorns and they could all perish in this battle."

"So could we," Nóe replied soberly. "Ashlynn, we are not here because we are obligated. We are here because we need to be, want to be." He looked at her. "Do you think that you are the only one that loves this land? There are men and women, children down there who are tired and exhausted. If you gave them the chance to leave now, to hide until this was all said and done, I know not one of them that would take the opportunity to be away from this."

"When will you address the people?" Emiline asked.

Ashlynn took a breath, pressing her lips together in thought. "As soon as Cavalon and Nuala return. I want their report first." Thinking tactics now, she looked at Nóe. "Does everyone know where they must be, and when?"

"They do, even the elves and the unicorns."

The smile Ashlynn now wore was grim. "Thank you for being my general, Nóe. I could not have been so organized without you."

With a low bow, Nóe said, "Is has been my pleasure."

A cry in the distance, a loud trumpeting that had Ashlynn's blood racing with a desire to fly, turned their attention to the far horizon. Cavalon was fast approaching. When two Volarim broke away from him and turned for camp, Nóe became concerned. "Only two. Where's the third? Who did we lose?"

Seeing the two, Ashlynn shifted her eyes to the much keener of her dragon form. "Your scouts are the two that headed for your base," she reported. "Nuala is..." Her brow furrowed in confusion as she blinked, green eyes returning to normal. She looked at Nóe. "Cavalon has her on his back."

Nóe frowned, climbing up on the parapet wall. "She must have been injured." Without another word, he jumped into the air and flung his white wings wide. Catching the current of the winds, his body rose and soared away.

"Wait for me!" Ashlynn called a moment too late.

"Go on," said Emiline, taking the cloak back from her daughter. "I've seen you training and know what you want to do." Her smile was mischievous. "Show your people the kind of queen they fight with."

With a grin, Ashlynn gave her mother a quick kiss on the cheek and hopped up on the wall as Nóe had. "Here goes nothing."

"You're going to give some of them a terrible fright," Emiline chided, laughter in her tone.

"I know."

Ashlynn sprang from the ledge head first, hands together overhead. As the air rushed past her body, she heard screams and shouts from people below in the village. Then it all went silent in the moments her body changed. Arms fanned out and became wings, body now long and covered in scales of polished gold. She rose into the air with a triumphant cry. Some of those who had screamed in fright now began to clap and cheer, watching the dragon ride the winds above them with ease. Others, with hands still clasped to their hearts, were trying to remember how to breathe again.

She landed in the field where Nóe, Nuala, and the now shifted Cavalon stood. When Ashlynn was back in her human form the first thing she saw was a grinning Cavalon.

"Nice trick." The compliment was genuine and held a small amount of awe. "I didn't take you as the type to go out for showmanship."

The appreciation of her dive and shift caught Ashlynn a little off guard. "Thanks. It was more for me than anyone else. I wanted to see if I could pull it off."

"And if you couldn't?"

She shrugged. "I suppose I would be walking funny for awhile." In a rare moment of levity, Cavalon threw his head back and had himself a hearty laugh. Distracting as Cavalon's light mood was, Ashlynn remembered Nuala and how she hadn't been flying. She looked at the winged queen now, glad to see she was in one piece. "Are you all right?"

Nuala nodded. "I am. It was a small injury."

"What happened?" Ashlynn asked.

"It was an arrow to the shoulder. Nothing to worry about."

~*~*~*~

The tavern had become an established place of meeting and Ashlynn knew members of her core group would be awaiting them there. Sitting down at a table the others already occupied, Cavalon untied the cloak from his neck and let it hang off the back of his chair. "They couldn't see us," he said, "not when we were shifted. Misuzu's theory was correct." She beamed as Jaryn came over with a few more tankards of ale, setting one before Cavalon. "As soon as they realized something was there and brought their shields down, whatever those may be, they saw us."

"What we observed," continued Nuala when Cavalon took a long draft of his ale, "was that they cannot see us in our shifted forms, and we cannot see them in our human forms."

"Well that's helpful," said Jaryn with optimism. To toast, he took a swig from his own tankard.

Cavalon didn't seem so optimistic. "Not necessarily," he argued. "If we were able to figure it out, I'm sure they were smart enough to do the same."

"So what do you suggest?" Ashlynn asked.

The Badarian sat back in his chair with a puff of air between his lips. "I don't know," he admitted. "If they're thinking, they would be changing their tactics. Now that we know where they are and one of their current weaknesses, they're probably scrambling to rectify the situation." He looked at Nuala. "They were headed north instead of straight here."

244

She nodded. "Most likely after attacking the water dragons this morning they decided to sail around and attack you at your own beach."

Elas frowned. "Why would they do that? After today, you would think they understood we patrol the waters."

"They do," said Cavalon, "but when you swam away, in their eyes they defeated you." He shook his head. "It was the smart thing to do. If you had stayed they could have killed all of you. You made the right choice, kid."

"Your Majesties!"

Every face inside the tavern lifted and watched as a villager came rushing through the open doors. There was panic on his face. "They've gone mad!"

"Who?" several asked in one voice.

"The drags, the ones attacked this morning. They've turned on us and are attacking the others!"

The next moment sent a whirlwind of movement through the crowded tavern. Nearly everyone inside was running and heading for the outside. Only the tender and a few too startled to think properly stayed behind.

There were skirmishes going on all over the place. Men and women who had been on the side of the Celts all along now swung swords and axes at their kin. Some were fevered enough to try and fight with their bare hands, while others had shifted and were snapping and clawing like feral beasts.

From the roof of the tavern jumped one such dragon. It landed on Kenayde and tore four long gashes down the left side of her face before anyone could react. Elas shifted in the next second and threw himself at his fellow water dragon the moment he heard Kenayde scream.

Cavalon scooped her up as soon as the two dragons rolled away, snapping and tearing at each other. He rushed her inside with Tasarin close behind. "I can take care of her," said the elf quickly. "Go help the others."

There was a maddened panic outside. The dragons had turned on their own so quickly that several people had been killed before anyone could really grasp what was happening. Cavalon ran back outside in time to see Elas shifting back into his human form, standing over the body of the dragon he'd killed.

"Get him locked up!" barked Cavalon. "If they were infected with something, there's a good chance you are too."

"No! I need to make sure Kenayde is all right!"

"He's right, Elas," said Ashlynn. "We will make sure Kenayde is taken care of. Go. You need to be in a cell with no water nearby and no chance of escape."

He nodded, pained. "I've been feeling it, Ashlynn. All day. I'm sorry I didn't tell you, but I've been fighting it."

Ashlynn put her hand on his shoulder. "Keep fighting it. You are going to be fine." She looked at Misuzu who stood nearby. "Bring him up to the castle and make sure he is secure before you rejoin us." Looking once more at Elas, her eyes were compassionate. "We will figure this out. Go now."

He still had enough presence of mind to go willingly with Misuzu, both of them running for the castle. "What now?" Nuala asked. "We thought we had healed them."

"Surface healing," reminded Cavalon. "You said it yourself." He looked at Ashlynn. "Whatever got them this morning hit them with more than cuts and bruises."

She growled. "Try to kill as few as possible. We will figure out what to do once they are all subdued."

~*~*~*~

Only half of the Gaels that had been attacked in the ocean ambush were able to be saved, leaving them with less than thirty water dragons. A day later and all that still lived were locked into a dry section of the dungeon. Elas was in his own cell, pacing back and forth and running a hand through his colorful hair. Kenayde watched him, face lined with worry. The gashes running from temple to jawline were red and swollen but no longer open and bleeding. Seeing her had fevered the pace at which Elas moved and troubled Kenayde.

"Is there nothing we can do for him?" she asked her sister quietly.

"We thought we had," Ashlynn answered, just as softly. "That is the problem."

Tasarin frowned. "I need a sampling of his blood before I can come up with any reasonable solutions. Right now, all I can give you is my best guess."

"Which would be?"

He looked at Ashlynn. "His blood has been poisoned. All of them have been. It gives them thoughts that are skewed and misleading, and it gives them a fever of anger the likes of which I have not seen before." His gaze went back to the ever-moving Elas. "I doubt he can even hear us speaking anymore."

Kenayde didn't want to accept it. She stepped forward and wrapped her fingers around the bars. "Elas, you're going to be okay." He turned and growled in her direction.

Gently, Ashlynn pulled her sister back. "He knows you're there, Nadie. A part of him knows it and that part wants you to be far away from him so you will be safe."

Tears prickled Kenayde's eyes. "Is he going to be like this forever?"

"No," Ashlynn promised boldly. Cavalon was coming down the corridor with a look on his face that said he needed to speak with her. She looked up at Tasarin. "Take blood from one of the sedated dragons and get to work. I want results as soon as you have them." With Kenayde, she joined Cavalon to head back outside.

"The ships are on the horizon."

"What?" She looked up at him in shock. "What do you mean? Both you and Nuala told me they were just heading north when you saw them."

He frowned, shaking his head. "I can't explain it, just like no one can explain what's happened to those men and women down there. Nothing is making sense."

Kenayde looked panicked. "That means they will be here before nightfall."

"We finally gathered all the bodies of the slain from yesterday," Cavalon said stiffly. "No better time than now to try and rouse your troops."

"Lynnie." Kenayde stopped and touched her sister's arm to make her pause as well. "Before we face what is coming, I want to go below. One more time... just in case."

Ashlynn frowned and took Kenayde by the shoulders, ignoring the look of confusion on Cavalon's face. "Nothing is going to happen to you. Nothing is going to happen to either of us."

"You don't know that!" There was pain and fear in her eyes, the wounds on her face only enhancing her desperation. "Please."

It was hard to argue with the quiet plea, but Ashlynn sighed. "We don't have time, Nadie."

Clearly frustrated, Kenayde's brow wrinkled. "Maybe you don't have time, but I am making the time. Go on without me. I'll be out shortly." Without waiting for an answer, Kenayde hurried away from Cavalon and her sister.

She made her way through the castle, down quiet hallways and empty staircases, until she reached her destination. Making sure that she was not being watched or followed, Kenayde glanced quickly over her shoulder. There was no one she could see or hear. Looking up, her eyes found a framed painting of a field of lilies. In the background, soaring through the sky were two birds. Reaching up, she ran her fingers over the texture of the painting. It was rough like a rock found on the beach, smoother than something found in the ground but too rough to have been polished by the ocean waves for very long. Her gaze traced the ornate gold frame and her fingers moved to now touch it as well. With a gentle tug at the bottom right corner, a very small door that was seamlessly hidden in the wall swung open with a grumble of stone against stone. Again she looked around to make sure no one was watching. When she felt confident in the fact that she was alone, Kenayde turned herself sideways to fit through the door. As she pushed it closed behind her, the frame corrected itself, looking as inconspicuous as the wall behind which she had disappeared.

It was dark and cramped behind the hidden door, but a hard and concentrated thought from Kenayde had torches alight in blue and gold, leading down the narrow passageway with their strange and comforting light. She squeaked quietly, proud of herself and her accomplishment but sorry there was no one there to see what she had done.

There was no carpet there, no paintings or flowers to decorate. This was Altaine at its birth; nothing but cobwebs, stone, and iron to hold the torches. Ashlynn frequented this particular passage when the time provided. Kenayde took this path each time she visited the castle, as did Wessely. It was a secret place where the servants and guests of the castle could not disturb, even with their good intentions. Having to push through the clingy webs told her that the last time anyone had been down there was the previous year, right before she and Ashlynn had sailed for Caedia.

The stairs led down into the mountain. Soon, the sound of her feet on the stone was accompanied by the slow trickling of water falling in tiny unseen rivers. The air grew stale and thick, but they continued their wordless descent. Upon reaching a window covered by dust and bird filth, Kenayde stopped to undo the latch and fling open the dirty glass. Fresh, cool air tumbled inside as though it had been waiting for that very moment. She filled her lungs and looked out over her city. From where she was, the knotwork of the streets could be seen and found by someone knowing what to look for. She was not yet at the same level as Altaine village, but not so far above as the main part of the castle. The winged could easily see this window if they were searching for any discrepancy in the rock. Otherwise, it would go unnoticed.

Farther down, the natural light guided her to the level she sought. It was nothing exceedingly fancy, but it was indeed a spot where magic dwelt. The room was no bigger than an anteroom, but gave life to a small secret garden. The floor was lush with green grass year round, said to have been blessed by one of the faery kind to stay that way. Kenayde knew it was no faery, but the magic of the Earth Elemental that kept everything alive here. Thistle and heather dotted the ground, and morning glory ivy climbed tenderly up a stone dais in the center of the room. Kenayde walked to it and brushed the dust aside. Beneath the thick covering were inscriptions in Gaelic. They were the vows her parents had made to each other the day they were wed. Looking fondly at the writing, Kenayde traced the letters with a finger.

This room had a past of many uses. For her grandfather it had been a place to store his most valued treasures. Nir had used it as a place to escape and read or write, where no one could disturb him. Once he'd married Siobhán it had become their room to share together. They had made private vows to each other here, before making them publicly to anyone else. Now it was a place of escape for their daughters. Ashlynn used the room simply to speak to her parents, and sometimes to feel safe in showing her weaker emotions. For Kenayde, it was a place to come and speak to the memory of her parents, and to pray to the Giver.

"You would be proud of Ashlynn," she said to thin air. "She's become such a fine queen and a woman many look up to." Bending, Kenayde picked one of the flowers. It was shaped like a star burst, and smelled like peppermint. "I know you can hear me no matter where I talk to you, but nowhere else feels the same as this room. I miss you." She stroked the long petals absently, rubbing the softness between her thumb and forefinger. "So much has changed since we left. Not here so much that I can tell, but in us. I remember leaving Oceana on my own last year and coming here to see Lynnie and meet Briac, feeling so small and wanting to appear so big. I remember seeing the castle, thinking I was in over my head, but knowing there would be no turning back." She smiled to herself, sitting at the base of the dais to face it. "I came in meek and timid, but willing to do what was needed in order for Ashlynn to sit on the throne. She deserved to be there, desired it, and I wanted it for her just as much. That day changed my life forever."

The oils from the petals made her fingers slick. She touched them to her neck, just under her ears for a natural perfume. It was a clean smell and one that would last to give her small reminders of this moment throughout the day. "Coming back here after all that we've been through made me feel like that child was missing. I had none of the fear of what I was about to face, but the fear of what was to come from what we had done. I so wish you were here." Her chin angled up as though she'd heard a sharp reprimand, her brows raised. "That is not to say that I'm not thankful for Mama and Papa. Sometimes, I just wish you were here as well. I wonder how this all would be, were you both still alive. Would Ashlynn still be as independent as she is? Would I still be happy in the background?" Looking back down at her lap and the flower, she sighed. "Unproductive thoughts, I know, but they never go away."

Her mind wandered to Elas, all alone and pacing in his cell. She touched her wounded face absently and wondered what her parents would have thought of him. Would they have turned from his scarred figure or would they have been as embracing as Wessely and Emiline had been, even after all of the water dragons had been infected with a rage that they did not truly feel? Thinking about it gave Kenayde a small pang of sorrow in her core. Though she'd never known her mother, never had the chance to, there would always be a part of her that longed for her. "Mother, I pray that I make you proud. Not only as your daughter, but as a woman and someday a leader. I pray that this responsibility that will pass down to me at Oceana is something I learn to love, and that I will be a queen worthy of her position. I know that day is far from me, that there is a much greater thing before me that draws closer even now. Be with me and keep me strong in my fight. I wish the same things of you, Father, that I make you proud of me." She paused to take a slow breath and shook her head, realizing what she was doing. It was pure habit to pray to the spirits of her parents, though her year at the monastery taught her that the one she should pray to was the

Giver. They were once there. There were living people to testify to that fact. The Giver was just...faith. Faith had to keep her eyes to Him, as well as her prayers. "Forgive me," she gently entreated, taking a moment to gather her thoughts.

"I am frightened," she admitted after a moment. "One of my greatest flaws is that I make plans for the immediate future and don't fully think through what will come of my actions. I am much like Ashlynn in that respect. I knew there would be a battle after Tadgh's death, but I didn't expect a war. Perhaps I am as naive as they say. I certainly didn't expect to lose Briac and to gain new friends." She lifted one hand to concentrate again, her thin brows coming together in determination. Fyre came forth and wrapped around her fingers and palm like a glove. It was such a strange thing to find comfort in because she'd never let herself think about or truly explore her own abilities. She was perfectly happy being the powerless second born. Her purposeful ignorance, however, might lead to her destruction if she was bested in battle.

"Meeting Luella...I know You have some grander plan in mind than I could ever hope to understand, at least so I have read and been told, but I pray for guidance." The fyre went out and she dropped her hand. "I pray for courage to do what must be done and the strength that a good fighter will need." Leaning forward, she rested an open hand against the cool marble base of the dais. "Most of all, I pray I lose no one else close to me. Keep watch over them. Take me if someone has to be taken." She mused in her thoughts, however, that if no one had to be taken, she would not complain.

Draping the bottom of her winter cape over her arm so as not to step on it, Kenayde carefully stood before letting it fall with a rustle. She leaned forward and placed a gentle kiss by the Gaelic etchings, reminding herself to bring down something of Briac's. This would become the room of remembrance, as well of that of thought and prayer. With one foot on the bottom step, she turned for one last look at the room and smelled the peppermint on her skin. The flower was tucked into her hair as the window was closed, and she made her way back upstairs.

"If I could have your attention," Jaryn was saying as Kenayde made her way to the crowd of warriors. Chatter and discussion quieted slowly, eventually leading to everyone turning their attention on their king. "I may not have what it takes to make a stirring speech, but there is something I'd like to say. We don't fight alone, dear brothers and sisters. Never let us forget for even one single moment that we have the Lord of all the universe on our side. David wrote many times to the Giver in the scriptures. Many of my favorite verses come from him, but perhaps my favorite is a complete psalm." He laughed and said, "Don't worry! I won't recite the whole thing."

To a quiet wave of laughter he began with a loud, clear voice. "The Lord is my light and my salvation, why should I be afraid? The Lord is my fortress, protecting me from danger - why should I tremble? When evil comes to devour me, when my enemies and foes attack me, they will stumble and fall. Though a mighty army surrounds me, my heart will not be afraid. Even if I am attacked, I will remain confident.

"I will hold my head high above my enemies who surround me. "

Somewhere, in a place that was impossible to find without truly searching for it, one lonely piper began to play a tune. It stirred in the hearts of the natives like a cool hand to a fevered forehead. Where the energy had been electric before and full of high emotion, now silence and humbleness rested. Heads bowed sometime during Jaryn's speech. Some had even fallen to their knees in prayer. The few who remained standing closed their eyes and bowed their heads when he began to pray.

"Gracious Heavenly Father...I am almost at a loss for words to say. I'm so very thankful for the men and women that surround me right now. It has been a blessing to learn more about them and to come to know them all as family, though my heart aches that it is out of necessity that we have grown closer. Lord, you know what we face this night. You know the enemy that speeds to our shores to threaten the very lives we hold onto. This war began under the guise of vengeance. Now the truth of it comes to light, and You know we fight for more than land. We fight to preserve what is good and what is right. We fight for the privilege to pass on the stories we have been told, the stories of You. As Your followers it is our duty, and one we gladly accept.

"Be with us as we charge into battle. Hasten our arrows, strengthen our armor, keep our aim true. Be with us, dear Giver, in every moment, and let us not forget Your presence. We don't go blindly into battle thinking we will win without losses. My heart already weeps for those that won't see the morning light. But I pray for them. I pray they know You and Your holy Son. Giver, you sent him to die for us, to cover our multitude of sins. Thank you. Thank you for always thinking of us, for giving us second, and third, and fourth chances when we need them. Thank you for caring for us as Your children. Thank you simply for loving us. We praise You, Father, even in the middle of this turmoil. Follow us now into the night, and be our protection. In Your precious name...Amen."

That closing word was repeated in a unified voice. Eyes opened, and men and women rose. They looked to their king and queen while as the piper continued to play.

"We're down half the water dragons we had to begin with and almost twenty others who died in their attack." Jaryn told Ashlynn quietly, looking at the bodies of those killed that had been brought together. Most were human, but there were small bodies of dwarves, tattooed skin of the Nagin, a small handful of elves, and one unicorn. Since there was no time to have any sort of regular service for them, a funeral pyre was the best they could do.

"Ashlynn, you've got to speak to them." Jaryn looked at his wife. "I'll stand beside you as their king, but they wait to hear from you and they are starting to feel the first real prickles of fear."

She looked out over the faces that were now too numerous to fit solely in the tournament field. They were outside the village now, a sea of beings united against the oncoming evil. This had been a hard hit to their confidence and it showed on every face. "I don't know what to say," she confessed in a whisper.

Jaryn slipped his hand into hers. "They're all feeling what you're feeling, love. Tell them what you would want to hear if the roles were reversed. Tell them you know what they're thinking. Reassure them. If you have faith, then so shall they." He smiled, guessing at her thoughts. "It's not me they want to listen to. Give it a go. You'll be brilliant."

Taking a deep breath, Ashlynn took a few steps closer to the pile of bodies that would soon be lit. Her eyes ran over the lifeless faces of her own villagers and those that would remain unfamiliar to her. These people would never again feel the warm summer sun on their skin. They would never hear the laughter of children, or taste the sweetness of a kiss from a friend or a lover. It made her sad, but it also sent a flutter of anger through her.

"My fellow Celts." Her voice was loud and didn't seem to fit the environment. She tore her gaze from that which gave her such stirring feelings to look into those faces that eagerly awaited what she was going to say. "Yesterday we suffered a blow we were not expecting. This, perhaps, makes the weight of the pain of it that much greater to bear. Husbands and wives, sons and daughters were lost, and for that we will grieve. Yet even as we lament their passing we know there will be more to come.

"I ask that you not bear ill will to those that brought this damage upon us. It is those that brought the damage to them that will have our fury." Murmurs of muffled excitement rippled through the crowd. "Before we know it, the enemy will be on our shores and we will be defending all we hold dear. You have seen those black masts on the horizon and know this night will not be spent in rest but in action. Tonight we fight. Not for ourselves but for our children and our children's children. We must bridge together and forget our differences." Her green eyes swept the faces before her, stopping meaningfully when she spotted Sabari and the dwarf she stood next to. "We are not many races gathered here. I see one people unified by a singular goal."

Jaryn squeezed her hand, his encouragement giving her strength.

"People of the ancient line, people of the old lands, listen to me now! A dark comes with the threat to extinguish the light we have promised to carry through the generations. This land has been invaded many times before, and every time we have fought to preserve and protect that which is precious to us. We rise to meet this threat once more, and once more we will triumph!" This time the murmurs were louder and the crowd gave more audible support. "For years, the name we bear has been spoken as an insult. But no longer! The tale of this battle will be told for generations over, and in every nation across the world. No longer will the Gaelic name or the Celtique name be a curse, but a praise!

"We must band together as one. We are brothers and sisters and we will protect one another until we no longer draw breath. By our blade, the enemy shall fall!" Ashlynn felt the adrenaline push through her veins and she drew her sword, raising it high. "Let us remember our fallen friends and honor them with the death of their enemies. The rivers of the Isles run clean today but on the morrow, they will run red with the blood of our enemies!" She had to yell to be heard above the noise now. "Tonight, we fight for survival! Tonight, we fight for redemption!"

CHAPTER TWENTY-TWO

The village of Siness was completely silent. There was not a single window with a candle burning, not a door open to visitors in the fading sunlight. For all it looked, the village and it's castle had been abandoned. Those aboard the approaching fleet knew better, though the stillness made every one of them nervous. Perhaps it was supposed to look like they'd run, allowed themselves to be driven away to avoid a fight. Laidley wouldn't have believed it for a second. With the reply Ashlynn had sent his squire home with, he knew she was in wait for him and his men. No matter how she'd prepared, he was confident in thinking she was not prepared enough for what he brought with him.

Waves lapped against the ship, the only sound in the darkening night. Merrik was beside Laidley, casting a surveying eye on what lay before them. "It is too calm," the older man said lowly. "They will wait for our feet to be on the shore before they attack."

"What would you suggest? We have the cannons. That would cause enough chaos for us to reach land."

The older man shook his head. "No cannons. They would do damage, yes, but there would be no substance to it. We have no choice but to go ashore now. Drop anchor here and send out the boats."

This idea made the young king nervous. "What of the water dragons? Should they attack again..."

"By now they should only be attacking each other." Merrik took a breath. "Still, we will send out a test."

From two other ships, four smaller boats were lowered, each holding six men. With three on each side they rowed toward the beach. It wasn't until they were midway between the ships and the land that there was movement in the water. Something, *several* somethings slid into the black deep with the long, sinuous bodies of snakes. The men stopped rowing momentarily and drew their swords. They searched the dark water, waiting to be attacked. When nothing happened they re-sheathed their weapons and picked up their oars once more.

And then sea exploded around them.

Several dragons leaped from the depth with sharp talons and hungry jaws. Too quickly taken over to draw swords again, the men beat helplessly at the creatures with their oars. The sound of the paddles against the hard scales of the beasts rang out like a thrush beating a snail shell against a rock. It was a fruitless sound that was too quickly followed by screams of terrified men and the cracking of wood. Those aboard the ships lifted lanterns and torches high to see, though there was no need. They knew what had happened and it was only confirmed when pieces of the boats slapped against the ships' hulls.

Laidley pointed to the shore. "Look." The dragons, nearly incapacitated just hours before, slithered out from the water and climbed up the embankment. "How is that possible? You said they would be mad!"

"They should be." Merrik cursed. "It would seem we are not the only ones using powerful magics."

Laidley looked at his captain, confused. "What?"

Something new moved on the beach and bought Merrik an excuse for not answering. He pointed and said, "Your Majesty."

"What?" The young king saw the figure standing out on the white sands, alone and seemingly unprotected. Laidley narrowed his eyes. "Someone give me a scope." One was passed to him and he pulled it to its full extension before putting it to his eye. "It's...Luella." He lowered the scope in disbelief. "It is my sister."

"Do not be fooled. She is not alone." Merrik moved from the stern to speak quietly to a small man with dark skin dressed in brown and black. The man nodded sharply before hurrying away. Returning to Laidley, Merrik's lips were pursed. "Remember, my King, she turned against you. It would be folly to feel anything but what you feel for your enemies towards her now."

Laidley felt pin pricks of guilt in his stomach; Luella, his sister, but also the person he'd always confided in most, stood vulnerable before his army. He had a sudden longing for the days of his childhood when any argument would be forgotten in minutes and they would be close again. How had it come to this?

The anchors had been set without word from Laidley and all waited now to see what would happen. With just one woman, surely enough of them could make it ashore. "Highness, if I may make a suggestion." But there was no time to speak. Laidley watched in great distraction as fires crawled their way down the beach, following an oily path and blocking off the village beyond it. There was no foreseeable way for even Luella to escape the flames. With each passing moment, the fires grew hotter and reached higher. He swallowed hard, wondering if she'd been sent as some sort of offering or, if rejected, a sacrifice.

She was illuminated, framed in a blaze of light and had all the attention on her that she sought. She grew in size, face elongating into a maw with sharp teeth, arms extending and growing talons while wings sprouted from her shoulder blades. She gave a terrible call into the night and used her abilities to turn the red and yellow flames around her to the blue and gold of her fyre.

There was not a man watching aboard those ships that was not paralyzed. For a moment no one dared to even breathe. It was Merrik who moved first and sent everyone into action. "Fly!" he commanded in a guttural yell. A blackness that had no distinct shape or form flew past him from each ship in a hurtling speed toward the dragon on the beach.

Luella stood strong, wings fanned out and bracing herself for the impact.

She didn't expect the stinging pain that sliced her with every little black thing that flew past her.

"Luella!" Tasarin was darting from his hiding place just up the beach, but Cavalon tackled him down. "Let me go!"

"They'll kill you!" Cavalon yelled. "She's a dragon and look what they're doing to her. What do you think would happen to you?"

"I do not care." The elf shoved Cavalon away and got to his feet. He would have kept running forward had he not been surprised by what was happening. The black shapes, small as insects and big as bats, flew past Luella in cutting darts and straight into the wall of fyre where they were consumed in terrific screams of pain. "The fyre," he muttered. Turning his head, he looked at Cavalon with demand. "Raise a fyre in front of her! Whatever it is that flies at her now cannot withstand it." Looking around, Tasarin called for Suule. His unicorn had seen what was happening and was already thundering across the beach before Cavalon could even think to raise the fyre to shield anyone. Luella's strength gave out and she could no longer hold onto her draconic form. Suule whinnied in anger and pain when the blackness attacked him, but fyre quickly flared at the front of the beach to protect him. Luella fell onto the curve of Suule's back and managed to pull herself up, clinging to him as he brought her from the beach and into the village.

Tasarin was close behind, pausing only at the edge of Altaine Shire. It was there that Wessely waited with the front line of the army. "I cannot explain it," the elf breathed. "The creatures flew right into the fyre as if drawn to it and it killed them."

"Good," the king commented. "Go after Luella. Make her drink the elixir you made for the dragons. Emiline will be able to help you."

"I will return as quickly as I can."

Wessely watched the elf go before turning to the men at the ready with him. "It will take them a few minutes to get ashore and when they do they will be timid. It has been proven they can hurt us, but proven also that we can hurt them. Do not advance until you have my word." A cold wind rushed in from the sea and Wessely looked up at the rusting branches of the hulking tree hanging over all of them. "Especially you." The branches moved as if in answer and he could have sworn he saw a glint of teeth in the moonlight as Ashlynn, camouflaged within the wood and leaves in her shifted form, gave him a wide grin.

Inside homes that lined the edge of the village, men and women were armed and ready for the fight. Now that the time was truly upon them, fear was simply a word. Adrenaline ran through their veins and made them a little jumpy. Wessely knew he had the strongest of them all with him. He prayed they would remain calm enough to think rationally and not simply charge forward without thought.

Someone was running up the wide path to the village and everyone froze. Upon seeing it was Cavalon a collective breath was let go. "They're coming our way," the Badarian reported.

"How many?"

"Suffice it to say that we're well matched in numbers."

As they spoke, thick clouds rolled in overhead at an unnatural speed. The blazing light of the sinking sun was set to gray and then black. In a nervous motion, everyone looked around and Ashlynn moved within the tree. "That can't be good," muttered Cavalon. Dark shapes flew above in a whisper, this time in discernible shapes. "Dragons." Cavalon waited only a breath before running deeper into the village. Seconds later, chaos broke out.

Riders were being flown into the village in droves, leaping from beasts blacker than pitch with crimson eyes. These men, jumping to the ground below, straightened to show nothing of themselves. There was no face among the black, all skin was hidden in clothing. Nearly everyone was caught off guard and numbers were quickly lost. In the sky, the Volar were attacking the dark dragons with everything they had. Unlike the Gaels, these shadowy dragons felt the pain of arrows and spears. When they were hurt they fell, or disappeared into ash.

Laidley stood on the beach for a long moment and just watched the madness. His long red cape swirled behind him when a bitter wind swept in from the sea. Above, snow began to fall. Mixed in the snow was ash from the fallen black beasts. He looked like a little boy lost, the picture of his sister turning into a dragon and then being assaulted and falling playing over and over again in his mind. This was nothing like he envisioned. There was a certain ritual to war, rules that needed to be followed. He turned to look at Merrik, enraged by the gleam in the older man's eyes.

"You could have killed her!"

Merrik gave no pause as he tore through one of Altaine's villagers with his sword. "A simple casualty of war. It is her fate to die."

Startled, Laidley jumped back as a man was thrown out onto the sands,

257

burns on his face and body that singed cloth and flesh. "*This* is how I will win this war!" Merrik shouted. "Come out with your Gaels and your swords. Fly with your winged comrades and people of the earth. You cannot defeat me! No one can defeat me!" In a crazed motion, Merrik drove his sword into the burned man's chest to ensure he was dead.

The young king's eyes were wide. The man beside him was not someone with whom he was familiar. Lines that had been on his face were no longer there. The leg he'd favored slightly since his days as a young knight did not seem to bother him anymore. "What have you done?" But Merrik didn't hear him. He was watching with wicked glee as more dragons glided through the night with even more riders. "What have you done!"

Finally hearing him, Merrik tore his gaze from above to look at Laidley. "What have I done?" he asked. "Does it matter? You wanted to defeat the Gaels and so we shall."

"Not like this," challenged Laidley. "Not with magic and - and demons. Not at the expense of my sister's life. She could've been saved!"

"She is one of them!" Merrik rounded on Laidley, his face wild and mad. "Didn't you see what she became? Your *sister* indeed. A bastard child from a secret affair. She is one of the Elementals you wanted to destroy. Be the king you wanted to be and get rid of them! *You will fight!*" As he said this, Merrik took Laidley by the shoulders and pressed his face close to his own. Laidley tensed in his grip and the pained expression he'd worn twisted into a feral sneer. Letting Laidley go, Merrik threw his head back and laughed. He watched as Laidley drew his sword and walked up the beach, preparing to enter the melee and join in the fight.

Misuzu and Cavalon were back to back, Cavalon with a heavy two-handed broadsword, Misuzu with twin daggers. They were surrounded but optimistic. It was not only men of Caedia that they faced but also the men that belonged to Merrik. "I was thinking," said Misuzu casually. She lunged low, swiping her daggers at the legs of one attacker. "When this is all done and over with I may stay here awhile."

Cavalon swung his heavy sword and met another, the metallic clash ringing in the night and mixing with similar sounds. "Oh?" he grunted, ramming his elbow into his assailant's rib cage. "How do you think your mother will feel about that?" The young knight punched Cavalon's stomach and got no reaction but a smile. Then he got Cavalon's fist to his face and met the ground.

"I think she will be all right." Misuzu jumped to miss a leg swinging out to try and knock her off her feet. She kicked the man in the jaw and vaulted over his shoulders in a flip. As soon as her feet were on the ground, she spun and drove both daggers into his back. Cavalon turned and Misuzu ducked so he could cut the head off another attacker. "She is never home anyway," Misuzu finished, yanking her daggers free. "Duck."

Cavalon bent and Misuzu rolled over his back. She drove her foot into the stomach of a knight, then spun in a graceful swoop to slice open his stomach. Now their circle of attackers was down to two – another knight and a black assassin. "Knight," Misuzu claimed. She charged at him and he ran, leaving Cavalon alone in the crowd with a single dark enemy.

"Just you and me, pretty." Cavalon twirled his sword in one hand, and the two men moved in a slow circle to size each other up. Both took a swing at one another, weapons hitting together so hard that there were sparks. Cavalon took a step back, trying not to let surprise show on his face. He spun, aiming a hit at his enemy's midsection but found the other man completely gone. The Badarian stumbled, having nothing to stop his momentum. He looked around, confused, and felt his feet being tugged downward. "What the..."

A black gloved hand was reaching up from the snow and ash covered ground to pull him down by his leg. Cavalon couldn't break free no matter how hard he tried. A second hand reached up to grasp his sword, keeping him immobile unless he let go of the sword. "Cavalon!" He looked up to see Nuala overhead. She loosed an arrow, her aim true enough to shoot through both hands. The same screaming that was heard on the beach bubbled underground. Cavalon pulled his leg free, clumps of partially frozen ground coming up around him.

More screams, furious, rang through the village. A quick look around showed him Kenayde struggling with her own attackers. Between them were multiple skirmishes. Thinking quickly, he looked up at Nuala. "Can you lift me?"

She'd seen what he had and nodded. With an arm through her bow, she flew low and took Cavalon's hands in her own. He used her like a swing and flung himself over the crowd to land right beside Kenayde. Since the black demons had taken his sword, he was forced to fight by hand. With Kenayde using both a sword and a dagger, they had the enemy at bay in no time. "Thanks," she panted. "That is the second time you have saved my life."

"I thought that's what family did."

Kenayde smiled, something out of place among the dirt, blood and bruising on her face. "Family?"

Cavalon rolled his eyes. "Don't go all mushy on me now. We're kind of in the middle of a war, here."

~*~*~*~

259

D. E. Morris

The tavern had been set up as a make-shift triage. Wounded came in and Emiline worked with various other skilled healers to see to injuries. Whether it was the elvish spell of illusion on the building that was keeping Laidley's men away or the grace of the Giver, no one knew, but they were thankful none the less. Tasarin hadn't left Luella for more than a few minutes since she'd been brought in unresponsive and bleeding everywhere. While Emiline worked on dressing some of the more personal wounds, the elf went to his unicorn.

Suule was enraged, snorting with flared nostrils and stamping the ground. Tasarin swiftly examined his wounds. "You are lucky, my friend." The elf ran a hand over the shallow cuts under the white fur, blood already dried and flaking. "I do not know what is in your blood that drives this poison away, but you have my eternal thanks, as do the men and women you have spared today." A picture of Elas came to his mind and Tasarin nodded. "Time will tell. He was the last to be treated this morning, refusing to be healed until the others were. His stubbornness may cost him in the end."

"Tasarin." Emiline was at the door and beckoning him to follow her.

Tasarin nodded and ran a hand down the length of Suule's neck, then pressed their foreheads together. "Go now. Find Ashlynn and protect her. If she should fall, all will be lost." Suule snorted and reared before running off into the night, and Tasarin hurried inside and straight to Luella's cot.

Her eyes were still closed, but the blood had been cleaned from her body. Emiline came over with a small vial of dark liquid. "I tried to wake her to give this to her, but she would not respond."

"I will try." He took the vial with a thankful smile for Emiline. She touched his shoulder and moved on to be helpful elsewhere.

When the water dragons responded well to the salve made from Nuala's ground Phoenix feathers, there was optimism that the poison would be eradicated. Then when they had all gone mad, Tasarin turned to the only other thing he could think of that would work. Suule was not pleased with the idea, nor were any of the other unicorns. Though once he explained that their single fallen kin in the surprise attack would simply turn to ash in the pyre anyway, permission was given. Tasarin was allowed to take blood, the thing unicorns were most hunted for, and make an elixir. Once ingested, the water dragons slowly returned to themselves. Not one of them was free from shame and sorrow at the realization of what had happened. It was because of this guilt that they volunteered to be the first wave of the assault. Everyone knew what a high risk it was, but they wanted to make up for what had transpired.

Looking at the vial now, Tasarin felt a lump in his throat. He had to remind himself that this blood, this healing blood that cured ailments nothing else would even touch, could be the only thing that would save some of them before the night was over. He ran fingers lightly over the cuts on Luella's face, anger turning his usually serene eyes cold. Laidley would not win. He would not triumph tonight over their lands, least of all, over Luella.

"Luella." He spoke her name with a gentle firmness, his hand at the back of her neck to lift her head slightly. "Luella, I need you to open your eyes." She didn't respond and he tilted his head. "Luella...open your eyes. I cannot help you if I do not see the beautiful blue of your eyes."

Pain rippled over her face and her brows came together. Though her eyes didn't open, tears formed at the edges and ran down the sides of her face. She whimpered and turned away.

Tasarin moved to sit on the cot beside her. He touched a cooling hand to her cheek and held her hand as she cried, leaning down to feather a kiss over her brow.

"It burns," she managed through her sobs. She pulled her hand free and covered her face. "It hurts so much."

"I know, my love. I know. I have something that will take it away, but I need you to sit up so you can drink it." Still she cried behind her hands. The gentleness was not working, and Tasarin knew he needed to be more stern to make her comply. It was for her own good. "Luella, listen to me. I know you are in pain, but right now you need to sit up. I can take it all away, but you need to do as I am telling you."

For a moment it seemed as if she would simply lay there and cry, but eventually Luella lowered her hands and opened her eyes. It was an instant regret for the elf, asking her to look at him. He had never seen so much pain in a gaze, and worked to push his anger down as he helped her sit up. "Drink this," he whispered, putting the vial to her lips. She kept her eyes locked with his until the bitter thick liquid touched her tongue. She started to sputter and he jerked the vial away. "You must drink it," he commanded. "There is no other way."

She panted, fighting the stinging and searing all over her body, and took the elixir to drink it herself. Her eyes clenched shut and she threw her head back to drain the vial. When it was done she coughed into her hand. Tasarin took the empty bottle and put it aside, then moved closer and wrapped his arms around her.

"I was so afraid," Tasarin admitted quietly. "If Cavalon had not stopped me, I would have been out there to shield you."

"It would have killed you." Fresh tears fell as she wound her arms around him.

"Everything is going to be all right," he promised, running a hand gently over her hair. "Just breathe. Sit here and breathe. I will stay for a little while, though I cannot stay for long." She lay back and he brushed her tears away. "Give it a few minutes and you will feel well. I would wager you will feel well

261

enough to be rightly angered and want to be out there yourself."

"I'm sorry if I hurt you."

The sudden change of subject had the elf blinking. "Hurt me? You did not..."

"Not now." She shook her head and raked a hand through her messy hair. "I hurt you when I left with Cavalon."

Tasarin looked down briefly. "It was necessary. I see how much stronger you have grown and the confidence you have in yourself. I was being foolish. Never before have I cared for someone as I do you and I let it get the best of me. If there is an apology needed, it should be coming from me."

She wet her lips. "Out on the beach, I thought...I felt like I was dying and the only thing I could think of was how sorry it made me that I never told you that...that I love you."

He looked at her, feeling her fingers intertwine with his. Luella looked at him searchingly. "Did you hear me?"

"I did." Tasarin blinked and took a breath, then another. "I keep trying to find words to reply with." His gaze fell to their hands, hers looking so much darker than his in comparison. "I love you," he told her, looking at her face. "I loved you that first night."

"When we stayed up until dawn talking," she agreed with a small smile and a nod. She touched his face and he leaned forward, kissing her lips tenderly. For a moment they held each other, faces close together. Nothing else needed to be said then, they just needed to be there with one another. It would have continued if a violent invasion of bloody images had not been thrust into Tasarin's mind. He sat up, touching his temple. "What is it?" Luella asked, tensing.

"I have to go. I need to help. How are you feeling?"

She was already getting to her feet, pulling her hair back into a messy knot. "Ready to fight."

CHAPTER TWENTY-THREE

Mei Xing could have been in the middle of a performance for the way she was moving. Her eyes were not quite closed as she spun and jumped, slicing through the air, clothing, and flesh with razor sharp fan blades. Like a blind person would use their other senses to figure out where objects and people were, Mei Xing let the air speak to her. She could feel the subtle changes in temperature and flow. From that, it was easy to know where to strike, when to pivot, and when to block. She was lithe and graceful, her expression never wrinkling in labor or exertion.

Nearby, Ashlynn was doing her best not to get beaten down in her human form. It felt as though every enemy knew she was the one to go after and tried to do just that. She caught a glance of Mei Xing out of the corner of her eye and envied the woman's confidence. When it became apparent that Ashlynn's sword was not going to be enough, a thought had blue and gold flames clinging to her blade. She'd forgotten that the flames themselves acted as a magnet to the enemy and when they began to rush toward her, she cursed and ran until she could see no way out of her predicament. Surrounded, she sliced through the enemy with a feral zeal. Something white appeared out of nowhere and she watched as Suule reared up, slamming his powerful hooves down on one of Laidley's men.

"How is Luella?" she asked, blocking a strike. "One for bad, two for good." With a quick swing of his head, the unicorn answered by stabbing one man in the chest with his brilliant horn, another in the eye. "That is what I like to hear," Ashlynn panted.

"They're coming from everywhere!" Nóe's voice came from above. "I do not know who these black ones are but they fight against Laidley's men now as well."

"What?" Ashlynn looked up in disbelief.

"They are taking orders from Laidley's captain." A spear shot by him a little too close. Anger sparked in his eyes and Nóe disappeared to go after whomever had thrown it.

"We're here!" Luella ducked under Ashlynn's raised sword, her own sword in hand, and took the head of a knight from her brother's courts.

"Are you all right?" Ashlynn asked with concern.

"Never better." The two women clashed swords in a moment of unity, then pivoted and split off in opposite directions.

Tasarin was over closer to Mei Xing. "We need to regroup!" he yelled.

"And where do you propose we do that?" Ashlynn got a kick to the center of her back and was sent sprawling to the ground. Luella was quick to cover her and kill the man who'd kicked Ashlynn while Tasarin helped her up.

"The tavern," Luella suggested. "The spell the elves put on it is holding. They didn't even know we were there."

Ashlynn nodded. "The tavern, then. Let's find the others and get there as soon as we can."

As it happened, not everyone made it back to the tavern. Ashlynn looked around at those who were gathered. All of them were covered in blood and dirt, with torn clothing and cold hands and feet. The night was already wearing long and the snow was coming faster. "It tried to pull you into the ground?" she asked, staring incredulously at Cavalon. She rubbed a hand over her heart, trying to ignore the aching pain that had started there just moments ago. "What are we fighting?"

"Demons," Elas said. "Clearly."

"How are you feeling?" Emiline asked him.

He looked at her somewhat sheepishly. "Fine, thank you."

"They fight against one another now," Kenayde told them all. "I saw the black ones, those with Merrik, turn against one of Laidley's men because he was in the way."

Luella crossed her arms. "Where is Laidley?"

"I have not seen him," answered Kenayde.

"What about Merrik?" Jaryn asked. He noticed Ashlynn's actions and frowned. "You feeling all right, love?"

"Fine."

Kenayde shook her head. "I have not seen Merrik, either."

"What can we do?" Ashlynn instinctively looked at her father, grimacing when she saw the long gash over his left eye. "Anyone have any suggestions?"

"The fyre worked," Cavalon offered. "They're attracted to it even though it kills them instantly."

Kenayde shrugged. "So we set the place on fyre."

Nuala looked at her. "What do we do with everyone else? Only Elementals can live through that."

"We need to gather them into one place." Cavalon's brows had drawn together in thought. "If we can figure out how to do that we can just get rid of them in one fell swoop."

"What about the bodies?" Misuzu asked. "I know you said you wanted to wait, to have a big ceremony for everyone that will be lost after the battle is over, but what if you set the fyre now?" She looked at Cavalon. "You said they are attracted to it, right? If the fyre is big enough they should flock to..."

She didn't finish. Her mouth slackened as her eyes rolled back in her head and her legs gave out. Emiline caught her before she hit the floor, her grip on the younger woman tightening when her body started going into convulsions. In the very same instant Ashlynn's knees buckled and she fell to her hands with a cry, looking like she was going to be sick. It was Cavalon who figured it out first. Panic widened his golden eyes. "Mei."

He ran from the tavern without a look back. Elas and Wessely ran after him, swords drawn. "Mei!" Cavalon bellowed out into the night. Darting in front of him, Elas and Wessely fought off any that tried to get in his way. "Mei Xing!" There were bodies strewn everywhere and it was impossible to find her.

"Cavalon!" He looked toward Elas and saw the younger man point. Following the line of sight, he experienced a rage he hadn't felt in a long time.

It was with blindness he fought and ran, and eventually fell to the cold wet ground before Mei Xing. "No," he moaned, gathering her small body into his arms. "No, no. Mei, come on. Wake up. Mei, open your eyes." Her head rolled to the side and revealed a long open wound along the width of her neck. Steam rose from spilled blood that was still warm. It could only have been a surprise attack; she was too skilled a warrior to be taken down otherwise.

It made sense now, the way Ashlynn felt the pain of her passing. Misuzu collapsing was her receiving the power of the Air Elemental. Cavalon gripped Mei Xing's body tightly, nuzzling his face into her hair as he stood with her. Wessely and Elas continued to fight around him, as did many of the villagers. Though she had not been there long, they understood the gravity of the loss. In a circle of protection, Cavalon made his way back to the tavern and down inside.

"What happened?" Jaryn asked, crouched beside his wife on the floor.

Ashlynn looked up with tears shining on her face. "I felt her go. No pain I have felt could ever match that." With help from Jaryn, Ashlynn got to her feet and went to Cavalon. Mei Xing's hand was cold and limp when she took it and pressed it to her lips. "My sister. I have only just found you and now you are lost to me."

"In her death comes a new birth." Cavalon looked around. "Where's Misuzu?"

"With Tasarin and Luella." Ashlynn's eyes took in the Badarian's face and saw her own sorrow reflected deeply there. "Cavalon, you're bleeding."

"I'm fine." He lay Mei Xing on an empty cot, gentle as though she were simply sleeping. "Enough of all this messing around. We end it now. Are you with me?"

Though she was still shaken, she nodded. "Of course."

"Come on. We're going to need Misuzu."

Luella saw them coming and stepped in front of Cavalon, wiping tears from her face. "She knows, Cavalon. She cannot think straight."

"I don't need her to think." Cavalon hardly met Luella's eyes as he moved her aside and walked to where Misuzu lay in tears. "You have to get up, Misuzu. I know you're hurting, but you'll have time to feel that later. Your mother is dead, and unless you get up and help us fight right now, we may all join her."

It was a cruel thing to say and Tasarin glared at him. "She just lost her mother."

"And I just lost my sister," Cavalon snapped, fire in his eyes. "Do you see me curling into a ball and weeping? Get up, Misuzu. Right now." He took her wrist and pulled her into a sitting position. His hands took her face and made her look at him. "Listen to me. She's here, I got her inside. Her body is safe, but her spirit is gone. I know you're thinking you want to go with her, but you give up on me right now and no one makes it out of this alive. You need to get up and fight. Get angry and use that. Use that raging fire you have inside you and help us win this. Do you hear me?"

She nodded between his hands and he loosened his grip on her to wipe her eyes. "Thank you, Cavalon."

"Thank me when this is all over." He kissed her forehead the way a father would kiss his daughter. Turning toward everyone watching, his expression was hard once more. "Let's go."

"Ashlynn!" Nuala ran down the stairs and inside, panting and holding a hand to her neck. "Something approaches."

"What now?" she growled, running past the winged woman.

"You all right?" Cavalon asked before he passed her.

Nuala nodded. "I will be." She ascended the steps beside him, Misuzu just behind. "Whatever comes is a living fire."

There was confusion on Cavalon's face, but hope peeked through Misuzu's misery. "Badru."

The snow was falling faster now, the ground a gray, slushy mess. Bodies of men and women, broken, bleeding and unmoving were everywhere. In the sky there was a light in the darkness. Just as Nuala said, it was a living flame. Now that it was close, those who recognized the form knew it was another Elemental.

The Fire Dragon flew over the village with a ferocious cry, flames streaming from his hulking form like a cloak billowing in the wind. Faces from every army turned skyward and cowered at this new addition to the battle. The dragon wasn't as large as Cavalon, but there was something fierce about him. His feet came down to land on a roof, pushing off of it with such force that the thatching caught flame before falling in on itself. The dragon did a tight circle in the air and dove, spewing flames at anything that moved.

"He doesn't know who the enemy is!" Ashlynn yelled. "He's killing anyone he can!"

"Nuala." Cavalon turned to the winged woman. "You're born in fire. You're the only one who would be able to get close enough to communicate with him. For some reason, Elementals can't speak to each other through telepathy. You're going to have to get to him and touch him to open communication."

Nervous turquoise eyes lifted skyward, following the erratic path of the new dragon. "I can do it," she confirmed. Leaping into the air, she gave a powerful flap of her wings and shot off into the night.

"Our turn." Cavalon looked at the three women with him. "We need to take to the skies as well. Misuzu, I don't know if you'll feel the normal pain of it. You've been shifting all your life, so I pray you'll be spared from it."

She shook her head, tears still wet on her face. "I will not know what to do."

"You will." He gripped her shoulders. "We all felt that way our first time, but as soon as you're changed, it will be second nature."

Luella breathed deeply. "Are we ready?"

Ashlynn nodded confirmation and the four of them parted ways at a fast run. As soon as one had clearance from people and buildings, the shift came and the dragons took to the sky. Misuzu had no trouble with the change, and found Cavalon's words to be true. It was like any other shape she'd ever taken, but with a sense that the form belonged to her just as much as her feline and human forms. Seeing the sky now spotted with the Elementals, other Gaels shifted and took to the air.

Nuala flew close to the Fire dragon, the intense heat from the flames rolling off his body making her sweat in the bitter cold night. He saw her and turned to snap at her. With a quick fold of her wings, Nuala darted below his neck and to the other side of his body. He saw her and snapped again. Her wings fanned and caught the current, lifting her high and out of his reach. Banking, she glided sideways and landed on his back. He cried out his anger into the night and Nuala braced herself for the voice that would surely be yelling and cursing at her.

Off my back, you flying peacock!

You are killing our people!

What is your point? He swooped low, blowing a stream of fire at a group of terrified soldiers and killing them instantly. *I am not here to help you birds.*

267

D. E. Morris

We are on the side of the ones you came here to save!

The dragon rose higher in the air, taking the time to process the words in his head. *You are with Cavalon?*

Yes! She looked to the side and pointed. *See! They come to you now. It is time to act as one. Let them show you who you fight.*

The other dragons flew over him and around him, dancing in the air as a sort of greeting. Cavalon trumpeted loudly into the night, the others doing the same in answer. In a tight formation, the dragons dove and split from each other to fight, Badru following Cavalon. Nuala flung her wings and caught the upward current to take her from the dragon's back. In a flashing explosion of light she became the Phoenix. Her high cry had many of her people flocking to her, ready for instructions.

~*~*~*~

Merrik walked through the crowds of people flailing swords and staves and maces, looking as though he were simply taking a stroll. His own sword was drawn and when anyone got too close to him, a Celt or a man of Laidley's, there was no hesitance in dispatching him. He saw ahead of him a wild tangle of blonde curls and sneered. It was the Gaelic queen he sought, and here she was before him. Her back was to him, leaving her wide open to his advancing. Merrik lifted his sword and prepared to lunge forward but his blow was knocked aside by a man stepping in front of him and slamming the hilt of his sword into Merrik's jaw.

Wessely took a step back, righting his sword and standing in front of his wife to protect her. She'd left the tavern to aid some of the wounded on the field and was now trying to get back, but it was complete madness with the fear the dragons put into everyone. "I will lead him away," Wessely said in a low voice. "Try to run."

Straightening, Merrik touched his jaw and grinned. "King Wessely," he purred. "For a moment I thought I was looking at your brother. I did not realize how similar you were in appearance." Dark eyes went to Emiline. "This must be your beautiful wife." He twirled his sword. "How sad that I must make a widow of you tonight. Unless I decide to be kind and let you join him in the afterlife."

He advanced and drove his sword into Wessely's with a loud clashing. Wessely was just as skilled as the older man and knew how to block almost every single move that was made. Neither held back, using all the force they had as they swung and struck. More than once, one was knocked to the ground and had to stand with a cold and slush covered sword. Emiline couldn't find an out that wouldn't put her directly in danger, and she was forced to stay and cower.

With the cold numbing his hands, Wessely was starting to struggle in the match. In an attempt to end the fight he lunged, but Merrik was too quick and pivoted, sending Wessely to the side and slamming his elbow down onto the middle of Wessely's back. The king went sprawling on the ground, his sword sliding just out of his reach. Merrik raised his own blade for a killing blow, but Emiline distracted him by throwing the helmet of a dead man at him.

"Wrong move," growled Merrik. Instead of going after Wessely, he turned for Emiline. Realizing what she'd done, she turned to run. Merrik was quick to catch her and wrap an arm snugly around her waist. Behind him, Wessely had recovered and reclaimed his sword, but found it hard to get through the mass of people fighting. "Pretty little queen," Merrik said softly. "You will be first to die and I will let your husband watch." She struggled in his grasp as he turned both of them around. Wessely was powerless to watch as Merrik shoved Emiline away before quickly plunging his sword though her chest.

Wessely's cry was despairing and he froze, watching Merrik pull his sword free so she could sink to the ground. He stepped carelessly over Emiline's body. "That was invigorating," He took a deep breath, enlivened. "I killed your brother, and your bride. Before the night is over I will kill your children. And now I will kill you."

Merrik took a step forward but stopped quickly, his eyes going wide. His breath caught in his throat and he looked down. Three arrows found their mark in his body: one through his stomach, one through his chest, and one through his shoulder. In shock, he turned around to see Kenayde who was nocking another arrow and readying herself to loose it, Sabari beside her with two arrows in her own bow. He gripped the arrowhead coming from his stomach, then sank to his knees, finally falling to the ground beside Emiline's body.

In an instant the black warriors exploded to nothingness and a path opened up for both father and daughter. Wessely beat Kenayde and shoved Merrik's body away as he pulled Emiline's limp body into his arms. He sobbed openly and unashamed, pressing his ear to her breast. There was no heartbeat and he wept into her shoulder. Kenayde fell to her knees beside her parents. Weeping, she threw her arms around Wessely and forgot about the battle going on around them.

High above, the dragons and the Volar now had no enemies in the air with them. Without a word, Gaels and Elementals shifted back to their human forms in a majestic flourish, the Volar landing beside them. They took up weapons and fought against the humans that were under the command of Laidley. It was now an evenly matched battle.

"Merrik's men are gone," Ashlynn called, shoving a knight away from her before lunging with her sword. "That must mean he has been killed."

"You have to find Laidley!" said Luella, getting knocked on her rear in the snow.

"Who is Laidley?" A tall man with skin the color of cinnamon and wearing long, colorful robes, ran a spear through a man.

"Laidley is the high king in Caedia now," Cavalon explained. "I saw him closer to the castle. Follow me!"

Jaryn was the first to find the young king and faced him with such a wrath that he was almost unrecognizable. He'd seen Kenayde and Wessely with Emiline. Adding Mei Xing's death to it, Jaryn was more than ready to make sure Laidley never saw another sunrise.

"So you are the high king of these lands," Laidley said, feet spread wide in a stance of defense. "How many losses have you suffered tonight?"

"Too many," Jaryn growled. Nóe landed just to his right, a long thin sword in his hands. Nuala, along with several other of the Volar, landed as well and formed a circle of protection around the three men, fighting off those that would try to interfere. With dawn only a few hours away, the others arrived just in time to see Jaryn and Nóe charge forward to attack Laidley together.

They worked as a team against the young king, but he was highly skilled and dodged almost every one of their moves. Even with one man coming at him from the left and the other on the right, he was quick and hard to best. A glimpse of his sister, bedraggled, soaked, and with a beautiful blood stained sword in her hands, momentarily distracted him. She was a courtly woman, a lover of fine gowns and pretty jewelry. He'd seen her attacked by those things Merrik controlled and knew she shouldn't have lived. Yet there she was, fighting, striking and taking her blows like a man.

Nóe's sword sliced open Laidley's arm and he growled loudly. His attention returned to his battle and he moved to retaliate at the same moment Nuala cried out in pain. Nóe couldn't help but turn around. He saw his wife bleeding on the ground, left arm slashed to ribbons and left wing severed. He rushed to help her as she reached out for him, attention completely shifted. Laidley ducked a lethal swing from Jaryn and lunged with all his strength, driving his sword through Nóe's back and piercing his heart. Nuala watched, frozen, with a scream building in her throat. Badru dispatched the two men who had injured her and Cavalon helped her to her feet. She tried to launch herself away, desperate to get to Nóe and struggling with Cavalon. Her blood was all over him now, but he didn't let her go.

"You can't help him," he told her firmly. She clawed at Cavalon, trying to break free, but his grip on her remained firm. When she realized he was not going to let her go she screamed her husband's name once, and sagged against Cavalon, completely broken and drained. In the cold, the heat of her body was felt instantaneously. "Nuala." She was warm and getting warmer. Their earlier conversation came back to him and he remembered what she'd told him about dying when she so chose. "No, Nuala, you need to stay here. You cannot leave your people without a leader." She looked up at him for a moment, then became flame and cinders in his arms. He cursed when the fires faded and her ashes flew away on the wind.

It was now up to Jaryn. He was faltering but so was Laidley. Both men were tired, yet determined. "It wasn't supposed to be like this," Laidley wheezed, clutching a stitch in his side as Jaryn paused for breath. There was compassion in Laidley yet. Seeing Luella had brought it out in him. But Merrik's power had been great indeed and fought against the humanity still left within him. His weary frown turned into a sneer, his words becoming taunts. "Your people are dying all around you. Surrender now and you may be spared."

Jaryn laughed tiredly. "Who do you think you're fooling? You'd kill all of us, given the opportunity. This is our land, our heritage. Do you think we'd actually give that up and hand it over to you?"

"You would if you were smart." Laidley advanced with sword raised, smashing the hilt of it into Jaryn's face before the other man knew what was happening.

Jaryn stumbled back, blinded by blood where the skin above his left eye was split. He felt hands pulling him away and only briefly saw Luella rush past him.

"Sister." Laidley and Luella faced each other, both wearing similar expressions of weary determination. "How could you turn against me?"

Luella shook her head sadly. This was exactly where she said she hadn't wanted to be. If Laidley was to die, she didn't want to witness it. She could only hope now to reason with him and end things civilly. "You left me no choice, Laidley. Merrik turned our father into an evil man and I knew you were going to let him do the same to you."

"Merrik made me a great king!" Laidley looked at his sister with sadness. "You could have had part of it. You could have had anything you wanted in Caedia, but you left. You left and forced me to become what I am."

"No, brother." Luella dropped her sword, leaving herself open to attack. "It was you who left. The moment you chose war over family, the brother I knew, the brother I grew up with, was no longer there."

"I was tired of being the whelp! Tired of never being loved! Never would I have measured up to Father. Never did I measure up to you, the perfect daughter." Laidley also lowered his weapon, seemingly forgetting everyone and everything else going on around him. "All my life I fought, struggled to be recognized. Father hardly looked twice at me, and Mother...she was too weak to even care. No one but Merrik thought I could be anything."

Luella took a step closer, obviously wounded. "I thought you could be. I *knew* you could be. Laidley, no one supported you like I did."

Laidley looked down, his drive replaced with exhaustion. He hardly moved

271

when Luella framed his face in her hands. "I came here to kill you," he told her, sounding like a child with a heavy heart. "Luella, you do not belong to me anymore. I saw what you are. I cannot let you live."

"You can," she told him gently. "There doesn't have to be a war between us, Laidley. You fear them, us, because you do not understand."

"No." He shook his head and her hands dropped. "No, you do not understand." He looked at her with sorrow, then stepped back quickly and gripped his sword tighter.

Luella scrambled for her own sword and swung up when she felt it in her grasp, blocking what would have been a killing blow. "Laidley, it doesn't have to end this way."

But it was clear from his face that he couldn't hear her any more. He dropped to the ground and swung out a leg to knock Luella off her feet. She landed with a thud and looked up in horror to see Laidley advancing on her with his sword raised. Instinct took over and she struck out with her blade.

Laidley's sword fell to the ground and he staggered back, clutching the hilt of the ornate Claymore as it protruded from his stomach. Betrayal was on his face and when he opened his mouth to speak, blood tricked down his chin. There came a sudden clarity to his eyes and he looked upon Luella with love. She got to her feet and held his shoulders, tears coursing down her cheeks. He staggered, his face a mask of pain. A sob caught in Luella's throat and she shook her head. "Brother..." She followed him down as his knees hit the ground. With his last breath, he fell forward into her embrace.

CHAPTER TWENTY-FOUR

The morning sun did nothing to warm the hearts of those left standing. What had been gray wet snow as the night began was now stained red. It was sticky and clung to exposed skin like syrup as the bodies were gathered together to be burned. Ashlynn felt numb from the inside out. She'd lost her mother, a sister, and a very old friend all in one night. Had she anything left in her, her eyes would have been red from crying. As it was, no one had any tears left to shed.

Once Laidley had fallen, many of his remaining men fled for their ships in hopes of reaching home without attack. Cavalon and Badru were eager to dispose of them, but Ashlynn told them to let the ships be. The war was over. No one else needed to die. Some of the Caedian warriors surrendered, immediately laying down their weapons and pledging fealty to Luella, now the last claimed descendant to Tadhg's bloodline and their rightful queen.

Sabari's body had been found not far from where she'd stood protecting Kenayde and Wessely as they mourned Emiline. She was cleaned by her remaining people and wrapped in pelts and tied with leather thongs to be taken home. Her father would want to mourn his daughter and have a proper ceremony for her. Ashlynn wished she could travel to Alybaen with the Nagini to tell their king how valiantly his daughter and his people had fought, but there were others with whom she would need to spend time as well.

Many had perished. The dwarves, elves, and Volar suffered just as much loss as any of the rest of them. There would be no rejoicing in the Celtique nations for a very long time.

People stood together in huddles, drawing strength and comfort from one another. Everyone had lost someone. Friends, lovers, and children were being piled together to be given final rites and their bodies disposed of. The numbers were too great for any kind of burial at sea or on land. They knew the necessity of what was to happen, though it was a hard thing to watch.

"This night has been long for us all," Ashlynn said to her people when the carts were still. "We have all suffered greatly and will never feel the same." She saw Emiline in her mind, lying so peacefully next to Nóe and Mei Xing as they rested inside the castle awaiting their own ceremonies. Now a sob caught in her throat and she found she could not go on. Jaryn put an arm around her shoulder and kissed her head.

"The Giver has granted us victory," he continued for her. "Though no great gain comes without loss. We will carry the names and the faces of our loved ones with us always, and do them the best service we can with our lives. We will carry on, go forward from this day. Not one of us is free from a scar to the soul, but I pray you don't let it disable you. We *will* be whole again, and we will help each other through this great time of suffering. Let us now say our final goodbyes and know our loved ones are watching us from above."

He gave a nod to Cavalon and the Badarian set the bodies ablaze in blue and gold flames. This time there was no pipe being played, no beating drum as there had been at Briac's service. The only music now was the sad chorus of weeping and the snapping of the unnatural flames that consumed those who were lost.

Inside the castle later in the day, Ashlynn and her new extended family held a private service in an open tower for the three people they'd all come to love and would never see again. All of them appeared peaceful, at rest as though they were simply sleeping on beautiful beds of wood and rich fabrics. But when Ashlynn touched Nóe's face, held Emiline's hand, pressed her lips to Mei Xing's forehead, there was no warmth of slumber. Only the cool pallor of death returned her farewell affections.

While everyone was saying goodbye, Ashlynn caught the sight of a dying spark behind the spot Elas stood with his arms around Kenayde. Nuala walked slowly toward the group, healed and looking as though she had not seen battle at all. Yet there was a hollow look to her, a sunkenness under her eyes and a weight of sadness pushed down on her shoulders. She went to her husband and kissed his lips, tears falling freely over him. If only the Phoenix within her was stronger. If only she could wake him. Moving back, she stood beside Cavalon and leaned into him. His arm went around her shoulders and she wept without shame.

The bodies were wrapped in the fabrics they lay on. This time it was Ashlynn who sent them on their way. The tower filled with heat intense enough to make them forget the winter chill, but it lasted only a few seconds. They all moved inside where they huddled as one group, mourning, holding one another, giving tearful and silent thanks that no one else had been lost.

One frigid morning, several weeks after the battle had been won, Ashlynn gazed down at her kingdom from one of the open spires of Altaine. It was the place she often went to think or be alone, the place where she said goodbye to her mother and her friends. It helped with the daily sickness she'd been feeling accompanying the promise of new life in her womb. Today she wasn't sure why she was out there; she wasn't feeling ill or restless. Jaryn joined her and slid his hand into hers, the heat of his skin warming her chilly fingers. Silent, he looked down into the village as well. People were rebuilding, fixing what had been damaged and bonding together to help one another. Had the destruction not been so great it would have been heartening to see.

"It gets a little better each day," he said at length. "We get a little bit of our strength back."

Ashlynn nodded slowly. "Maybe on the outside. On the inside, we are all still just as damaged." Jaryn squeezed her hand, but said nothing. "It's not over Jaryn. I can feel that it is not over."

"What do you mean?"

She reached up to brush hair from her face. "I don't know how I know, but there is more to come. We may not see it in our lifetimes, but my gut tells me that this was just a glimpse of the things that will have to be endured." Tears filled her eyes; they came to her easily now and she hated it. "There will be so much more death before we can rest." She touched a free hand to her stomach. "I fear the world we are bringing this child into."

Jaryn took her in his arms and held her tightly. "One day at a time. It's all we can do. We won this time, and I believe we would win again if battle were upon us. And our child will be safe, my love. So long as we both draw breath, you know nothing will happen." He inhaled deeply, letting the cold air sting his lungs. "All we can do is live each day, praying as we go that we're doing what the Giver would have us do. We cannot forget that the things that look like a mess to us are perfect masterpieces to Him."

Against his shoulder, Ashlynn nodded. She took a few steadying breaths before straightening. Jaryn's words were wise, but she could not push her worries aside easily. "I'm cold," she said, changing the subject. Her fingers searched for his again and they turned for the inside.

She would not say anything more on the matter for now. Instead she would remain vigilant, and she silently promised her unborn child that she would protect him or her, whatever it may take.

D. E. Morris

EPILOGUE

No matter how much power he had or restorative ability, it still hurt when Merrik had three arrows spear through his body. He had a clear memory of laying in the cold snow, feeling wet flakes fall around him and over him. They clung to his lashes, melted against his skin while there was still heat there and ran in warmed little streams down his face. He could taste the blood that coated the insides of his mouth, hear the weeping and the clash of metal as the battle continued around him. He could even remember the murky sky above when he'd been shoved away from Emiline's body. After that it was a blissful darkness. No pain, no cold. Just darkness.

And then there was a thread of consciousness, something that reminded him that he was more than a thought or some strange memory that belonged in the back of someone's mind. He had power. Great power. Remembering this was like remembering to breathe after holding air in for too long. He didn't know where he was, didn't even really remember *who* he was, and it didn't matter. That life had passed. Now he was on to the next, the better.

At the time of his coming into power in the bowels of Castle Montania he understood that the knowledge he newly possessed would be indispensable. It came back in filtered thoughts. In the unending darkness he came to accept that this was just another pause in a journey that had been going on for generations. He was just another spoke in the wheel.

There were texts written long ago, perhaps as far back as when the scriptures were written for the first time; secrets; answers to long left unanswered questions. They had all been together once, bound in a book the way the Elementals were bound together in ways they did not yet even know themselves.

He needed that book.

Darkness was turning into an ugly gray, gray slowly ebbing away to make

276

room for light. Morning. The sky was clear and there was just a hint of the moon still left to fade away. Merrik stood to look around and get an idea of his surroundings. The sea was before him, a long plane of grass behind. Mist clung to treetops on an island just across the way. He could have been anywhere. A quick run of his hands across his chest proved that he was uninjured.

A wind came at his back, warm and embracing. Clearly this day was not the same day as when he'd died. The question was, had he gone backward or forward? It would be found out all in good time. For now Merrik simply smiled to himself and let the wind play with his hair and his clothing.

He hadn't felt this good in a very long time.

ABOUT THE AUTHOR

Diana began writing at the age of fourteen, following the lead of her father. She'd always enjoyed reading and quickly fell in love with writing as well, creating worlds that were easy to get lost in and characters that were relatable. She presently lives in New Hampshire with her cat Gallifrey, and is working on a supernatural YA novel, as well as continuing work on the next books in the *Age of Valor* series.

If you enjoyed this book, please consider leaving a review on Amazon and Goodreads.

Made in the USA
Middletown, DE
20 April 2017